THE SKY RIDERS

AN INVENTORS WORLD NOVEL

OTHER BOOKS BY CHRISTOPHER HOPPER

The White Lion Chronicles

Rise of the Dibor

The Lion Vrie

Athera's Dawn

The Sky Riders (Inventors World Novels)

The Sky Riders

Raising Thendara *(coming soon)*

The Berinfell Prophecies
(with Wayne Thomas Batson)

Curse of the Spider King

Venom and Song

The Tide of Unmaking

THE SKY RIDERS

AN INVENTORS WORLD NOVEL

BY CHRISTOPHER HOPPER

SPEAR HEAD

NEW YORK · BALTIMORE · SEATTLE

Published by Christopher Hopper in alliance with Spearhead Books.

Exterior and interior layout and design by Christopher Hopper.

Illustrations by Christopher Hopper, taken from his original Moleskine notebook on
The Sky Riders 2008-2013.

Author photo by Jennifer Hopper | www.jenniferhopperphoto.com

ISBN-13: 978-1492167723

ISBN-10: 149216772X

Printed in the United States of America.

To my Daddy, Peter.
The man who fell from the sky,
from whom I inherited my love for all things that fly.

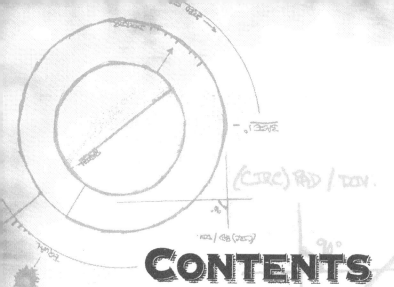

CONTENTS

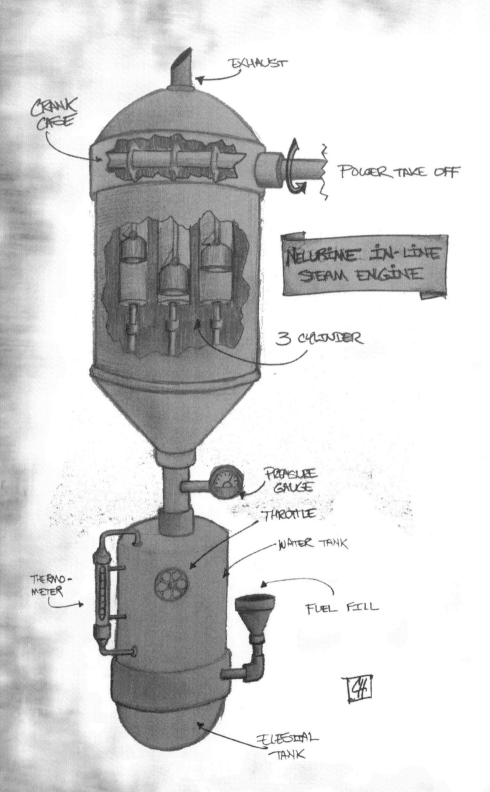

EXHAUST

CRANK CASE

POWER TAKE OFF

NELURINE IN-LINE STEAM ENGINE

3 CYLINDER

PRESSURE GAUGE

THROTTLE

WATER TANK

THERMO-METER

FUEL FILL

ELESIAL TANK

THE NORTHERN RANGE

THE SHOALS

FAIRVALE

CHRISTIANA

KNIGHTSBRIDGE

PREVAILING WINDS

BELLRIDE

DUNMORROW

THE MOORS

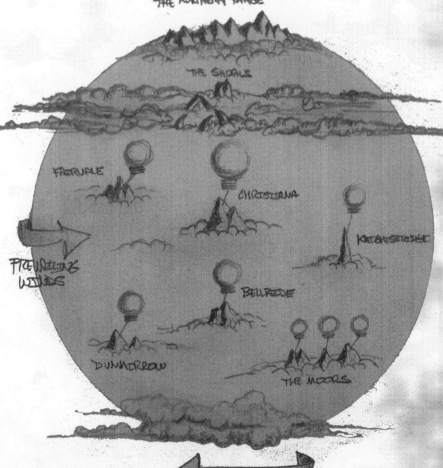

ROTATION

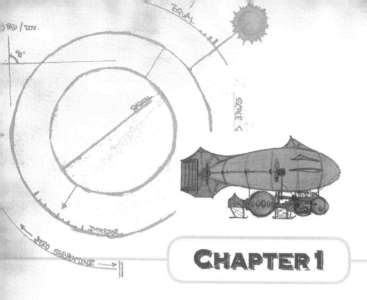

CHAPTER 1

IT'S EASY TO forget about everyone else when you live in such a dangerously beautiful place. A glorious world in constant peril of never being. I lean over the railing and study the toes of my leather boots as they hang off the upper deck. One misstep, and it's all over. 3,000 feet to the endless cloud-floor. It stretches on to the horizon, meeting the warm glow of the twin suns; no need to wear goggles or cream this early. Still well within the safe hours. But we're never safe from gravity. Or the clouds.

The clouds. Always watching from a distance. Like a million sets of eyes looking up into my soul. Examining me. Calling out to me from within the ancient haze. Waiting to devour. And within it, the sickening feeling of death. The betrayal of every Sky Rider that's ever plunged to his end. The very thing that brings so much beauty into life is also the one thing of which I'm most afraid. Or as with Mom, the most disappointed. Dad should be too. But he never seems to be.

My thoughts drift to flying, as they always do. Freedom. Alone in the sky, just me and Serio. No one to bother us. Nothing but open air. My only true escape from people. From memories. And yet, the clouds remain, ever below me. Reminding me. Looking at me. Waiting for me.

"You coming, Junar?"

I pull my eyes from the twin rising suns to see Dad. "Sorry, Dad." I push away from the railing and adjust my scarf.

"Never gets old, does it?" he asks with a grin.

"Nope," I reply. "Neither does breakfast." I knew that would make him smile.

"Well said. Ready?"

I nod, and we head toward the square. Ever since I was a little guy, he's taken me here on Saturdays. Picking up supplies for the Guild, buying flowers and, as is our tradition, grabbing something to eat from any one of the numerous vendors. I love coming here with Dad. And as far as I can tell, the feelings are mutual. It's special. Not every teen has this with his old man.

And not everyone gets to grow up to be just like his father, or *wants to* for that matter. But one day very soon, I'll be just like him. An Ace Pilot. For now we wear the same matching lambskin, flight jackets, the only difference being Dad has the Ace patch—5,000 hours aloft, 100,000 pounds of nelurime collected, and a victory title—while I have the First Year badge. *Apprentice.* His jacket is more worn-in too. Got that rough look to it. Like mine will have one day.

We walk over a few foot bridges suspended between the wealthier housing platforms before turning in toward the deck's center square. *The market.* In the market, anything can happen. Fights between merchants are always fun, as is the occasional tussle among customers. Pickpockets. Politicians. Pretty girls. Every now and then I even get to see the *Brologi* called in to subdue an agitated mob.

We take our seats outside *Basra's* among a small cluster of outdoor tables, always preferring the open air to those tables stuffed inside. A wide awning, yellowed from the suns, spans above us as the waitress offers menus.

"Need these?" she asks. "Or the usual?"

"The usual," Dad replies.

"Thought so."

The market is on the top deck of Bellride, as are all markets in the floating cities of Aria-Prime. Top decks get the most light, and a full view of the balloon matrix. *Real estate here is expensive,* Dad always points out. Heard him say it for years. *Basra's* sits midway along a line of shops to one side of the square, which means I always have a great view of the action that takes place beneath the myriad of brightly colored booths. It's cold out, and Bellride is flying leeward to the southeast; a crisp spring day. Still, it doesn't keep families searching for bargains, street performers cartwheeling down the aisles, and any number of squawking birds or nosey sheep from passing in front of our table. Normally, I'd be entertained. But today a small, shiny object catches my eyes beside one of the table's legs. I reach down and retrieve it.

"What do you have there?" Dad says, leaning forward.

"Not sure." I lie. But Dad knows exactly who made this, just as much as I do. "*Somebody* dropped it, I guess." The thing is square. Mostly. And fits easily in the palm of my hand. It's adorned with two bulbous buttons and slightly separated brass plates, revealing more than one spring within.

"Looks important," Dad says.

"What do you think it is?" I ask.

Dad takes it up, turns it over a few times, then gives it back. He lowers his voice. "Only one place something this meticulous could have come from." And I know exactly what he means. My eyes must betray my knowing, as Dad raises a finger to his lips.

Inventors.

I lean toward him, lowering my voice. "Why would they be out here?"

Two copper plates slide between us. "Lamb skewers and chop-chop," the waitress says with a grin.

Two men sit at a table outside an eatery a few stalls down from the father and son. Both are dressed down, skilled at the art of disappearing when needed, but more accustomed to being noticed than not. They order only a pitcher of water, preferring not to risk dulling their senses with the lethargy that comes from heavy eating, and pass the owner enough *liir* to leave them alone. What they endeavor to do today requires the utmost care, and they can afford neither food nor company to distract them now.

The older of the two had arrived fifteen minutes after the first. On purpose. "What have you observed? Anything?" the elder inquires.

"They just got their food," says the man with the darker complexion. "Nothing out of the ordinary."

"And the boy?"

"He's there with Leif as planned."

"So it's just as you expected," concludes the elder.

"Yes. You brought the letter?"

The elder flashes a folded parchment from within his cloak, then tucks it back inside. He takes a breath, opens his mouth as if to say something, then pauses, his words seemingly caught in his throat.

"What? What is it?" the dark man asks.

"I'm questioning your judgement on this one," says the elder. He casts a long look across the market at the pair. "Are you sure he's up for it?"

"My lord, you surprise me. I was under the impression you had been briefed."

"It is the briefing that gave me doubt," replies the elder. "No personal connection to us, no family lineage amongst the Order. I'm concerned that the truth will be too much of a shock."

"You're worried that he'll turn."

"In a word, yes," says the elder. "But as you've pointed out, his talents are too notable to ignore. He'd be a remarkable asset to the Order. But still, betrayal seems imminent."

"And what if he does?" the dark man says, more as a statement than a question. "The skies can be perilous, you know."

The elder *tsks* his subordinate. "There are easier ways to break a man."

"The boy?"

"That's one method. Among others." The elder turns from

the table and gazes through the menagerie of people to spy on the unsuspecting pair. "He has many cares we could prey upon, and we have many enemies to blame."

"How is it?"

"Great, Dad," I reply with my mouth full; he never minds like Mom does. "Yours?"

"As always." He pats his stomach.

I keep looking down at my new toy; I know he's trying to get my attention off it.

"So, son," he asks, "what does the Headmaster have planned for you next week?"

"For one thing, he's scheduled a children's tour before Festival tomorrow." I'm sure my face is less than enthusiastic, as is my tone.

Dad smiles. "Just remember, you were that age once," he says, waving a mutton finger in my face.

"I know, I know. It's just sometimes—"

"Sometimes one of those little runts will grow up to be an Ace...just like you."

I feel a wide smile break through my displeasure, then look down. "Thanks, Dad." My eye catches the strange gadget again. Seriously cool. I'm not even hungry anymore. Which reminds me.

"I also asked for some time off," I add. "To repair a saddle."

Dad eyes me. "Let me guess: something a little above your capacity to fix?"

"Let's just say, I might need some help." I pick up the gadget and twist it at Dad.

"You'll make any excuse, won't you," Dad says, nodding to the device. "Alright, son. Have at it. Just be careful, and don't—"

"Don't get followed, I know." I wipe my mouth, push my plate away, and start in on the contraption.

Third floor. Room 34. Three knocks. Pause. Two more.

The bolt slides back. Door opens a crack, still chained.

The man in the hallway dips his head.

"Did you deliver it?" asks the old man inside.

"It's done. The boy retrieved it as we thought."

"Good, good. Come in."

The door closes a moment, chain slides back, and then opens fully into a rented overnight room. A small bed occupies one corner, while a dresser and writing desk fill the other. The far wall holds a large window dressed with a thick drape on either side and, before it, atop a wooden tripod, stands a gleaming, brass telescope. The old man walks right back to the telescope, which he has focused to a point clear across the market. After a brief spy into the eyepiece, he steps back declaring, "Ah, marvelous! Come, come, have a look."

He steps away, allowing his understudy to peer in, though the term *understudy* is often a misnomer with these two. Both are well on in years, their only difference—besides the younger being rather portly—was a fraction of theoretical experience on a level most couldn't even conceive, in this case mastered by the *professor* and taught to the *understudy*.

The understudy peers through the eye piece. The boy is already fumbling with the device. Even the father seems interested. "It is hopeful," he says, looking back to the professor.

"Hopeful! I should think so!" He claps. "Quick, man, don't take your eyes off him. Not for a second."

The understudy returns to the eyepiece and waits. Then starts mumbling to himself.

"What's that?" the professor asks, stepping closer. The understudy doesn't reply, but plays with the focus ring, then reaches up and drops a brass-ringed filter into the chamber further up the telescope's body. Instantly his view changes and he can see within the device in the boy's hands. "Simply amazing."

"What? What is it?" the old professor asks, wringing his hands.

"Have a look."

The professor steps up and squints. "It's as if he's figuring out the sequence—"

"Without having the faintest idea what he's doing," concludes the understudy.

"Precisely!" The professor says, nearly knocking the telescope over.

"Easy there..."

The professor steadies the instrument, then throws his hands in the air again and exclaims, "Do you have any idea what this means?"

"He has the gift," the portly understudy says.

"He has the gift!" says the professor.

I've been working with the gadget for about five minutes, I think. Dad is trying not to be interested. I can tell. He's playing with his food. But he's looking at me.

Click. Something inside moves. "Hey, Dad, I think I figured it out."

"Woah, really?" He sits up, wiping his mouth. "Lemme see."

This contraption is mine, somehow. I mean, it's not really *mine*, I know. It's *theirs*. But playing with it in my hands, I feel as though I've invented it...as if I'm rediscovering how I'd designed it. *My invention.* "Watch, Dad." I turn what I've deemed the *top* plate to the left. Depress a glass button. Turn it clockwise. A spring releases. Slide the *bottom* brass plate northward. Then an internal click. A small ejection of steam hisses from between my hands and I drop the device on the table.

Dad and I both look on as, without my assistance, the object begins to shift in shape, its four edges folding back to reveal a small compartment containing...

"Another red paper fox," I say. That settles it. To anyone else, it'd be underwhelming. But to me, it's the bona fide mark of the Inventors that I've grown accustomed to. An animal long since deceased from Aria-Prime, it's said to have roamed the surface back before the cloud-floor forced everyone above. Cunning and quick. I'd add this folded paper to my growing collection. The one only Dad knows about.

Dad reaches over and withdraws the folded shape of the fox, as small as a quarter-liir coin. "Always peculiar," he says. He leans back examining the artful paper-miniature, his mood changing. Not quite sad. More thoughtful. Regret? I've seen it a few times before. Different than how he looks at Mom; this look is more like he's remembering something. Long ago.

Something behind me catches his eye. He places the fox down and sits bolt upright, looking at someone. "Can I help you, gentlemen?" he asks. I would turn around, but two men are standing behind Dad, both wearing heavy cloaks with hoods.

"Dad?" I nod past him. We both exchange glances. *Surrounded.* Yet in that same moment, I see a posture change in the men behind Dad as they notice the men standing behind me. It seems this encounter wasn't planned by either party. And then there's a rumbling sound. Dad notices it. So do the strangers. They raise their cloaks' flaps and reach for crossbows. Dad's eyes widen; I bet ten liir the men behind me are producing similar weapons.

"Down!" Dad reaches across the table to shove my head down, wrenching me out of my chair.

My ears ring a beat after my head hits the deck. Not from the blow to my temple, but from a loud concussion in the middle of the market. Something blasts against my body. Dazed, I squint through a tumult of overturned tables and fumbling people. Screaming. Wood splinters, brightly colored fabrics, bodies running. And fire. That's never good.

Someone steps on my ankle. The pain makes me focus, makes me see Dad reaching toward me. "Stay low, and follow me!" Not rising above a crouch, he runs into *Basra's*. I roll over, gain my feet, and pursue.

Once inside Dad is withdrawing his crossbow, deploying the arms, and slamming a bolt home in the lock. His hands work smoothly. Efficiently. He takes three more bolts and slips them into the leather brace on his forearm. While he never worked Saturdays, he always insisted that his *responsibility to the public never took a day off.* And today that public will be grateful.

I'm pressed against a wall and risk a glance out a shattered window, broken from the blast. Suspended between the deck and the balloon matrix hovers a C-Class Airship. Shoot, I've never seen anything fly *inside* the city before! Are they insane? The roughly painted insignia on the canvas balloon tells me all I need to know: a crimson flag, crossed with a cutlass—weapon of choice for the *Zy-Adair.*

Sky pirates.

Plunder 'til death bid thee still.

Nimble and remarkably stable, the C-Class is modeled after a Hidlebach, but not exactly; it has some things the Hidlebach designs lack. Twice the prop propulsion for one thing, and an extra passenger compartment with window-mounted weaponry and underbelly, bay style doors. *Which are opening.* Six ropes uncoil, and a half-dozen figures slide swiftly to the deck.

"Stay here, and keep away from the doors and windows."

"But Dad," I shake my head a little, ears still ringing, "I want to—"

"Do as I say, Junar." He looks at me for a moment to make sure I get it. Which I do. I run my fingers through my hair, frustrated. Then he ducks out of the restaurant, and takes a position behind an overturned table. He peers over the table's edge and aims his crossbow. A bolt streaks across the market and impales a pirate as he is about to touch down. The assailant drops the last five feet and *thuds* to the wooden deck in a heap.

Dad's second bolt speeds off as a blast comes from the C-Class' gunnery compartment. The table he's behind explodes, bits of shrapnel spraying into the restaurant. I pull back behind the wall, covering my face. I wave the smoke and splinters away from my head and look to Dad. He's fine, having rolled out of the way, but his last shot went wide, gaining the attention of the intended target: a tall pirate brandishing a cutlass in one hand and an electric *nelurime* pistol in the other.

The pirate sees Dad sprinting to more cover and raises his gun. A sizzling blue charge shoots out of the brass tube as the pirate absorbs the recoil. Tendrils of lightning cross the air and terminate at an awning pole with an explosion. The fabric cover bursts into flames and settles atop a few people still too afraid to clear out of the market. Dad runs to the bystanders' rescue, kicking at the awning, yelling for those trapped beneath to escape. That's when I notice the pirate take aim at Dad. The scum! He knew Dad would try to save the bystanders, and flushed Dad out like a grouse in mountain brush.

"Nooo!" I scream as I tear from my cover in the restaurant. The assailant turns to look at me. As do the remaining four pirates. Shucks, so I may have been a bit hasty.

"What are you doing?!" The words are hardly out of Dad's mouth when a second and third electrical charge comes careening toward me. I dive. The restaurant's doorway erupts; sparks and bits of brick spatter my head. More screaming.

Move, Junar! I look up, the pirate moving toward me. *Move now!* I scramble to my feet, stumble forward as a fourth blast rips into a cloister of chairs. I trip, rolling head-over-heels into a fruit stand.

Blinded for a moment by the colorful tent that's collapsed on me, I hear the distinct sound of metal splitting bone. Then a choked cry for help. I struggle against the cloth, then flip it off to see a fallen pirate tearing at the crossbow bolt in his neck. I give Dad a nervous look; by my count, he only has one bolt left.

Three of the assailants have taken cover behind a table, but the fourth is stalking toward me. I can't get up fast enough, fumbling through the wreckage. I can hear the pirate's leather flight-boots squeaking against the wooden deck, and the swooshing of his canvas pants. I glance up; his eyes glare at me through tinted glass goggles. He holsters his pistol, then raises the cutlass over me.

I start kicking, praying to Talihdym that I'll deflect his blow. Sword comes down fast. But just as fast, the glass over his left eye explodes, a metal shaft protruding from the brass frame. The pirate drops the weapon, which clatters harmlessly off my legs, and pitches forward into a lifeless heap.

I crawl backward from the corpse, then hear Dad's voice yelling, "Get out of here!" He's taken cover behind a vendor's stall, waving me off; his crossbow's unloaded, but he's still holding it with authority. I'm not going to just run and leave Dad alone, so I hide, weaving back to *Basra's.*

The owner and his wife are huddling behind the counter. "My Dad's got everything under control," I say confidently. The wooden deck explodes just twenty feet behind me, berated by the boom of the airship's cannons. I yelp and jump over the counter to join the couple.

"Does he now," states Basra. I manage a timid smile and a half-laugh.

There's more shouting from outside, but not that of frightened civilians, or pirates. Perhaps the men who'd surrounded me and Dad earlier? Clearly they had weapons, but they hadn't stayed to fight. I risk a glance over the counter. The market is a charred mess of smoldering sales-stands and fabric, interlaced with a few dead bodies including the three pirates Dad dispatched. The voices that now command the square belong to the *Brologi. The Chancellory Police.*

Sure, Dad and the Aces from the Guild have responsibilities to uphold the law and defend the people against violence, just like this. But most Zy-Adair attacks take place in the skies, rarely—if ever—this close to a floating city. Dad is as good as any with his crossbow—but from the saddle of a felrell, not in a street fight. *That*, he'd always tell me, *is where the Brologi hold their own.*

I watch as two dozen Brologi file in from all four corners of the square, taking up defensive positions on one knee. The worn "B" insignias on their dark helmets and hardened leather armor is stuff of legend among the younger kids of Aria-Prime. Shoot, even us older teens are still enamored with them. Twenty-four crossbow strings click back into their locks, and a rattle of nocking bolts echoes around the market. Eyes hidden behind darkened sun visors take aim down their weapons.

"Loose!" comes the command, and with it, the remaining pirates are riddled with metal rods, each marauder spinning lifelessly to the deck. The Brologi then turn their attention to the airship, but stay their weapons; a missed shot would risk igniting the C-Class blimp, or worse, traveling further up into the balloon matrix; such a mistake would be catastrophic.

Instead, four troopers dash into the market's center and

take to the ropes. They ascend hand-over-hand with startling speed. Feeling less intimidated, I give a parting wave to Basra and his wife and swing over the counter, venturing into the square. Apparently I'm not the only one watching the Brologi climb: the pilot must be watching too. Not only have the airship's props been engaged, starting it forward, but one of the ropes uncoils from the passenger bay, cut free. The Brologi trooper flails, plummeting back to the deck with a sickening *thud*. The remaining three continue to climb, undeterred.

I watch in amazement as the ship turns for one of the taller buildings on the square's perimeter. I'm not sure it can clear the structure. But then I suppose the pilot doesn't care to. *Dash the Brologi across the building's face.*

Basra's voice comes from behind me, "Climb, you blasted 'Logi, climb!"

Dad's yelling my name, running toward me. But I only take my eyes off the drama above for a second. Dad gives me a quick side-hug, then turns to watch. The airship is dangerously close to the far side of the square now, close to the old hotel.

"Come on," Dad urges from between his gritted teeth. "You can make it!"

All at once another rope leaves the housing, uncoiling like the body of a headless snake. I hold my breath. The Brologi falls...

...then catches an adjacent rope.

"Can you believe that?" Dad punches me in the arm. Now that I'm alright, Dad is remarkably at ease in this situation, almost enjoying the troops' death-defying display. But I suppose he would be; neither heights nor Zy-Adair faze him. *All part of the job*, he'd readily admit. Dad and the Brologi are like brothers in arms, even if they are from different Guilds.

The three Brologi are just a few feet from the bay doors. The highest of them withdraws his crossbow and fires up into the compartment. A beat later, a man in flight gear tumbles from the airship, a cutlass spinning free from his hand. By the time his corpse bounces off the hotel and lands on the deck below, the Brologi are safely inside the compartment.

The ropes slap against the face of the hotel, then slide out of sight as the C-Class roars away from the square and heads over the rest of the city. Dad and I walk forward, hoping somehow to follow the airship. But the skyline swallows the bulbous craft, as well as the remaining Brologi tracking from the deck.

"Let's go!" I say. But Dad catches my arm.

"They'll handle it from here, son."

He holsters his crossbow and turns to help some people to their feet. I sigh, casting a last glance to the empty space between the building tops and the balloon matrix.

We've helped three people up when I hear rumbling. Loud. The airship is swinging back into view, hurtling over the square! Dad looks up with me and points; the port engine is on fire. The ship is losing altitude.

"Everyone out of the square!" Dad hollers, waving his hands toward the closest side street. Whatever pandemonium swept through the market before is now amplified tenfold. The thought of an airship flying inside one of the floating cities is one thing, but crashing into it while on fire is quite another.

"What do we do?" I yell at Dad. He looks to me, then to the airship, then to the troops refilling the square.

"Those troops up there need to get the balloon free of the ballast," he says, eyes scanning the cockpit. Shadows move within; the Brologi are still fighting whoever's inside. "And if they can't, someone else will have to."

"Well, who?" I ask.

"I suppose these are the moments we're born for," he replies. "Fly or die."

"Fly or die," I answer.

24

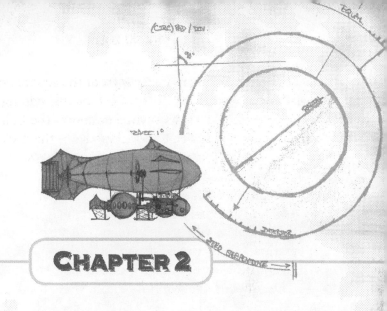

CHAPTER 2

THE CRIPPLED AIRSHIP circles the square in a wide, lumbering arc, struggling to stay off the tops of the buildings much like an overgrown pigeon trying not to succumb to its obesity. The Brologi in the cockpit seem to be fighting with more than one adversary. Clearly, no one is flying the contraption.

Dad looks at me, then back to the airship. "Come on, Junar. This way."

Dad runs across the market, leaping over wreckage. I follow, keeping one eye on the ungainly ship, the other on the chaos of the square. How so much devastation met our peaceful square *twice* in a matter of moments is bewildering.

I remind myself to breathe as Dad darts into a four-story building and up a darkened staircase. I follow him and hit the first landing out of breath. He's already around the corner, down the hallway, and bounding up the next set of stairs by the time I clear the corner. I pass by the numbered doors, all rental rooms, then mount the next set of stairs. The second floor finds me winded, and Dad is heading to the third. I can hear the C-Class humming outside, its one good engine straining hard. By the time I reach the top floor, Dad is nowhere to be found.

I cup my hands to my mouth. "Dad?"

"In here!" He has kicked in a door at the end of the hall. I run down, wheezing, legs cramping. He stands in a small room beside a blown-out bay window, a brass telescope collapsed on the floor. "She's coming around!"

I tear my eyes from the mesmerizing optical device on the ground and look to where Dad points: the airship is completing its first circuitous route around the market.

"Quick! We've got to get on the roof!"

Dad is out the window faster than I can think. I rush after him, my shaky hands grasping for the ledge just outside the window. My feet push off the sill, and soon my head is craning out far above the market, looking for Dad. I ascend carefully, finding the wood siding rather easy to climb. The airship is getting closer.

"Take my hand." Dad reaches down for me. A strong jerk, and I scramble up on the flat roof. "When she comes around, I'll need you to boost me up."

"You got it," I say, still on one knee.

"Then get off the roof, son. There's no telling what could happen."

"What about a weapon?" I ask.

He casts me an uneasy glance, then brandishes his fists. "These'll have to do," he winks. No wonder everyone loves my dad: the guy's a real hero. "Here she comes."

Still on my knee, I cup my hands for his foot. Sure enough, the airship heads right toward us, ropes dragging. With any luck, Dad will catch a rope as high as I can hoist him and be up inside to help even the odds in no time.

"Steady..." he mumbles. His leather boot is firmly in my grip and his hands are on my shoulders. "*Steady...*" The airship is closer now, the sound of the good props cutting the air like a milling saw. I glance over my shoulder and see clearly into the cockpit: two pirates going hand-to-hand with two Brologi...the third trooper must be down.

A beat later and the front of the balloon is directly overhead, the ropes and the cargo bay doors coming up fast. "Now!" Dad yells.

I thrust Dad's foot upward with all my strength, straightening my knees and throwing my weight up. The engine is loud in my ears, almost drowning out Dad's grunt as he leaps for a rope. I spin around and follow Dad with my eyes as he climbs into the belly of the beast. I let out a holler and pump my fists, chest tight with excitement. Raising an arm to shield my eyes against the prop wash, I lose sight of the airship. The wind plays with my hair, and I smell the warm, pungent exhaust from the nelurime engine mixed with the smoke from the burning one.

When I look again, the vessel lurches to starboard and changes course. Dad is on the bridge, must be. Whether by accident or intent, he's taking the ship away from the square. And toward open air.

All the action will leave me behind if I stand still, and I'm not leaving Dad on his own. Not now, not when he needs me most. So I start after the airship. Running. I know I'm crazy. Probably impulsive. But I'm *just* running, haven't committed to anything yet. The ropes drag across the tops of the buildings in front of me; I'm catching up. Still running.

The prop wash is heavy again, making my eyes water. I blink furiously, then notice there's a gap between buildings up ahead. And it looks wide. Maybe wider than I can jump. Probably a street below.

The engine continues to strain, smoke making me cough. The ropes are only a few feet in front of me. Gap's closer. And definitely wider than I can jump. I should just stop now. This *is* crazy. And I know Dad will be so mad if I do what I'm thinking of doing.

But it doesn't matter. He needs me to see this thing through with him. To make sure he gets out alright.

My mind's made up. I buckle down and pump my legs. One eye on the C-Class, one eye on my footing. *Make up ground.* Faster and faster. The building's edge is coming up. I'm so close to the ropes. Mere feet. The airship speeds to the far side of the opposite roof. Ropes skittering off the ledge, my feet follow.

Then, empty space. Deck below me, I see people look straight up.

I search for a rope. I fall farther than I anticipate, but my hands meet a line. Grab it. Pain flares, skin burning to slow my fall. I clamp down harder, and swing out beneath the airship. Four stories below, I hear a woman scream from the deck.

I look back up and climb hand-over-hand. *Made it.* Then there's a building coming toward me from across the street. No wonder Dad wanted a boost! It's coming on fast. *Climb, Junar.* I pull quickly, arms screaming. But I'm still too low. I pivot my hips to face the building, then lift my legs and run my feet up the wall. My head nearly bashes into the bottom of the airship's fuselage as I crest the building's edge and summit the roof.

Now on the next building, I release the line and run, dodging air vents and clotheslines. Lungs burning. What have I done? This is *beyond* crazy. I feel like I'm losing control, like my actions have gotten out ahead of me. Faster than I can think. Dad is going to kill me for not thinking. But I can't leave him. He'll thank me. If I live.

Just ahead I see another gap coming up. *Already?* I reach out for my same line, miss it, then latch on. There's no time. I pull my legs up and swing out over the span. Spinning around a few times, I attempt to gauge the distance to the next roof top. Fortunately it's a few feet below me. Rather than drop down, I decide to hold on as long as I can.

Climb! Hand-over-hand, I pull myself upward, legs kicking. I glance below and see the roof drop away to the street. *Faster!* I realize the building ahead is much taller than the previous ones. So tall, in fact, that I'm sure the airship won't clear it.

Arms straining. Sucking in smoke and exhaust. Now just two feet below the cargo hold, I swing a leg up and in, then pull myself the rest of the way up. I lie on the metal deck for a deep breath before we hit. The collision jars my head, pitching me forward and into the bulkhead. Shadows and sparks fill the cargo hold as the airframe skips along the roof, throwing me about. A deep grunting comes from the bridge. *Dad.* I no sooner think his name than he bursts through the metal door.

Disbelief fills his face. "Junar?"

"Hi, Dad." I've never seen him so surprised.

"What—what are you...never mind! We've got to get out!" He hoists me onto my feet, the hold filling with the noxious smell of smoke and nelurime. The airship hits another roof line. Dad holds onto me and grabs the door frame. I catch a look inside and see one Brologi struggling with the helm, two others flat across the floor. And three Zy-Adair, all unconscious. Or worse.

"Lieutenant, it's now or never!" Dad yells over his shoulder.

"Go, sir! I've got this!"

"Leave her be, Lieutenant. She'll make her way just fine," Dad orders back. But I can tell by his voice that he doesn't believe it.

"Yeah, right into the city, sir," the Brologi says, shaking his head. "Someone's got to hold these controls."

I shoot a look out the shattered glass windshield. The ever-present gap between the skyline and the balloon matrix is widening. *The city's edge.*

"Tie it off then, Lieutenant! Come on!"

"That's no good, sir. Too unstable." As if to emphasize his point, the airship's one remaining engine starts sputtering, jerking the aircraft further to starboard, and then dipping down. The lieutenant wrestles with the controls, straining against the sinking pull. He looks back at Dad. Then his head turns slightly; while I can't make out his eyes through his darkened visor, I know he's looking straight at me.

"Get out of here!" the lieutenant roars, then turns back, body stiff against the flight yoke.

I look down through the cargo bay doors. A city street disappears, replaced by one final roof not more than ten feet beneath us. Beyond this roof, I know, is open air. And below *that*, the cloud-floor. It's now or never.

I'm still contemplating a jump when a solid blow catches me between the shoulder blades. I sprawl out the cargo hold, then flip head over heels from the jarring impact with the roof. I taste blood in my mouth, ears ringing.

I sit up, patting myself down. *Everything in one piece.* Then spit, blood and saliva. Dad is already on his feet, somehow running to the building's edge. I stand up, dizzy, but manageable.

"No! No! No!" Dad shouts, pumping a fist at the sky. "What are you doing?"

A sickening feeling churns in my stomach as I realize just what the lieutenant is doing. The airship shoots out from over the city and then pitches forward. Heading straight down. Away from people. Away from the balloon matrix.

I approach the edge of the building as far as I dare, right foot forward. Then look down. A trail of black smoke follows the ship as it hurtles toward the cloud-floor, starboard engine growling to a redline whine.

All Dad and I can do is stand and watch as the craft races onward, growing smaller and smaller with each passing second. Slipping below the cloud-floor would have been the more humane route, the lieutenant blacking out and eventually suffocating in the toxic cover, but the bleeding fuel lines finally spit refined nelurime near enough to the engine that it explodes.

The secondary explosion, however, is far greater, as white-hot engine metal tears through the canvas balloon, igniting the hydrogen gas within. Black and orange fire clouds burst outward, followed by a heat wave we feel on our faces. Metal, fabric and wood burn with the luster of the suns until only a blackened skeleton remains, disintegrating into the cloud-floor.

Two men stand on a balcony amongst a throng of onlookers, all of them straining over the railing on the outer deck. People whisper beneath their hands, others openly wondering at the Zy-Adair's attack, and all in bewilderment as the airship explodes over the cloud-floor. A few women whimper in the arms of their husbands, and more than one parent scolds a child who gets too close to the railing. Slowly, the crowd begins to thin, opening a chance to talk a little more freely.

"Blasted sky pirates. What were they doing here?" asks the dark man.

"I'm surprised you didn't order the raid yourself," the elder chides.

"Nonsense." Too late does he realize his superior is insulting his wayward practices. He gestures with his head to the father and son, now standing on a roof's edge high above them. "Still don't think he's the right man for the job?"

"He has fine abilities, to be sure," says the elder.

"And...that's all? Listen, if he backs out—"

"If he backs out, it's your mess, not mine."

The dark man stares, thinking through his elder's threat.

"And I mean that." He pokes the dark man's chest. "Plausible deniability. This *never happened*. You'll go down with your ship." A distant, third explosion from below emphasizes his point.

"I understand."

"I would hope you do."

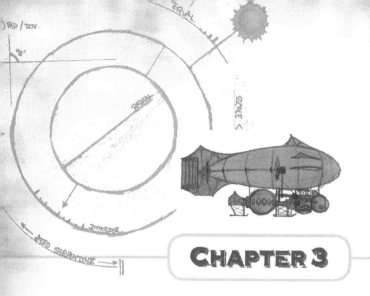

CHAPTER 3

"*Hey, hey! Stay* out of there!" One of the six-year-olds is climbing into a feed bin. "You want to be bird food?" I could think of easier ways to get rid of the buggers. But I'd lose my apprenticeship should any of them conveniently come up missing; getting kicked out as a First Year newbie is not ideal. I brush some feed from his mock-pilot jacket, the kind every kid on the tour gets to wear, then lead him away. "Stay with the group, got it?"

"But I wanna' see the big birdies!"

"You will soon enough." I kneel down, eye level. "But your parents would appreciate it if you didn't get *eaten* by them at the same time."

"Eat—eat—eaten?" he says.

"You *are* about the same size as a sheep," I add.

"A she—she—sheep?"

I nod and push him toward the twenty other *Junior Cadets* in the middle of the tack barn. They look around, wide-eyed, as Lance explains all the various parts of the aviary equipment. It's a fairly impressive hall for those who've never seen it before. Shoot, I still think it's pretty cool: open beams supporting the A-frame style roof, perch and tethering bars jutting out from the walls, and fresh hay littering the floors. Add in there the smell of freshly tanned sheep skin, fermenting bird feed, and the acid smell of dung, and anyone could guess what I smelled like after my studies every day. Good thing Mom was a Guild lifer. Not that I cared too much what she thought anyway. It just made living at home a little more tolerable.

Even cooler is all the detail in the barn; inscriptions and swirled carvings adorn anything made of wood. Then they are embossed with gold. While I'm about as good with a carving knife as I am with a cooking pot, I still admire the Carpenters Guild and their work. One word: *tradition*. I can't read the symbols, nor can my parents for that matter. It's the *Old Script*. But just seeing it up among the rafters, littering the wall boards, makes me feel important…like what I'm doing here is part of a much older way of life. Understand it or not, I can *feel* it, and that is infinitely more important in my mind.

As much as these tours bore me to death, I can't help but remember with nostalgia my first trip as an Honorary Junior Cadet more than ten years ago. Granted, Dad had taken me to work more often than his superiors would have liked (something you can do when you're an Ace), but actually being *on* a Guild-sanctioned tour—slapped with an official title, albeit superficial—made me feel legit. Like I was one of the elite…one of the *Kili-Boranna. The Sky Riders.*

Lance is done showing them how the main harness rig— the pilot's lifeline—works, and passes the runts off to me. "All yours," he says with a wink.

"You shouldn't have." But we both know that despite our display of indifference we'd rather be here than anywhere else in Aria-Prime, even if it was only giving tours. Of all the Guilds to work for, none were as esteemed or as sought-after as the Kili-Boranna. Or as deadly.

While both our families have been standing members of the Guild for generations, it did not mean automatic induction; we had to prove ourselves like any other apprentices. The only difference was that being a Sky Rider was in our blood. Where others dreamed of soaring through clouds and racing around mountains, reality bound them to metal-smithing or carpentry or farming; *we*, on the other hand, were *born* to be Sky Riders. We know the sights, sounds and smells of this industry better than anyone else alive, save only our parents. And one day our children will know it too, but that'll be a very long, long time from now.

"Alright, everyone." I raise my hands to gather their attention. "I need you to zip up your coats and pull down your goggles. We're going outside." The class giggles with excitement at my pronouncement, half of them forgetting they're even wearing eye protection at all. Once they are bundled up, we tether their belts to the safety line, then stand them directly in front of the enormous aviary hangar doors. The little bundle of kids are visibly shaking, faces looking up. Pilots normally use the barracks door for entry into the hangar, but for tours, we use the bird entry gates. And not the inset common-door, I mean the *actual* bird gates. It's all for effect really; anything that needs doors *this* big must be awe-inspiring. And the *felrell* certainly are.

I nod to Lance, then say, "Hold onto your helmets!"

Lance and I heave the doors forward. A gust of cold wind buffets the little group, sending a dozen on their rumps. But still they look on in wonder as we press the doors wider, our backs and shoulders burning. When at last the hinges refuse to go further, Lance and I turn to the kids, waiting for *the look*. Fighting the wayward gusts that sweep through the hangar, the little Junior Cadets gather their courage and step forward.

"Wait for it…" I say to Lance. It's the first little boy—the one from the feed bin—whose jaw goes slack first, shoulders drooping. "And…there it is." I smile, folding my arms.

Lance laughs. "Gotta love it."

Others try to mouth words of enthusiasm, but nothing intelligible comes out. Sure, everyone on *the islands* sees a felrell. Every day. But very few ever see them this close. Birds aren't allowed anywhere on the islands but in the hangars. Too dangerous.

"Watch your step now," Lance says as he clips himself into the safety line. "One hand for you—" he waves to them, then grabs the red cord that traces every gangway in view— "the other for your work."

"And stay away from the edge!" I add. "It's a long way down."

The hangar itself is spectacular. Basically, a huge, round room with a domed ceiling. No windows, no other doors, and no floor. Just open air. 3,000 feet straight down to the cloud-floor. We've had plenty a visitor get sick right on the spot. I hate cleaning up puke. Hate losing someone over the edge more. Thus the safety line. 'Course *we* don't use it much, but we're trained to. What with *Steward Regulations* and all. *The Houses* always get in the way. *Meddlers.*

Bellride's aviary hangar resembles every other island's in that it's on the lowest level of the city, the last deck before the cloud-floor. This, of course, is because the felrell prefer flying *up into* their nesting grounds. Thus the gaping hole. But where each hangar differs is in the unique construction style and ornate carvings, as well as the emblems of each fleet of Kili-Boranna: the flags, banners and draperies. Varies by city. Our flight patches are different, as are our scarfs and tack emblems. *Kar-Bellride*, as it is known, is built in the traditional *Apoc* style. This means little to anyone who hasn't studied it. Basically, just lots of exposed metal and timber catwalks, and walls smeared with textured mud. I think it's a cool mix between the rustic older styles and the more modern metalworking.

The red safety lines follow the carefully engineered catwalks along the hangar walls that turn in and out of the nests—square rooms stacked two high, all the way around the hangar's perimeter. Thirty nests in all. And in the nests? *The magic.*

I never get tired of looking at these creatures. Magnificent, really. Dad always says that anyone in this business doesn't do it for the pay. Or the glory. They do it because they love to fly, and they love the birds. I've always understood that; probably got it from Dad. Felrell are mesmerizing, with their eyes the size of a man's torso. Wingspan of thirty-five feet. Shoot, they can eat a man as fast as they can gut him with a talon, swallow him whole in a single snap. What's not to respect about that? But fear turns to awe when you realize they can be *tamed*, at least to a certain extent, and allow a man on their backs. To fly.

"This is Serio," I say, standing in front of a nest along the port side of the hangar. The amber bird pulls its head from beneath its wing and blinks, cocking its head so one giant eye hovers arm's length above the closest child.

"Is—is he *yours*, mister sir?" The boy is peering straight up, probably convinced he's about to be eaten. I know I would be. Kid's the size of Serio's eye. Yet still asked his question. *Brave little guy.* Pilot material?

"He sure is, little man. But takes a lot of work before you gain your bird, ya know."

"So you ride him?" asks a little girl with braids dropping out of her oversized flight helmet.

"That's the idea." Lance grins. "But they're all resting for now. They don't take to flying much, except at dawn and dusk."

"Shoot, occasionally a high noon trip, but that's just for fun," I say as I pat Serio on the neck, then make the sign of sleep to put him back to rest. "And if we do, we have to be quick. The noonday suns are just too dangerous to be out in for long. That's why you little guys wear your protection layer." I tap the invisible cream on the back of my hand. Serio takes one more look at the kids, coos—more like the bellowing blast of a deep horn than the lilt of a simple homing pigeon—and places his head back beneath the fold of his wing.

"I wanna ride one!" says the first little boy. "Can I? Can I, *please?*"

"Easy there, Ace." I pat his helmet-covered head. "Maybe on your next tour. Seeing them up close like this is a pretty big privilege."

Like I said, I don't mind the tours so much. The kids always make me laugh and give me an appreciation for what I'm allowed to do. *It's a privilege, not a right*, Dad always says.

A few minutes later, while I'm explaining how the various pieces of tack work, I notice a man out of the corner of my eye. "Then the pilot will clip the lead line into the harness rig and—"

"Excuse me," says the man. "Ap Leif?"

It's a messenger. Must've found his way through the tack room and saw the hangar doors open. All the other pilots are in the barracks resting or on break. Newbies never nap. Not even Second Years.

"Yeah, that's me." I excuse myself from the kids, and meet the man as he peers over the edge of the hangar floor. "Easy there, sir. Don't want to have to look for my message in the clouds."

The man steps away, shaking off a chill. "It's not for you," he says above the wind. "One of the apprentices just said I could find you back here."

"Oh, OK. So it's for...?"

"Your father." He reaches into his satchel and lifts out a parchment envelope, then hands it to me. *Leif ap Jeronil* is penned on the front, and on the back flap, a wax seal. "From the House of Stewards, Kili-Boranna—" he pauses— "in Christiana."

I look up. I'm sure there is more than a little surprise showing on my face. "Christiana?"

"The one and only. I trust you will deliver the letter to your father then?"

I nod. Still in surprise.

"And I can tell the sender that the person who took delivery was..." He trails off, waiting for my name.

"Sorry. It's Junar."

He writes it down on his pad. "Junar ap Leif." Dots something. "Done." Looks up at me. "Have a good day."

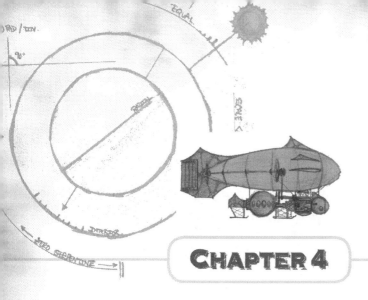

CHAPTER 4

"DAD! DAD!" WHERE is he? They said he'd gone home early to see Mom. Only one problem; no one's home.

We live on the bottom level where most pilots live. Not the best deck, but not the worst either. You get more sunlight than the middle decks, but it's still cramped, unlike the top deck which has a clear view of the balloon matrix. When Dad made Ace Pilot, he got offered a house up there. Oh boy, did Lance trip when I told him! Only the wealthiest people ever get that sort of real estate. Dad turned it down, of course, something I don't think Mom has forgiven him for yet. Typical. But we still have an outer lot. And my bedroom? It's got a big bay window that looks right over the edge. Mom wouldn't allow the bars to come off the glass until I turned eighteen. But when I got into the apprenticeship program Dad vouched for me. *A perk of the job*, he'd argued.

Mom still hates it.

My stomach is growling, so I throw the envelope on the table, rip off my jacket and goggles, and stoke the heater. Another perk: *never have to pay for top-grade nelurime*. I throw a spade full of refined crystals in the fuel tank, then latch the door. A quick twist of the master valve and *whoosh*, the little unit pumps out the heat. I fill a pot with water and drop it on the stove; yeah, I always say I'm not good in the kitchen, but what teenage boy doesn't know how to make *marso soup?* Noodles, some spices and a few vegetables from the cooler, and you have a happy boy.

I sit down, slurping the stuff, and stare at the parchment... the wax seal.

What could Christiana want with my Dad? Sure, he was only the best pilot in Aria-Prime, biased son that I am. But *Christiana?* It had to be a dinner. Award dinner with the Council of Houses, I bet. For saving Bellride from the Zy-Adair. Shoot, maybe even a Steward position! But he'd never take the job change. Not dad. He lives for the harvest. He lives to fly.

The envelope is calling my name. If it wasn't wax sealed, I'd—

"Hey, son!"

I spin around. "Dad!" I can't get my legs under me fast enough, knocking my bowl over as I reach for the letter.

"Woah, flyboy! Easy with—"

"It's a letter! A message from Christiana! The Guild Steward!"

He looks as surprised as I did.

"A letter? Christiana?"

"I know, I know!" I say. "Just open it!"

"Easy, son." As he takes the letter, his giddy grin betrays any sensibility of adulthood. "Now what would Christiana want with me?" he says to the letter.

"Gotta be an award banquet. Saving Bellride yesterday. Or your performance this season. Your numbers are off the charts!"

He dismisses my praise and turns to the wooden table. He slips off his leather flight jacket and peels off his helmet and gloves, goggles still around his neck. I get his chair, then sit beside him as he tears open the seal. But he stops short of pulling out the message. "I think we should wait for Mom."

"*Mom?* What? Nah."

He eyes me.

"I mean…yeah. *Mom.*" A deep sigh. "Of course we should."
I don't understand how he can be so considerate of her.

Dad lays the envelope back down. And we both sit there.
Staring. Father and son. And wait.

"We could head back to the aviary. Make a run."

"Dad, it's eleven o'clock. Any felrell we try and wake—"

"Bite our heads off. I know."

Another long pause. We don't say anything. Just look at the
wax seal. The official seal of the Guild in Christiana.

"Ah! I can't take it!" Dad steals the letter off the table.

I sit back, eyes wide. "But…what about Mom? What
about—you're actually going to open it?"

"What do you think?"

"Groceries! What does a lady need to do to get some male
help around here?"

"I gotcha, Mom." I swing down the steps, hands gripping
the banister, and meet her at the door. Even manage a hug.

"Well, I say, what's gotten into you, Junar?" She pulls away.

"Nothing. Just…thanks for going to market."

"*Thanks for going to market?*" She casts me a crooked smile.
"Junar ap Leif, what's gotten into you?"

"Nothing, Mom. Promise."

"You're up to something." She laughs. "Here, take these—"

"Got 'em." I pick up the bags and set off for the kitchen.
Dad is at the table. Mom leans over and kisses him on the cheek.
But that's not good enough for Dad; as fast as a felrell snagging a
sheep, he wraps his arm around her waist and pulls her close. I look
away. Give them a moment. Not that I don't dream of doing the
same to a girl someday, but—I mean, it's my *parents*. Plus, I hope
my wife won't be as—

"What's gotten in to you boys?" she says.

I look back to them. Dad pulls the envelope out of his shirt.

"What's this?" she asks, taking the letter.

"Read it, Love," Dad says.

40

I walk around the table as Mom unfolds the parchment. Her eyes are quick. And with every line, the anticipation seems to grow. Until...

"Oh, Leif!" What comes next is a nearly indiscernible stream of semi-thoughts punctuated with a hand to her chest or fluttering beside her face. "I—I can't believe...but you'll be flying against...can you do that? I mean—of course, but...*a new house?*" And then she lunges for Dad, arms around his neck.

Dad winks at me and gives a thumbs up.

Mom suddenly pulls back. "Wait, you are saying *yes*, aren't you?"

"Ha, my dear Sondra, need you even ask?"

"*Oh, Leif!*"

And thus begins our new life, one I can't even begin to dream of.

Goodbye Bellride. Hello Christiana.

But breaking the news to Lance is not something I'm looking forward to. Festival is going to be a long one tonight.

Bellride's sanctuary is packed, as it is every Sunday night. It's full of the *Children of the Light*, all looking to the stars through the open ceiling of the circular amphitheater. The music is more jovial than usual, as if the minstrels in the center floor are expressing my emotions. But I know that's not logical. So I write it off as being my positive disposition.

I'm singing a familiar song, one of a hundred I've sung since infancy, but my mind is otherwise engaged. Eyes searching for Lance among the flowing banners and waving hands. He's two sections to my left, four rows up. Apparently he's already spotted me, because he waves when I make eye contact.

Man, this is not going to be easy.

Eventually the music stops, and Temple Bellride's High Priest waits for everyone to be seated before he begins his homily. The air is cool, so all the families are bundled close together, listening intently to the message.

"We once were bound in darkness," he recites, dressed in his thick, magenta robe. *"But now we dwell in perpetual light, a boon from the generous hand of Talihdym."* A number of people voice the agreement, their voices faint in comparison to the echoing of the Temple Priest's. *"Where once we were pursued by death, a squalid cloud that snuffed out the flame of mens' souls, we now stand as conquerors, free spirits, enlightened by the wisdom of the skies, and called Children of the Light."*

Lance makes some gestures to me. To anyone else, it's spastic. But to us, it's our code. *Fifteen minutes after Festival. No guests. Aviary dome.*

The Temple Priest's voice grows stronger. *"We have risen above the murk and mire of death, delivered by the Great Talihdym. He, who always rescues his Children, a great deliverer who is ever faithful, has brought us to this home above the clouds, close to his presence, bathed in the radiance of the Suns, cradled in the comfort of the Moon. And within the very clouds that were meant to snuff out our life's flame, therein lies the sustenance of our civilization, the source of Life that we, to this day, worship Talihdym for blessing us with."*

No one's ever told me what we got delivered *from*, not exactly. Other than the clouds, which I get. But seems to me Talihdym makes clouds. So it's never made sense. How could he deliver us from the stuff he made? Our ancient ancestors used to live on the surface of Aria-Prime, they say, but then the nelurime clouds arrived, and forced all of us to the mountains. Eventually the clouds filled the whole world so thick that we could never return, and we found ways to survive on the peaks above the clouds. When we outgrew the peaks, we took to the air, and the Age of Invention was born. Ironic that the very clouds that threatened to kill us contained the very energy that has sustained us. *Nelurime.*

"And so it is we worship, with outstretched arms and open hearts, the One who has secured our place in the Light. Forgetting all that is behind, and looking forward to the eternal horizon of hope, we live free."

"We live free," replies the whole amphitheater in unison.

We live free, from what? And how did our ancestors live? What was the surface like? I imagine it was awful and intense.

Bondage is the word the priests use. *Bound to the land*. But that's all. It's not that I mistrust the temple priests, it's just that there seems to be so little of our history passed down. Shoot, I suppose it's so long ago now that few remember. I get that. I don't even know what the Old Script on the archways of Kar-Bellride says. But still, with something so important, I'd think someone would remember. At least I hope they would. The priests know. But they say it takes a lifetime to impart their knowledge to the next generation, that's why only those in their Guild understand it all. OK, so they're not really a *Guild*. Something separate altogether. But it's never interested me beyond weekly Festival in moments like this, so I'm fine with knowing that I'll never know. Just so long as it doesn't affect the Kili-Boranna and my career of becoming an Ace. The priests keep us focused on our purpose, and we do the rest.

"*So we pledge our lives,*" calls the High Priest.

"*We pledge our lives,*" reply the people.

"*To live lives worthy of our freedom.*"

"*To live lives worthy of our freedom,*" everyone says.

"*And in so doing, honor Talihdym, God of the Skies.*"

"*We honor the God of the Skies.*"

With our last pronouncement, the minstrels strike up their playing once again. People begin clapping, singing, waving their hands, all in honor of the invisible God who's all around us.

I know Talihdym is there, like they say he is. But I don't see him. Don't feel him like everyone else seems to. Shoot, I *believe*. We wouldn't be here without him, certainly. But I don't see him working daily like everyone else claims to. Or at least like the priests claim to. I believe in things that work. That make sense. Wings in the wind, creating lift, defying gravity. *The miracle of flight*, I believe in that. And I'll ride it all the way to the top. If Talihdym is there, he knows what I want.

"So, you're really leaving, aren't you, 'Nar," Lance says as he lies down two sticks to work on his nelurime route. We're sitting on the aviary dome, playing cellwurk. Aren't supposed to be up here. Servicemen only. But what a view of the lower level! Houses in every direction, sprawling out from the center of the deck. Level Two just above our heads. And the setting suns in the distance, clouds on fire, sparkling with nelurime in the coming twilight.

"Yep. Really am," I confirm, preparing to play the hand I've been building for the last two turns. The sticks represent flight routes, and connect cloud cards and city cards. The more nelurime and timber you can harvest, the more cities you can build. Build six and you win. I can tell Lance is bummed. Not about the game. About me leaving. Shoot, I'd be. "But I'll come visit."

"Yeah, sure," he sighs.

"Bro, I know it won't be the same, but I'll come back, and you know you can come hang with me whenever you want."

"Whenever the Guild Steward lets me, you mean." We both laugh a little. *Like that's gonna happen.*

Anyone who's ever had to say goodbye to a best friend knows how hard it is. You smile, talk about how easy it will be to see each other, and make the best of the situation. But you both know deep down it's years between visits, if any. No one really travels to other islands on Aria-Prime; you just kinda live your whole life in one place. If a friend leaves, it's permanent. You move on. Life moves on. And you become different people. Things aren't ever the same. Not really. It'd happened to Lance and me before with other friends; just never thought it would happen to us.

I play my hand and build a new island, effectively cutting off his route in the same action. He smiles, then looks up at me. "So, you gonna race?" he asks.

I'm glad to hear him change the subject to something we both love. *The Champions Race.* "You know it, bro!"

"Now I'm *really* jealous," he says with a smile.

It's what every flyer dreams of as soon as they find out what flying is. The ultimate test of skill, training and courage—the Champions Race hearkens back to ancient times, run annually for hundreds of years as the greatest race on Aria-Prime. It predates what few written records we have, so the only surviving accounts are oral. Long before there were such things as Guilds, the race was used as a means of ranking flyers, created to select the lead pilot for the harvest and determine the strongest birds in the fleet. While the Guild Stewards do all that today, the race lives on as testimony of our heritage and a plumb line for who, in fact, are the greatest pilots on the planet.

Banned for a number of years in my great-grandfather's generation as too many pilots died, taking nasty falls into the clouds, the Champions Race was eventually restarted after the advent of the harness rig. Made it virtually impossible for a pilot to leave his bird. A pilot has to be completely inattentive to safety procedures in order to fall; that, or equipment failure. Rare. But it's enough of a possibility that rigs are retired after sustaining any damage at all—weather related, age or otherwise. Uninhibited gravity is a flyer's worst nightmare. *Reliability is never an accident*, Dad always says. And it's that mantra that helped him win three years ago. Earned him his Ace title, along with his harvesting record and time aloft.

"Only another three months until graduation," I say, tapping my First Year patch. "I figure I'll sign up to race once I'm a Second Year and get that permanent position."

"You'll smoke 'em, 'Nar. No one can touch you," he says, abandoning the game and tucking the pieces back into his bag. I smile. Could never find another friend like Lance.

"Thanks, bro. But you and I both know there are some pretty amazing pilots out there who—"

"Why don't you just sign up when you get there? There's no rule saying apprentices can't race."

"Woah, Lance. Apprentices don't fly it. You know that. Come on. Name me one apprentice who's ever won. Who's ever *finished*."

"I would, but you haven't raced it yet."

I put my arm around his shoulder. "Well, remind me to tap you as my flight leader when I do." Lance is one of a kind. And, truth is, I'm really going to miss him. Not sure how teens are in Christiana, but Bellride's produced one of the finest pals a guy could ask for right here.

Yeah, everyone sees me as the outgoing sort, *a real go-getter*, our Steward tells my dad. But somewhere in me, I hate the crowds.

And meeting new people. Shoot, I'm afraid of people, period. Sure, they're always around, just like the clouds. Always watching, never sleeping. But how do you find a friend? I mean, a *real* friend. One that won't betray you? Lots of acquaintances, but no one like Lance. Besides Dad, Lance is the only one who gets me. Went from highchairs to harness rigs together. And soon, I fear, I'll be on my own.

"I'll be your flight leader," Lance adds. "But only if you fly *this year*. Promise me, *this season*."

"Bro, I'm not—"

"Promise me." He puts his hand out; Lance sure knows how to bug a guy.

"We'll see." And we shake. "Thanks, man," I say, then we both look out at the ever-changing sky. There's a long pause as reality clambers back onto center stage.

"So, when do you leave?"

"Three days. Mom's already started packing. Dad's probably down below now, sorting through his gear."

"You need any help?"

"With what?"

"With being the son of the world's most famous soon-to-be *Timber Pilot!*" Lance punches my shoulder.

No one's said it to me quite like that yet. Shoot. Timber Pilots are the most acclaimed felrell pilots on Aria-Prime. Truly a unique breed, they're part flying-ace, part forester, part warrior. Theirs is a dangerous but glorious mission, enough so that even being *asked* is an honor rivaled by little else. And none other than the Chancellor himself has the authority to invite a pilot, a request you never turn down; it was one of the only Guild-related activities that he ever had final approval on. And for good reason.

The precious timber—a commodity that directly allows for the expansion of all the floating cities in accordance with our world's ever-growing population—is harvested from the Northern Range, a series of heavily wooded mountains on the pole of Aria-Prime. So what's the big deal? Plenty. To even *get* to the Northern Range, one has to fly through the *Shoals*, a series of arch-like rock formations that jut out of the cloud-floor. And no use flying over or around them; the upper reaches of the northern hemisphere are perpetually cut off by a storm system we call the *Wall*, a system so tempestuous that the only route through is afforded by the minimal cover the Shoal's sparse geography provides. Navigating through them is only for professionals, and returning with timber is only for Aces. It's also the place where most people believe the Zy-Adair hideout. Though I don't see how anyone can actually live a comfortable life there. Probably why they're so foul-tempered.

Once there, the Timber Pilots have another opponent to face: the legendary *Lor-Lie. The winged wolves.* While they aren't unmanageable, they can bite a man's torso off if given half a chance.

And what does the pilot get as a reward? Well, a massive pay increase for one thing. And a huge house, for another; presumably the main reason Mom is so positive about Dad taking such a dangerous promotion. It's always about what *she* gets out of the deal, anyway. But Dad can handle her and the job, though I still don't know why he stays. He could have any woman he wants.

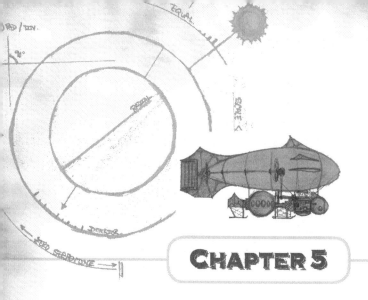

CHAPTER 5

As MUCH AS I love the felrell—and it's true, there's no creature like them—I love *flying* even more. Add in a healthy dose of technological ingenuity, and it's quite the attractive mixture. Sure, the Council secretly frowns on the *Inventors. Misfits. Curmudgeons. Aloof hermits just looking to get rich.* I've heard it all. But none of it sticks. *Different*, I give them that. But how can you *not* be different when you can come up with such glorious contraptions?

My first trip to meet one of the Inventors inside a real lab was when I was five. Dad needed the locking mechanism on his harness fixed. Jamming issue. Yeah, normally a metal-smith would address the issue. But a metal-smith didn't create *this*, and therefore is clueless as to the method of repair. That's what the Stewards hate most: the Inventors make useful tools that only the Inventors know how to fix. As I grew older, I argued that the Inventors should just be ascribed as a new Guild. But Dad told me never to breathe a word of that again. *Bad blood*, he said.

The Inventor's lab was surreal. I had never seen anything like it. I mean, I was five, so I hadn't seen much of anything. But

I'm seventeen now, and still marvel. Lights, tubes, beakers, welding torches, heaps of metal, drawers of bolts and screws and pins. Glass panes everywhere, and shelves of trinkets. It seemed like whatever the old man put on his work bench, no matter how haphazard or chaotic, would leap to life as a creation worthy of inspiration. And everything, it seemed, was steam powered. *The* wave *of the future*, I remember the old man saying at the time, his hand stretching out in front of my eyes.

Of course, I later learned it was Hidlebach himself. He died a year later. Completely alone. Was found in his dark hovel with his musty lab coat still wrapped around his body. No one even knew how long he'd been dead. So whenever I fly here to Knightsbridge, my thoughts always drift back to that first meeting.

Most flyers avoid these spires. I mean, avoid flying *directly through them*. The accelerating drafts and thermal declination create some pretty unsavory winds. If you don't like high winds. That, and the tight spaces make for short bursts of really intense flying.

All the more reason for Serio and me to appreciate them.

Most Inventors I know are night people. Most likely hate the light altogether. So the majority of Inventor dwellings—at least the ones I know of—are tucked away on the west side of the pinnacles, away from the rising suns. I learned a while ago not to bother them in the morning.

I've heard of a larger enclave hidden in the center of the rock formations. I've never been invited there, to the *Center Community*, as someone referred to it once. Apparently a little too sacred for me. *Invitation only*, I'm told. Meaning, *you have to be an Inventor*. But I feel privileged enough to even show up here. I mean, show up without a welcome party. Let's just say that most people who dare come to these caves walk away with singed whiskers. Dad told me that the House of Lords once proposed to exterminate the Inventors years ago, long before I was born. But the attack didn't even last the afternoon. These hermits can spit fire, blow things up and move boulders. Not the nicest people. At least they're nice to me. *Misunderstood* might be a better description. Aren't we all?

The only two hovels I've ever been allowed in were

Hidlebach's as a boy, and this one, owned by Dr. Maurice "Haupstie" Haupstien. With a wide, semi-bouldery landing for Serio, his cave is about forty feet to the rear of the flat rock, the entrance nearly out of sight. Wouldn't even know it's here if you hadn't seen it before. Dad introduced us a few years ago when I continued to show interest in meddling with Inventor technology; that's when my paper fox collection began. The introduction was secret, of course. But unlike other things, Dad isn't afraid of getting caught with the Inventors. If only he'd use the same determination to get out of a bad marriage as he does to pursue illegal friendships with Inventors, maybe life would be different for us.

A metallic, growling whisper crackles to life from somewhere in the darkness up ahead. *"Who's there?"*

"It's me, Dr. Haupstien, Junar ap Leif."

The tone of the voice changes, but the grating effect stays. *"Ah, Junar! Come in, son. Come right in!"*

Gears churn somewhere beneath me, then a blast of steam. A tall sliver of light appears ahead; I look behind me to catch Serio's eye. "Be good," I say, and give him a slight nod, as both my arms are busy with the saddle. I duck into the darkness, and bump against the door. It opens a second later to a squat, round figure bumbling toward me.

"Junar! What a nice, nice surprise," he says through a pipe clenched in his teeth.

"Hi, Haupstie." I fight the harness through the door frame.

"Here, here, let me help you with that," Haupstie says, quickly taking up the saddle; he's short but surprisingly strong. The smell of sweet tobacco fills my head.

"Thanks," I say. "But before you accept it, this one's a Guild saddle."

"So there's no liir."

"Right. And I totally understand if—"

But his look stops me cold. Perhaps I overestimated this venture.

"I know, I know. I'm just saying, I'll pay you for this one myself if I have to. I'll be able—"

"My dear boy, not everything's about money, you know.

Plus," he adds, "I have other ways of exacting payment from the Guild. Don't you worry. Off we go!" He hauls my saddle away as I ease the door shut behind me. I pull my goggles down around my neck and peel off my helmet, running my fingers through my matted hair. Gloves come off and I stuff them in my jacket. The hallway is meticulously carved, a granite burrow illuminated by cage-ensconced lights along the walls. I watch as the light filters through the swirling smoke of his pipe, casting the corridor in a pale haze. The sound of hard rock beneath my feet changes to a padded muffle once we reach a long thoroughfare of red carpet.

I follow Haupstie's bounding steps around a sweeping turn and emerge into a vaulted room lit by a massive glowing orb in the ceiling. The space is bursting with every metallic odd and end imaginable, accompanied by the permeating smell of machine oil and oxidizing iron. A low hum comes from a brass box against the far wall that Haupstie calls an *electrical generator*. One of his newer inventions. Bundles of cables snake away from it to various places around the room.

This is his workshop. Or *laboratory* as he prefers it. And anyone can see why. From floor to domed ceiling, contraptions spill from their shelves and cubbies, sporting gears and tubes and brass plates and buttons and levers and switches and springs and wires. His *experiments*. Ladders of various heights run along the perimeter on wheels, making every possible locale accessible to Haupstie's portly physique and stained, knobby fingers.

In the room's center, surrounded by four remarkable glass-pane walls, sit a cluster of tables. Each workbench is illuminated by thin rows of light in the floor and articulating, brass work-lamps from above. The glass panes themselves are scribbled over with writing. Numbers and calculations mostly. A few intriguing sketches. Haupstie's scribbles change every time I come here, always something new.

Haupstie passes through the gap between two glass panes and plops the saddle down on what seems to be the only open work space. The remaining area on this table boasts vices, bags of tools, wire-framed stands cradling glass tubes and bubbling beakers, supply bins, and more than two sources of open flames. While the floor outside the glass-enclosed workspace is immaculate, inside my boots crunch on bits of solder, metal shavings and a few screws. In here, cleanliness is not a priority. Only *creating*.

The only real heat comes from a large furnace in the back, its red glow adding to that of the orbs above. Steam hisses from valves and gauges around it, brass tubes snaking out of the workshop into other hidden recesses of Haupstie's lair. But warmth is the last of Haupstie's concerns; this is his *forge*. Surrounding it stands a dark anvil, a rack of hammers and pliers, his quenching basin, and a marvelous invention of hoses heaped around a metal canister that he calls a *torch*.

Haupstie dons a strange leather cap spouting a series of articulated arms, spring-loaded pinchers, and various sizes of optical lenses. With one hand he cinches up the strap beneath his double chin, then flips down a monocle.

"These Guild saddles always get beaten to a pulp," Haupstie says. "Shame."

I nod, captivated as always with the shelves of undeveloped inventions and spare parts. I pick up a brass spring that's seen better days.

"If you don't mind me saying," Haupstie says, looking over his monocle at me, "you could have easily repaired this one yourself. It's well within…" But I suppose my look of interest in his magical lab silences him. "Ah, yes. Very good."

"What's this one do?" I ask of an invention that looks half-done. A brass box with a few knobs, containing filament bulbs and more wires than I can count.

"Ah, yes," Haupstie says, looking up, "that one there will change the way we communicate. One of Dr. Hidlebach's last pieces. Never completed, though. Such a shame," he mumbles, resuming his examination. "Such a horrible shame."

I put the spring down and move to a basket filled with clamps and hoses and glass bulbs. "It puzzles me," I say, staring at the collection of novelties, "why you Inventors are not the lords of us all."

Haupstie looks up again, his mood changed.

"I mean, you can do anything. Look at this place! And life

is better for it. Shoot, *all of humanity's* better for it! If only you'd fight your way out of seclusion and take your rightful place—"

"Careful, son," he shakes a chubby, oil-stained finger at me. "Those words are not welcome here."

I put the basket back. "Sorry. It's just that—"

"It's just that you speak of things you're not educated to. And wiser men are better suited for the task."

"Then educate me! I don't understand how all this can be so forbidden!"

"All of this—" he waves that finger— "has glory enough for itself."

"Riddles. Always riddles with you."

"And not with you?" he retorts. His mood is so mercurial sometimes. "Were you not planning on telling me about your invitation to Christiana?"

"Christi—hey, how did you know that?"

"Please," Haupstie says, focusing back on the saddle. He swaps out a different monocle over his right eye, and places a large green one over his left. "Our *seclusion*, as you call it, affords us more privileges than you might think."

I stare at him, baffled.

"Well? Are you just going to stand there? Quick, hand me that torque-wrench."

I move to the other side of the glass enclosure and see the tool he's indicating amongst a pile of metal scraps. I point at it to make sure.

"First off," I clarify, "it's not *my* invitation. Dad's getting the promotion. Secondly, there's no riddle about it. Dad's the best there is. The Guild's just doing the obvious thing."

"The obvious thing?" Haupstie smiles, taking the wrench from me. "Funny you'd say that."

"What? Why?"

"Just not every day I hear the word *obvious* and the *Kili-Boranna* mentioned in the same sentence."

"Yeah, yeah. So it's been a long time coming. I know what you mean. But I suppose there's some level of bureaucracy in any Guild."

"My dear boy, the Guilds are bureaucracy themselves," Haupstie says, twisting on a metal plate beneath the pommel.

"What's that supposed to mean?"

"Never as they appear. Never *obvious*, as you put it."

"Listen, all I know is it's Dad's big break. Like I said, it took a while. But it's here now and he's taking it."

"And so are you."

"So am I?"

"Oh, don't be naive, Junar. They're getting the whole package. Your Dad, your Mom…"

I scoff when he mentions her.

"*I saw that!*" he says, his finger pointing at me. "They're even getting *you*, Junar ap Leif. Flying's in your blood, and the Guild knows exactly what it's doing, believe you me. Sure, it might be hard on you at first. New environment. You'll have to prove yourself all over again. But the truth is that they want you just as much as they want your father; you're a good long-term investment in their eyes. And in the end, you'll have to choose."

"Choose?" I step away slightly. "Choose what?"

"Choose between what's best for you, and what's best for others. We all do."

"Look who's speaking in riddles now," I say, crossing my arms.

Haupstie stands up straight, hand to his lower back. He flips one monocle up and glares at me, his wrinkly old eyelid arching over his eyeball. "What if there was another way for you?"

"Excuse me?" I ask, not sure if I'm more disgusted by the question or by the eye.

"What if you were born for something else?"

"You mean, if I wasn't born for flying?"

"Not flying," Haupstie replies. "Just…not the Kili-Boranna."

"This is crazy talk, Inventor. The Guild is my *life*."

"Yes. But what if you had another life?"

"Why? What else would I possibly do?"

Haupstie stops. Just staring at me. Unmoved.

"Wait, wait, wait," I say, moving out from the center cluster of workbenches and glass. "Are you actually serious?"

"You have the gift for it," Haupstie says, looking around his laboratory.

"Please, you've got to be kidding me."

"I'm not at all. Neither are the others."

I stop, hands on my hips. "*Others?* You've discussed this with other Inventors?"

"Of course," he says. "We've been watching you for years."

"Oh, so now you're stalkers too?" I'm exasperated. "This is crazy talk. I mean, in a strange way, I guess I'm flattered. But someone doesn't just *change their Guild*. It's got to be the same way with *you people*." Bad way of saying it. "Sorry. I guess what I mean is, don't you have your own kids? Successive generations and all? You know. Why an outsider? I'm not one of you."

"No, you're quite right. You *are* an outsider. But then again, so is anyone who hasn't been invited to see what we see."

"What you see? What are you talking about?"

Haupstie unclasps his chin strap and sets the cap aside. He walks between two of his glass panes and moves toward the glowing hearth of his forge, hands extended. "Junar, what is your job?" he asks over his shoulder.

Trick question, right? "My job?"

"What do you do, I mean, for the good of humanity?"

"You sound like our philosophy teachers."

"Then humor me," he adds, rubbing his hands together.

"Well, when you say it like that, we help provide light and heat to our civilization."

"By harvesting nelurime."

"Yeah, by harvesting nelurime."

He turns around and mumbles, "I suppose it's one way of redeeming the past."

"What's that?"

"Never mind," Haupstie says, warming his backside. "Do you ever dream of more?"

"More? As in, getting promoted? Like Dad?"

"No, no, no!" Haupstie rubs his rump. "Confound those Guilds! What do they teach you these days? Can't you think on your own at all?"

"Maybe you could be more specific."

"More specific? You actually need me to spell it out for you?"

"No, but, perhaps if—"

"If there's more to live for? If life is more than just nelurime and felrell and floating cities and timber from the Northern Range?"

Right now I'm thinking maybe the doc has been stuck in here a little too long. "But, Haupstie, that *is* life," I say. "As is marriage and a child—"

"Ah, yes. And *a* child. Tell me, do you think that's normal?"

"Pregnancy?"

"Pregnancy." Haupstie throws his hands up and moves back into his fold of workbenches. "Seriously. Do you even have eyes?"

"Well, last I checked, I—"

"Don't answer that." He picks up the saddle and heads toward me. "You are meant for more than *this*, Junar," he says, plopping the saddle into my arms. "All of you are. I'm simply offering you another path. To see life from a different perspective. And to do more with your own."

The saddle is suddenly heavier than before. "I appreciate that, I do. Really, Haupstie. And I'd love to come and work for you, to be in here every day, learning. But I'm meant for the clouds. To fly. I don't think I could ever leave that, or my family." He doesn't seem very satisfied with my response. "Maybe I could come here a few times a week after chores and watch you, and you could, you know…"

"It would be hard for you," says Haupstie, lowering his eyes.

"But if I came straight here right after—"

"It would be hard for you to live under *their* system after you see what there is to see from *these* eyes," he says, pointing to his old sockets. "These eyes have seen more in this lifetime than…"

There's a long silence as the doctor's expression grows distant. Then cold.

"Haupstie?"

"What's that?" he says, looking up.

"Something about what you've seen in your lifetime?"

"Never mind that now," he replies, and starts turning me around. "You have a Guild to get back to and a promotion to endure."

"I'll be back to see you soon," I say. We walk down his hallway.

"Yes, yes, yes, that's all very good."

When we get to the door, I stop and turn around. "I'm really honored by your invitation, Haupstie. Truly, I am."

"So is a pig when it's offered more slop," he says. Definitely upset. Didn't mean to ruffle his feathers.

"Uh, OK."

"Just take that saddle back and tell them you got it fixed," he says.

"I owe you one," I say, trying to smooth things over.

"You owe us far more than you'll ever know," he says, taking a puff on his pipe. "All your people do."

"Yeah...OK. Well, I hope you have a great night."

"See you soon, young Junar," Haupstie says, slipping back inside the door. "You know where to find me." The door closes, cutting off a thin wisp of smoke that disappears into the shadows.

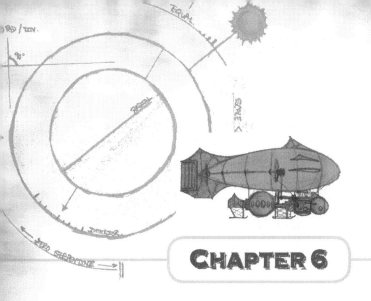

CHAPTER 6

"YOU ALRIGHT, SWEETIE?"

"Yeah, Mom. Just daydreaming." My breath is fogging up the starboard portal window; I've been absently tracking a speck along the horizon. I rub the glass with my sleeve, then rest my elbow on the cold brass frame. The clouds are always so beautiful from this altitude; funny how something so breathtaking can also be so deadly.

"You miss home?"

I clear my throat, never turning from the window. "A little, I guess. I mean, it's *home*, right? I'm supposed to miss it."

"Very true."

Can't tell her what I'm really thinking. Barely want to admit it myself. But above the desire to be left alone looms the frustration of bringing *her* into our new world. Wanted to leave all the painful memories back in that house, with all those things we spent all week packing. But it isn't the house or our possessions that hold the memories, I know that. It's *being* with Mom. "I'm looking forward to Christiana, though. I mean, what's not to love?"

She squeezes my arm. "It's going to be incredible, don't you worry."

"Yep. Incredible." And it is, I know it. *Christiana*. It's the floating, capital city of Aria-Prime, for crying out loud. But will I be swallowed whole? I mean, it's a whole new life. New places. More people. And making new friends. *Friends*.

"Son, why don't you go grab a snack from the aft?" suggests Dad. I love how he knows just how to break up an uneasy moment. Grandpa always used to say that *we can't even worry on an empty stomach*. Boy, was he right. Dad and Mom both lean back so I can slide by, trying not to bang their knees. Then it's a left turn down the aisle-way of the A-Class, straight back to the brass desk holding the snacks.

I'd learned a lot about the A-Class airship in school, but then I'm always easy to teach when it comes to anything relating to flight. The passenger pod is a bulbous tube decorated with red velvet and brass, with three chairs on each side of the aisle, four rows. Outside, the large gas-filled balloon above has horizontal and vertical stabilizers further toward the bow, and a massive vertical, articulating fin in the stern for steerage. The airship's second-generation *Nelurime In-Line Steam Engine*, or NILSE for short, provides power to two sets of propellers situated on the sides of the balloon: one set amidships, the other at the stern. The A-Class can hold up to twenty-four passengers and three crew, not bad as far as passenger airships go. Our belongings are in tow on a B-Class, twice as big as this one, but better suited for transporting goods. A freight carrier really. And entirely more slow. The Guild paid for the move and the tickets. Which means all the snacks I can eat.

I pass a few of the other passengers on our relatively light flight and smile, trying not to look awkward as the airship rises a little. *Thermal*. "Pardon me," I say, catching myself on an older woman's seat back. She nods with a smile, and I continue to the rear. No sooner do I ask a female crew member for a sweet bar at the desk, than the co-pilot starts speaking from somewhere behind me. Back down the aisle-way his head is sticking out of the forward hatch.

"If I can ask you all to take your—"

The airship drops at least a dozen feet and everyone gasps. I feel weightless for a split second, then bounce into the crew member behind me.

"Please, please, take you seats everyone," continues the co-pilot, now rubbing his bruised head. "Straps on. We're entering some unexpected thermal differentials." The airship leaps up, rising abruptly enough that the poor co-pilot spills out of the hatch and onto the passenger pod deck with a *thud*. The stewardess races past me and helps him to his feet. The co-pilot thanks her, dips his head in embarrassment, and climbs back through the engine room into the pilot pod.

I pick up one of the spilled sweet bars from the pile on the floor and make my way back to my seat just as another fluctuation buffets the airship. Thermals are all a part of flying. Sure, I feel much better on the back of a felrell; they eat thermals for breakfast. Air temperature fluctuations are nothing to be scared of, but I can tell plenty of people behind me are scared. The gentleman across from us is waving for a vomit pouch.

I sit down, lock my lap-strap, and tear open my bar. Take a bite, then gaze out the window. Only another hour, they say. I stop chewing. The speck on the horizon. In the time it took me to leave and come back, it's become three distinct objects. I squint. They're what the Inventors called *speedships*. Light, nimble blimps that use a smaller balloon as an anti-ballast and stubby wings to generate additional lift and provide direction. Unlike the larger airships which keep their crew and passengers out of the cold, as well as protect them from high-altitude sun exposure with tinted glass, the speedships position the two-man crew out in front of the balloon in an open cockpit. The engine compartment is situated aft of the balloon for balance, and the propellers are affixed to the belly of the balloon amidships to keep the vessel upright. I'm told their steam engines are *estimated* to be twice as strong as any we use, and can provide greater torque. Which equals one word: *speed*. The reason their speed is *estimated* is because no one knew for sure; speedships don't belong to the Guilds. They don't belong to the Inventors either. When I point out the unmistakable markings on the balloon's port and starboard surfaces to Dad, that's when Mom starts screaming.

The Zy-Adair.

"Keep your heads down!" Dad shouts, shoving hard on Mom and me. It feels like the market attack all over again.

The rest of the pod's in pandemonium. But my heart's racing too, so I can't blame them. My excitement level is somewhere between paralyzing fear and boyish wonder. Are my hands shaking?

"Everyone remain calm!" comes the stewardess' voice. "Please remain seated!"

"Dad!" I shout.

"Head down, son!"

"We're totally exposed up here," I say, calculating this A-Class' armament. "I don't even think we have any defe—"

"I know, son! Just stay down," Dad orders.

Dad's crossbow is packed back in the B-Class, locked in its case. Banned anywhere else except when on a Guild-sanctioned sortie. Dad yells something with his teeth clenched. He's ticked. And that's one version of my dad I know to stay clear of. Mom puts her hand on my foot. *Leave him be*, I can hear her saying. That's what she always says. Probably because she's had so much experience with him being ticked.

A shadow passes in front of my window, dimming the whole side of the pod, accompanied by a deafening rumble that shakes my seat.

"What do you think they want?" Mom pleads, as if Dad is the knowledgeable authority on pirate activity.

But Dad just shakes his head. "All the goods are in the B-Class," he says. His eyes track something out the port side. "Back there you idiots!" he seethes.

"Sir, please stay seated and keep your head down!" Those are the last words the stewardess speaks as glass explodes from one of the port windows. I sit bolt-upright and strain around my seat back, barely able to make out her chest as she falls—her blouse is peppered with red holes.

"Head down!" Dad yells, shoving me forward again.

Another window shatters, this time preceded by a loud *boom!* somewhere outside. The rest of the windows explode from the blast, and the passenger pod is jarred to port.

A man cries out. "My leg!"

I see Dad spin around, looking toward the man. He unlatches his strap and gets up.

"I'm hit!" the man cries. "Please! Help me!"

Mom is praying next to me, lips moving fast. Hushed words. Then Dad's voice. "Junar!"

That's enough to launch me from my seat. I jump over Mom's arched back, leap from the row, and land, crouched at Dad's side.

"Son, get my knife out," Dad says. Both his hands are covered in blood, covering the man's wound. I look into Dad's face for reassurance. Everything is going to be fine, just like back in the market, right? Dad squints, eyes shifting away. "Junar, my knife!" Shoot. I withdraw it from his left jacket pocket where he always keeps it. "Cut off a good length of the strap from a seat there. Then get me some clothes, shirts, anything. We need to stop this bleeding!"

More blasts go off, riddling the hull with loud *pings!* that make my ears ring. I can't even begin to imagine what's causing all this damage. The pirates are shooting something at us. But I don't see crossbow bolts anywhere, just puncture holes in the fuselage letting in outside light. I cut through two strap ends with Dad's knife and pass them off, then take off my jacket and shirt, handing him both.

"More!" he demands. I look around for anyone willing to part with garments, but everyone is panic-stricken. I glance out the windows as another two bursts put more holes in the pod. I wait for the volley to finish, then leap over Dad and kneel by the slain stewardess. I remove her linen jacket and hand it back to Dad, my hands sticky and red.

Someone else shrieks. *Pain.*

"Junar! Relieve me!" I'm back at Dad's side in an instant, replacing his hands with mine on the man's leg. "Keep the pressure on. The tourniquet should hold." He stands up, moving to a woman in the row behind ours. Suddenly there's a hand on my shoulder.

"Here, let me," Mom says. "Go help your father. Quickly."

Her voice is strong, but I can see she's crying. She kneels beside the man's torso and slips her hands beneath mine. She looks up at me again. "Go."

I spin around just in time to see another dark shadow block out the suns.

"*Down!*" Dad cries. I follow orders and hit the floor just as the seat cushion above my head bursts open. Feathers everywhere. I take a deep breath, then feel my head. "You OK?" Dad asks.

"Yeah, Dad. All here."

Then things go from bad to worse. Real fast. The airship lurches forward, everyone hitting the seat in front of them. I fall into Mom, then we both slide down the aisle-way, grabbing onto seat legs. The dead stewardess slams into me from above, knocking my hand free from the chair leg. I hit Mom again, and we all careen further down the center of the pod before colliding with the bulkhead. The back of my head is on fire, striking the lower rim of the hatch. Behind the hatch, I hear the unmistakable sound of metal scraping metal. Steam hissing. Then an explosion that shakes the whole airship.

"Dad, I think the engine's out!"

"Stay put!" He points to me. The pod pitches forward even more, people screaming. I feel the drop in my stomach; the airship is losing altitude fast.

I reach up and try the hatch.

"Junar, what are you doing?" Dad yells. I only give the wheel a half-turn when the whole hatch busts loose and falls away. The roar of open air frisks my hair and threatens to suck me out.

It's gone. The whole cockpit. The engine compartment. *All of it. Gone.*

Tattered lines swirl overhead, the only sign that something once hung from the balloon. And where they're attached further up, I notice black stains. Burn marks. And flames fighting to stay alive.

"It's on fire!" I yell, but I can barely hear my own voice. "Dad!"

"I heard you!" he yells back, then swears.

"He heard you, son!" Mom adds, not helping.

Whatever input the pilot last gave the ailerons, they're locked. I look down through the hatch, watching the cloud-floor approach. We're descending straight for it. It's begging me to come in with its unseen, pleading eyes. If we pass into it, we're dead within thirty seconds. Not that it matters much. If the Sky Pirates don't shoot us, the flames will ignite the gas in the blimp. That's one big *boom* we won't recover from.

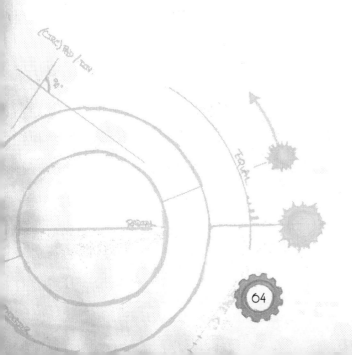

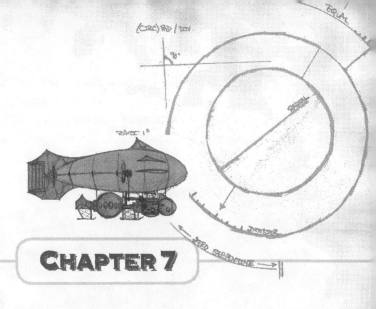

CHAPTER 7

JUST WHEN I think the fire is smothered by the winds of our rapid descent, the canvas lining bursts into flames. I can only assume the entire balloon is engulfed. Which means the last cords holding the passenger pod are too. If the gas doesn't explode, then we'll be weightless in a matter of seconds.

Dad drops down beside me at the hatch. "Knife!" he demands, holding open his red hand. I put the blade in it.

"What are you going to do?" I yell. He has a wild look in his eye. "Dad?"

He pushes me and Mom aside and puts a leg through the hatch.

"Woah! Dad!"

"Leif, my love!" Mom protests. "What in Talihdym's name are you doing?"

"Stay here," he shouts, touching Mom's face. "I'm going to cut us free from the balloon."

I glance past him. The clouds are coming up fast. "But, Dad!"

"That balloon goes, we all go. At least we'll have a chance if—"

"Leif, no!" Mom looks mortified, an expression born of confronting death.

At least we'll have a chance if what? I don't see how an exploding balloon differs from having *no* balloon.

Dad bends down and kisses her, then gives me a nod. "These are the moments we're born for, son," he says. "Fight until there's nothing left to fight for." He grabs the back of my neck, pressing his forehead against mine. "Fly or die." Then he reaches around the outside of the pod and pulls himself out and up.

I look after him, but risk falling out. I'm too shaky. I have no idea how this is going to end in anything less than death. Everyone is screaming. A minimum of three people are seriously wounded, and all three crew are dead. At least our descent has got the pirates off our backs; no more shooting, or whatever it was.

I crawl to one of the starboard portals and look up. The wind whips against my face, eyes watering. Bright sunlight. I can see three silhouettes chasing after us. They aren't letting up. And they won't, not until we're all dead.

Snap!

The airship shudders. Dad must have cut through one of the cords. Or the fire has. How many more? This is crazy. I'm actually rooting for my Dad to cut us free from the balloon and send us plummeting to our deaths. I look back to Mom. She's kneeling on the floor. Praying.

Snap!

Another rope severed. Then another. With the third, the entire passenger pod pitches sideways. Those not strapped into their seats are airborne, slamming into the port side of the hull. More screams, terror. I catch myself, hands around the busted window frame. Glass shards feel like hot metal pokers in my palm. I swear under my breath like Dad.

"Mom, see if you can cover the forward hatch!" She looks up at me. "That was three lines. If Dad cuts two more on the starboard-side, we'll be angled straight down! Don't want anyone falling out!" Not that it matters, I guess; a free fall into the cloud-floor is a free fall, period. You die no matter what.

Mom props herself up and looks around. A free seat cushion lies near her. She grabs it and starts to wedge it in the hatch.

Snap! Snap!

Two lines?

"Everyone hold on!" I yell.

The whole pod tips just as I suspect. Bodies slide down the port wall and collect at the bottom beside Mom. Passengers shout from broken bones; at least that's what I assume the breaking sounds are from.

Only one cord holds us up now, I imagine. Bet Dad won't even need to cut it. The weight will be enough. Or the flames.

Then it hits me. *Dad!*

I scramble over the chairs, climbing them like a ladder. The highest window I can reach is straight above me in the aft. "Dad!" I have to reach him. Make sure he's OK. "*Dad!*"

"I'm here, son!" he says just outside the portal. I poke my face out, the wind banging my head against the frame. Then he yells instructions at me. "Stay below! Last line!"

"Don't you fall for me, understand?" I order him. It's a line commonly heard in the hangar. Every flyer knows it; every flyer jokes with it. And every flyer knows it's the one accident you can't walk away from. *Don't fall.*

"Wouldn't dream of it," he replies.

I can only see his leg hanging over the side. Can almost touch him. Then overhead, a black form blocks out the suns. Closing fast. Too fast. How can their ships manage such speeds?

I pull my head inside just as one of the speedships comes within a few feet of us, then plunges past us. I scarcely know what to think. The pirates are screaming. I hear their voices. Taunting us in our demise.

Suddenly I hear a howl from atop our pod. "Yeah, baby!" Dad cries. "Bring it on!"

I look out the window again. The second speedship is drawing level with us when a massive bird descends on the enemy balloon. Its talons dig deep into the canvas and squeeze. A cacophonous pop followed by a violent explosion sends the bow and stern flailing away from each other, leaving only canvas tatters in the grasp of a felrell. And a smiling Sky Rider on its back.

Dad whoops again from on top, and I join him, releasing a frenzied shout. Mom looks up at me in panic. "No, Mom! It's OK!" I exclaim. "The Kili-Boranna are—"

Snap!

One of the most uneasy feelings in all the world is the initial sensation of free fall. In one instant, your stomach tightens as you get that sour taste in your mouth and the hair on the back of your neck stands up. Some people faint. Others vomit. But as our pod breaks free of the balloon, all I see is the light of the suns streaming through our ship, like long fingers flicking a spinning top faster and faster.

Silence.

Followed by a deafening concussion. The balloon explodes overhead.

The pod shoots further down, jarring everyone within. Spinning. Bodies pinned against the hull. Ears ringing. The hull shudders. I'm so dizzy, light shafts spinning faster and faster. Can't lift my head up.

Clouds. We're heading right for them. How much further? Five hundred feet. No, less.

Dad.

There's no way he can hold on…not with the spinning… not with the balloon exploding. I fight the blackness creeping in around my vision. The light is dim here. Yellow, shimmering. We're in the clouds, laden with nelurime. The gas is already working me over. Consciousness fading. And then another jarring motion. The spinning stops. I'm pressed between two seats, my chest caving. Have we landed on something already?

I blink. There's a huge talon in the portal over my head, another in the portal two rows down. I struggle to keep my eyes open. But the air…is so…so…

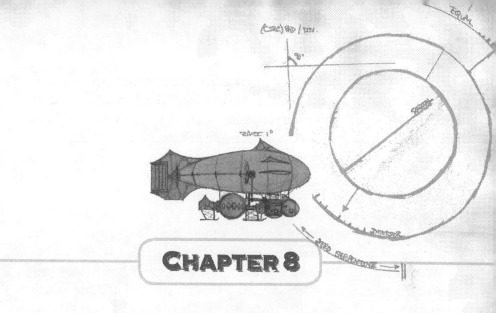

CHAPTER 8

I'M TOLD I slept through the night; I wish my head felt like it'd rested that long. The light hurts my eyes, and my head is throbbing, barely able to focus on what the nurses are telling me.

"Woah, woah, please don't sit up that quickly, sir," says a pretty voice.

"I'm fine, really." I pull the sheet off my legs and swing them off the bed. But two of the nurses won't let me get up. And understandably so. They explain I'm one of the few people in all of Aria-Prime who's not only survived a direct midair attack from the Zy-Adair, but has traveled *into* the cloud-floor and lived to tell about it. Dizziness overtakes me and the women help me back into a more relaxed position.

Most clouds contain marginal amounts of nelurime. Nothing that will kill a man. And these are the ones we harvest. But not the cloud-floor. It's something altogether different—a dense field of caustic clouds that covers the entire surface of Aria-Prime. There's no going through it, unless you intend to die on your trip down. The vapors of the cloud-floor are so lethal that at thirty seconds of exposure you're unconscious. At forty-five seconds, you're brain-dead. And the big rub? Well, they're full of nelurime. A great harvest field. That's why they're so yellow. Sparkly. But neither bird nor man are welcome there, so the Guild has a strict "no fly" rule despite how much we might be able to harvest from them—that is, *if* you can survive the run. And when I say *strict*, I mean lose-your-wings strict. Forever. Go join another Guild, 'cause you ain't working for the Kili-Boranna anymore.

Thus the floating cities, tethered to the places where mountain peaks poke through the top of the cloud-floor. Six mountains, to be exact. From smallest to biggest they are Knightsbridge (the spired peaks); Dunmorrow; my home island of Bellride; the three small peaks of The Moors; then Fairvale; and finally the capital, Christiana. The first floating cities that the Inventors started creating were simple, of course—nothing like what we have today—and had lots of mishaps. The balloons were thin, the woodwork unstable. But over the succeeding generations, the technology improved. Eventually, the land on the mountains was given over entirely to farming and herding, while the floating decks were committed entirely to habitation. The massive cables that keep each city from floating away are virtually indestructible, as are the nets full of massive balloons—also known as the *balloon matrix*. The cities always drift with the prevailing winds, taking them off center from the mountain peaks, usually twenty or thirty degrees, depending how the engineers have the compensation cables rigged. This allows for cable swings to transfer workers and supplies with ease. I've never ridden in one, but I hear they're a blast.

"Young sir, you really should rest a bit more," says one nurse.

I look from her to the other two nurses at the foot of my bed. The room is dim, brass pipes running across the ceiling. Something is whirring. Then an elderly man whisks into the room, notebook permanently folded into the crook of his arm.

"I'm sorry, he just won't stay down, Doctor," says one adamant nurse. "So restless in that brain of his."

"Now, now, Dolores," says the doctor, "he's fine." The old

man has a kind smile.

See, ladies? I'm fine.

"Thank you, nurses," he adds. "That will be all."

They leave. But I hear one nurse contesting down the hall, "...I still say he needs more rest..."

"Well there, young man," the doctor says as he hops up onto my bed, his two white tufts of hair bouncing with him. "Seems you and your father are quite the heroes! Mother, too."

Why hadn't I thought about them? "My parents. Are they alright? Where are—" My head starts pulsing from the effort.

"Easy there. Everyone's fine. Safe and sound. And in remarkable shape, I might add, given the circumstances."

My hand is burning. I'm not sure why I hadn't noticed before now. I raise it up to see it wrapped in a bandage.

"Got quite a laceration there, you did. Should heal right up though, quick as copper."

"Copper?"

There's a knock at the door. I look up.

"Hey there, flyboy."

"Dad!" This time I *do* sit up too quickly. "Woah—"

"Gotcha," Dad says, his arm under me in a second. The doctor is still sitting on my bed, steadying my waist.

"Didn't think we were gonna make it out of that one," I say.

"That makes two of us," Dad says, helping me recline. "Almost didn't."

"It seems to me that you both owe your fellow pilots a great deal of thanks."

"You can say that again, Doc." Dad smiles. "Why, if it wasn't for them—"

"And you cutting that gas bag off us," I add. Dad winks at me. Then continues.

"But if it wasn't for our brothers, we'd be—"

"Dead!" The doctor throws his hands up in the air. "Suffocated! Splat! Or worse!"

Dad and I stare at him. "Worse than dead?" I ask. Awkward silence. "Thanks for that, Doctor...?"

"Doctor Remkovich. Pleased to meet you both," he says,

offering his hand.

"And you," Dad and I agree.

Dr. Remkovich slips off the bed, pushes up his spectacles, then pronounces us both in good health, all things considered. Dad wears a sling around his left arm; me, white gauze around my head and hand. "I presume you'll have quite the reception tomorrow, what with yesterday's escapade and all," says Dr. Remkovich. "As if your arrival here wasn't grandiose enough." He produces a thin, brass plate, two inches square. "If you should need anything further," he says, handing the plate to Dad. We both thank him, then the old man dips his head and slips out.

Dad looks at the plate, flipping it over. Etchings on the card spell out words. *Level 10, Inner Deck, Home 24, Sub B. REMKOVICH.*

"What is it?" I ask.

"Guessing it's his home address."

"On a card? That's unusual." He sure was an animated little man. More lively than any doctor I've ever met.

"Well, what do you say? Time to get outta' here?" Dad asks.

"Shoot, yeah!" Almost forgot. "What about Mom?"

Dad chuckles. "She was outta' here last night. Had to see our new house and get it ready. Truth is, I don't think she likes hospitals any more than you or me. That, and she is pretty strong. It would take an entire nurse ward to keep her down. How I love that woman."

"Totally." My attesting isn't entirely genuine, however. I just don't get how he can love her after all she did. But having almost lost her, I'll be happy to see her. I guess.

Dad helps me up, slowly. I take a second to gain my balance, then we start toward the door. "Hey, Dad?" He pauses. "What you did back there, and how you risked your life for everyone, well… what I mean to say is, I just…I love you."

"I love you too, son." He kisses my head, then we sign out.

I was expecting a cool new house. What I wasn't expecting

was a mansion. "Are you sure this is it?"

"That's what the message says." Dad pulls the parchment letter out of his jacket to double-check the address. For both our sakes.

I leave Dad's side and race toward the front bridge—an arch that spans the gap between the main road and the house's foundation platform. Then I run up to the front door, bursting through.

"Easy there, pilot man," comes the soft voice from my childhood.

"Mom!" She stands against a wall in casual clothes, hair up, and a towel slung over her shoulder. Despite all my misgivings, I pick her up off her feet. She beats me with the towel, probably happy for my sudden change, albeit temporary, we both know. The door closes behind us. Dad walks over and we all embrace.

"We should all thank Talihdym for today," he suggests. "And for yesterday." We do. Right there on the spot. For keeping us alive. Shoot, I'd never been so grateful. I squeeze my parents more during this prayer than I ever have in my life. You do that when you almost lose someone you love...when you almost lose yourself. It seems fitting that before we did anything else in this new house as a family, we prayed. I only hope it has a strong effect.

"So, boys," Mom says, grinning, "who wants a tour?"

The house is unbelievable. As on Bellride, we're given a plot on the deck's perimeter; unlike Bellride, we have a three story home on the top deck! Yeah, that's right. *Three stories on the best level.* Oh man, it's too incredible. The kitchen can seat, like, twenty-five people. Everything is shiny, new copper and brass, streamlined pipe conduit, and more gauges than I've ever seen. Feels more like the bridge of a C-Class cruiser than a kitchen. Mom is clearly excited. And I'm happy for her. I am. I know I should be. But I'm also happy for me.

Each floor has a living room, each with an independent nelurime heater, tinted glass windows, and brand new sheep-leather couches. Mom and Dad's room is on the second level. It's cool. They have their own bathroom, and a huge closet that Mom can walk into; of all things she thinks *that* is almost as cool as the kitchen. Go figure.

There's a guest room, three bathrooms, a grand family room, and a master study for Dad. But my room is on the third floor.

I open the door. Pitch black. "Anyone know where the light is?"

"Right here," Mom says behind me, and flicks a switch to my right just inside the door. A motor springs to life, then the sound of gears. And in the center of the room, huge slits open up along a dome, like massive curved flower petals overlapping one another. Soon the six petals recede into the walls, revealing a crystal-clear domed ceiling with a perfect view of the balloon matrix.

"Unreal," I breathe out.

A ladder stands in the middle of the room, ascending to a wide wooden platform with a brass railing.

"Go ahead, son," Dad says. I look back at him, then to Mom. They're as happy for me as I am for them. I hug them both, then dart for the ladder. I can't climb fast enough. Up top there's a bed, a desk, and a knobby, antiqued lamp stand. There's also a reading chair, book case, and…

"A telescope? Oh, you've got to be kidding me! This is…is awesome!"

"Had it ordered up especially for you, flyboy," Dad says, beaming.

"You guys are incredible. This *house* is incredible!"

"Oh, it's truly a blessing, Leif," Mom says, hugging Dad for the hundredth time, then kisses his cheek.

"You're a blessing, Sondra," Dad says. I wince and look away. A blessing to whom?

"Oh, I almost forgot," Mom says, hand to her chest as she turns to Dad. "Tonight!"

"Tonight?" Dad repeats.

"The guys are coming over."

"The guys?"

"What guys, Mom?" I ask from my platform.

"You know," she gestures. "*The guys. Our* guys. Kar-Bellride

Kili-Boranna!"

"What?" Dad and I both reply in unison.

"They are?" asks Dad. "You're kidding me. Sondra!"

"I said I'd throw them a *thank you* party. For saving our lives and all."

Dad reaches over and holds her face in his hands. "Sondra ay Linell, I couldn't have married a more wonderful woman."

I look back to my copper and steel telescope.

No, Dad. You probably could have.

Dad usually doesn't talk this long about anything. But everyone knows it's from his heart. "All I can say, guys, is *thanks*. Thanks for always watching my six, for looking out for my family."

"And for catching you in midair when you tried flying without a bird!" says one of his buddies.

A chorus of laughter.

"Well said, Bronn," Dad says, laughing. "Won't try that again unless you're around." Then Dad looks to each of them. "A truer family a man has never had."

"A toast!" Everyone turns. It's Dad's wingman, Gerold. "To our very own Ace of the Skies, and forever a Bellridian flyer!"

"Don't forget where ya came from, Leif-Bird!" adds Bronn.

More laughs.

"To our very own, Leif ap Jeronil, the luckiest flyboy in Aria-Prime, and one amazing friend," says Gerold with his mug raised high. "Fly or die!"

"Fly or die!" Vessels clink, then silence as our guests take deep drafts. Dad even gives me a chance at his mug. The dark ale of the Bellridian Kili-Boranna is a brew made in the wings of the tack barn, out of view from outsiders. This batch they shipped over just for tonight. Of course, shipped *secretly*; no alcohol allowed on the islands. But the Kili-Boranna can get away with small pleasures like this; who's going to fight them? Bitter, and drunk only on special occasions, the ale will always remind me of home.

How everyone fits in this kitchen is beyond me, despite its

impressive size. But we pack them in. We're putting Mom's new masterpiece through its paces on the very first night. Mom has extra help from all the other wives, of course. The food is exceptional, as is the company. For nearly dying the day before, I have never seen Dad and Mom so happy in all my life, as if everything in the past is forgotten. *Almost.* Here they are, surrounded by their closest friends, and Dad at the top of his game. Life can't get any better.

And for me? Well, I'm pretty happy too. Lance made the trip out. Not that he had a choice. Apprentices are *required* to attend Guild transfers. We do all the dirty work and heavy lifting in the move. And I'm glad to see him.

"Cool telescope!"

"Yeah, Dad said he ordered it especially for me."

"An RL-24h. *Radial Luminary, Twenty-Four Helix.* Man, these things are expensive!"

"Well, my Dad *is* the number one paid pilot in Aria-Prime now, ya know."

"Don't brag, feather pants. I know." But Lance can't hide his huge smile. He looks through the eye piece. "So cool."

"Thanks."

He steps away, then sits down in my new reading chair. "All I can say is, nice digs, bro. You got it made."

"Well, at least *here* I do. One of the apprentice liaisons of Kar-Christiana is downstairs. Told me all newbies get hazed pretty bad."

"Hazed?" Lance sits up. "Like, beat up?"

"Something like that."

"But you're—"

"Almost Second Year. I know. I said the same thing. He said it doesn't matter."

Lance looks down. "Sorry, 'Nar. Welcome to the big city, I guess."

And big city it is. I put Christiana's balloon matrix at four times the size of Bellride's. I've never seen anything so big in all my life. And there it is, soaring right above me as I sleep.

Unlike Bellride's measly four levels, Christiana has ten. *Ten!* And each twice as big as Bellride's. The houses are bigger, the paths are bigger, the bridges are bigger...even the food is bigger! And I can't wait to see the hangar. If it's anything like the polished glass and steel architecture I've already seen, I'm sure the bird home is ultra modern too. Hazing or no hazing, Serio will be there. And so will Dad. I'll manage.

A knock on the door. "Come in."

"Hey there, you two." It's Mom. "Everyone's heading back to the hangar, Lance. You want to stay here for the night?"

"Nah, but thanks, ay Linell. The Steward will have my hide. You know how it goes."

"Indeed I do."

"Night, 'Nar. Sleep good." He pounds my good fist.

"You too, man," I reply. "Thanks for coming. I mean it. Really means a lot."

Lance slides down the ladder, then looks up. "I'm just glad you're OK. Now stay that way, would ya?"

"I'll try," I say as I flex my bad hand. Pain. "I'll try."

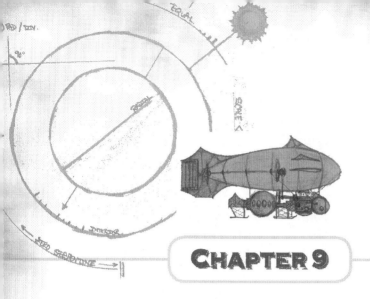

CHAPTER 9

DAD, MOM AND I set out from the house. Suns are barely warming the eastern sky as we cross the bridge onto a main deck and head toward the center of the level.

It was a short night. My head still hurts from the cloud gas. Focusing on stuff is way easier, but every now and then I feel like I want to vomit. They did say it would take a few days to wear off, I remind myself. Not fun stuff. Mental note: *never get near the cloud-floor again.*

We pass cluster after cluster of sleepy houses, broken up by the occasional open market or business district; even proprietors find it too early to be up yet. I would protest the early hour again, but I know it would only antagonize Mom, and we all knew where that would end.

The wind is a few clicks above *calm* today; no storm systems in the forecast either. So the only thing to hear in this sleeping city is the eternal creaking of deck joints flexing in the breeze. I suppose if someone hasn't grown up with it, the sound would be tremendously annoying, but the groan of the boards has a calming effect for those born in the air. Not sure how I'd sleep without it.

Nelurime lamps light the way until the suns are up, directing us over long bridges and winding suspension routes. While the smaller cities, like Bellride, are mostly constructed of one solid deck for each level, a city as large as Christiana is made up of dozens of platforms, each connected together by various means to form a single level. Mom isn't as keen on the idea of seeing the level below while traversing a bridge—or even worse, the next *three* levels. That's hundreds of feet straight down. She grabs my hand, cutting off my circulation. But I can't blame her. Just because you're born in the air doesn't mean you're immune to a fear of heights; that's something reserved for those of us who work in the air every day. For someone like me, looking down on top of a hundred houses layered over one another is amazing.

Aside from the wooden platforms that make up each deck, Christiana is held together by brass, tin, copper, and a new compound the Inventors are calling *steel*. Hard to make, but extremely solid stuff. Polished daily, the railings glimmer in the yellow light, as do the rooftops, the archways, the benches, and every bit of hardware that holds the houses to the deck. On the outer perimeter of each level, tinted glass windowpanes are suspended over sections of the path to serve as resting spots, shadowed from the light of the suns. These are crucial during the hottest hours of the day, or when you forget your protein cream. Sunburns are nasty things to recover from out here. I've had my share, and rarely forget to cover up.

Finally we arrive in the center of the top deck, and Dad points out the cable swing network. It's a massive convergence of cables that radiate in all directions, lines that can speed passengers from one side of the city to the other with ease. Or *vertically*, as was our case this morning. The main structure that holds all the cable swings sits to one side of the large vertical and horizontal bundles. We enter the building and take our seats in the first swing. Must be twenty swings all lined up and ready to go.

"Hands in," Dad says. He's used cable swings before, but this is a first for Mom and me. Everyone on Bellride walks; grand staircases connect the decks, which makes for good exercise. There just isn't a need for this much convenience.

Each swing is a small metal box with two pairs of bucket seats facing the same direction. Two arms on the box's port side arc overhead where they meet the *syncrolinkage*: a gimbaled gyro with a locking clamp and wheel assembly. The syncrolinkage not only connects the swing to the cable, but maintains the swing's orientation, no matter what angle the cable runs at. Aside from the two doors on the swing's starboard side, the only other notable attributes are the curved glass windshield and the deployment control panel which consists of a metallic red lever, a blue lever and a translucent green button.

"Looks simple enough, Dad," I say.

"To operate, but not to build. Geniuses."

I love Dad's deep respect for the Inventors. That's where I get it from. Though he never admits it publicly. Wouldn't want to be labeled a *dissenter* needlessly. Can earn you bad points with the Guilds, even among the Houses for that matter. And while everyone attributes the cable swings to the *Giloti*, or the *Metalworkers Guild*, those on the inside know the Guild buys the contraptions from the Inventors, and then pays enough to keep it quiet...*forever*. At least that's what I've picked up while doing repair errands for broken felrell equipment. How the Inventors tolerate us stealing their ideas like this makes me wonder what their motives are. Maybe it really is money, like everyone says. Though I doubt it, given how much Haupstie has helped me at his own expense. But one has to wonder how they sleep at night when others constantly take credit for their work.

"Make sure your lap straps are secure," Dad says. "Here we go!"

Dad throws the red lever first. This activates the gear assembly that moves the swing in line with the continuously running cable—one big loop from the top of Christiana to the bottom. In this case, the cable shoots straight down, right through the center of all ten levels. Next, he moves the blue lever that controls the servos, getting the syncrolinkage in place for a grab.

"Might want to hold on to something," he says, then hits the green button.

The syncrolinkage clutches the secondary cable, part

of a spring-loaded recoil system that absorbs the initial jerk of momentum, and then *whoosh!* We're transferred to the primary, high-speed cable. Mom gives a little squeal beside Dad up front as the swing drops out from underneath our stomachs. Dad puts his arm around her.

This is too cool. The first level whizzes past us, and suddenly we are 100 feet above the houses of level nine! I peer over the side of the swing as the roofs race upward. We're past them in a second and through the hole in the deck. Arriving over level eight, I look out to the horizon; the morning sky of blues and oranges hovers between two levels, vanishing in a blur of black, then reappears in level seven.

I look up front as Mom tightens her jacket around her neck a little more. Then grabs Dad's arm again.

We pass through eight levels in a matter of moments, then Dad looks over at Mom and back at me. "The stop is a little more abrupt."

"What?" Mom asks over the wind. But Dad leaves no time to explain. On purpose.

He presses the illuminated green button again, this time turning it off. I look over the side and see a small structure coming up fast, and below it, a huge net. I can only guess why: to catch out-of-control swings that miss their stop. Not too comforting. Beyond the net is the cloud-floor.

"Hold on!" yells Dad.

Dad throws the blue lever and the syncrolinkage comes undone. Meaning, we're free falling. Mom grabs Dad's bad arm. He winces. Then the sensation takes a violent reverse, as if my stomach has dug into my heels. Our swing leaves the primary cable for the secondary, and we slow to a near-standstill. Coming to a complete stop, there's a soft *click* beneath us.

It's over.

Dad pulls the red lever back to starting position and our swing slides away from the cable. The doors open automatically, but Mom won't let go of Dad. She's still clutching his left arm, eyes closed.

"Sondra, baby," Dad urges her. "We're safe."

She looks up. A bit ashamed. "Ah, right." Nervous laugh. Typical Mom in a new situation.

We all climb out of the swing and start along a path following shiny metal signs that point toward the aviary hangar. But in all honesty, no one needs a sign.

Halfway to the far side of the deck stands an immense round structure nearly 100 feet tall, like half a ball protruding from the deck. The building is made entirely of dark, metallic panels, with every other one appearing semitransparent. Presumably windowpanes. Bronze cables crisscross the surface, making it appear like a domed fidtchell board, but instead of square, every panel is hexagonal. Brass pipes lace up the sides in pairs, then disappear over the summit, presumably carrying water or waste to various parts of the interior.

Attached to the main building stands a secondary building, smaller but no less impressive than the first. The tack barn, I assume, but it can hardly be called a *barn*. Like the first building, this one is round, but smooth, maybe brass. The way it shimmers in the growing light makes it hard to tell.

Where the surface meets the wooden deck closest to us, there's an oval door. No handle.

"How do we get in, love?" Mom asks.

"We knock, my dear." Dad raises his hand and raps the hard shell. I thought it'd ring like an enormous bell. But it doesn't. Just a muted *thud*. I wait behind them, Mom holding Dad's good arm. My hand still hurts pretty bad. But the Doc says it will heal fast. Here's hoping.

The door opens.

"Ah, ap Jeronil." The man checks a pocket watch tethered to his grey, wool vest. He's lean, and unusually tall. "Right on time, I see. As expected." The man is neither enthusiastic nor dull. *Professional* would be the best word. And in that, confident. And why shouldn't he be? This is the prestigious gathering of Aria-Prime's greatest, most renowned flyers. The Kili-Boranna of Christiana. "And ay Linell, I presume?"

"Indeed." Mom extends her hand.

The gentleman shakes it politely. "Reginald ap Daramore,

Personal Assistant to the Steward, at your service."

"Honored," says Mom.

"And my son, Junar," Dad says, stepping aside.

"A pleasure, young Junar."

"Pleased to meet you too, ap Daramore," I say, making sure my handshake is extra firm, like Dad taught me.

Reginald turns back to Dad. "My instructions are to escort you first to your rooms in the barracks, and then introduce you to a few of the crew. Of course, your ladyship will need to wait in the tack barn." Clearly they're holding on to the name "tack barn" for nostalgia's sake—this place looks more like the Chancellor's Hall. "From there, the Steward will have breakfast with the three of you in his study."

"And our birds?" I ask, hoping to confirm what I learned last night at the party.

"They were flown in yesterday, as a matter of fact," answers Reginald. "Fed, washed, and ready to show. You have Kar-Bellride to thank for their care."

"Thank you very much, Reginald," Dad says, "you've truly gone out of your way for us, and at great expense, especially considering all that our trip's entailed."

"Nonsense." Reginald brushes the comment aside.

"Still," Dad presses, "if you're a testament of the Guild's efficiency, I look forward to a long life here."

"As do we, ap Jeronil. As do we."

With that, Reginald ushers us out of the cold morning air and into the tack barn, grander than anything I could imagine. Must have enough equipment for outfitting and repairing a hundred rigs. And then some. There are shiny, metal silos filled with feed, repair rooms, dozens and dozens of bird stalls; the Guild even has its own slaughter house for butchering sheep and fowl.

Unlike what I assumed, the brass dome is not metal at all, but glass, tinted gold on the outside. It lets in dim, filtered light that compliments that of the nelurime lamps, each fixture hammered from wrought iron and mounted along the metal beams that crisscross the immense space overhead.

There's not a smudge on anything, not even a single piece

of straw on the floor. The place is immaculate. Simply stunning. Whatever standard operating procedures these guys hold to, Kar-Bellride stands to learn a thing or two.

Reginald escorts Mom to a sitting area, serves her a steaming mug of coffee, then shows Dad and me through a windowed door into the locker room. He leads us through the maze of showers and toilets all cast in white marble, then stops at the lockers, handing us folded slips of paper with our combinations on them. The warm steam filling the space feels good, and I'm even more pleased to find out they had a sitting room designed just to lounge in. A *steam room*, Reginald calls it. "Relaxes the muscles," he says.

We leave the steam of the locker room and ascend an enclosed, spiral staircase. On the third level we pass through a wooden door and enter a long, carpeted hallway with a dozen doors on either side. We're in the main hangar now if my guess is right, out of the sight and smell of the tack barn. Reginald stops before a shiny mahogany door with brass hardware.

"Your room is number 3," Reginald says to Dad, "as per your request. Your key, sir."

Dad unlocks the door and walks inside. The spacious, carpeted room has a floor-to-ceiling window, angled in line with the natural curve of the building's exterior, presumably one of the massive metallic panes I saw from outside. Dad's room faces toward the outer deck. It has a comfortable bed, reading chair, and an oak desk with a copper colored lamp, as well as a mahogany wardrobe—way more luxurious than the sparse accommodations at Kar-Bellride.

Then to me, Reginald says, "I'm afraid this will be your only view of the pilots' quarters until you're inducted. Apprentices stay in the barracks above the hangar. No key needed, all one big room. I don't suspect you'll be there long, though: from what I hear of your flying, you'll be graduating within a few months."

His vote of confidence fills me up pretty good. Just because I make Second Year doesn't mean I'm guaranteed a spot in the cast, but it tends to lock in an apprentice's association with a particular house, so when a spot does open up, the Second Years are brought up. Until then, you stay a Second Year. One guy in Bellride was a

Second Year for three years straight. I watched him every day when I cleaned stalls as a Page. I knew it had to be rough on him.

"We'll save that tour for later," Reginald says as he references his pocket watch again. Like I said, *professional.* "Don't want to keep the Steward waiting."

Back down the stairs and through the locker room, a route which I don't think I'll have memorized for quite a while, we pick up Mom and head into an ancillary hall with a plush, burgundy carpet that turns left to a set of sliding brass doors. Reginald presses a button inset on the wall, and waits.

"What does it do?" I draw near.

"A *steam elevator*, sir," Reginald cites without turning round. "Will replace the cable swings soon enough. Easier on the stomach. And far more safe. A *refined* way to traverse Christiana."

"That'll be a relief," Mom says.

A short series of digits light above the frame until a soft bell chimes. The doors open revealing a small, red velvet room with gold trim. Reginald steps aside. "After you, your ladyship."

Mom and Dad both hesitate. There's nowhere to go.

"It's a moving room," Reginald reassures them, "no need to fear."

Mom straightens the coat draped over her arm, cautiously stepping inside. Dad follows, then me. Once inside, Reginald presses one of several numbered buttons. If my assumptions are correct, we're headed to the bottom floor. The doors close, and a single overhead light illuminates the room. It smells clean, like metal polish.

I feel the steam elevator start to descend; my gut barely notices the shift away from the deck. A steady hiss emanates from somewhere above our heads. We pick up speed, then a soft chime rings every time a new button lights up beside Reginald. Finally our moving room comes to a gentle stop. Not nearly as much fun as the cable swing, but Mom is far more pleased.

The doors open. Mom gasps and Dad holds her back.

The distinguished man before us, sitting politely at a tableclothed breakfast setting, is hovering in mid air. The cloud-floor is a few thousand feet beneath him, with nothing between them.

Sensing our acute unease, as I'm sure he does of every first-time guest to this particular chamber, Reginald whispers something to Dad. It's the floor. And all the walls, for that matter. Made entirely of clear glass. The room is quite literally attached to the underside of Christiana's lowest deck. Only the ceiling is opaque, made of copper, and fixed with a dozen recessed light bulbs. A grand writing desk sits to one side of the room, an elongated reading chair to the other, and a book shelf, ordered by color, if not alphabetically, directly between them.

"Sir, I present Master Leif ap Jeronil, his wife, Lady Sondra ay Linell, and their son, Junar, Apprentice, First Year."

The man stands up and, as if walking on air, comes around the table. The firm sound of his shoes' soles gives the only indication the floor is indeed solid enough to walk across.

"Completely safe, I assure you," he says. His opal colored hair is oiled back over his scalp, his eyes sharp and discerning. Tall, elegant, and suited to his high, open collar. "The only one like it in all of Aria-Prime. Come, come." He extends his hand toward Mom. "My fair woman, I am Lucius ap Victovin, Kili-Boranna Guild Steward at Kar-Christiana." And with a single, fluid motion, he takes Mom's hand, sweeps it to his lips, and releases. I see Dad raise an eyebrow.

"And you, my good man, are what we have spent all this liir on?" Lucius' eyes look Dad over from top to bottom. "Remarkable." He sticks his hand out, silently insisting Dad shake it.

"It's an honor to meet you," says Dad.

"The honor is and ever will be mine," says Lucius, letting go first and turning to me. "And Junar—" he cups my shoulder— "your reputation precedes you, young man. Not unlike your father, eh?"

"He shows much promise," Dad says with a low voice. He's being unusually subdued. Extra cautious?

"Much promise, indeed," Lucius agrees. Eyes back on me. "Reginald here will introduce you to your Headmaster, though I doubt he'll be teaching you much." He pauses. "But first, we dine!" To Mom: "Have you eaten?"

"Only a cup of coffee in the—"

"Only a cup of coffee?" He looks from Mom to Reginald sternly, then back again. "You are our esteemed guests." Lucius walks back toward his breakfast setting. "Come, come. Sit and let me get to know our newest flyer and his beautiful family." By that he means Mom. At least he's looking straight at her. *Figures.* She does have the tendency to produce lust in other men. Still, I can't help but feel protective somehow. Then scorn myself for feeling guilty about something that's clearly her own fault.

We sit down, Dad making sure to pull out Mom's chair before Lucius attempts. Reginald begins breakfast service: fresh coffee, fruit juice, then toast, bacon, goat cheese. Expensive tastes. And poached eggs. Not my favorite, but if the host likes them...

"So, Timber Pilot?" Dad starts off. "May I ask why?"

"You may, and then I would ask, why not?"

Dad shows a slight smile. "But there are dozens of notable pilots out there. Landrews in Knightsbridge, Felix from The Moors—"

"Come, come, my good man," says Lucius. "Denial does not become us. We are both men of action, men who cast risk aside as easily as a lesser man a corn husk. You have better numbers than any single pilot on the planet."

See, Dad? Told you so.

"And yet you remain in Bellride. Unnoticed."

"He's noticed," Mom contests.

"Yes, but by those that matter?"

Mom's face flattens. She forces a forkful of eggs to her mouth. Hates them poached as much as I do. But Lucius is right. Dad does need to be noticed by those here in Christiana. He deserves to. More than anyone else I know. Mom has to see that this is his big break—his *only* break. And hers. Even she has to see her ticket to luxury in the risk. *I mean, look at all you get, Mom. It seems life's been about you anyway. Why not willingly embrace it now instead of hide behind your mock concern for your husband?*

"The fact is, I simply had to have you here, Leif," adds Lucius. "I need a thinker. Someone willing not just to fly the Shoals, but someone who can *lead*. Who can face the Lor-Lie as easily as you face the Zy-Adair. And someone who can handle the pressure of overseeing the largest timber harvesting operation in the world."

"Wait, *oversee?*" Dad holds his fork in midair. "But I thought—"

"Thought what?" Lucius sits upright. "That you'd mix in with the lower pilots? Take orders from a younger, less skilled aviator? Shameful."

"Oh, Leif! That's marvelous!" says Mom.

Well, *she's* happy for him. But Dad doesn't seem convinced.

"Steward ap Victovin, I—"

"Lucius, *Lucius. Please.*" The Guild Steward dabs the corner of his mouth with his napkin.

Reluctantly, "*Lucius*, that's very kind of you, but I hardly think I'm ready for such a position. Certainly you have better, more experienced—"

"Nonsense!" He takes a nibble from his toast. "The only way I know to replace a good man is with a better one."

"Replace?" Mom raises her eyebrows.

"Captain Lofton. My second-in-command. No one told you?" Lucius' countenance changes dramatically. He looks to Reginald, who takes a deep breath and stands up a little straighter, if it were possible. "Lost, I'm afraid," says Lucius. "It was…a terrible accident." He pauses. I can't tell for whose sake. "A log fell atop him. He knew better than to pass below the convoy mid-flight."

"How dreadful." Mom looks down.

"Awful indeed, my dear woman," Lucius says, searching for Mom's eyes. "Your husband *did* tell you about the dangers involved with this career, did he not?"

"Well—yes, of course. I mean, well not every danger, I'm sure."

"It is not for the faint of heart," Lucius says, touching Mom's elbow. "And judging from the injuries you sustained just to get here—" he looks to both Dad's and my bandages— "I am assured more than ever that your family is a strong one." A chill goes up my neck. "The strongest Bellride has ever known."

"Steward—*Lucius.*" Dad puts his silverware down. "The point of fact is—well—I'm very honored by your generosity, what with moving us here, the raise, the new home and all, but I'd rather not—"

"Do not be foolish, man. This was not my decision alone. Even the Chancellor had to give his approval. You know that."

"The Chancellor, Leif?" Clearly Mom doesn't know *all* the rules governing these sort of promotions.

"There, you see? Even your lovely bride perceives the reason here." He's still touching Mom's elbow. "Come now, my good fellow. There is no one in all of Aria-Prime with your set of skills. These are the moments we're born for!"

Born for? Hey, that's Dad's line!

"Yes, the Chancellor." Dad plays with his chin. "He's certainly important."

"Yes, and you'll have your introduction with him and then the proper lead time, training and plenty of guidance too. But I need a man, a *real man*, to carry the weight of this position." He places his fist on the table. "Are you up for it?"

Dad looks at Mom. Then to me. Takes a deep breath.

"I shan't ask again, Leif," Lucius adds.

Dad. Say something!

Lucius waits. He's not moving a muscle, his cards played.

Dad!

"I won't disappoint you," Dad says, sticking out his chest.

Yes!

"Marvelous!" Lucius claps his hands together. "Let's finish here. Then, to Festival and the ceremony!"

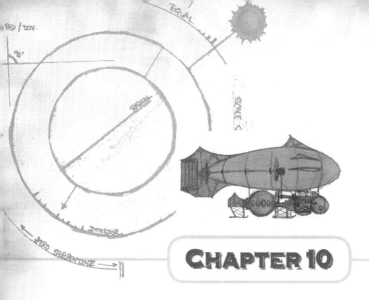

CHAPTER 10

THERE ARE PLENTY of reasons why I like Dad's induction ceremony, and very few why I don't. Massive crowds aren't really my thing. All these people in one place at one time…I'd rather be in the tack barn pitchforking hardened bird dung. Can't think straight with all these eyes looking at me. Watching. But I have to admit, being the center of attention isn't all that bad. Plus, it gives me a chance to see and be seen by all the most important people in Christiana. Including the Chancellor. And the girls.

"Ooo, now she's pretty!" Mom points out, yelling in my ear above the cheering crowd. Since my whole life has been about the Guild, I haven't thought much about girls. Until maybe right now. Wow.

"Mom, cut it out," I say, rubbing my ringing ear. While Mom might be a flirt herself, she *is* right in pointing out the good-looking girls. That *she* is pretty; and so are all the other *shes* standing just in front of the stage, each trying to get my attention. I don't know much about Christiana, but one thing is for sure: I could get used to this.

We're standing on a wide platform surrounded by Christiana's elite, looking out over the largest audience I have ever seen. And for good reason; there's nowhere else in the world that this many people can be assembled. *Champions Stadium.*

We're at one end looking down the length of the field. Two identical seating sections swell up to our right and left, sweeping into the sky like felrell wings. Must be more than half the world's population here. Reginald tells me each section holds 5,000 people, and another 3,000 on the field. As if that isn't enough, there are even more people standing outside the stadium. And not a single one of them has stopped cheering since the parade began.

This Festival makes the weekly one on Bellride look like a pitiful group of younglings attempting to throw a party. Beyond extravagant! Then again, they tell me this isn't normally how Festival is on Christiana; it's usually in the Temple, and with fewer participants. But seeing as how everyone considers Dad a gift from Talihdym Himself, they've combined the two activities with good reason for celebration.

To one side of the stage, a mass gathering of minstrels produces more music than I've ever heard. Steady beats and playful melodies serenade an endless line of wheeled carts moving down the center of the field. All manner of colorful creations explode from their beds. The people pulling them are dressed just as vividly as those mounted atop their architecture. Traditional feathers explode out of everyone's costumes in bold colors: fuchsias, blues, yellows and white. Grand headdresses, flowing capes, decorative masks. And the rhythmic music shakes the air, beating the deck hard enough that I'm sure the balloon matrix is vibrating overhead. I scan the crowd to see everyone singing and clapping in full celebration. It's a tribute to Talihdym, God of the Skies. And why shouldn't everyone be grateful? We are the favored of Aria-Prime, the Children of the Light.

With the parade line finally filing out of the stadium, the Chancellor calls everyone's attention back to the stage. He makes some speech about how blessed we are as a people and how much we've been given. Mentions something about Dad's heroics back in Bellride and his "prestigious" Ace Pilot's record. I'm blocking most of it out as there's a really cute brunette in the front row batting her eyes at me. Then I hear Dad's name as the Chancellor introduces him, and the cheering erupts once more. Deafening.

Chancellor Opius, quite old, bald, and adorned with liver spots, acknowledges my Mom. Then he makes a grand show of kissing her hand, clutching it in the midst of his billowing, burgundy robes. Must be the thing to do around here, though his action is far more grandfatherly than Lucius' could ever hope to be. Then the Chancellor shakes my hand, giving me a slight nod. The people shout all the more.

It's funny to think all this commotion is essentially over nelurime and timber. But they *are* the lifeblood of our civilization, so it's at least understandable. Nelurime only comes from one place: the clouds. A product of the surface gases of our planet and the power of the suns, nelurime is an ancient gift from Talihdym, used in producing heat, light and energy. And without timber from beyond the Shoals, we can't expand; our Life Control laws make sure our population is never ahead of supply. So we, the Kili-Boranna, keepers of the felrell, are the only people capable of managing the animals that harvest both nelurime and timber and, in effect, keep our people alive.

I'm lost in a few sets of blue eyes as I hear the Chancellor's voice say Dad's name, which yanks me back to reality.

"...And Leif will be taking his lead flight tomorrow morning!" More cheers erupt from the stadium.

I look to Dad. What happened to the Steward's promise of training, practice and lead time? Perhaps the Chancellor is ill-informed. Surely the old man is not a flyer...couldn't possibly know *all* the ins and outs of training for such an undertaking. Or maybe it's just a puffed-up promise to energize the people. A political stunt. Which I don't like. Not that the people need any more energizing. Dad smiles at the multitude and waves. I can tell he's tense about the pronouncement though.

"But, alas, I have said too much. Shall we not hear from our esteemed hero?"

Esteemed hero? Wow. To say Dad is getting the royal treatment is a complete understatement.

He walks up to the large diaphragm *phonocapsule*–another of the Inventor's creations, this one magnifying a person's voice. Clears his throat. No one hears his first attempt to say anything. There's simply too much noise. Bedlam is more like it. The girls are still screaming off to my immediate right. Dad tries again after the Chancellor prompts him, then raises his hand to the masses.

"Thank you, to everyone, thank you, for making us feel so welcome."

"We love you!" someone cries out, endorsed by a few more screams. Mom is clearly beside herself, almost giddy. Of course, I can tell she's mildly put off that the screams are from women. Serves her right. But at the same time, it serves her own pride. Wife of a national celebrity. Not bad.

To say I'm not enjoying this would be false. Who wouldn't?

"We–my wife and son and I–don't have words adequate enough to express how we feel." Dad looks to Lucius, who's standing beside Mom. "I'm obviously very appreciative of the Guild's extreme trust in me, and grateful for the opportunity of a lifetime. And to the people of Christiana, here's to our new lives among you. Friends, and now family. Fly or die!"

One would think Dad had just been elected Chancellor. Might as well have been.

I can't even imagine my good fortune! One minute I'm mucking stalls in Kar-Bellride, giving tours to sub-human lifeforms masquerading as future adults, the next, thousands of people are cheering my name. OK, *Dad's* name. But now a whole bunch of girls know mine. Or at least what my face looks like. Either works.

Dad waves and steps away from the podium. I have never been so proud of him. My Dad. Ace Pilot of Kar-Christiana, the greatest Kili-Boranna pilot ever to fly the skies of Aria-Prime. And I, his son.

Life has certainly become interesting, real quick.

With the induction ceremony complete, the Chancellor escorts us backstage along with his retinue of advisors, Lords and

Stewards, and congratulates Dad again. "We're really just thrilled to have you here, Leif," he says, clasping both of Dad's hands. "And we're overwhelmingly pleased that you've accepted our offer."

"Please, Chancellor." Dad smiles. "The pleasure's truly all ours."

"Call me Opius, Leif. Titles are not becoming of friends."

Friends? Shoot. Go, Dad!

"Opius. Well, this has been more than incredible already," Dad says. "This, I mean, and the new home and everything."

"That's all the Guild's doing, I'm afraid. Credit where credit is due."

"But surely–"

"Leif, you should know, I am schooled in flying felrell as much as you are in bureaucracy. I stay away from the dealings of the Guilds as much as possible, and I much prefer it that way."

Probably explains why he announced Dad was taking lead *tomorrow morning*. But I can tell Dad is still uneasy about it.

"The structure allows me the distance I need to make the wisest decisions for *all* of Aria-Prime, not just a few special interests."

I see the Chancellor glance toward Lucius, deep in conversation with members of the Council.

"Lucius oversees all things Guild-related. They operate on their own, accountable to the rest of the Council, yes. But thank me only for approving their request; it is your brethren to whom you owe the esteem which you improperly bestow upon me."

"You are most gracious," Mom interjects, taking his hands.

"And a pleasure meeting you, Lady Sondra." He kisses her cheek. Again, unlike Lucius, it's very fitting. I look to Dad: no issues there. Where Lucius just rubs me the wrong way altogether, the Chancellor seems quite the diplomat. Beloved by his people, adored by his men, elected leader of the Council, and now friend to my family. Is this really happening?

"And you, young man," he says, putting his hands on my shoulders, "we're expecting great things from you." Then he leans in close to my ear. "And if they give you too hard a time over there, you make sure to let me know. One needs friends in Christiana.

Trust me."

"Thank you, sir."

"You're most welcome." Opius shakes my hand, then dips his head to Dad and Mom. "Leif. Sondra." And with that, the Chancellor returns to the company of his advisors and is led out of the stadium, leaving us back in the care of the Guild.

Reginald steps beside us. "Master Leif, shall we return you to your home now?"

"In truth, Reginald," Dad says as he turns to Mom, "and if it's alright with you, my Love, I'd rather get right to business."

Boy, am I glad to hear this! Last thing I want to do is help Mom unpack more boxes.

"It seems there's some miscommunication about how soon I'm starting," Dad says, looking back at Reginald.

"All such issues need to be taken up with the Steward, I'm afraid," says Reginald. We glance over to Lucius who is still surrounded by his retinue, inaccessible.

"Have at it, dear," Mom says. "You know I have *plenty* to keep me busy."

"And I better go introduce myself to the Headmaster," I say, trying to sound reluctantly responsible. "Betcha they don't do things the same as we do on Bellride."

Reginald consents and offers Mom his arm. "Then I shall escort the Lady back to Ravenmoore."

Ravenmoore. Dad's new name for the property.

"Why, thank you, Sir Reginald," Mom says, threading her arm through his elbow.

No doubt she's thrilled to be with him.

The trek back to the hangar takes longer than I expected. The cable swings are jammed with people, thousands waiting in line. One of Lucius' men works some magic and gets us toward the front of the line, but even then the swings are bogged down. But it's still better than having to wait here for an hour or two.

A few of the girls in line force brass pens and parchment

pads into my hands, asking for autographs. Autographs. I'm completely amused. What have I actually done? Nothing. Mastered the basics of flying, celestial navigation, aviary care, equipment maintenance, nelurime harvesting, and the hangar's standard operating procedures. Which means I know how to shovel bird dung like a pro. Oh, and how to slide down the dome of Bellride's hangar without dying. That's it. Hardly worthy of scribbling my name on a pad.

Shoot, OK. I sign my name for them.

Once on the lower level, it's a quick walk to the hangar complex. And unlike earlier in the morning, the tack barn is bustling with activity. Birds sit preening atop perches, reins and saddles are being oiled, feed is being shoveled from silo to wheelbarrow to stable bin, and everywhere Apprentices are prepping fresh birds for pilots departing on sorties while others take the reins of returning birds.

"I really need to get this issue sorted out," Dad says to me.

"Go ahead, Dad. I'll be fine."

"I presume that's your Headmaster over there," Dad says, pointing to a lanky man clad in a leather vest and baggy flight pants. The guy certainly fits the part of Headmaster—even from this side of the tack barn I can hear him barking orders to pupils about my size.

"Have a good time, son," Dad says with a hand on my shoulder. Then he takes off for the pilot barracks.

"You too, Dad," I call back.

Deep breath.

OK. Here goes.

I turn for Mr. Long Arms but don't make it far. Five steps and something hits me hard on the left side. My whole left side. I blink, nausea quickening in my gut. I'm about to vomit.

Then blackness.

My eyes open. Everything's blurry, light killing my eyes. I squeeze them shut, head throbbing. I think I hear myself moaning.

And then, an angelic voice.

"Hey sport, can you hear me?"

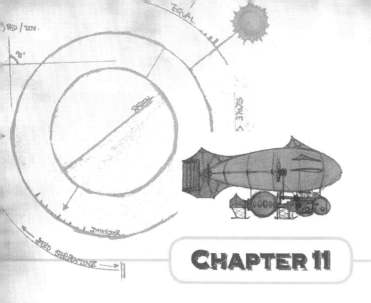

CHAPTER 11

"*HOW MANY FINGERS* am I holding up, kid?" she says. I still can't open my eyes against the shooting pain. But I'd like to see who's talking. At least I don't feel like I'm going to throw up anymore. Wait, scratch that.

"What was he doing walking in the zone?" says an older voice.

"I'm not sure, Headmaster."

"Idiot," says another person, younger. Male.

The *zone*, the main lane of incoming and outgoing activity. Most dangerous place in a tack barn. Bellride's is too small to be of any significance. But here, well, here it's apparently more important. Much more.

"How many, kid?" she says again.

I try opening my eyes. The smell of bird feces is strong. Helps me focus. But also makes the vomit climb higher in my throat. A few fingers floating in front of my face...then *her* face. Strawberry blonde hair. Wow. What was the question?

"How many, quick, before I hit you in the head."

"Two fingers," I say, then rub my head.

"Yeah, he's fine," she calls over her shoulder. Looking back at me: "Do they teach felrell wrestling back on Bellride?"

I don't get what she's talking about.

Wait, did I get clobbered by a bird in the zone? Oh man. Talk about embarrassing.

"Well, just watch where you're going, kid." She thrusts out her hands. "Name's Olivia. But you can just call me Liv."

For such a pretty face her hands are surprisingly rough.

"Sit him up," says Long Arms, the Headmaster.

Liv pulls me forward. I'm dizzy, trying to blink it all away. Stomach isn't right.

"Should be dead," says a teen standing beside Liv. Hands on hips, he's scowling at me beneath a red crop of hair.

"Shut it, Erik," Liv snaps. "Kid's new here, so give him a break."

There's a fourth person, an imposing form standing behind the Headmaster. Arms crossed: one's mechanical just below the bicep, made of brass struts with gears in the elbow, fitted with a leather glove; the other arm's muscular, a burly mass of weathered flesh. Tattoo on the side of his neck and cheek. A chest full of coir-broulli. *Hardened leather.* And a hefty crossbow slung around his shoulder...a shoulder adorned with a leather plate bearing the stitched "B" of his order. Brologi. He gives a quick nod. That's all. Then walks away. I would ask who he is, but I feel like throwing up now more than ever.

"You're not looking so hot, sport."

"Yeah," says Erik, "looks like the guy's about to—"

Vomit.

All over myself. Get some on Liv and Erik's boots.

Oh, for the love of Talihdym! I want to crawl between the deck boards and die. Great introduction, Junar. Just great.

"Erik, get him out of here and cleaned up," barks the Headmaster, scowling down at me. "And Liv, get rid of this mess. I want him standing on his own two legs in ten minutes. Report back to me."

"Yes, sir." Liv and Erik reply in unison, standing to attention before him.

"*Now!*"

Nice guy.

"So you're the new Ace's son, eh?" Erik throws a wet rag at my face. The locker room's big mirrors show my flight jacket covered in the Steward's fancy breakfast. Not so fancy anymore.

"That'd be me. Junar ap Leif, at your service."

"At *Dalfirin's* service is more like it." Erik crosses his arms and leans against the marble wall beside the row of sinks.

"The Headmaster?"

"The one. Tends to run the newbies through the ringer."

Perfect. But I expected as much.

"And don't expect any favors from me," Erik walks around behind me, wiping some puke from his sleeve. "You're on your own here." His fingers flick the spit onto the back of my neck.

"Then why are we still talking?"

He stops, and gets right in my ear. "Listen, you might be Second Year in a few months, but you're not from here. And if you're not from here, you don't belong here. And I don't like you."

"No one said you had to," I reply calmly. I look down and clean the last streak off my flight jacket. Bad move. First rule of being a newbie: don't ever let your guard down, not for a second. His hands shove me forward, my head collides with the floor-to-ceiling mirror behind the sink. A sharp crack of glass. Really getting tired of seeing black. I make myself keep my eyes open. Something warm runs down my face. Mirror has a red smear.

"If I were you, flyboy, I'd watch my step."

I try to think of something quick to fire back, but when I look up, Erik is gone. Cheap shot. I wring the rag out in warm water, pressing it against my forehead. Wincing from the pain, I look myself in the eyes, then shake my head. *Easy, flyboy.* Don't get riled up over nothing. Then I hear voices in the far end of the locker room. I put the rag down. Listening.

"What do you think of the newbie?" a voice says, echoing

against the marble tiles somewhere down one of the rows.

"Seems confident. We'll see."

Other apprentices? Great. More people talking about me.

"How do you think he'll handle the mission?" A metal locker door slams.

"I dunno. But can't wait to see the look on his face the first time." The voices laugh. "Always priceless."

"Think he'll make it?" The laughing dies down.

"If he doesn't, we both know what happens."

Footsteps. Coming toward me. Look preoccupied. I start dabbing my forehead again; I always forget how much head-wounds bleed.

"You looking at something, 'Prentice?" says a voice. Two pilots.

I look up, feigning ignorance. "No, sir. Just cleaning myself up."

The other pilot: "Good boy. Don't forget to wipe." I offer a hesitant smile.

The two pilots laugh, then turn the corner and push out of the locker room.

As they leave, I see one thumb at me over his shoulder. "Who's that?"

"How should I know?"

"So let's get a few things clear, shall we?"

I like clarity. Need some for the splitting headache I have. But somehow I doubt Dalfirin will be assisting me there. I'm standing in one of the felrell stalls in the tack barn. Wet bird crap up to my ankles. The strong ammonia smell is making my head worse. The fact that this stall is the *only* one in the entire barn that is not immaculate lets me know they've saved it. For VIPs. Like me.

"You're not your father," says Dalfirin. "And I'm not your friend." He stands in the stall with me, arms behind his back, oblivious to the overpowering odor. "I produce the most renowned flyers in all of Aria-Prime; there's nothing my pilots can't fly through. And there's a reason for that: if you're not the best, you don't graduate. No exceptions. Not even for sons of Aces. To me, you're neither a son, nor an Ace. And never will be."

"OK."

"*Yes, sir!*"

"Yes, sir."

He spits at my feet in disgust. This guy is a piece of work. But I can handle anything he can dish out.

"You're standing in this barn, washed and ready to work, at o-four-fifty-nine. No exceptions." The Headmaster starts walking side to side, boots sucking in and out of the mire. "I decide if you're sick, which you never will be. I decide when you have breaks, which you never will have. And I decide when you are done for the day. From now until you drop out, you belong to me." He stops and lowers his face into mine. "I own you, is that clear?"

"Yes, sir."

"*Yes, sir!*"

"Yes, sir!"

"Mistakes are not one of your options, Apprentice Junice."

"It's *Junar*, sir."

"*Excuse me?*"

Bad move. "Nothing, sir."

"Precisely. As I was saying, mistakes are not one of your options. You'll perform without failure. A lack of diligence is what gets Sky Riders killed. And none of the pilots I've graduated have *ever* been killed. Do you know why?"

Was this a rhetorical question? "Because they don't make mistakes?"

"*Are you questioning me?*"

"No, sir."

"*Why aren't my pilots killed, Apprentice Junebab?*"

"Because they don't make mistakes, sir!"

"*Because they are perfect!* If you are not perfect, you will be a perfect candidate for enrollment in one of Aria-Prime's many other Guilds. Or perhaps you like *inventing* things. Do you like *inventing* things, Apprentice Juneflee?"

"No, sir!" I'm light headed from all the shouting. And the smell. How much can this guy take? Keep your game face on, Junar. It's almost over.

"Is the smell getting to you?"

"No, sir!"

"Are you lying to me, Apprentice?"

Great. How am I supposed to answer this one? "Headache from earlier, sir." *Nice cover.* The dried blood on my forehead helps sell it. I hope.

"Then you wouldn't mind cleaning this stall, would you?"

"No, sir!"

"Report to my office when you're done." He walks out and watches the near constant flow of inbound and outbound felrell rushing through the zone. I'm sure he knows I have no idea where his office is yet. I look to my left, eyes settling on an old wheel barrow encrusted with dried dung. I glance around for a shovel.

"What's the matter, Apprentice Jujam?"

"There is no shovel, sir."

"Who said anything about a shovel?" He holds up both his hands and wiggles his long fingers at me.

You've got to be kidding.

There is no way I'm going to wash the smell from my hands, no matter how much soap I use. I finally turn off the hot water and dry them with a fresh towel, marking it with a red stain from my throbbing palm. Infected for sure. I find a fresh bandage in the medical supply locker and dress my hand, trying my best to copy what the nurses did.

Satisfied, I exit the locker room, the door closing behind me. I start across the tack barn, this time my head swiveling, though almost everyone has left for the day. The automatic feeders have been turned on for the night: a gigantic conveyor system with more gears and pulleys than I've ever seen. The thing kicks on every hour on the dot, spitting out steam and churning the woven treads that move seed out to every nest in the hangar. It's a super cool contraption. Yet another thing the Giloti have taken credit for, no doubt.

"Don't worry," comes a confident voice. "Stink that bad wears off in about a week." It's Liv. Floating toward me. "Um, you OK, kid?"

I nod.

Say something, you moron!

"Hi."

She laughs. "How's the hand?"

"It's nothing," I say, hiding my dressing behind my back.

"So I see you and Dalfirin have been properly introduced," she says, walking around me.

"You could say that, I guess. Erik, too."

"He's a peach, ain't he?"

"Peach?" Hardly the word I'm thinking of.

"So I hear you're almost done with your First Year, like me," she says.

"You're...you're a—"

"A pilot?" What a smile this girl has. "Yeah."

"I...I mean, it's just that..."

"I'm a girl. First they've ever let in, as a matter of fact. I know. Get that a lot. Feels pretty good, though, ya know? Doing things no one else has ever done before. *Pioneering*, Daddy calls it."

"Pioneering..." Man, I'm the real conversationalist today. I look down at my feet. Thinking.

"How's your head?" she asks.

"It's, ya know—ouch!" She's touching my forehead.

"Sorry. Guess I didn't see that when you woke up."

"Wasn't there then. A product of your *Peach*."

She furrows her brow, then clicks in the side of her cheek. "Gotcha. He's just playing tough guy. He'll lighten up. Promise."

"He doesn't bother me anyways."

"Sure he does," she insists. Is this an arguing match? "Well, listen, sport. For what it's worth, I'm sorry about plowing you over earlier." That smile again. I'm such a sucker for this girl.

"That's OK, Liv. It was an accident."

"But you were kinda right in the middle of the zone."

"Got it. Won't do it again."

She puts her hand out. Making amends? We shake.

"Anyway, who was that other guy?" I ask.

She raises an eyebrow.

"You know, big guy. Armor, tattoo, crossbow." Should I mention the arm?

"Oh," she says softly, "you mean Banth."

A long pause.

I squint. Waiting.

"Sorry. It's just...no one really talks to him. He's Brologi."

But Banth is unlike any Brologi I've ever seen before. More armor, and more scars. One real arm. And that ghoulish tattoo on the side of his head.

"So where's he from? I mean, that tattoo is crazy!"

"We don't really talk about him." For a girl with a wit and the mouth to match, that's saying something. "Aren't you supposed to be reporting back to Dalfirin now?"

She knows something she's not telling me. I can feel it.

"Yeah, about that," I say, "he said to report to his office."

"And I bet you have no idea where it is, am I right?"

I wink at her.

"He does that to everybody, don't worry. Well...I didn't tell you, but head through the locker room, stay right after the showers. You'll see a metal door with a brass push bar, a lot like the one that leads up to the Pilots' quarters. Just make sure you knock before you go in."

"Right after the showers, push bar, knock."

"See ya round, sport." She turns on her heels without waiting for my reply.

"Hey, wait a sec." I reach for her arm. "How do *you* know so much about the locker room when you're a—"

"Women know everything," she says as she pulls away.

I admire her for a few steps.

"I use it after everyone else has cleared out. And don't get any ideas, flyboy." She looks back at me. "I always lock it."

This is taking forever. Seems like the knock on the door will never stop echoing off the locker room's tile. I rap again. Then the door pulls open.

"Finally done?" Headmaster Dalfirin asks as he drops his monocle into his shirt pocket.

"Yes, sir!"

"Hardly. You didn't forget about the nests, did you, Apprentice Junick?"

Nests? Are you kidding me? "No, sir!"

"Then you're still standing here because…?"

I exhale fast. "Admiring the view, sir." I turn around, hungry for more bird feces.

"Suck up," he whispers as I walk away.

"Absolutely, sir!" I say. I see his reflection in the mirrors by the sinks. Could swear the Headmaster's smiling.

"Oh, and Apprentice June-June."

I spin around. If this guy is my key to flying, then I'll do everything in my power to do whatever he wants. Though, Liv is right. He's getting to me already. And I hate it. Because she's right? Or because someone's getting a leg up on me? In any case, maybe, just maybe, I'll *force* him to like me in the process.

"Might give you a shovel tomorrow."

I raise my hands and wiggle my fingers at him. "Who needs a shovel?"

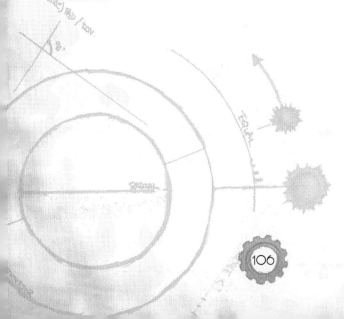

106

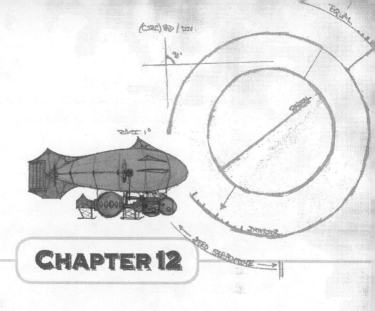

CHAPTER 12

WHETHER BY MY suggestion or his good nature, Dalfirin *let* me use my hands the next day. And the next. Can't be good for my cut; I know, because it's getting infected. The last two nights it's burned as I went to sleep. Guild Medic has been insisting I keep gobs of ointment on it. Yeah, right. But I just keep lying to myself that it's fine. That it's worth it. To fly again—*anything's* worth it.

I'd also be lying if I said I'm not jealous watching Liv and Erik suit up, saddle their felrell, and dive out through the hangar on their practice runs. Shoot, my only contact with Serio has been asking him to move out of his nest so I can clean it. Still bummed the Guild flew him here from Bellride. I wanted that mission myself. But even cleaning up after him is joy enough, I suppose. Love that stinking bird. Seems like he's the only constant in my life. Not that I don't love our new mansion and a little newfound fame. OK: a lot of fame. But that's on the street. In here, I'm a little higher than bird feed. But Serio treats me the same, celebrity or leftovers. I'm his rider and he knows no bias. End of story.

"Soon enough, old friend." I scratch beneath Serio's beak

with my dung-encased fingers. It's the second time I've cleaned his nest today, and every other for that matter...been at the chore for almost eight hours straight. And my arms feel every minute of it. "Soon enough."

I turn to hear a few voices hollering from somewhere below in the sky. Liv appears first, bursting up through the hangar from outside, her bird hovering to a near standstill, then alights on the hangar's landing rim. Erik comes right behind her, followed by two brand-new First Years that Liv and Erik have taken on maneuvers.

"I believe that's ten times in a row, Apprentice Erik," says Dalfirin. He stands above on a catwalk, hands behind his back. Didn't notice him. Wonder how long he's been standing there.

Erik lifts his goggles, exasperated. "She's just too fast."

"That she is." Dalfirin nods.

Not only is Liv the first girl ever to be allowed in the program, but she's apparently the one to beat.

I look back to Serio. "Think we can match her?" Serio just coos.

Liv slips her feet out of the stirrups and swings out of the saddle. Down her bird's wing she slides, letting her boots slap the wooden floor, making a statement. Her ride preens beneath its wing before she grabs the reins. Then she shoots me a wide grin from clear across the hangar. "When're you joining us, sport?"

Anytime you want, Liv. Serio gives her a head-tilt and squawks. "Couldn't have said it better myself, Serio," I say, patting him on the neck. I had never liked a girl before. Always flying. Always felrell. But Liv...something about her...

"We'll let the newbie prove himself tomorrow," Dalfirin declares from his own lofty perch. "See what our dung-boy can do."

I can't believe my ears. "Hear that, Serio? We're going out tomorrow."

"If he's up for it." Liv grins, then turns into the barn.

"Oh, I'm up for it, alright," I say, but Liv ignores me and keeps walking.

"You just watch yourself, flyboy," Erik calls out, climbing off his own bird with much less finesse. He almost trips on landing.

"Thanks for the warning, Erik, but I already know you're used to second place." I can see Dalfirin swivel toward me. *Amused?*

"Oh yeah? Well...you better get used to being *second!* I mean, *last!*"

I don't even give Erik the courtesy of knowing I hear him, and go right back to my chores. Tomorrow, I'll let my flying do all the talking.

"You here, Mom?" I kick my boots off.

"*Please*, don't slam the door, Junar. How many times have I told you?"

"Sorry."

"I'm in the kitchen. If you want to *talk* with me, come in here."

I slide in on my socks. Never had marble floors in Bellride. "Helmet."

I rip it off.

"You seem in a good mood," she says. "Care to enlighten me?"

Being stuck here while Dad's been away hasn't exactly been my idea of ideal, but the house seems to keep her in a pretty good mood, so I can't complain all that much. Dad never did work out the discrepancy between Lucius' *adequate break-in period* and the Chancellor's immediate start comment; seemed everything bowed to the Chancellor, as Dad was up and away the very next morning. "I have some good news," I say.

"Which is?"

"I'm going up tomorrow."

"Oh, now that's wonderful, darling."

"Yeah, isn't it?" Even my disdain for her lessens when it comes to flying. "Wait 'til Dad hears."

"He's still not back, love." She turns around behind the cutting board and produces a glass from a cupboard. Fills it with water, then hands it to me.

The cloud collectors work the same here. I take a long draft.

Tastes great.

"Thanks, Mom." I stare at my glass for a second. "Still not back?"

"He did warn us these trips would take him out as many as four days at a time. More if they had to clear a lot of trees."

I sigh. "I know. But the *first one?*"

"There's quite a lot we're going to have to get used to around here, isn't there?" She rubs her hand in my hair. Used to do that to me as a small boy. "My heavens, son. You smell as if you've rolled in every nest in the hangar."

"Pretty accurate, actually."

"Give me that jacket, and go get yourself cleaned up."

I give her a diligent, "Yes, Mom." She slaps me in the back with my jacket as I head for the stairs. I turn back and force a smile. I want things to be right between us, I do. But she acts as if they already are, and they're not.

"Get out of here, you mess!" She smiles.

If only I could forget that easily.

After I clean up, we share dinner together, then say our goodnights. I admit it's an early bedtime, but I just can't help myself. For one, I barely know what to say around her when we're alone anymore, and two, tomorrow is my day. Dad's had his promotion, but tomorrow...tomorrow is all mine.

Takes me two hours to fall asleep.

"How long have you had him, sport?"

"Dad raised him for me since I was twelve." I cinch the forward girth strap, then double-buckle the end. "He's been my bird even as a Page."

"Lucky," she says.

I can't believe I'm *actually* saddling Serio. *In Christiana.* He and I are in the stall just beside Liv and her bird, Aavian. And beyond her, Erik and Forn. My heart is pumping. I'm actually nervous?

"Nice Dad you got," she adds.

"Yeah, he's pretty much the best." I grab the reins off the perch and bring them to Serio's head. He takes the bit—by far the most intimidating task to learn on a felrell—and I throw the lengths of leather over each wing. "How ready are you, Erik?"

"More ready than you'll ever be."

"What does that even mean, Erik?" asks Liv.

"It means he's slow."

Slow, but meticulous. No accidents. The best pilots take time to examine their equipment *as they put it on*, not just as they take it off. Never know when you might find wear, corrosion or worse: a break. Erik can make fun of me all he wants, but I plan on flying for a long time to come.

With both girth straps tight, my saddle looks like a smooth lump on the back of Serio's neck. High-backed, and really quite comfortable, the Finlin saddle is my preferred seat, using ridged stirrup settings to keep the legs locked in, rather than the bulkier and more restricting waist strap on the traditional saddles. The stirrups are thinner and require the rider to use more balance on the balls of the feet, both to stay balanced and to keep from falling off when inverted. Building the muscles in the ankles makes them virtual *hooks* in the stirrups. Likewise, I prefer the thinner Stiletto reins and bit. Easier in the bird's mouth. Never understand how some pilots could be so heavy handed. A felrell will do anything you ask, but it's all in how you ask for it.

"How we looking, Apprentice Junbie?"

I climb up Serio's left wing, slip my left foot into the stirrup, and swing around. Clip in my tether to the saddle's locking mechanism. Gloves on, goggles down, reins wrapped twice around my fists, and a fresh layer of cream on my exposed skin. "All set, Headmaster." I knock my helmet twice. "Fly or die."

Dalfirin pulls around his bird, Stridon, and approaches the barn's exit ledge. Stridon spreads his wings and bobs his head, giving out a deafening shriek. Dalfirin looks back at us. "We'll head south, circle Bellride in honor of our new dung-sweeper, then return. Nice and easy, nothing fancy. And no nets today, just free-flying."

"Sounds good, sir," says Liv.

Erik nods.

I pull up the rear and watch as the first three plunge down through the hangar and into open air.

"You ready, boy?" I pat Serio on the neck.

He screeches, definitely happy to be heading out.

He walks up to the edge, and I peer over his right shoulder, straight down, 3,000 feet. Glorious.

I give him a sharp *he-yoh!* and Serio takes one hop, wings outstretched, diving out of the hangar. My gut rises. Hurtling toward the cloud-floor as fast as gravity can pull us. The wind roars through my helmet, my stomach relocating somewhere in my throat. Most First Years are taught to *flare* out of the hangar. Take it slow. And rightfully so. A clean drop means managing high speeds, which can be very unforgiving. And surviving a midair collision is rare; only a few of those pilots are alive at any one time on the planet. But Serio and I are quite the team. Been going on mock-sorties after hours just for fun ever since Dad let me on the back of a bird. Just because. It goes without saying that felrell like to fly. But Serio is an exception. He *lives* to fly. And that makes us a perfect match. While I love the Guild, and everything that goes with it—yes, even cleaning stalls—I *live* to fly too. The feeling of leaving the barn and taking to the skies is more exhilarating than any feeling I know.

We're falling straight down. Serio flaps a few more times, my legs spurring him on. Then a quick flick of my wrists tells him to fold his wings, the acceleration position bred into every raptor large and small. *Speed dive.* Used for hunting in their native state. Again, another technique only taught to advanced First Years. Goggles are essential here. Without them, a pilot can't see a darned thing. And how the first flyers ever stayed on without saddles still blows my mind. True heroes of the Guild. Most pilots have trouble approaching such speeds *with* a saddle. Thus the advent of the tethered waist strap.

Three forms pull level another 1,000 feet below us along the cloud-floor: our *targets*, at least as far as Serio's concerned. We're still gaining speed, well past terminal velocity of a free-falling human.

I ask him for more with a quick flick of my heels. "He-yoh, Serio!"

When traveling at over 250 feet-per-second, 1,000 feet comes up quick. Easy for a bird of prey to deal with, uncanny vision and all. Dalfirin is in the lead, then Liv, followed by Erik. I crouch low and point Serio just ahead of Erik. Three seconds later we dive in front of Erik, close enough that I can see his body jerk back in shock. Serio pulls up hard, flaring his wings to avoid sinking into some clouds. I grunt, then force myself to stand up in the stirrups. Stomach is down in my knees. I look up over my shoulder. Erik's veered out of formation. His bird, Forn, is circling back around.

"Good boy, Serio." I pat his neck. He arches up, shoving me back in my seat, and takes Erik's spot in the formation. Serio gives Liv a loud hello, to which she casts a quick glance over her shoulder. Surprised. She looks elsewhere for Erik, then smiles, seeing him a few seconds back, trying to catch up. A nod to me; apparently she doesn't disapprove of my antics.

We fly on, Erik now right on our tail. He must be steaming mad. I know I'd be.

Dalfirin still hasn't looked back yet, a sign of his confidence...or his complete disregard for his underlings. He and Stridon keep a quick pace, skimming the upper reaches of the cloud-floor, just out of harm's way. Christiana is almost out of sight, only a small floating dot on the horizon. And the suns are well on their morning climb across the sky bowl.

Serio is antsy under me. Growing weary of the tight line formation. As am I. Seeing Bellride creep over the horizon doesn't help things either. The memory of hundreds of flight hours surge back into my head. Probably Serio's too. Sifting the skies with nets laden with nelurime, skimming over the rock surfaces of the anchor mountains, and illegally buzzing between deck levels at dusk. Enough to stir anyone's blood.

As we approach the island, close enough to make out Kar-Bellride on level one, Dalfirin pulls back even with me. "You want to take the lead?" he asks.

"Are you kidding me? Sir."

Liv spins around. Smiling.

"Show us around, kid," Dalfirin replies, then drops back.
"Yes, sir!"

Serio screeches, flapping at my adamant heel-hits, then
rises out of formation. He surges over Liv and climbs even higher
as Bellride's balloon matrix fills the sky above us. The habitation
levels hang beneath it like tiny toy houses on planks of wood. I
bring in the reins; Serio answers, pulling back into a vertical climb.
My back presses against the saddle seat until my torso is hanging
off it, leaving my eyes to stare straight up into the darkest blue of
the sky. Serio's lunging beneath me, his wings pushing back the
air as easily as someone bounding up stairs. My stomach muscles
cramp. Holding steady. The space below my feet suddenly fills
with the facades of the city buildings I know so well, windows and
doors and streets and faces. From here I can smell the heady yeast
from the early morning bread and the thin odor from the nelurime
ovens. Then everything transforms into the faded red of the balloon
matrix as Serio and I race vertically up its northernmost face.

I glance over my shoulder, looking straight down at Liv,
followed by Erik, then Dalfirin. Taking up the rear, is he?

We're nearing the summit, so I ease up on Serio. We
follow the contour of the balloon, arching toward the center. A
few seconds later and we're on top, seeing what few Bellridians
ever will. Of course, the view isn't as spectacular as it is higher up;
from 25,000 you can actually see the curve of Aria-Prime. Hard
to beat that. Stars so clear, too. But nearly impossible to breathe,
so no one stays up long. Still, hanging weightless over Bellride's
matrix is pretty neat. Almost like I can jump down and walk on it.
Sure, I could. But more than one soul has fallen through the linen,
crushed by the ever-shifting gas-filled balloons that do the heavy
lifting to keep Bellride—or any of the other floating islands—
aloft. Not a pleasant way to go.

We pass the apex and begin the steep descent over the
south side. Rather than peel off and avoid inversion sickness, I
stick with the balloon's contour, pointing Serio into a dive straight
along the outside. My bum lifts off Serio. I flex my ankles to keep
my hips locked in the saddle. Serio screams something, and I let
out a holler too. Weightlessness turns into acceleration, forcing me

back into my seat again as Serio beats the air twice to gain control of our fall.

A moment later and the decks race into view. Serio rotates halfway through a barrel roll in order to prepare for one of our favorite fly-bys. I look up, watching three levels of Bellride whizz past, then feel Serio level out in a move I don't even need to initiate with the reins. The fourth and final level races toward us, appearing as if Serio is intent on smearing us across the outer-deck houses. I see at least three people out for a morning stroll; one woman has her hand over her mouth, looking up at me. I love this part. We descend under her, my head passing just ten feet under the deck trussing, narrowly averting an ugly decapitation. I hear the woman scream. Perfect.

I glance under my arm and see Liv run well below our line; Erik, likewise, takes a deep, cautious swoop under the lowest level of Bellride. But Dalfirin follows our tight flight path without so much as ducking. A seasoned professional.

Serio uses our momentum to glide straight under the heart of the city, passing to the left of the hangar opening, and just to the right of Bellride's anchor line. The sturdy cable, nearly ten feet around, sweeps all the way down to the east side of Mt. Bellride, some 2,500 feet below. There it plunges into a heart of bedrock, and finds purchase in a forged iron-trunk. Unshakable. Thinner cables run along it, providing easy passage to and from the mountain with swings. Most people never set foot on the mountains now— only those tending the steep fields, or the flocks, or those mining for ore. The islands are much more hospitable. Can't believe people used to live down there. So steep. And that's not even counting Knightsbridge: pinnacles rising straight out of the cloud-floor. No land worth farming or raising sheep on there. Just trade with other cities. Makes up for it with higher production of nelurime. And unofficial home of the Inventors, though no one talks about them. Except me, of course.

Serio and I race out from the shadow at the far end, flying away from the island a fair distance before coming back around. Now eye-level with the city, I realize how much I miss her; not even a week in Christiana and I'm already homesick. I'm such a lightweight.

I ask Serio for more speed and bank into a wide circle, sweeping around Bellride with a panoramic view of all four decks. A few more early risers see us. I think some notice me, arms waving. I wave back, as do Liv and Erik behind me; Dalfirin remains ever stoic, unmoved. It really doesn't matter who you are, son of the great Leif ap Jeronil or not—as long as you are flying a felrell, people love you. I might as well be the Chancellor himself, waving to a handful of citizens who feel fortunate enough to spy us on this clear morning. But still, I have to imagine some of them recognize me for who I am. Like the clouds below, someone is always watching.

We circumnavigate the island once, then I give a nostalgic salute to the city of my birth. "Come on, Serio," I say, pulling away and slowing to allow Dalfirin to reclaim his place of leadership up front. But he doesn't arrive. I look back to see Dalfirin still in the rear. He gives me the slightest nod. More? I can do that. I readjust my goggles, then tighten the reins around my gloves, the squeak of leather upon leather...the wound in my hand reminding me it is far from healed. If Dalfirin wants me to keep leading, then I'll give them all something to remember my first day with. Especially Erik.

With the suns warming the eastern sky, I see a storm front moving in from the west. Dark, heavy clouds. The first we've had in a while. Wherever there are storms, there are thermals. And complex cloud formations. Perfect.

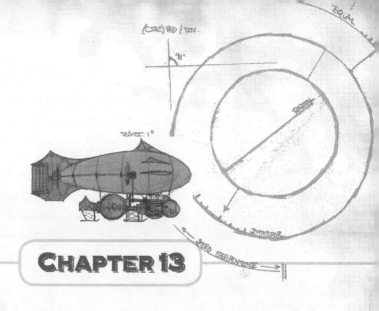

CHAPTER 13

Our line of four felrell races westward across the sky, beating against the prevailing wind and following my lead. Light behind us, a wall of grey in front of us. Dalfirin remains unmoved in the rear, seemingly compliant with my pursuit of the oncoming storm.

As we're a people who live in the sky, forecasting weather in all its various forms is second nature to us. And the closer we get to this air mass, the more I realize just how much of a menace it's shaping up to be. Gusts start buffeting Serio as we close to within 5,000 feet of the storm. Right on cue, a flash of lightning lights up the innards of the beast, followed by the first drops of rain. *Menace* is an understatement. If Dalfirin isn't pulling rank now, then I'm good to proceed. But I can almost feel him flying over me to turn us around. I look back...

...still holding his place.

Really?

Alright then. Here goes.

I spur Serio forward, driving him at the first thunderhead that materializes: an enormous column of dark grey, rippling moisture that's billowing upward. And expanding. Probably full of some good nelurime too. I have Serio bank to the left, talons painting long lines through the dense formation. An updraft throws me down in the saddle as we surge at least fifty feet up. Stabilize. Stabilize. A little rougher than I expected.

Another thunderhead just ahead forces us hard right. Serio rolls all the way over—my first inversion of the day. Another crack of lightning, this time in the open, illuminating the entire sky and, with it, a strange channel forming in the clouds ahead. Like a narrowing tunnel, daring us to come in.

I give Serio his head, letting him decide.

A tug forward.

Means he wants to go in. Serio beats the air three times, flares up, then pulls in his wings. We drop into the cloud tunnel, spiraling through stray threads of vapor. Completely encased in dim light and surrounded by churning storm cloud, we barrel into the front. Serio and I descend ever closer to the cloud-floor, lurking somewhere below. How far, I'm not sure. But that's part of the rush. That, and not knowing where this tunnel will spit us out...or if it even has an open end. Getting swallowed by a cloud formation isn't ideal. Many a wayward flyer has lost himself in a storm front, only to emerge disoriented and much further off course than expected. But still fine. Fine. Most of the time.

One pilot from Bellride, Rodgers as I recall, was in his first year of professional service to the Guild. Graduated two years before I was accepted into the apprenticeship. He went out on a solo mission, harvesting in the Lower Reaches, when he reportedly ran into a storm. Other pilots returning from the area pleaded with him to turn back. But they said he insisted on finishing the harvest...clouds fat with nelurime that day.

He was never seen again.

Storms aren't usually too dangerous. Challenging, sure. And the bigger ones are in the summer months, though less frequent. But most won't kill you. Still. The only reason I can figure Dalfirin is letting me lead the class into this one is because of pride. We're being trained by the best to be the best, right? Hadn't he said, "There is nothing my pilots can't fly through"? I intend to see if he means it.

Serio and I soar on, following the ever-shifting tunnel further into the bowels of the beast, wondering where it will lead us. The path rolls to the right, then shoots up, only to level off in a large chamber, shut out from the morning suns. The air is much warmer in here. Moist. A bolt of lightning connects the ceiling to the floor, producing a thunderous boom that makes my ears ring. I shake my head. Then look back.

Liv looks fearless, while Erik is definitely off his game. Nervous. And Dalfirin? Like he's preparing to take a nap, slightly annoyed that something has roused him. A good sign.

I lead the team around the chamber once, searching for the way out. By the time I make it back around, the tunnel we came through is closed up. Trapped.

Not good. Not horrible, but definitely not good.

Another flash and crack of lightning. There's only one option. Not sure how deep this storm is, and can't tell which way we've come from; likewise, there's no determining how close the cloud-floor is at this point. So I kick Serio and pull back on the reins.

"He-yoh!" I cry.

This storm has to have a ceiling, and we're breaking through the top. Serio responds with a lurch upward. I lean forward, grabbing the saddle as he shoves air beneath us.

Billowy grey clouds consume us, the fine mist soaking my face and lining my jacket with silvery beads that race across the leather. They gleam in the flashes of lightning like jewels decorating my coat. I ease up on Serio's head, asking him to hold his course—most times it's better just to let a felrell follow their instincts. Serio's gotten me out of worse.

Once on a harvesting sortie with Dad, we got caught in a storm. I had to drop the net from Serio's rig. Standard operating procedure if caught in a front. Gusts can tear a bird apart if it's still attached. And it's less expensive to replace a net than it is a pilot or a bird. Dad dropped his end, too, and we were separated for over forty minutes in the storm. I was sure we were going to die. But Serio wasn't going to let that happen. Not that day. He practically tore the reins from my hands and took us south...then into the bright of day.

I think I hugged that bird every day for a month.

Crack!

The muted world around me erupts in another flash of light, this one too close. Serio voices his annoyance, though I barely hear his call over the ringing in my ears. I know we'll get out. Right? Yeah. And the others? Of course. Except that we're in the thick of it now, and I can't see them. Which means they can't see me either.

Not good.

Then Serio cries out again, fighting against the gusting air currents.

That's it! I press my fist into the nape of Serio's neck, asking him to call out. A long blast pierces the air, following my command as trained. We fly on, jostled by more thermals in our pursuit heavenward. My face is soaked from the clouds, and I can taste the protein cream in the corners of my lips. Another flash of light from somewhere in the distance. I push on Serio's vertebrae again.

The blackening clouds are like grave clothes, keeping a corpse bound to its fate. Three more times Serio screams, hoping that those behind us will find the same resurrection we hunt for.

Higher and higher we climb, trying to outmatch the pace of our opponent. At last the shadows are fading, falling away into a sullen sewer trough of dismal grey. Then, as if someone flips on a nelurime chandelier, Serio and I are through, bursting into clear air. I'm sure he's breathing a sigh of relief as much as I am.

We gain another 250 feet, and then pull around, circling over the distorted cloud hole we made. Hoping. Waiting.

As we linger in a wide turn, I start playing through all of Dalfirin's possible reactions. I had bitten off a little more than I could chew. OK. *A lot more.* But my motives were innocent...if a little impetuous. Trying to prove myself? Maybe. But this is the kind of gutsy display Dalfirin wants. Right? Sure, Junar. If getting your classmates killed is part of the show.

Great. Just great. I'm going to get the kick-out that's coming to me. I know it as much as the feathers in my boots. But

Kar-Bellride will take me back.

I hear a felrell call. Followed by a black mass forming in the cloud cover. Liv bursts through a moment later, flicking her reins and yelling something to Aavian. She sees me above, then flashes a quick smile. Genuine? She joins us to starboard and picks up our wide, circular pattern.

"You're pretty brave, flyboy," she says, pulling her goggles up on top of her head.

"I'd like to think so," I reply.

Too strong?

"I'm just saying."

"Saying what?"

"My dad might not be as impressed as I am, trying to get me killed and all."

"Your...dad?"

As if on cue, Dalfirin bursts out of the clouds with a panic-stricken Erik in tow right behind him.

"Wait. You mean—"

"See you back at the hangar, flyboy."

The storm follows me all the way home. In more ways than one. I stay more than a few minutes in front of Dalfirin the whole return trip, so he hasn't said a thing to me. Not yet, anyway.

Here in the tack barn, Serio seems to sense the impending barrage and is creeping into an open stall, head down. I follow after him, hiding behind his neck, both of us soaking wet. Rain. And sweat. Cold fingers undo his girth buckles. Slip the bit out of his mouth. If I can put Serio away before Dalfirin returns, maybe I can give him some time to cool off. And I can disappear.

Too late.

Three more birds arrive, pieces of straw flinging about the tack barn. I peel off my helmet and run the fingers of my good hand through my hair. The city is already swaying from the high winds, rain pelting every building on the windward side. Only the nelurime lanterns push away the dark. Brush back some of Serio's large feathers, acting like nothing is out of the ordinary. But in truth, my chest is as tight as a harp string, heart beating as loud as a forging hammer. Maybe Dalfirin won't notice me?

"Junar ap Leif."

The voice cuts me like a mill saw splitting a board in two.

"Before me," Dalfirin orders. "Now."

I duck under Serio's belly, coming into the open, straight-faced.

Erik walks past me. "Now you're in for it, newbie," he says. But he looks away when I stare at him, still shaking.

"At least I can hold my own," I reply. The dig is uncalled for, I know it. But I'm not exactly thinking clearly. I see Liv step into a stall on the far side with Aavian. She raises her eyebrows at me. Not comforting.

Back toward the hangar, two Pages take Stridon from the Headmaster. Dalfirin turns and faces me, arms folded behind his back, a puddle of water forming under his black flight boots.

"You wanted to see me, sir?" I can see him working his jaw bone. Here it comes.

"*Wanted* to see you?" he growls. "Hardly." Then, with slow, measured words: "What, in the name of Talihdym, do you call that?"

I swallow. "Flying, sir."

"Flying," he repeats, clearly unimpressed.

"Yes, sir." The man never takes his eyes off me, drilling right through my head with his glare. Can he see my knees trembling? Maybe he hears them too.

"What part of *nice and easy, nothing fancy*, did you not understand?"

"Sir?"

Dalfirin clears his throat. I'm not sure I've ever seen someone so angry, yet so restrained. "Junar ap Leif, you're hereby relieved of your flying privileges until further notice. You'll be placed under the Pages for cleaning duty—four times, daily—and won't utter a *word* to any of your seniors until your privileges are reinstated...*if* I deem them so. Do you understand?"

"Yes, sir." Was that my voice?

"Speak up, son!"

"*Yes, sir!*"

"You're done for today, and can go home to your mother. I don't want to see your face around here until tomorrow morning. The only reason I am not sending you back to Bellride on the next airship is because your father is so highly respected. Consider it a *favor* of the Guild. But if you ever try anything that *stupid* again, I'll own your bird, and you'll never fly, ever...for *any* Guild. Am I making myself clear?"

"Yes, sir!" I think we're done.

"One last thing." He leans in, a hand's width away from my nose, hot breath filling my face with each word. "*Stay away from my daughter.*"

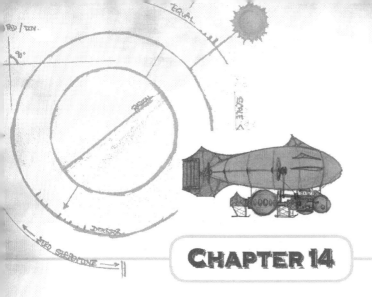

CHAPTER 14

I'M TOO COLD and wet to do anything other than go home, take a hot bath, and sulk. But with the entire day in front of me, home is the last place I want to be. Mom will be there. Tons of questions. I don't feel like talking.

The cable swing whirrs up through the levels, the city well into its late morning routine even despite the weather. Sure, the open air markets are shut down, but that doesn't keep people from going inside their favorite shops to do business. The motto of "one hand for you, the other for your work" is a way of life. Storms hit fairly often during the *dark season*. We're almost through it. But the real storm is about to hit.

"Well, hi there, baby!" Mom says from in the kitchen, making something that normally smells delicious. Stirring a wooden spoon in a bowl, while something else cooks in the oven. "You're home early."

"Hi, Mom," I say. *Smile, then get to the stairs, Junar. As fast as you can without being completely rude, which will just delay things further.* "Not a lot going on today."

Mom puts the bowl down.

"Going to clean up. See ya."

"Hold on right there, Ace." She comes around the corner, flour all over her apron. "I know when something's up with you. And something's definitely up with you."

"With me? Nope, all things are cool, Mom. No worries." My foot makes the first step, but she grabs my arm.

"Junar ap Leif," she says. I'm beginning to dread that name. "What happened?"

"Nothing, Mom!"

She lets go. How am I yelling at my Mom already? Silence. I want to turn, to run upstairs.

"You know, Junar, I can handle disrespect. But lying? From my own son?"

"You're one to talk."

Oh, Junar. Bad move. *But it's the truth!*

"What did you say?" She squints at me.

I turn away.

"Look at me!"

I won't.

"Look at me, now!" Her hand flies free and catches my far cheek, snapping my head back toward her. Hard. The smack makes my right ear ring.

I look up at her, face burning. "I got suspended."

Her eyes open wide. "Suspended?" She stutters to find the words. "What? Why?!"

"I don't want to talk about it!"

"I'm not asking you to talk about it, I just want to know what happened!" Her eyes dart away in panic. Then, "Oh, no." She inhales. "Your *father!*" Then covers her mouth. "What will he say?"

And...we're talking about it. "Mom, it's nothing. I was asked to lead the team on a sortie, and we got caught in a storm. Bad move on my part, reprimanded by the Headmaster. I'll be back flying in a week I bet."

"Oh, this is not good, son." She looks off into middle space somewhere, completely forgetting she struck me. Her own son. I deserved it, though.

"I know it's not good, Mom. I was there, remember?"

"Not good at all."

"Mom, seriously, I know. Can I just go upstairs and take a bath?"

She snaps out of her distant stare. "I'm not going to tell your father, you know."

"You're not?"

"Oh no—" she glares at me, finger pointing— "*you are.*"

"I am," I repeat, unmoved.

"He's coming home tonight."

"Tonight? But I thought—"

"Lucius stopped by earlier."

"Lucius?" But Dad's gone. That's totally inappropriate. Unless *she* invited him. How fitting. The Guild could have sent Reginald, surely. But she asked for Lucius.

"Said they were making good time. Oh, Junar..." She clasps her hands. "This is just the kind of thing I *don't* want him coming home to."

"I know, Mom. But it'll be OK. I promise."

"For your sake, I sure hope so, young man." She turns right, then left. Kitchen. "You get yourself cleaned up," I hear her call. "I'll...I'll call you down when he gets home."

Grounded.

Seventeen years old and treated like twelve again.

Just wonderful.

The hot water does little to ease my apprehension of *the talk* I'll have to initiate with Dad. At least Mom will probably do the favor of telling him I was in trouble despite her previously stated refusal to do so. Hate dry conversation starters. I can just imagine it now. "Hey, Dad, remember the Headmaster? Yeah. About that..." Nah, I'd much rather have him storm into my room and hand me my butt. Get it over with. Confrontation is one of my least favorite things in the world. And today I'm going three for three: Dalfirin, Mom, now Dad.

I basically sit around my room, playing the conversation through in my head over and over. I can plead my case pretty well, like the best of 'em. Wanted to impress the Headmaster, do my family proud, and had no idea the storm was going to be *that* bad. Totally an accident.

Right?

I climb the ladder to my bed for the twentieth time and lay down. I try napping, burn off some of the long hours. No use. The wind keeps me wide awake. Yeah, that's it. I sit up and reach for my telescope. Spin it around randomly and peek in the eye piece. Focusing. Focusing. Houses, roofs, sky. Something passes across my field of vision.

I pull away and look across the city to the far horizon. Filling the space between rooftops and the balloon—*there!* Birds! Dozens of them. I squint back into the telescope. *Felrell.* And floating beneath every two or three is what looks to be long bundles of tree trunks. Four, five at the most. *Timber.*

Dad! It's the Timber Pilots! Everyone's used to seeing the Kili-Boranna out and about with their long, nearly translucent nets trailing beneath them. If you don't look hard enough, you miss the rig completely. But trees? The birds are majestic, their wings beating the air tirelessly with slow, grand strokes. And the trees, giant dowels suspended in midair beneath them. Miraculous.

I gently pass the telescope over the faces, trying to pinpoint Dad. Ah, there he is. Right in the front, no less. Suddenly I feel my standing rebuke melt away, replaced with mounting pride for my father. The new Captain of the Guild. But saying his title in my head brings back my predicament: Captain of a suspended youth. If Dalfirin won't send me back to Bellride with my wings clipped, Dad will.

I push the telescope away, spinning it around the swivel twice, then plop down on my bed. Wish I had somebody to talk to. Like Lance. Or Liv. Oh, now *there's* trouble. Still not sure the bath had cleaned off all the spittle. *Stay away from my daughter.* With my ticket back to Bellride almost ensured, I don't think that's going to be a problem.

The outside door opens and closes. Mom's voice. Excited. The scent of whatever she has been preparing all day fills every room in the house now. And I'm hungry for it. *Can't even worry on an empty stomach.* Too true, Granddad. Too true.

I pace around my room, waiting for Mom's call downstairs. But it never comes.

My impatience finally gets the best of me, and I slip out through my door, down the first flight of stairs, around the landing, then quietly down the last flight. Not all the way. Their voices stop me. Brief mumbling, followed by long silences. No, I know when they're being romantic. And this is not it. Something is wrong. The only light downstairs is seeping out from the kitchen, spilling onto the floor. I slow my breathing and press the final few feet along the wall.

"They were just sitting there, Sondra," Dad says.

It's the first I've heard his voice in days. Missed him. So much. Even if his return means my punishment, he's justified in doing so. At least I have him back in one piece.

"I still don't know what to think of it," he adds.

"And the others?" Mom asks. "They just told you to *shut up and do your job?*"

Someone told Dad to shut up?

"Yes." A deep sigh. "Honestly, I don't really feel like rehashing it again. What I need now is clear direction."

"I'm…I'm not sure what to tell you, my love." She pauses. "I mean…what do *you* think you should do?"

Dad's pausing. No response. Probably running a hand through his hair by the sound of his breathing. That's where I get it from. Something is *really* wrong.

A chair creaks, followed by Mom's footsteps pacing around the marble floor. "You could set up a meeting with the Chancellor."

The Chancellor?

"That's one option. And a good one, dear. But I'd rather keep it between me and the Guild. I don't want anyone else knowing. I have to handle this…carefully." More footsteps. Then Dad grunts like he always does when Mom is rubbing his shoulders. "I don't think I'm cut out for this, Sondra. I really don't. Not this kind of pressure."

Cut out for this? What in the world is he talking about?

"We'll figure it out, Leif. We always do."

"To be honest, right now I wish we'd never left Bellride. *That* job I knew. Could do it with my eyes closed. No surprises. But this? And everything wrapped up in it? It's just too much."

I can't believe what I'm hearing. Can it be? Dad? Thinking of…of withdrawing his position *after his first mission?* No, something else is going on. Surely. Something he's not saying. Dad can handle any pressure.

"What they're asking me to perform, I…" Another deep sigh. "I just don't see how I can. I'm not like that."

I press my back hard against the wall harder. Heart beating in my head. Too much pressure? Dad? But if he steps down, that means…how can he do this to himself? To the family? To me?!

"I think you should go see Junar now, my love. He has something to tell you."

I make it up the stairs and into my room with a few moments to spare, just enough time to catch my breath, and act like I hadn't ever left my room.

Three knocks on the door. "Son? Can I come in?" I can't bring myself to answer. He steps inside. Then finds me up on my bed.

"Hey, Dad." How excited should I seem to be?

"Hey, there, Ace."

Oh, *anything* but *Ace.* Why's he being all nice? He knows I'm in trouble. And it doesn't make my disappointment with him any easier. "So how was it, Dad? Your first mission, I mean?" I feel like I'm lying by even asking a question I already know the answer to. Everything in me wants to blurt out a string of words I know I can never take back.

I slide down my ladder. The hug is half-hearted.

"It was alright," he says.

"Just *alright?*"

He shakes off my reply. "Mom said you had something you wanted to tell me."

I have plenty to tell him. "Yeah, I..." there's really no delicate way to put this, "...I got suspended."

His eyes widen. "You what?"

"Seriously, Dad, it's no big deal. It was an accident, I led the team into a storm—"

"An accident? What storm?" He points through an imaginary window as if it was still raging. "The storm earlier today?"

"I was just trying to—"

"Trying to—what? *Show off?* Junar...I mean, really. You could have gotten people *killed!*"

"Nobody got hurt, Dad."

"That never excuses carelessness! Oh, good grief." He spins around, hand on his forehead. "I can't *believe* I'm even having this conversation." He turns around once more, mumbling, looking like he might need something to brace himself with. "How could you let your dedication slip like this?"

"*My* dedication?" I've had enough. I can feel the words rising up in me and I can't stop them. Won't stop them. "What about *yours*, Dad? *You're* the one who told me to never quit, to always push myself and give it my best. But I guess those were just empty words, huh? What about *you?* Giving up so soon, *Leif?*"

My face feels hot. I have *never* in my life spoken like this to my father. But someone has to say it. If Mom won't, I will. Our future is on the line.

Dad spins around. "What did you just—?" He stops. Swallows.

My cheeks are wet, eyes blinking away tears.

"What did you say?" He takes a step toward me. "Were you *listening downstairs?*"

I stare at him.

"Junar! Answer me!"

"Yes, OK? Yes, I—"

"What did you hear?"

"I heard enough!" More warm trails run down my face, gathering around my nose and lips. I wipe them away with my forearm. "Enough to know you're giving up. That you think you're not good enough. And I can't understand why. *Not cut out for this? Too much pressure? Pressure?!* Are you kidding me, Dad? No one handles pressure like you! What was that stunt you pulled on our way here? Was that not enough *pressure* for you?"

"Junar...what you heard, it's not what—"

"No, Dad. You know, you were my hero. But now..." I don't even need to finish the sentence. I can see my words cutting him. Deep. I don't mean for them to. But I have to say what's in me. "... if you walk away from this, you're just another pilot like everyone else."

Are his eyes tearing up? I can hardly see. I look down.

"I don't want to walk away, son. But it's more complicated than that."

"Complicated?" He's not actually making excuses, is he? "Here's what's complicated: moving back to Bellride, like you wished for downstairs, and having to tell the *whole city*...having to tell *all of Aria-Prime* why *my Dad*—Ace Pilot Leif ap Jeronil—whimped out. Gave up on his dream. On *my* dream."

My dream? I didn't just say that, did I?

Silence fills the room for the first time since he's entered. I can hear my heart thumping in my ears.

"Is that it?" Dad says coolly. "So this is all about you, is it?"

"Not *all* about me, Dad. It's about Mom too. And you."

"Well, there it is." He turns around yet again, gathering his thoughts. "That hurts, son. It really does. I'm not sure who you think you are, coming off and speaking to me like this, but you have no idea what you're even talking about."

"I don't?" It's hard speaking through sobs. "Then explain it to me, *Dad.*"

He stares at me. Weighing something. Weighing the truth. For a man that's always taught me to tell it like I see it, he sure is having a hard time now. Faltering. And suddenly I realize I've seen this in him before. When he found out about Mom's affair. When he wasn't man enough for her, so she went calling on someone else. She always said it was about having another child, about being so mad at our peoples' policies on Life Control. Dad physically couldn't produce more kids, thanks to the system; so she went after some young stud who hadn't reached his life allotment yet (which never seems to move above *one*). She wanted another son like me. But it really wasn't about the children, was it? It was about Dad whimping out. He couldn't look me in the eyes then, and he can't look me in the eyes now. And here I am discovering that my father is no longer my hero. *A* hero, surely, but never again like he used to be.

"Tell me why, Dad!"

He's shaking his head.

"Tell me!"

"I…" Then that look of defeat. "I can't," he finally says.

"I knew it. So you *are* giving up on this job then."

"I'm not *giving up* on anything, son. I never would do that."

"Then what're you doing?"

He stares at me, my heart twisting inside. "It's just not what it seems, son. I…I can't tell you more than that." His eyes dart away, then he turns for the open door. There it is again with the eyes.

Quietly, I say: "You're a coward, aren't you?" Hot tears run down my face, voice trembling. "Face it. When you found out Mom had her affair with that other pilot. You didn't do anything. Because you were scared."

Dad keeps his hand on the door handle. Doesn't even turn around. It feels like minutes before he answers. But I've said all I want to say. It's his turn. If the truth is on his side, let him tell it.

"Yes, son," he says. "I'm scared." Then he closes my door.

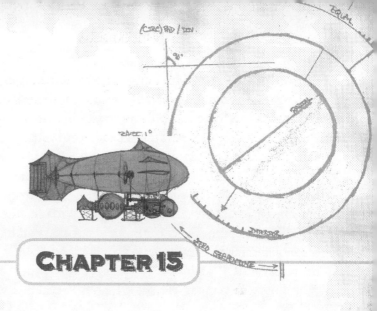

CHAPTER 15

IT'S BEEN A long few weeks. And the first time I ever remember *not* saying more than a few words to Dad each day. "Morning" and "G'night, Dad" are the extent of it, really. We haven't talked about the conversation in my bedroom again. And when Mom tries to bring it up, whether to be a busybody or genuinely trying to help, I refuse. I've even walked away a few times. If they aren't willing to be honest with me, then there's no discussion.

Dad's been on six more sorties to the Northern Range, and every time he returns, he seems more tired, more beat down, and half the man I knew a year ago. Shoot, half the man he was just five weeks ago. While he's always argued he'd never do such a thing and taught me to never do it myself, he still is: he's giving up.

The argument with Dad, however, has proven to be a powerful accelerant in my apprenticeship, you might say. Rather than turn me off to a prestigious career with the Guild, it's inspired me. To be better than him. Than he ever can be.

I don't mind cleaning duty. Anything that gets me out of the house is warranted relief. And each day that I endure the ridicule of the Sky Riders in the locker room is one day closer to getting my wings back. Being with the Pages isn't all that bad either. A good bunch of kids, the way I figure.

Actually, the part I find most unpleasant about Dalfirin's rules for me is the whole *no talking, no contact* policy. I'd forgotten about it only once, on my first day back, when I waved good morning to Erik. I'm sure if it had been Liv, I would've lost a hand or a finger or something. But Dalfirin made sure I didn't do it again, making me shovel the contents of every stall into the middle of the tack barn, after hours of course, and then shovel it all back into each stall. Only to clean them yet *again*, this time heaving the refuse out the hangar as usual. Lesson learned. I was grateful for the shovel.

I've taken to my chores, even embracing the additional punishment from the senior flyers. Working my back 'til it breaks is more like it. But it's paid off. Dalfirin not only repealed my suspension two days ago, but even gave me permission to speak to Liv. "Just watch yourself, Apprentice Jumble-Jon," is all he added. *Even back to calling me names.* Things are looking up.

Liv, Erik and I have picked up a few daily harvesting runs with the pros. Nothing extravagant; entry-level stuff, really. But the routine is welcomed, as is the flying. Sweeping clouds for nelurime is fun stuff. Our job is to arrive early, make sure everything in the barn is in order, then set out the pros' rigs. Once that's done, we set up our own. All nets are made of handwoven silk taken from worms on the anchor mountains. A single-flyer net is about 30 feet wide at the top, 60 feet at the bottom, and 150 feet long. Double-flyer ones are three times as wide; you get more nelurime with them, but they're slower since you need two birds working in tandem. The net's narrow end is attached to a control bar, which connects to the harness beneath the felrell. Folded over on itself to start, the net stays tucked underneath the bird until the pilot opens it up—usually once inside a cloud field full of nelurime.

The luminescent yellow hue of any cumulus clouds is a dead giveaway. A Sky Rider sweeps through the cloud, gathering the moisture on the silk until it reaches saturation. As soon as a net has left the cloud, the pilot has precious little time to get back to a processing hall—officially a *nelurime evaporation plant*, or *nel-vat* for short—before the nelurime evaporates with the water content. The felrell alights atop the vat, a tall, square building not far from the hangar (and in cities like Christiana and Knightsbridge, one of several), allowing the net to pass through a large cut-out in the side of the building. Once the net comes to rest, the engineers— taking great care not to bump the silk in any way—disconnect the bar from the rig and lower the net into a secondary hall. Here it's closed off from the outside, then heat treated, allowing the water to evaporate, and leaving behind a yellow crystalline powder along the silk threads. A few gentle shakes and the powder descends into a collection tank where it's further refined, packaged and prepared for sale.

Apprentices aren't nearly as efficient as the pros in harvesting. There's an incredible amount of skill that goes into navigating a cloud field, knowing what line to take, and knowing when the net is saturated. A good pilot on a healthy bird can make about five runs in the morning, another five at dusk. But an Ace like my...like a few flyers out there can make twice that many. They're the miracle workers of the sky.

As for finding new friends, I'm doing alright. Sure, at first Erik was my adversary. But he's softening. My little storm-chasing episode left him rattled. Showed him I wasn't a joke. He knows I can fly, and I know he can talk. We've reached a mutual understanding, staying out of each other's way, and sorta becoming—well—*friends* would be too strong a word, but perhaps *teammates* would be a better one.

I see Erik and Liv are chatting in an empty stall. I'm back from putting the felrell away after a good sortie. Two hours until suns are down. I walk in on their conversation as Erik says to Liv, "I'm not sure about that."

"Not sure about what, Erik?" I ask.

He looks up at me, caught off guard, as does Liv.

"Oh, hey, Junar," she says, brightening at my appearance.

"We were just talking about taking you to our spot."

"Spot?"

"No, we weren't, Junar. She's just—"

"Where a few of us First Years gather for fun." She flicks the hair off her shoulder. "To hang out. Talk. Ya know."

"Cool. I'd love to go." I put a hand on Erik's shoulder. "Thanks, bro."

He shrugs it off, casting Liv a look that could kill. "No problem," he manages to say.

We're dismissed for the day, and the three of us jump back on our birds and take off, heading southeast. Liv won't budge when I ask where we're going, Erik yielding even less, probably still ratcheted up that I'm being included at all.

We soar onward, cruising at about 4,000 feet, until the island of Knightsbridge rises into view. Though the smallest of all floating cities, Knightsbridge is no less than spectacular. With its balloon ever appearing as if it were about to be popped by the series of towering pinnacles straining toward it, Mt. Knightsbridge is more of a cluster of spires than a mountain, stretching over 2,000 feet above the cloud-floor. Perfect place for a secret hangout. And for a sect of rogue, but relatively docile recluses, obsessed with fits of creative tinkering. While most people only *speculated* that the Inventors made their homes in undisclosed caves scattered throughout the spires of Knightsbridge, I *know* they did.

Liv avoids the city—elevation 5,000 feet, due to the higher tethering point on Mt. Knightsbridge—and dives down well below the mountain's summit, banking right, followed by a wide left turn that brings us along the west side of the peak and toward a cluster of spires and outcroppings.

"We'll bring 'em down there," she says, pointing to a wide ledge half hidden in mist just 800 feet above the cloud-floor. Serio screeches, as if understanding her wish, and follows as Liv rolls over into a steep spiraling descent.

I can smell the scent of nelurime rising up from below, as well as something else very familiar, but can't place it. Clean, fresh.

We enter the shroud, each bird flaring onto the hazy rock outcropping.

"Well, this is it." Liv unties a small satchel behind her saddle, then slides off her mount.

"Looks like we're the first here," Erik says, glancing around.

"We should be," Liv replies. "We made good time."

I undo my tether and slide down Serio's wing. "Not to be ungrateful, but I can hardly see a thing, guys."

"You will, flyboy."

"We leave the birds here," Erik adds. "They'll be fine. Come on."

I leave Serio with the others, and we move north, following a narrow path bordered by the sheer rock face on the right and a perilous drop to the left. The path ducks into the mountain itself, a cave-like hallway, hiding us in darkness for almost a minute. I hear water dripping. It's musty and damp. Uneven ground. The glow of light ahead, an exit.

Finally we emerge into a truly marvelous creation. Ensconced in the folds of the mountain, but still visible to passers-by on a clear day, sits a bowl of boulders, small trees and a grassy sward, all centered around a shimmering pool of water. Fed from an artesian spring deep within the mountain, the water flows over the far lip of the pool, cascading straight off the side and down into the cloud-floor. It's what I was smelling before. Fresh water. Such powerful artesian springs are not uncommon—the one on Mt. Fairvale provides the island's drinking water. Most other cities using cloud condensers or rain catchers. But none of them plunge out into midair like this one. Or are nearly as serene.

"Close your mouth, Junar," Erik tells me.

Right.

Liv elbows me in the ribs. "Pretty neat, eh?"

I nod, wincing at the jab. "Totally. What do you call it?"

"Eldorfold," she says. "Come on."

The three of us follow the path down into the basin. Liv sits down on a patch of grass by the pool and pulls off her boots. Erik leans back against a tree and stretches out. Wanting to check the place out a little more before relaxing, I pick my way through the boulders on the right side to get a better view of where all the water's going.

"Careful." Liv looks up. "It's a long way down."

I edge as close as I dare, then peer over. A beautiful white plume descends into the open. A few circling egrets snap at the falls. Something worth eating in the water? Eventually the falls disappear out of sight within the cloud-floor.

Content, I look back to the others, deciding where to get comfortable. Choosing the more appealing of the two, I sit close to Liv. Not *too* close. But enough that we can talk.

She takes a swig from a canteen in her satchel, then tosses it to me.

"Thanks," I reply, not sure how to feel about my lips touching where hers were a moment before. "Erik says others will join us?"

"Yeah, a few more First Years from some of the other islands."

I sit back and enjoy the scenery. It's super cool here. "Man, I never knew about this place."

"That's because Bellride isn't invited," says Erik from across the pool. He asks for the canteen with his hand.

"Really? Why not?" I cap it and toss it to him.

Liv removes a loaf of bread leftover from lunch and tears off a chunk, then hands me the loaf.

"Only the three biggest Guilds are allowed to come," says Liv. "The Moors, Fairvale and us." As if on cue, about half a dozen silhouettes cross in front of Eldorfold, the setting suns casting a warm glow around the unmistakable shape of felrell. "Speaking of which..."

"Not even apprentices from Knightsbridge?" I ask.

"Nope," says Erik. "They produce a lot, but they're still small in number."

"And who made that rule?"

"It's just the way it's always been," Erik replies rather sharply.

"Still—" I look around— "I didn't even know about this place. Not even a rumor."

"That's because Sky Riders don't snitch," says Liv.

Moments later, five other teens enter Eldorfold. Erik and

Liv wave a casual hello. The new arrivals pull off their helmets, strip gloves, and make themselves at home.

"Well, looky here, who's the new guy?" asks one of the smaller boys.

"You haven't heard, Finn?" another in the group whispers. "Christiana? Leif ap Jeronil?"

"Sure, I have," says the one called Finn. "Are you daft?" Then it dawns on him. "Oh, I get it. You're the Ace's son."

"That's me," I say with a slight nod. Just the comparison makes me sick to my stomach. They have no idea that, at his current rate, Dad is probably a week away from resigning. And I'll be back at Bellride. Don't want to get comfortable here in Eldorfold.

Finn pauses, everyone apparently waiting for his pronouncement over me. "Well, he's as welcome as any if Erik and Liv say so."

"Name's Junar," Liv says with a smile. "And, yeah, we say so."

I stand up as Finn walks over and offers his fist and forearm. "I'm Finn, from Fairvale," he says as he leans in with the flyer's forearm embrace. "This is Danos, The Moors." Danos locks arms with me, too. Then Finn introduces the other three: two more from Fairvale, one from The Moors.

"Nice to meet you guys," I say, then sit back down and pick up my bread. They seem alright. Finn is a head shorter than everyone else, dark hair and face like a chubby mountain weasel. Loud. Probably obnoxious. But definitely a leader; everyone seems to respect him.

"So how's your day?" Liv asks, looking to Finn.

"Alright, I guess. Had some weather spill down from the Wall." The Wall is that perpetual storm system that circulates around the planet's upper reaches. Fairvale's closer to it than any of the other islands; they often get hit hard if the wind changes out of the north. "Lost a pilot, we did."

"Seriously? Who?" asks Erik.

"Nelmen. Was a Fourth Year. Pretty good, actually. Kinda caught us all off guard."

Thought it was a good place for me to chime in. "Man,

sorry to hear that."

Finn stares at me, saying nothing. Awkward. Did I say something wrong?

"We're *all* sorry to hear that," Liv says, coming to my rescue.

"Thanks, dame." Finn glances back at me, saying, "Thanks, Ace."

I nod. That was weird.

"But that's not the worst of it."

"Oh?" Liv sits up, as do I, curious as to what could be worse than losing a pilot.

"The Zy-Adair attacked last night."

Erik is nearly on his feet. "Last night? But we didn't hear a thing about an attack."

"You wouldn't. It was a raid," Finn adds. "Broke into our tack barn. Stole a bunch of gear. The Guild wants to keep it quiet. You know, don't want the citizens to panic."

I can see Liv's brow wince. "That's odd. What would pirates want with felrell tack?"

"Dunno." Finn shakes his head. "We wouldn't have even known they were there had not one of our Pages sounded the alarm. Stayed up late, doing extra chores. He was about to lock up. Poor kid's really shaken up over it."

"How many?" asks Erik.

"Kid says two. Maybe three."

"Maybe?" Erik asks.

"He's shook up, OK?"

"Sorry." Erik raises his hands. "Just checking."

It's clear that Finn's a little rattled too. Not that I blame him. Zy-Adair are bad news, no matter how you cut it.

"What do the Brologi say?" I ask, hoping I might be allowed to join the conversation this time.

Finn drills me with his beady eyes again. "They're investigating. Most likely just a gang of them playing tricks. Trying to rile us up."

It's definitely odd. Usually pirates don't do anything *unless* they can be *seen*. Make trouble to prove a point. Put fear into the islands. But a secret mission? Not that I'm an expert on the Zy-

Adair, but it doesn't fit.

"Junar knows a thing or two about pirates," Liv states. "Don't you, Junar?"

Liv! What are you doing?

"He and his Ace Dad rescued a bunch of passengers during an attack," she says.

"With help from the Guild in Bellride, of course," adds Erik. Always correcting wherever he can.

"And he and his Dad took down a modified C-Class that attacked their market back in Bellride," she adds.

"Woah," says Finn, looking around. "I heard about that rescue, just didn't know it was you. That's some fancy stuff there, eh, boys?" The others nod. "So you and your Pops are quite the pair, are you? You fly like him, too?"

"I can hold my own."

"Boy, can he!" Liv pipes up, then leans back on her elbows, glancing sideways. Is she blushing a little? "I mean, he can handle himself. Right, Erik?"

Erik replies with a scowl. Still sore at me.

"Handle himself..." Finn strokes his chin, coaxing imaginary facial hair from places it won't grow for another year. "Handle himself enough to fly the Champions Race?"

"Ha!" Erik spits, sitting back against the tree, more than amused.

"Finn, come on," says Liv. "He's new...no need to egg him on."

"I'm just saying, Liv. It's not every day an Ace's son is a First Year. Could be quite a show."

"Not a smart move for apprentices, Finn," she replies. "Or have you forgotten about the Finisher's List?"

The *Finisher's List*. It's exactly what Lance and I had talked about before I left Bellride. Him wanting me to race; me reminding him few apprentices had ever signed up; both of us knowing that none of them ever finished. *Ever.*

"Oh Liv, come off it," Finn scoffs at her. "Don't tell me you wouldn't love to see something like that happen in our class. He'd surpass his old man in one day!"

Surpass my old man? With everyone watching?

"Or die trying," Liv shoots back.

"Well, I say he should do it."

"Erik!" Liv scolds him.

"What? He should!"

The three of them continue arguing, Danos and the rest jumping in with their opinions. It's seven against Liv, and this is one fight she isn't going to win. Whenever a bunch of teenage males get bent on a contest, there's little anyone can do to stop them. Except their mothers. And as far as I'm concerned, *my* mother has no say in it.

With everyone watching...

"I'll do it."

The arguing ceases. Everyone stares at me. Liv especially.

"What'd you say?" asks Finn. He turns to the group. "What'd he say?"

This is it. This is my way of making a name for myself... of distancing myself from my dropout Dad. Oh, sure, no one else sees him as that. But they will. And while he's busy tucking his head under his wing and drifting back to Bellride, I'll be taking his place. As an *Ace*, earlier in my career than *he* ever obtained it. Than *anyone* has.

"Junar...I don't—"

"Ahh, let him be, dame!" Finn interrupts. "He's got it in him. Look at the boy! That's fire!"

"You got this one, Junar!" says Erik. Vote of confidence? This is a first.

Liv is on her feet now. Fists balled up. "Junar, I'm telling you. This is a bad idea."

"Thanks for the concern, Liv. But I have to do this."

"No. You don't."

Erik stands up. "Liv—"

"Shut it, Erik!" Liv snaps.

He looks as though he's been shot through with a crossbow bolt. She walks within a foot of me and stares me down.

"Junar, I'm telling you, you're going to get hurt. Or worse. Whatever your reasons, it's not worth it."

No one dares interrupt her now, I'm quite sure. I know I wouldn't. But I've made up my mind. Her words are directed at me, so I will be the only one to answer. But she's not through.

"If you really want to be pressured into this—" she gestures to the guys behind her— "by *them*, then fine. That's your choice. But I'll have no part in it."

I take a deep breath. I like her. Really. Not sure how much yet, but I like her, a lot. However, this is *my* future we are talking about. I don't expect her to understand. After all, she's already carved her future out of impossibility: the first female Sky Rider in history. That's something no one will ever forget. Plus, she's right: it is *my choice*.

And I've made it.

"I'm flying," I say without looking away. "But only under one condition: this stays right here. Nothing gets to my dad, nothing gets to my Headmaster. No one blabs about it until I say so."

"Secret's safe with me," says Erik. "Fly or die."

"Fly or die." The others respond.

Except Liv.

I see indifference cloud her eyes, her fists relaxing. She grabs her boots, stuffing her feet back in. Then picks up her satchel and grabs the canteen from Erik. "You're not who I thought you were, Junar."

"No blabbing, Liv," I remind her. She glares at me, and tries to say something. But I cut her off. "Remember: Sky Riders don't snitch."

She jerks back, slapped with her own words. Pulls her helmet on. Then, without so much as a wave or a nod, she turns for the path and disappears around the corner.

"Women," Finn scoffs. "Can't live with them—"

"And neither can the felrell," Erik concludes.

We all laugh. At least on the outside.

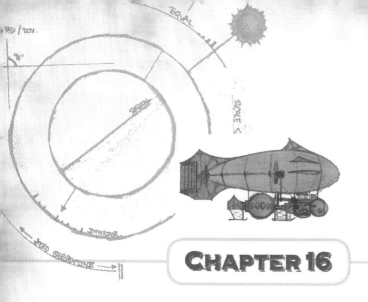

CHAPTER 16

THE DYNAMIC IN the tack barn has changed a lot over the last week. Suddenly Liv wants nothing to do with me, and Erik has practically made himself my best friend. Even Dalfirin seems to be lightening up on me. Has Liv told him? Though, I highly doubt my enrollment in the Champions Race would be something he'd endorse. Safety is everything to him...something I should have taken into account before I took the team into the storm. Still, I can't help but think that if he does indeed know, perhaps my desire to prove myself has somehow raised his perception of me. As a man.

But regardless of their reasons, I welcome Erik and Dalfirin's newfound acceptance of me. I'm no longer the rookie. I'm *in*.

And Liv? She'll come around. Eventually. Especially after I've won. Surely she'll understand once I explain everything to her. She'll see. Wish I could've just blurted it all out to her back at Eldorfold. But for all the doubts I have in my Dad, I'll at least give him the dignity of telling the Guild himself. That he's leaving.

That he can't handle the pressure.

And me? I'm here to stay. I've found a place to belong, and to prove just what kind of pilot I can be. *The best.*

Dad continues to get worse every time I see him come back from a mission. Brooding. Depressed. And always tired. He tries talking to me a few times, but it's just superficial, really. He never can come out and admit the truth to me. Granted, that's got to be hard for any father to confess to his offspring. I give him that. But the point is, he hasn't. And he won't.

So my mind is made up. And I'm sure my disapproval shows. But how is a kid supposed to handle his hero not showing up for game day? He has the talent, he has the drive. But he doesn't have the courage.

When he isn't around, Mom is having all sorts of moods, all of them upset. She yells at me for the slightest thing. Leave my dirty clothes on the stairs *once,* and she flips. We don't talk. Just holler. She throws things too. Breaks plenty of her glass bowls *by accident.* This is how she acted before my baby sister was born, when the Council found out about the pregnancy. Heard her screaming at the Brologi when they came to take her away. Came to "keep the population in balance." Ironic. She wanted a boy. But she brought it upon herself, knowing full well what would happen to an unsanctioned life. Life is only convenient when the system can sustain it. We procreate when the resources are there. That's it. To do otherwise is to invite hardship on everyone, most of all the new life. And such selfishness on Mom's part was met with the end it deserves: extinguishing the reward. Hey, I don't say I agree with it all, but rules are rules, and she knew that. We all do.

Needless to say, my house is the last place I want to be. So I spend almost every waking moment with the Guild. And more than one night sleeping there. Serio's nest is plenty wide for the two of us, and he is more than warm enough.

I excel at Guild life, doing everything Dalfirin asks of me and then some. If my world is crumbling around me, then I will make this my life. Kar-Christiana is my home now, and I will become its greatest asset. I will become its champion.

When Dad finally stops trying to make efforts to speak

with me altogether and Mom is anything but nurturing, I decide to move out. I take my flight bag and a few changes of clothes, then leave. I want to go back for the telescope in the middle of the night. Its functionality outweighs the distinct tie to Dad. OK, maybe not entirely. I know he loves me. I know he wants to make things right. But he can try harder. Maybe my leaving the house will make him see this means a lot to the family. That it's not too late to stick it out.

The only times I see him after that is in the tack barn when returning from sorties up north. *Defeated* is the best word to describe him. He looks at me occasionally. I can feel his eyes on me as I put Serio away. Dumb bird always gives me a pouty look. *Go talk to him.* But it's just my imagination talking.

Finally we bump into each other in the locker room, towel around his waist coming out from a hot shower.

"Hey, son."

I glance at the floor. "Hey, Dad."

Not quite sure how to describe what I feel in this moment. Part of me wants to hug him, towel and all. Part of me wants to just keep walking right past him. *Later.*

"Listen, Junar, I know that—"

"No worries, Dad, we're cool." I wave a hand through the air.

He catches my wrist. "No, son. Listen to me. Please."

"Are we back to this again?" But I'm too stunned to pull away.

Dad looks around, then whispers, "I'm going to speak with Lucius."

My eyes go wide. He's going to ask for help? Or is he giving his official resignation? I just stare at him, waiting. He lets go of my wrist.

"I'm not sure how it's going to end. I just wanted you to know that..." His eyes dart around. Is he seriously going to cry? "...that I *tried.*"

Longest pause of my life. *Say something, Junar!* I swallow. It all comes out in a jumble. "Well, thanks for telling me. Let me know how it goes. I'll be here in the barn if you want to talk with me."

That's all you can say? I feel like a fool. But what am I supposed to say? His choice, not mine.

"Night, Dad." I turn on my heels and push the door open. I swear I hear him say "I love you" as it closes.

I go to bed feeling convicted. Very convicted. Even Serio's scolding me. *Ease up on him, Junar! It's your* dad, *for crying out loud.* But no matter how hard I try, I can't seem to forgive him for what he's done...for what he's about to do. The fact is that any complaint on his end will demote him, possibly indefinitely. It means a huge insult to the Guild, to the Chancellor even, if it ever becomes public knowledge that their prized flyer turns out to be second rank. And that's being kind, at best. So it'll stay amongst the Guild. A long, bitter reminder that they've made a mistake, and that's all Leif's fault. As much as I want to console him—and he deserves as much, I suppose—I have a future to think of. Selfish? Well, what else do I have, really? At some point, a boy has to become a man and make his own decisions, regardless of his father's. And distancing myself from the humiliation he is about to bring upon our family name is my only way out of this.

The moon reflects off the cloud-floor and casts a pale light into the hangar. Only the cooing of sleeping birds and a steady, southerly wind is audible above my soul-searching cries of my heart. Seems as good a time as any to pray. And even with that thought, I feel embarrassed, like I've been ignoring Talihdym all along. Like He would not condone my behavior. But if I can't pray to Him, who else do I have?

"Talihdym, I know You're up there, listening."

Serio stirs.

Quieter.

"So, I just want to ask You, if You could help my dad, that'd be great. He really needs it. And You, sure as anyone, know I can't do anything for him."

Won't do anything, is more like it.

"Just…be close to him, I guess. He's a good man."

The best.

"And I know he's trying, but somehow, his efforts simply aren't…well…good enough."

For whom?

Why am I praying like I'm verbally avoiding the questions I already know the answers to? *So frustrating.*

I roll over and pull the wool blanket up tight around my neck. I *will* get to sleep. Eventually. Talihdym will do something, I'm sure of it. Maybe Lucius will be gracious. Give Dad some sage advice, or ease up on the frequency of the sorties.

Or send the whole family back to Bellride.

Morning arrives, and while I tell myself it's a new day, the memories from the night before linger in my head like an overplayed song—impossible to ignore. But not impossible to drown out. Work. Dedication to the tasks at hand. Being the best. These are loud efforts, with power to suppress. And I freely give myself to them. Hiding in them.

"Well done, Junar."

I look at Dalfirin. *What, no nick-name?*

"I must say, you've really taken to your work in these last several weeks." He examines my harness repair once more, just to be certain. Broken girth lines are nothing to skimp on. "But tell me—" he withdraws his hand and places his arms behind his back— "doesn't your mother miss you? With you sleeping in the hangar and all?"

Random question. I run my fingers through my hair. "Miss me? She's just glad to have some peace and quiet back in the house."

"I see."

Is that a good *I see?* My heart's beating in my ears.

"And your father?"

"Eh, we see each other all the time here in the barn. You know, father and son, working together." I try to sell it as best I can.

"I see."

Again? Not good. Less than enthusiastic.

"Junar—" he steps closer— "is everything *alright* with you? Your family?"

Why the care all of a sudden? "Uh, of course. Why?"

Dalfirin stands there, looking down on me. Certainly knows how to make a guy sweat. "Just call it a hunch," he says.

"Well, thanks for asking." I reach over and heave the saddle off the blocks. Looking back, the Headmaster is halfway across the tack barn floor. "Well, that was weird."

"What's weird?"

"Woah!" I drop the saddle. It's Liv, standing outside the workshop. "You just scared the bird crap out of me."

"Easy there, sport," says Liv, "I'm not going to bite." Yeah, right. She comes in and stoops down to my saddle. "So, you afraid of my dad or something?"

"Not really." I shake my head. "I mean, no."

She picks the saddle up with practiced ease and dumps it in my arms. "There ya go, kid."

"Thanks." I stare at it. "Hey Liv, you wanna hit Eldorfold with me later on? The guys are going and I thought—"

"You thought wrong, flyboy." She winks and turns to walk away.

"So that's it then?"

She looks over her shoulder, her hair twirling about her head. "What's it?"

"You're going to be sore at me until the race is all over?"

"Who said anything about when the race is over?"

Dang, she's brutal. "Liv, I'm just saying—"

As if it's not enough to have the Headmaster up in my face, I need to have his offspring for round two. Suddenly Liv strides back toward me and sticks a gloved finger an inch from my nose. "You listen to me, Mr. Cocky." *Mr. Cocky?* "You want to go off and prove yourself to the world? Fine. Be my guest. But there are better ways of doing it without getting yourself killed."

"Like what?"

"Like owning up to your parents and standing with both of

them instead of running like a coward."

I blink.

What did she say?

I try and speak, but no words come out. My face suddenly feels hot. I look around the barn, wondering if anyone is overhearing our conversation from this corner of the room. I open my mouth again but she cuts me off.

"Like everyone doesn't know about your Mom's past, or see that this new job is taking its toll on your Dad. And you're obviously in a fight with your Mom, and probably your Dad too, because who chooses a bird's nest over a house like the one you've got, kid? Come on, Junar! You think we're all blind? Well, do ya?"

She had me. And it hurt. I don't even know what to say, caught in the worst awkward pause ever. I can't lash out at her, because none of it's her fault. And I won't lash out because I desperately want her to like me. But she has no right to speak so disrespectfully about my parents like this. That's over the line. I open my mouth.

"Just what I thought," she spits in disgust. "You got nothing to say." She turns on her heel and storms off. I just stand there, holding the saddle, my arms burning.

What just happened here? I look down at my repair on the girth straps, suddenly wishing I could repair my family as easily. More footsteps. Erik appears in the workshop doorway.

"By Talihdym, what was that about?" he asks.

"Her Highness, just getting in line behind her father to exact her pound of flesh from my hide."

"Well, she should. Seems the old man's going soft on you lately."

"Think it's the race?" I ask.

"Wouldn't doubt it," he says, then takes the saddle from me and carries it over to the rack. "We still on for tonight?"

"You know it."

"Awesome," he says, leaning against the saddle post. "The guys are flying in ten degrees before suns set."

"I'll be a few minutes late, I think."

Erik looks at me a little funny. "Why, what's up?"

"Ah, just some stuff I need to take care of. Meet you there."

"Alright, Ace. Whatever you say. Have a good day if I don't see you 'round. Fly or die."

"Fly or die."

With Erik's sudden charm, I wonder if he just wants me out of the way. The race is the easiest way for that to happen, if I think about it. Thus his raving endorsement of my participation? While I can't prove it, obviously, I at least appreciate him easing up on me...and I certainly will enjoy his face when I win. For his sake, I hope he at least places a good bet on me. Unless, of course, he *likes* losing his precious First Year stipend.

I'm going to be late to Eldorfold. An Ace's rig needs some looking at. While I'm still not a huge fan of my dad, I know he is of me. Always recommending me to other pilots and everything.

Best repair dog in the city.

Oh, my son can fix that in ten minutes flat.

They couldn't help you? Go see Junar.

Shucks, almost makes me feel guilty. And I don't mind the extra liir in my pocket. Even one job a week means a little extra spending money. Would have spent it on Mom before. Not anymore. I'd spend it on Liv too, if I thought it'd help her out of her dark cloud. But that's not happening. So much for the women in my life. Means I can save it, I guess.

"Your pops says you're quite the repair Ace," says one of Dad's guys. 35 years old, I'd say.

"Yeah, well." I shrug off the compliment, then look over the guy's harness. It's an old one. Manual locking mechanism. Busted. "Looks like your compression spring is rusted clear through."

"But you can fix it?" he asks.

"It's pretty old...ever thought about getting a new one? I hear that—"

"No can do, kid. Gift from my old man."

Really? You have to bring fatherly sentiment into this? One of these days it's not going to sting so much.

"Well, I'm not sure I can find the parts around here," I say, wiggling one of the hinges. "Might need to make something. Or, worst case, take it to—"

"Worst case what?" The man's face flattens. Even though the guys know the Inventors make half the stuff we use, Dad still warns me about bringing them up in public. Or in private. Never know who might brand you a dissenter.

"Worst case," I say, "is you might need to take it home and put this one in a display case."

He looks at me, then to the harness, then back at me. He's not buying it. "Tell you what, kid. I'll pay you thirty liir just to see if you can fix it. You keep the money no matter what, even if it's through one of your—*you know*. And if you get her working again, there's ten more where this came from." He places six five-liir coins into a small leather pouch and hands it to me.

"You have yourself a deal, sir."

"When can I expect it?"

"Hey now, you can't rush a fix like this."

He chuckles. "Your pops said you were a quick one."

My pops. "Yeah…I try."

"Well, you know where to find me. And ten more." He winks. Thirty liir plus ten is exorbitant, even for an antique harness repair like this. He knows as well as I that the only person fixing this saddle will be an Inventor. And I'm more than happy to take it. If everyone wants to stay away and leave their dirty work to me, well, that's just fine by my flight log. If I stopped flying, Talihdym knows I'd probably be an Inventor myself.

But first, to Eldorfold.

"What took you so long, Ace?" asks Finn. Everyone's sitting in a circle down by the pool.

"Harness repair," I say, nodding a greeting to the others. "Erik didn't tell you?"

"Yeah, I did," says Erik, "but you never told *me* what you were doing, Mr. Mysterious."

"Details, details," I say as I make my way down. They open up a space for me to sit, but not before I splash a handful of cold water in my face, washing off the day. "OK...so what's the news, Finn?"

"Word is all the Timber Pilots are signed up to race, everyone but—" He stops short, face frozen.

"Go ahead," I say. "Say it. *Everyone but my father.*"

"Sorry, Ace. I didn't want—"

"You can't hurt my feelings any. I know he's not flying."

"Yeah, well, I..."

"Any more First or Second Years?" Erik saves him.

"Not yet. So far our boy Junar here is the only competitor from among our prestigious rank and file," says Finn. All the other guys from Fairvale and The Moors pound my back, congratulating me.

"I haven't proven anything yet, guys." I wave them off. "Relax."

"Proven? Why, just to *sign up* takes guts!" says Erik.

"Thanks," I reply. "But I'll need more than guts to stay up with this lot."

"A kiss from Liv might do," says Finn, puckering his lips. I'm blushing.

"I wouldn't be so sure," adds Erik. "The Queen isn't too fond of our young Ace at the moment."

The guys all pity me with mock concern.

"She still sore from last week, eh, Junar?" asks Finn.

"You could say that," I reply. Everything in me wants her to like me. Wants her to see my point. But a piece of solid iron would have a better chance of bending at this rate.

"Ah well, no worries," concludes Finn. "She'll come around when she sees you cheered at Champions Stadium."

"Yeah, jealous of all the screaming girls," Erik adds. The other guys laugh. "So you think—"

Finn raises a hand. "Woah, what's that?"

We all sit up from our grassy seats.

"What's what?" Erik asks.

I hear it this time too.

"There it is again," says Finn, his ferret-like eyes squinting. Sounds like heavy stones grinding against one another.

"Mountain quake?" I ask Finn. I'd heard of them happening before, but obviously we never feel them up above.

"Nah, too quiet," he says. "Plus, the ground ain't moving." The sound is rattling up from somewhere below us, around the far side of Eldorfold toward a sheep path we never use.

"What's down that route, anyway?" I ask.

"Nothing," answers Erik. "We never go down there. Just wraps down around the mountain and dead-ends with the cloud-floor. Nothing to see."

"Unless you want to suffocate," Finn adds. "Or maybe see some sheep carcasses."

"It's just falling stones," says one of the other guys.

Finn wrinkles his brow. "I'm not so sure." He eyes the sky to measure the fading light. "Got another half an hour before suns set." Then he looks to me and Erik. "What d'ya say, boys? Feel up for a little hike down?"

"I'm game," I say, standing up.

"Me too," says Erik.

The other flyers decline, not wanting to travel back home in the dark. So they say their goodbyes and walk out to their birds.

Finn zips up his flight jacket, then leads the way. Erik and I follow him to the other side of the wading pool, edging near the falls overlook. We hug the cliff on the right where a narrow sheep path materializes around the rock wall.

"Easy does it," Finn calls back. "Need you healthy for the big race."

I smile.

"What about me?" asks Erik from behind.

"We need you in case Junar here needs someone to keep all the girls away after he wins."

The sheep trail is a lot steeper than I imagined it might be. Not that I'd expect a path around Knightsbridge's anchor mountain to be anything less than precarious, nor would most people consider this an *actual trail*. It's just that most Sky Riders don't spend a whole lot of time hiking, so my legs aren't used to this. And judging from Erik and Finn's breathing, neither are they. That, and as we edge closer to the cloud-floor, the gas is starting to affect us. First the smell, sterile and pungent. Then, the dizziness, which makes it even harder to stand on cramping legs.

As daylight fades, the trail folds back into the mountain's face, and we're walking through a deep bowl. Dozens more sheep paths come down from above, merging with our own. The walkways are like tiny tendrils of smoke emanating from the fire's source. The reality is that there's any number of ways to transit the steep spires of Knightsbridge. No wonder the Inventors make their homes here. Not only can you forget a cave, but you can forget yourself. Haupstie's hole is on the east side of the mountain, and much higher than any I might spy in here. I look straight up, spinning slowly, the pinnacles reaching toward the dimming sky like long, black fingers of an ancient crown. Impressive.

"I think it's this way," Finn says, pointing the way out of the bowl.

Our trail breaks free from the myriad of other paths, and in a few more paces it emerges to hug the far side of the mountain again, a sheer drop to the cloud-floor, not far below. "Watch yourselves, boys," says Erik, holding onto the rock wall off his right shoulder. "Getting tricky down—"

Finn raises his hand, then spins around, whispering. *"Footsteps!"*

"A sheep?" I ask.

"Person! Person!" Finn corrects.

A person? Someone actually coming up? Can't be. From where?

"Quick." Finn points back up the trail. "The boulders back in the bowl. I think we can find cover."

"You think?" Erik asks. "Let's hope so, 'cause there's no way I'm out-running anyone back up this thing."

The footsteps are closer; we all hear them.

"Shhh! Just go! Go!" Finn turns us back, waving his hand.

Going up is much harder. Thighs burning.

We make it back to the bowl and Finn cuts in front. He walks among some of the smaller boulders, trying to find anything we can fit behind. Then he points. "There! Look!"

With the bowl quickly losing its color in the fading light, I can only see a dark sliver in the far rock face. Erik and I follow to where Finn is trying to slide in.

"How far back does it go?" I ask Finn.

"Just come in!"

"Get in there," Erik orders, half pushing me.

I turn sideways and slide in, shuffling my feet further back. It smells musty, plus the odor of some creature's excrement.

"Come on! They're almost here!" Erik says, nearly knocking me over. I'm in about as far as I can go, pressed tight against Finn. Any more and I'll get jumpy. But Erik's in now, so that's all that matters.

"No one make a sound," Finn whispers.

A silhouette comes around the trail and into the bowl. Big, masculine. Carrying something. No one else follows. So just one person. It's too dark for me to make out the face; plus Erik's really blocking my view. The figure pauses and looks around. Then turns on a new path, passing a foot away from us. He heads up his route without so much as a nod in our direction.

Once he's out of sight, the three of us let out our breath. It suddenly dawns on me that I don't even know why we're hiding. We have as much right to be here as anyone. Don't we?

"Is it clear?" Finn breathes. He nudges me in the ribs.

"Hey, is he gone, Erik?" I ask.

Erik peeks his head out, then waits a few seconds. "All clear," he says. We all spill out of the crack, wiping sweat from our foreheads.

"Well, that was creepy," I say.

"No kidding," Finn confirms.

"So, could you make out who it was?" I ask Erik. "Get a good look at 'em?"

No response. Erik's just standing there. Staring in the direction that the stranger left.

"Well, could you?" Finn echoes, getting in his face. "Both your big heads were in my way."

"Yeah," Erik finally says. "I did, actually."

Finn throws up his hands. "Good grief, man. *And?*"

"It was Banth."

Finn and I look at each other. I turn back to Erik to be certain. "As in *Chief of the Brologi, Banth?*"

"The one," says Erik, still looking up the steep hillside. "And he was carrying something. Something really strange."

Finn grabs Erik's arm. "By Talihdym, are you going to make us pull everything out of you?"

Erik looks at him, then to me. "He was shouldering a bag... with a human foot coming out the top."

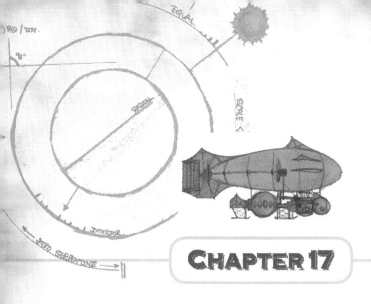

CHAPTER 17

"A FOOT? COME on, Erik," Finn says, punching him in the shoulder.

"No, I'm serious! I know what I saw."

"Yeah, probably something that looked like a foot," Finn says, then lifts his hands to point an imaginary crossbow at Finn's head. "Like the heel of his crossbow! *Thwap!*"

Erik bats Finn's hands away. "Think what you want. But you didn't see what I did. It was a foot."

"Guys," comes my feeble attempt to reign them back in, "the better question is, *what is Banth doing all the way down here?* I mean, the cloud-floor is just below us, right?" We all look to where the trail descends from the bowl. The smell of nelurime is strong. "And even if Banth had a secret meeting with an Inventor, no one's hovel is this far down, is it?"

Finn looks at Erik, then says, "Only one way to find out." With that, he's walking down the trail again. I'm not sure it's such a good idea, especially with it getting so dark now. But we all know we can't go home without finding out where Banth came from.

Going past our furthest point, the trail narrows, hardly

more than a thin ledge, forcing us to press our backs against the rock face. It's steeper too. The three of us shuffle along, squinting and blinking against the growing haze, until we simply can't go any further.

"I can't see ahead," Finn says, then coughs. The dark clouds swallow up any remaining light beyond.

"So he walked up from the clouds," Erik concludes with a mocking tone. "I don't believe it." But with a rock wall against our backs, and a plummet to certain death beneath our toes, there's simply no other explanation: Banth emerged from the cloud-floor.

I wipe the tears from my eyes. Getting really dizzy. "Well, unless you boys want to hang out here and taunt death, I suggest we head back."

"Roger that," the others agree.

It's my second time since leaving Bellride that I've breathed that much cloud gas, and I don't like it any better. How anyone can tolerate it for more than the half-minute it takes to pass out is beyond me. So being back at Eldorford is a welcomed relief, especially since it means I can rest my legs.

The good news is that wherever Banth was heading, it wasn't to Eldorfold; our hideout is safe. Had he arrived here by felrell, this would have been the only place to land. But Brologi use airships to traverse Aria-Prime, which means docking on the island above, or more likely in this case, on the mountain's tethering platform.

"Let's keep this one between us, boys," Finn says, splashing water in his face. Erik and I nod. "Until we know something more."

"No use looking like fools," I say, "spouting on and on about *Banth appearing from the cloud-floor.*"

"Who'd believe us?" Erik asks.

"Precisely," says Finn. "Let's get home."

We head through the tunnel and mount our birds.

"Night, Finn," Erik says. "Race you home, Junar?"

"Actually, I have something I need to do while I'm here." By what I can see of their moonlit expressions, you'd think I just said Banth and I were good buddies who steal people's legs. "Relax, guys. It's a Guild thing. Fixing an Ace's saddle." I tap the extra seat behind my own. "Seeing a guy here in Knightsbridge."

Their faces relax. Slightly.

Finn was suspicious enough to assume correctly. "Having an Inventor fix it, is more like it."

He's a quick one. So I concede. "I've used them more than once, and—"

"We don't need to know." Finn raises his hand. "I'll pretend I didn't hear any of this."

"Oh, come off it, Finn," Erik scolds. "You know you think they're cool."

"Cool or not, we'd be kicked out of the Guild for *life* if they knew we were even talking about this." Then he corrects himself, looking straight at me, "If they knew *you* were talking about this."

"And stalking a Brologi through the clouds on Knightsbridge wouldn't do the same?" I propose. "Or worse." I draw my finger across my throat. Finn doesn't reply. "Seems we have more than a few secrets between us now," I add.

"And we'll keep it that way," Erik says. "Right, Finn?"

Finn takes a deep breath. "Right."

"Have a safe flight home, guys," I say.

"And you have a safe..." Finn fumbles. "A safe time with your *repair man*. Fly or die."

From the air, Serio and I watch Erik and Finn head west, then double back to face Knightsbridge and her massive balloon matrix. My eyes scan the mountain spires again, eyeing the familiar route into the Inventor caves. I imagine the bowl we discovered to be below many of them.

"Good to see you, my boy," Haupstie says from inside the door, his pipe clenched in his teeth. To the saddle he says: "Locking mechanism busted?"

"Uh, yeah. Exactly."

Haupstie eyes the broken component. "How much extra

did he pay you?"

"Thirty liir. Another ten if I get her fixed proper."

"So much?" Haupstie squints, then looks up at me. "I'll fix it for five, you keep the change. We have a deal?"

"Roger that!"

By the time Haupstie has the saddle on one of the workbenches in his laboratory, I'm sure he has it figured out. "Let's see here." He gives the saddle a once-over, examining every square inch of the item. "A pretty hefty man, this Ace?"

"Uh, yeah, as a matter of fact, he is." Did I mention Haupstie's perceptive?

"Hmmm, and a bit of a nervous flyer, too."

I rub the back of my neck. "I guess."

"So, tell me, young Junar, how is life in Christiana?" His face is floating three inches over the saddle.

"Was a little hard at first, but I'm getting used to it." I take the liberty of moving around the perimeter of his work space, eyeing the equations on the glass panes. "You know, new friends, new Guild, new home."

He affirms me with a slight *hmmm* and a nod, eyes still searching for the problem. Is he expecting more of an answer from me? I follow the red carpet right up to the floor-to-ceiling shelving, fingering a basket full of strange parts that resemble brass teardrops the size of apples.

"Any problems?" he asks.

"Uh, nope," I say without turning around.

Awkward silence.

Then, *"Busted!"*

I spin around, then blurt out, "OK, like I was really going to come right out and say I wasn't getting along with my parents! Come on, Haupstie!"

He looks up from the saddle where he's pointing to the broken locking mechanism, eyebrows raised. "Excuse me?"

Whoops.

"So there's restlessness in Junar's home?"

I grind my heel into the carpet. "It's not so bad."

"Bad enough to lie to a friend?" *Friend* might be stretching a bit, but I'm honored he thinks so.

"Bad enough that I'm hoping it all just goes away," I reply.

Haupstie cocks his head, staring at me through two different monocles, eyeballs bulging. It's weird. "Young Junar, a felrell saddle's problems only go away when we either put the effort into fixing the saddle, or throw it out. Otherwise, pilots die."

"Haupstie, we don't normally throw out a saddle, you know that."

"And we also don't throw out people."

It's suddenly stuffy in here. I look down at the carpet, trying to think how I can go outside and get some fresh air. Must be all the smoke from his pipe.

"Would you like to talk about it, Junar?"

"Nah, I'm good."

"Good," he says, tinkering with the saddle again. "So what started it all?"

"I said, I'm good."

"Come now, that's absurd. No one is *good* when they are at odds with their parents."

"I'm not at odds with my parents."

"You're also a terrible liar," he says. When did this guy take up counseling? I keep walking around the outside of the room, making my way toward the furnace. "You have a friend who they don't agree with?" Haupstie throws out a guess. "Maybe a new *girl*?"

I wave him off without looking. "No. And the one I like would probably take their side if I did anything stupid."

He grunts, takes a puff, then tries again. "Disrespectful to your mother?"

"Yeah, but that's not what started it."

"Ooo, now we're getting somewhere!"

I look over at him. He's unscrewed a control arm of the locking mechanism. He secures it in a vice. Can't tell if Haupstie's talking about me or the work.

He picks up a pair of tongs and twists hard on the piece. "Needs some heat!"

In one fluid motion he uses the tongs to pop the broken

control arm from the vice, wheels around, glides to the furnace, and meets me there just as I arrive. He's extremely nimble for such a stout fellow. The forge's iron door flies open and he shoves the small metal form into the heart of the beast, Haupstie's face cast in a bright, orange glow.

"It just takes a little warming up, you know," he says over the roar of the fire. "Then you can work it more easily."

I think he tells me this every single time I bring him something that needs retooling. I nod. As I always do. A bit of *crazy* in him. But isn't it in all Inventors? Maybe that's why they're outcasts. Still, I like him.

"So—" he looks up at me— "you're not as beloved on Christiana as you were in Bellride, is that it?"

"Uh, at first..."

"That's not it then," Haupstie interrupts. Thinking. Then, "Did Dad have a say in demoting you for something?"

"What? No, no." I wave him off again.

Haupstie pulls the work from the heat, now a living-red hue. He places it on the anvil, bumps the furnace door shut with his shoulder, and picks up a small hammer. Then he starts yelling over the pounding. "WELL, I KNOW YOUR NEW GUILD STEWARD IS A BIT OF A CHEEKY FELLOW."

"What's that supposed to mean?" I yell.

"HE SAID SOMETHING OBSCENE? I KNEW IT!"

"No, no! I'm asking you what you mean by that!"

"OH, NO? HE ATE THE SPLEEN OF YOUR CAT?"

"Could we just wait until you're done to keep talking?"

But Haupstie stills his hammer before I finish speaking. "No need to shout at me, boy—" he pulls the pipe from his mouth— "I'm only trying to help."

Face in my hand. "This is ridiculous."

"No, it's working quite well, in fact," he replies, staring at his craftsmanship. "I think we're nearly there." He quenches the metal in a tank of black oil, then lets it sit. "This leaves me only one other conclusion."

"Haupstie." I motion for him to raise his monocles. The absurd-looking cap is bad enough, but having two giant-sized eyes glaring at you—both different sizes—is pretty hard to take seriously.

"Right, so sorry, lad." He shoves them up.

"You were saying?"

"Ah, yes." He turns back around and plucks the control arm from the tank with the tongs. He rubs it with a towel, then tosses it to me. By instinct, I think I'll get burned, but I know better from past experiences. It's cold. I do still, however, get oil on my hands and flight jacket. "Look good to you?" Haupstie asks.

Strangely, I can actually see exactly what he's done: used the present body of metal and hammered it out to take the place of the previously existing catch hook. Simple fix. Ingeniously simple fix. "Yeah, looks really good. Most people would have replaced this altogether."

"Most people discard what they don't think is working properly. But the wise look to mend what has already proven to be trustworthy."

I look up from the control arm, staring at him. Are we still talking about inventions?

Haupstie takes the piece from me with a rag, wipes it down, then returns to the saddle. I walk back around the perimeter of the room while he reattaches the metal arm.

"Right as reality!" he exclaims a minute later. He stands back, blowing out a steady plume of smoke.

"Thank you so much, Haupstie," I say as I pass between the panes of glass.

"It's my pleasure, Junar." I reach to pick up the saddle, but Haupstie catches me by the wrist with a plump, oily hand. "Remember, things are not always as they appear. Sometimes things break for a *reason*." He blinks at me. "To remind us of where we've come from, and what we need to do to correct the past."

Crazy old man.

"Oh, right. OK. Well, thanks again, Haupstie." At least he's a kind old man. I heft the saddle in my arms and turn around, careful not to bump anything. I move back into the hallway, and I can hear Haupstie's feet padding along the carpet behind me. His main door opens up with a hiss.

I look up to the sky bowl of stars. Seeing their silvery flicker against the black sky suddenly makes me remember. "Oh, payment! I nearly forgot." I shift the saddle's weight onto my hip and reach into my jacket pocket, pulling out the small pouch of liir the pilot paid me with.

"Tell me, boy," Haupstie says, "have you thought any more about my offer?"

"Offer?"

I struggle to open the pouch beneath the saddle.

"You know, of becoming a *tinkerer*," Haupstie says, producing a small, red paper folded in the shape of a fox. "Of joining us."

"Ah, yeah, well, not exactly, but…"

"Here," he says, handing the fox to me. "For your collection."

I struggle to reach the folded paper from under the saddle. But just as I take it, Haupstie swipes the pouch out of my other hand.

"Thank you kindly," Haupstie says.

"Uh, Haupstie, that's *all thirty liir*," I say rather timidly, not wishing to offend him. "I thought you said you just needed five."

"And I thought you said you just needed a saddle fixed." He winks and slips back into his cave, the door latching shut behind him.

Had I not been holding the seat I probably would've fingered a fiver out to him, as previously agreed upon. But his statement offends me. Convicts me. Haupstie wasn't content to fix my saddle. He wanted to fix me.

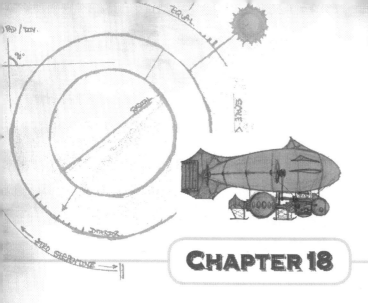

CHAPTER 18

BY THE TIME I get back to Christiana, it's almost midnight. I bring Serio into the tack barn and remove the repaired saddle and then my own before walking him back into the hangar for the night. I notice the south quadrant of birds are missing from their nests, their coos absent from the typical evening's song. The Timber Pilots.

"Gone on another mission," says a voice from behind.

I spin around. "Steward ap Victovin, I was just—"

"My apologies, Junar, I didn't intend to startle you," he says. This guy is even creepier in the dark, if that were possible.

"Forgive me. The hour got late, and—"

"Yes, yes, Junar. No need to explain." He waves my words aside with his hand. "I understand the impetuous nature of youth. We all need a *joyride* once in a while." He leans in close and whispers, "*Your secret is safe with me.*"

"Thank you, sir." I think? "So, my father, he's left again?" I indicate the empty quadrant of felrell.

"Yes, yes," Lucius says. "He is our best now, you know.

Asked to lead every mission."

So Dad's talked to him then? Is everything actually smoothed over? Of course, if he hasn't, I don't want to blow things for him—*that* would be a disaster. Though I doubt it would make anything worse. It's bad enough, no matter who spills the powder. How to put it…

"So, my Dad's doing alright for the Guild?"

"Why, of course, Junar," Lucius says. Even in the dim torchlight I can see his brow furrow. "Is there a reason he shouldn't be?"

My heart lodges itself in my throat. "Ah, nope. Just, ya know, want to make sure my family is, is…bettering the Guild, is all. Ya know."

Lucius stands over me, looming. "I see."

"Well, I should really get back to putting Serio away. Still got some cleanup to do so the Headmaster doesn't skin me." I start leaning into Serio, hoping he'll move on cue. "It was an honor to see you, sir. And thanks for keeping this, you know, *our secret*."

"Indeed."

I make it only a few steps.

"Oh, and Junar, are you still rooming in Serio's nest? Heard there's some *trouble* at home."

I stop and turn back, hoping my face is beyond the reach of the tack barn lamps. "No trouble, sir, just trying to stay committed to my work here. Plus, you know: *moms*."

"Mmm, quite. Well, might I suggest you pay your mother a visit? I'm sure having a man around the house while your father's gone might do her some good."

"Uh, yeah, sure thing, sir."

"Tonight," Lucius adds. "Sleeping in hangars is for riffraff, not the son of Christiana's Ace pilot."

"Right, tonight then." I swallow hard and wipe my brow. "Got it, sir." But when I look up, the Guild Steward is already walking toward the steam elevator to his office. Serio's preoccupied with watching Lucius too. "Yeah, I don't like him either, boy," I whisper. I untether Serio's lead and let him find his way into his nest, then return to the tack barn and put the saddles and reins away. The repaired Ace's saddle will remain in my locker until he gets back from up north. The Guild-borrowed seat he has isn't as comfortable as this one, but it's better than flying bareback.

After making sure everything's in order, I wander back to the hangar and toward Serio's nest, contemplating the Guild Steward's instructions. I don't care what he wants, there's no way I'm going back home. Not for a while, anyway. At least until Dad figures out what he's doing and Mom is ready to not inadvertently kill me with a kitchen knife. Guild Steward or not, I'm not leaving. And no one knows how to hide in hangars better than the children that grow up in them. Lucius will be none the wiser.

Serio jerks me awake. It's still dark. Then shouting.

"*Move! Move! Move!*"

I leap to my feet, but hastily, stumbling over Serio's wing, only to collapse back into the nest. I can't focus. Blinking. I'm sure Lucius has discovered me.

Still, sleep is pulling away from me like an onion getting peeled, layer by layer. The voice, it's coming from the tack barn.

I crawl forward and peer around the corner of Serio's stall to the hangar doors, opened by two pilots. More flyers are running into the hangar. "Bad news, Serio. We've been ratted out." Serio flicks his head back and blinks an eye at me.

I wait to be arrested, standing up and dusting the straw off my clothes. Instead, pilots race into stalls and pull their birds to life, half-dragging them into the barn to be outfitted.

"Be right back, Serio." I pat him on the neck. "Gonna find out what's going on." I slip out of the stall, down the gantry, and stop just to the inside of the hangar door.

"We're out in five!" declares Dalfirin, tapping his pocket watch. Beside him is Reginald, Banth and the Guild Steward himself. The entire company of flyers are busy rigging their birds and preparing for—

"And be sure to take extra bolts!"

Preparing for a battle?

A blow to my shoulder. I'm knocked to the floor.

"Look out, kid!" a man exclaims. I roll out of the way as a pilot leads his bird past me.

"What's going on?" I ask from the floor.

"Attack, up north. Sky Pirates. All hands."

"Up north? You mean—"

"The Timber Pilots got ambushed."

I've heard people talk about time slowing down just before a bad injury, or when you receive bad news. I've never had it happen before. But then again, I've never had really bad news.

Dad.

I roll onto my side, and before I even get to my feet, I know exactly what I'm going to do.

The last pilot has barely dropped out of the hangar before Serio and I are bolting into the tack barn. Less than a minute later I have his saddle and reins in place. "Stay here," I say, running to the locker room, through to the barracks, and then to the armory door. Sure enough, it's been left wide open. Inside are dozens of bare locker closets, stripped of their crossbows and bolt quivers. I walk past three rows of them before finding one with the doors still closed. Inside, a crossbow. I snag it and the quiver, then turn to leave.

"Just what do you think you're doing?"

"Liv!" Someone else appears just behind her. "Erik!"

"Going somewhere?" she says, nonplussed.

"Yeah, north. Sky Pirates attacking the Timber Pilots."

Erik looks at Liv. "Hey, that's not what you told—"

"Never mind what I said," Liv says, raising a hand. Looking straight at me. "Don't think for a *second* you're just going to leave and fight the Zy-Adair."

I move toward her. "Don't think for a second you're going to stop me."

"Wasn't planning on it," she says. "You're not leaving *without us.*"

"What?" I say.

"What?" says Erik.

"It's *my* Dad up there too, ya know," Liv says, then steals the crossbow and quiver from my hands. "Fly or die."

The suns are warming the eastern horizon as we climb to 5,000 feet above the cloud-floor. The way I figure it, the pilots have a ten-minute head-start on us. If we fly fast and stay high, it won't be long before we see them, and—once they encounter the enemy—we can enter the fray undetected. If Dad's in trouble, no one is going to keep me from helping him.

Then it hits me. I'm quite possibly risking my life to come to my father's rescue. The father I was about to disown only hours before. Haupstie's words come floating back to me. *The wise look to mend what has already proven to be trustworthy.* "Well, Serio, here's my chance to appear wise." How ironic.

"Look there!" Liv points. A speckled mass hovers just below the horizon. I see the rhythmical movement of wings.

"Come on, boy." I lean forward in my seat. "Give me some more!" Serio responds, beating the air ever harder. While a large team of flyers moves more slowly, smaller units, as in our case, are far more maneuverable, which means only one thing—the only thing that matters at a time like this—*speed*.

"Get all you can out of 'em!" I holler over the wind.

"We're with ya!" Liv replies, slightly behind.

Erik nods too.

For as hard as Serio is working, we're making only small gains. The good news, however, is that we're not losing sight of the main contingent. That would be bad. Really bad.

Before long, the suns crest the horizon and begin their long journey through the sky bowl. I have never pressed Serio this hard. I know he's fatigued when my heel-kicks stop prodding him faster; he's *already* flying as fast as he can. How much further to the Shoals is anyone's guess. After all, none of us have ever been there. And once we get there, then what? It's the most dangerous flying anywhere on Aria-Prime. Then again, if I'm going to complete the Champions Race, I'll have to run them at least once, if not more. Nothing like hunting Sky Pirates in the Shoals for good practice.

But somehow I have a feeling we'll never make it that far north.

The speckled blotch of pilots and felrell disperses. At first, I think we're losing sight of them, but then a second wave of large dots enters the scene. And that's when Liv, Erik and I all realize they're engaged.

Zy-Adair.

With the main force no longer advancing, we cover a lot more air, sprinting headlong toward the battle. Within minutes, we're nearing the sounds of the conflict, but oddly, they seem mostly one-sided. The Kili-Boranna are outmaneuvering the pirates with ease, climbing up one side of their speedships and down the other, aiming their crossbows at the cockpits or trying to puncture weak spots in the balloons. The pirate defenses, however, are far superior. The Zy-Adair are relying on their nelurime pistols to dispatch any felrell that get too close.

But soon the two forces part ways, with the Kili-Boranna continuing on to discover the fates of their ambushed pilots, and the Zy-Adair...to escape? But the pirates outnumbered the Guild significantly today. And they *never* retreat.

Plunder 'til death bid thee still.

Something's off.

CHAPTER 19

"NICE MORNING FOR a haul," says the pilot to starboard. "Eh, Leif?"

But Leif is in no mood to talk, and brushes off the comment with a look in the other direction. He's still anxious from the unsettling conversation with Lucius the night before. It had not gone well. Not at all.

Dawn's coming and he's tired from flying all night, as is Bouja, his faithful felrell; a same-day run up and back through the Shoals is insane. It's absolutely senseless to force such a long flight into one day, especially flying straight through the middle of the night with no stops. Does damage to birds. Does damage to men.

"You want to leave? Whatever for?" Lucius leans forward over the table in his glass-floored office. Leif isn't sure if this is a rhetorical question or not. An awkward silence fills the glass room, suns setting in the west.

"Well…"

"Leif, I would suggest you think very carefully about what you say next," adds Lucius.

Leif clears his throat to the side, and then continues. "I cannot participate in what you've hired me to do."

Lucius waits for more.

"Mind you, I don't fully understand it all, but—"

"But you would rather go back to Bellride."

"Indeed, I would, sir," says Leif.

Lucius frowns and sits back in his squeaky leather chair. He steeples his fingers, rapping the tips in rhythm. "You have created a rather odd dilemma for me then, Leif."

"Yes, Steward, I understand."

"No, I don't suppose you do. You see, you now know what few others do. And knowledge, as you know, is a most powerful weapon. *Ideas.* What people perceive as reality—whether true or not—is the most powerful thing. And keeping *that* stable is the basis for order within any civilization."

Leif stares at the Steward, not sure what—or even how—to respond.

"My dear Leif. The dilemma is quite simple, really. What you know can *never* become common knowledge. And I have no insurance to the contrary if I let you go."

"Insurance," Leif repeats.

"Quite so. If I let you go, how can I be sure this little issue you've been privy to stays between us?"

"You have my word."

Lucius laughs out loud. "Your *word.* If I've ever met a moral man, you're twice as simple as he."

"Sir?"

Lucius stands up and leans over his desk, nostrils flaring. "Your *word,* dear Leif, *is not good enough.* Things are at work around you that you cannot possibly fathom, and one misplaced word from you could destroy...well..." Lucius relaxes and falls back into his chair, which squeaks again. "You could destroy many peoples' lives."

"I understand."

"Let me be clear, Leif. If I let you go, I must have absolute confidence in your silence as to the things you've seen."

"I already told you—"

Lucius reaches into his desk drawer and produces a small knife with a black handle and a double-sided blade. "The human skin," he says, placing his finger on the tip of the blade, "is remarkably resilient. Holds us together, keeps out infection, and maintains our body temperature. Yet, it's only seven-tenths of an inch thick. Or thin, however you want to look at it. Either way, for all its resilience, one only needs to apply a few pounds of pressure with a metal point to puncture the skin."

Instantly a drop of blood appears on Lucius' index finger.

Leif winces.

"And that one tiny drop of blood, my dear Leif, is all the information needed to bring my wrath upon your life."

"But I already said I'd give you my word."

"I don't care about your *word*, Leif. I care about the things that you'd bleed for. That you'd *die* for."

Leif hesitates. "I—I don't—are you talking about *my family?*"

Lucius lays the knife on the table and licks his finger, studying Leif's face. "You haven't told them anything, *have you*, Leif?"

Leif balls his fists. "Why, you *conniving, arrogant*—"

"Ah, ah, ah, careful, Leif," Lucius says, bringing the knife up.

"I should kill you right here and now." Leif clenches his teeth.

Lucius sighs, then looks down the blade at Leif. "Very well," he says, sitting back. "I'll let you return to Bellride on one condition. There is a new shipment ready for picking up in the Northern Range, and I need it by tomorrow morning."

"Tomorrow morning? But that's impossible."

"Then I suggest you rally the men immediately."

If he was *leaving* so soon, there was one thing Leif needed to do before he was gone. A secret. For his family. For his son. "Very well. Is that all, Guild Steward?"

"Quite. It shall be your last errand for me."

"And then I'm free to return to Bellride with my family."

"You have my word," replies Lucius.

"Your *word*," repeats Leif. "And that's supposed to be good enough for me, but mine isn't for you?"

Lucius looks down, clenching the knife in his hand. Measured and methodical, Lucius glares back beneath a furrowed brow. "I said, you have my word."

The pickup was easy enough. Instead of each bird taking only one log, a team of five all lock in to a central bundle of timber. Not a common technique, but for larger shipments, it's the only way to carry them. Leif flies center point on Bouja, directly above the bundle of logs, while the other pilots fly the four points surrounding him like a compass rose. The tow-lines run from an underbelly rig on each bird down to the main belts around the timber.

Leif shakes the memory of his frightening talk with Lucius from his mind. "Almost home," he whispers to Bouja, "then the nightmare is over."

Light continues to push away the black sky, when Leif notices something coming toward them on the horizon.

"You see that?" Leif yells over the wind to no one in particular.

His pilots look, squinting.

"Wild felrell, if I had to guess," says one of them.

"They'll move," says another.

But Leif doesn't buy it. "No, there's no undulation. Too steady." No one replies, but all are looking on. Something doesn't seem right. Leif lifts his flight goggles, thinking they are dirty, then blinks to clear his eyes. "It almost looks like..."

"Like Zy-Adair," says one of his men.

"I guess I didn't want to be the one to say it," Leif says. He withdraws a brass telescope from his pouch and extends it. Eye to the glass. "Sky Pirates," Leif confirms. Then, more hesitantly, "I count at least six airships. A few speedships too." He blinks and takes another look, heart beating faster. "Maybe more, it's hard to tell." He stows the telescope and pulls his crossbow from off his hip, laying it across his lap. "Better get ready for a skirmish, boys. Seems this shipment is more of a prized commodity than we thought."

None of his men move.

"Kili-Boranna," Leif orders, *"ready your weapons."*

But still none of them respond. Leif looks to port and starboard, but his pilots are fixed on the airships racing toward them.

"Men! Draw your weapons!"

The airships are closing the distance fast. That's when Daren, the lead felrell pilot flying point, turns around and glares at Leif, then forward again, eyes on the foremost speedship. Daren raises a hand...

...and waves the pirates off.

At once the Zy-Adair peel away from their course and double back, heading due south.

"What in the name of Talihdym is going on?" Leif demands, taking aim at his lead pilot. "Daren, what have you done?"

Daren mumbles something, but won't look back.

"Speak up!"

Daren glances to his right and left, nodding slightly. The other three pilots respond with nods of their own, then reach down and pull the quick-release levers on their saddles. Used in case of emergencies. To jettison payload.

"Traitors!" Leif yells, firing his crossbow at Daren. The cables disengage from the harnesses. All but Leif's.

The four felrell shoot skyward while Leif and his bird plunge out of the sky. Leif releases his crossbow, and reaches for his own quick-release lever. But he can't grab it. The wind is violent, Bouja flailing. Feathered wings whipping. They're plummeting toward the cloud-floor. Leif still can't get his hand on the lever. Then he feels Bouja begin to spin, bound to the monstrous anchor. Closer to the cloud-floor. Dizzy in the thinning, yellow light, Leif finally gets a gloved hand on the lever. Then he pulls with all his might.

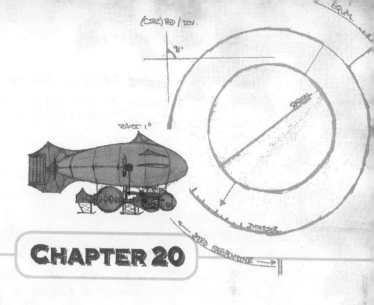

CHAPTER 20

THE FIRST AIRSHIP nearly collides with Liv, a pirate blasting at her with a nelurime pistol. She evades the vessel with a violent peel-off to port. I lose sight of her after firing my own bolt at the cockpit. The blot misses. My heart sinks. Then Liv reappears to the stern.

The remainder of the fleet is still heading toward us. We have enough room to fly over them and join the rest of the Guild.

"You OK?" I yell.

She gives me a quick salute, then circles back around with her crossbow at the ready. Clearly, Liv isn't about to let that attempt on her life go unanswered.

And that's when all the questions begin. Can Liv, or any of us, for that matter, actually kill someone? Can we send an enemy to his grave, impaled by one of our crossbow bolts, or cursed to sink below the cloud-floor? While the topic has never actually come up, I can only imagine that Liv and Erik's response will be the same as mine if asked to defend those we're loyal to. Those we love.

Give me the crossbow.

But in the heat of battle, does anyone think about such

things? The implications? The haunting that others talk about? That last shot I took at the cockpit was my first ever aimed at a person. But I expected to miss. Now I'm preparing to engage the enemy for real.

Liv races after the airship, staying clear of its prop-wash by choosing to fly up and over the balloon. The engines on this modified A-Class are much louder than the ones on the ship that bombed the market in Bellride. But then again, that'd been a C-Class, and it wasn't at full speed.

I track right behind Liv, my crossbow gripped in my right hand. I let the reins go limp over my forearm and withdraw a bolt from my hip-quiver. My left hand lays it in, shaking—from the wind—and pulls the string back to the lock. It was easier than I remembered.

Almost to the bow of the balloon, Liv rolls over, flying inverted. She's held to her saddle only by her stirrups and safety line. She raises her crossbow and aims over her head. As soon as the cockpit comes into view, Liv lines up the sight with the pilot's head and unleashes the bolt. I drift past the airship's starboard side and look down. The pilot is slumped forward with a feathered stick protruding from the top of his helmet. With his weight now pressed against the flight yoke, the airship noses forward into a dive and plummets toward the cloud-floor.

Liv and I come about only to find the entire Zy-Adair fleet barreling toward us.

"*Dive! Dive!*" I shout. "*He-yoh!*"

Erik, Liv and I duck under the host of airships, engines thundering overhead. Static blasts charge the air as the pirates take aim at the birds. In return, our crossbow bolts litter the canvas balloons like quill-skewered pigs. A moment later, we reach the far side of the fleet and cruise into open air.

"Wanna circle back?" Erik asks.

Liv looks at me.

"Didn't see any Timber Pilots in there, did you?" I ask.

A grave expression comes over both of them. They shake their heads.

"I didn't come to kill pirates, I just came to make sure my

Dad—"

"Junar, look." Liv's pointing again, this time to another speckled mass on the horizon. Moving toward us. Slowly. No one speaks as we coax our birds on, flying even farther north. With every beat Serio makes, my stomach cramps in my gut. I'm apprehensive about meeting up with the Timber Pilots. Assuming this was them. But why? Dad is fine.

I try to make out Dad's form as the cast gets closer, but it's impossible from this distance. Perhaps he'll see me first and wave. I watch for a raised hand.

I notice the expedition isn't hauling any timber. Must have let it go in the ambush. Smart thinking. They would've been like sitting ducks tethered to those logs, reducing a felrell to little more than a hay-eating D-Class airship.

We're closing on them now and I can make out the flyer's forms. I think I see Dad. My heart skips several beats. He's OK! Thank Talihdym!

Wait.

No. It's someone else waving to me: one of Dad's lead pilots. Daren.

Liv, Erik and I descend, flying beneath the main cast. Procedure. Then we circle around to join formation from behind. It's as we come into the pattern that I realize there's no familiar voice greeting me. Only stoic men riding in silence. My eyes search. Every pilot. Every bird.

"Where's my Dad?" I ask. Growing frantic. I repeat myself, emotions running toward the edge of my control.

The lead pilot drops back and slides in beside me. "Junar ap Leif?" Daren asks me. I see blood coming from a hole in his jacket, his hand covered in red.

I yell a third time, *"Where's my Dad?"* I'm trying to read his face. But all I see is a blank expression, half-hidden by his flight goggles. That's when he begins to shake his head slowly.

"I'm so sorry, my boy," Daren says.

Wait, what? Sorry about *what?* No...

"Where is he?" I ask. "Back in the Northern Range?"

Daren stares at me.

"Why'd you leave him behind? No problem, I get it."

"Son, listen—"

"Wait," I say, not even sure I'm the one talking anymore. "You're not really serious. That he...he's..." I look down into my lap, gloved hands tightening around my leather reins.

"There was nothing we could do, lad. The pirates attacked. Your father and Bouja took heavy...they fell beneath the cloud-floor."

"It—it can't be. I mean, he was just home, just told me he was going to have a meeting."

"We're all sorry, kid. Really."

My chest is about to explode, blood rushing to my face. I can't feel anything. Only aware of a deep hole expanding inside me, rushing to consume everything within. Then somewhere from the deepest seat of my soul, a groan stirs, dark and miserable. It births in my belly, rising up through my throat like a column of fire. When it hits my mouth I can barely hear it, my ears already ringing from some other sound.

I feel my face rock into the back of Serio's neck, my hands limp on the reins. His feathers are hot and wet, my face damp. Aching. Motes swirl through my vision, so I clamp my eyes shut. But the stars remain. I sense Serio pull out of formation, and I'm glad for it. I just want to be alone.

Tears fill my goggles, their warmth pooling against my skin. I'm laying here for...for...I don't know how long, arms hanging over Serio's neck. Sobbing. Grieving. Trying to keep air in my lungs.

I don't even know why I'm still on Serio. Everything in me wants to go wherever Dad has gone. To heaven. To Talihdym, *God of the Skies*. What's the point of even returning to Christiana? To Bellride? Neither will ever be home to me again.

Mom.

The thought of her finding out breaks me all over again. The weeping is painful. I can see her face, see her crumpling in the kitchen. On her knees. Crying out to Talihdym. Clutching her apron.

Oh, how my heart hurts. I cry openly, finally ripping off my goggles and dropping them into the abyss which has claimed my father's life. I don't care about my possessions, about my appearance. About myself. It would be so easy to roll off Serio and join Dad. And the way I figure it, I have to. I have to say I'm sorry. I have to make right the way I left everything. What is the last thing I'd said in the locker room? *Well, thanks for telling me. Let me know how it goes.* Then a *Night, Dad,* and I just walked away.

What horrible words! My last words to him! I'd been mad. Upset. Totally selfish. And perhaps justified? But none of it is worth his life. I take it all back. Right now. And he needs to know. No, *I need to know.* To make things right. How can I possibly go on living?

Talihdym! Where are you?!

But I feel nothing. No presence. No rescuing love. Just emptiness.

Without sitting up, I slip my right foot, then my left, out of the stirrups. My left hand finds its way to my belt and undoes the safety line. I'm flying free, and soon…falling free.

"Hey, what do you think you're doing, sport?" an angelic voice says beside me. I slowly open my eyes. Her hair has come undone from beneath her helmet, whipping in the breeze.

"Liv?"

"Junar, I know you're messed up from this. And I'm sorry. So sorry. But I'm also here to make sure you get back in one piece. So you're going to sit up, slowly. And put your feet back in the stirrups, and clip in again."

I haven't moved, head still resting on Serio. "Liv, I can't. I can't do it."

"Yes, you can, Junar."

"I want to go be with him."

"I know, but that's not what he'd want. Neither would your Mom." She pauses. "It's not what *I* want either."

I think I hear Erik say, "Me neither," but it's too distant. And I don't care what either of them want anyway.

"He's gone, Liv. Gone. *Forever.*" I can feel more tears bleed from my eyes, blown across my face by the wind.

"But forfeiting your life won't bring him back, Junar," Liv

concludes. A shudder sweeps over my body, enough that I slip out of the saddle. Liv screams. It startles me, as it would anyone. Everything is silent, save my own heartbeat in my ears.

Staring over Serio's shoulder to the cloud-floor…seems a long way down. And buried there, *death*. My father's dead corpse. The finality of it all grips me. No, *strikes* me. My left hand flinches, reaching for something to grab.

Then it hits me: *I don't want to die*. I very much want to live. And I want to climb back on the saddle as my left hand finds the pommel again.

No sound. No rushing air. No birds chattering or people talking. Just absolute silence.

Then there's Liv, reaching down for me. Yelling something at me. Probably profane. Cursing at me to get back in my seat. Even with her twisted face, she's beautiful. And I know I'm meant to be with her. I want to *live* for her. And I want to keep flying.

A dark shadow passes overhead and a hand grabs me by the collar of my flight jacket. I'm hoisted upward and dropped back in my saddle. All the sights and sounds rush back. I look up.

"You're welcome!" Erik yells from overhead, now peeling away on his bird. "You can thank me later!"

I wave, still too choked up to speak, then see Liv pass Erik a thankful glance. Her eyes return and rest on me. "You good for the rest of the trip?"

I nod. Deep breath. "I think so."

"Well, I know you are," she says, smiling. Then pulls ahead to let me and Serio draft.

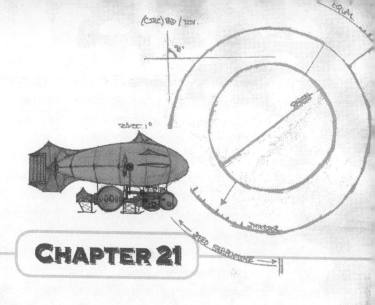

CHAPTER 21

I'M IN THE tack barn putting my saddle away when the barrage of condolences begin. "Sorry for your loss," must be mentioned at least once by every single pilot in Kar-Christiana. Then finishes with, "If you need anything, let me know." Really? That's all you can think to say? What I *need* is my father back. I find their condolences more irritating than comforting. They grate on my soul. But what else is someone supposed to say to a grieving person? I thank each them each.

Soon the wave subsides and a melancholy air fills the tack barn. No one shouts orders, out of respect for the fallen flyer. My Dad. Only one pilot was injured. Daren. But no one else was lost in the ambush, though a number of pilots sustained burn marks on their jackets from nelurime pistols.

"He died saving my life," says Dad's lead pilot, Daren. His chest has been wrapped by the Guild Doctor, his wound deemed non-critical. "He was a true hero," he says, extending his hand. "Again, if you need anything..."

"Not anything you can give me," I reply.

Daren nods, a firm lower lip pressing out. "I understand. Still, if there's something I can do, you know where to find me. Fly or die."

Our motto suddenly has a whole new meaning.

While I appreciate Daren's gesture, none of it helps. I already know my father's a hero. I don't need some pilot to inform me of that. And I don't need his help.

Steward ap Victovin is the last to pay his respects. "My dear boy, we are all deeply saddened by the loss of your father." He places a hand on my shoulder. "Truly, he was one of the greatest pilots this Guild has ever known. And furthermore, he died in the face of battle, protecting his men." Lucius hesitates. "He will have a hero's funeral by week's end, I promise."

Why's that so hard for him to say?

"Thank you, Guild Steward," I reply. Haven't even thought about a funeral. I just want all of this to end, to forget about it. But telling Mom is still ahead of me.

Lucius nods and walks away, then interrupts his own steps. "Tell me," he states over his shoulder, "you didn't go home last night, did you. Stayed in the hangar with your bird. That's how you were able to leave with the others, wasn't it."

Is he seriously going to reprimand me, given everything I've just been through?

"Uh, yes, Guild Steward. Turns out I fell asleep while taking care of Serio's—"

"Never mind, boy." He waves his black-gloved hand. "It will all work itself out." Then he walks back toward the barracks.

I stand there until Lucius disappears, feeling extremely uneasy about his last comment. What did it matter if I stayed against his wishes? In normal circumstances, sure, I get it. But he really has the audacity to bring that up? I'm mad. Didn't like him before, don't like him now.

"Hey, flyboy," Liv says, coming around the corner with her hand on a beam. "You OK?"

I clear my throat and kick some loose straw.

"Gosh, sorry. Stupid question, right?" She smiles nervously. "Listen, I—"

"Yeah, fine. I'm fine."

She looks over her shoulder toward the barracks. "Everything OK there?" *Lucius.*

"He's a creep," I say. "I don't get him."

Liv laughs. Love it when she does. She has a great laugh. Possibly the only beautiful thing in my life right now.

"Yeah, good thing he isn't involved with the day-to-day stuff down here. We'd all be miserable."

I nod in agreement, then say, "I just have your father to worry about with that."

She laughs again. Then takes a step toward me. I can smell her scent. Sweat mixed with yesterday's perfume. "Listen, sport. I know my words won't make your dad come back, but—"

"But they do make me feel better, Liv." I step closer.

"Let me finish, Junar. I—"

Suddenly Dalfirin appears behind her.

Oh, crap.

"Junar, come quickly," Dalfirin says, face stone cold.

"What is it, Headmaster?"

"Everything's OK, Junar. The last thing you need is more bad news, I know. Just know that your mother is fine."

"My mother is—*what's going on,* sir?"

"Ravenmoore was attacked last night. Raided. You need to come quickly."

The windows are blown out on the lower level, and the front door is wide open. Two Brologi stand guard on our front deck. And I can hear voices from inside. Then weeping.

"Mom!" I take off running over the bridge to the house, Dalfirin waving off the guards as we approach. Once through the front door, the devastation assaults my sight. Furniture flipped and torn apart. Books strewn about. Mom's immaculate kitchen looks more like a metallic garbage heap then a culinary space. The walls are gouged in numerous places, exposing the hollows between rooms. Every light, wire and pipe is dismantled.

"Mom!" I yell again, this time sensing she's close.

In the kitchen, speaking with the Brologi Chief, Banth.

"Oh, my baby!" Mom covers her mouth and tries skirting the wreckage. But she trips. I reach for her hand, which she takes, but falls into my arms. Collapse. A new wave of emotions spills over her. *Oh, my baby, my baby.*

"It's OK, I got you, Mom. Everything's going to be alright." Mom weeps so hard she shakes. Her legs give out, and we sink to the ground. Her overflow makes me start crying again. But I must be strong for her. I must be. I can only assume this isn't just about the house. "You know about Dad."

She looks up, eyes swollen and puffy, just long enough to give me the slightest nod, then presses her head into my neck. "I'm so sorry, I'm so sorry," she mutters. "I'm so, so sorry."

I hold her there, letting her broken heart spill onto me. I'm just glad she's alright. As for the house, I'm mystified.

A new voice is talking on the deck, then one of the Brologi guards says, "Inside." Lucius walks in, looking around in genuine surprise.

"What in heaven's name?" Then he sees me and Mom holding one another on the floor. "I came as soon as I heard," he says, looking to catch my mother's eye. "I'm terribly sorry, Sondra. Junar." Then to Banth he says, "Do you have any leads on who did this, Chief?"

Banth looks to one of his men helping oversee the investigation; the Brologi comes in from the next room holding a weapon. My heart sinks. The pistol consists of a rectangular brass slide on top with a bulbous cylinder spool beneath it just forward of the grip. A glowing blue button protrudes from the rear above the thumb, and two copper pipes run down the sides of the slide. A single optical lens adorns the top of the weapon, delineated with crosshairs. The signature of only one group.

"Zy-Adair," Lucius says with a set jaw. "Two attacks on the same family in the same night."

"Coordinated, it would appear," says Banth, emotionless. Does the man even have a soul?

"But what were they after?" Mom says, lifting her head and

sniffing back tears. "Why would they want to kill my husband? To destroy our home?"

"More likely to *kill* you than destroy your home, Sondra," Lucius corrects. "You were lucky you spent the night at a friend's house, and that Junar here stayed in the hangar." Lucius looks at me for a brief second. Is that regret I see flash in his eyes? He'd been so adamant last night that I come home...

Banth steps forward and says, "Your husband posed a threat to the Zy-Adair. Not only was he an asset to the Guild's health, but he wasn't afraid to go after them, as he's proven before."

"The Sky Pirates—" Lucius strokes his chin— "they don't let such actions go unpunished, you know."

"So this is punishment?" Mom cries. "Punishment for saving innocent lives?"

"Heinous, I know," Lucius says. "Despicable. And it won't go unanswered. Will it, Chief?"

"No, Guild Steward," says Banth. "We'll be coordinating a response with however many pilots you'd like to contribute to the effort."

"Very good. I look forward to hearing your plans." Lucius looks back to Mom. "My dear Sondra, would you mind if I had a word with you on the porch?"

Does this man have no scruples? Mom pulls away and looks up at me, smiling, then whispers, "I'll be right back." Lucius offers his hand, but she relies on me for support instead. The two of them walk out the front door, and step to the side.

I look at Banth. All I can think of is the sack Erik saw him carrying with the foot sticking out. *Murderer.* That two separate pirate attacks happened against *my family* in the same night seems outlandish. Impossible even. Dad was no more a threat than any other Sky Rider. More likely it was *Banth* who'd done the dirty work. Framing Dad for something. And probably under Lucius' oversight. I don't trust that man with my own bird seed. Nor do I trust Lucius. I nod at Banth, heartlessly thank him for his help, then quietly emerge onto the front porch.

"So you're sure a courier didn't show up?" Lucius asks Mom.

"For the second time, *I'm* sure, Guild Steward. I should

think I'd remember my husband's final note being delivered to me, don't you?"

"Indeed," he says, stretching the word. He's going to give himself a blister if he keeps rubbing his chin.

"Why don't you just ask the courier yourself?" Mom adds.

"Ah, we are locating him now. Seems he's a bit hard to track down. I'm quite sure he'll have the letter, though, and I'll make sure it gets to you myself. I'm only sorry you could not have it now. I personally feel at fault, as I was the one who summoned the courier for his errand." Then Lucius notices me standing behind him. "Ah, young Junar. Again, my deepest apologies."

"You already said that once before, Guild Steward." I'm in no mood to pander to him. Something's off. And what is the worst he'll do, kick a fallen Ace's son out of the program? Not without losing all manner of respect. *And* having me as an archenemy.

Lucius *harrumphs*, then adds, "We'll have some cleaners come take care of your home. Good day." He bows with his hands pressed together. "Sondra. Junar."

The next two days are laboriously slow. Teams of workers come to help Mom and me piece our home back together, and with them come gifts of furniture and appliances from the Guild. Dalfirin has given me some time off too. At least Mom and I have something to do together. We don't talk much. Mostly she just breaks down crying and needs me to hold her. I shed plenty of tears of my own, but not in front of her. One sight of me crying and it sends her into a tailspin.

Lucius checks in on us twice, each encounter awkward and cryptic. The letter—and the courier for that matter—still haven't materialized. Liv and Erik also stop by, bringing Mom flowers. I want them to stay longer, but they always have to get back to the barn. Seeing them makes me realize just how much I value their friendship, even as new as it is. Lance will be coming in for the funeral on Sunday Festival. Seeing his face will mean the world to me.

But above every other self-thought going on in my head, one elevates itself above all the others. That I may have been dreadfully wrong about Dad. At least partially. *He died saving my life,* Daren said. *He was a true hero.* Even if Dad had been afraid of the new job, afraid of the Shoals, afraid of the Lor-Lie beasties, and afraid of the Zy-Adair, he died fearlessly. He died protecting the lives of his men. And *that* was *courageous.* In the end, he was strong. I was wrong. And Haupstie was right: Dad hadn't given up, at least not on his men.

I pound my pillow at night, screaming into it, pleading with Talihdym to give my Dad back, if even for a moment. Just long enough to say I'm sorry. To say I'd been wrong about him. But Talihdym never answers me. Eventually I exhaust myself, sweat pouring down my face, and I fall fast asleep. It's like this every night.

The time at home also allows me to process what's next. Where to go from here. The Champions Race seems meaningless, and avenging my father's death the priority. The Zy-Adair will pay for his murder in blood. And I pledge my life to extracting it from them. I'll find new ways to hunt them, invent new weapons, and take the battle to their front door, no matter where they hide. I'll join the Brologi if I need to, or simply launch out on my own. Maybe even become an Inventor. The details will come. But for now, it's enough to know that I'll give my life to a new cause. That, and guarding the relationships that really matter most to me.

. Which brings me to Liv.

The way I figure it, telling Liv I'm backing out of the Champions Race is worth quite a few points toward getting her to like me again. Of course, telling her that I want to spend the rest of my life hunting Sky Pirates is likely to equally undo the effect. But that will work itself out. Eventually. She'll see my point and—given her personality—most likely join me.

By the fourth day the house is well on its way to looking more normal than not, and Mom has improved tremendously, though still weepy if I so much as look at her wrong. With the funeral tomorrow, I'm ready to venture back to the tack barn. And to see Liv.

"Good to see you," a few of the Aces say, hitting me in the arm.

"Thanks," I acknowledge. It feels good to be back. In truth, the Guild is where I belong. And as much as I want to be home for Mom—correction, *know I should* be home for Mom—this is truly *home*. The smell of fresh hay mixed with felrell sweat and metal girders are the small comforts I look forward to. That's how somebody knows they're addicted to a Guild: you love everything about it, even the dirty jobs.

"Hey there, sport," comes Liv's voice. She has a shovel full of dung hovering over a wheelbarrow. I wave and walk over. Man, she looks good. Even cleaning out stalls. "How's Mom?"

"She's doing better," I say. "So is the house."

"And you?" She drops the dung and turns back into the stall.

"Eh, ya know, doing OK, all things considered. Just really wanted to get back here to see—"

"Serio? He's been missing you, that's for sure," she says, scraping something crusted on the floor. "Dumb bird sure has it bad for you, sport." She flings another shovel full of crap into the wheelbarrow.

"Uh, yeah, Serio. He's doing alright?"

"Won't stop eating. Think he misses flying, to tell the truth."

"I believe it," I say. "Hey listen, Liv, I've been doing a lot of thinking and I—"

"Don't mention it, sport. You would've gone after *my* dad with me. It's what we do."

"Ah, yeah. I guess what I mean to say is—"

She raises a gloved hand. "Eldorfold. After chores. You good with that?"

"Uh, yeah! That's perfect!" *Overexcited.* Relax, Junar. Act normal. "Want me to tell Erik?"

"No, no. Just us."

"Just us," I repeat slowly.

If my jaw is on the ground I won't be surprised. The truth is, I just want to tell her about the Champions Race. But she seems to have something else in mind. And to say I'm nervous would be an understatement. A girl like Liv wanting to fly solo with a guy like me? I look over both shoulders, hoping *Daddy* isn't watching. This feels like a setup. Crash and burn, baby.

"Easy, sport," Liv says, putting her hand on my shoulder. "He's out working the Pages. Don't worry. He said I can talk with you."

"Really?!" Overexcited *again*. "I mean, really? That's alright, I guess."

"So, see you there?"

"See you there," I reply as she throws the shovel at me. I catch it an inch from my face.

"Mind finishing for me? Got more chores in the hangar, and we'll get done sooner."

She can ask me for anything and always get a "No problem, Liv."

"PS: Welcome back, Junar." She walks away, holding my attention. And my heart.

Liv and I stagger our departures so no one will be any the wiser. Not that I mind, but if our relationship has any hope of lasting, I want to get things right. Want her to understand who I am, and why I'm going to do what I'm going to do. Liv has quite a will, and I don't want to cross it again. Ever. That much is clear.

She takes off fifteen minutes before me and, once Serio's rigged, I drop out of the hangar and head east.

The flight seems unusually long. Anticipation, I guess. Never talked with a girl *alone* alone. Like, just us. Always people around. My hands are shaking the reins as Knightsbridge comes into view. Serio's getting irritated and snaps his head a few times. I go through everything I want to say. Trying my best to order my thoughts. But when Serio finally lands on the ledge, I've nearly forgotten everything I want to say. And by the time I come around the path into the clearing and see her sitting on the grass, my brain is absolutely useless.

"Hey, kid."

I wave, not sure I can talk properly yet. She's so pretty.

"Good flight?"

I nod.

"Hey, what's wrong? You OK? You look like you might be sick."

"*Do I?*" Is that my voice? I clear my throat. "Do I? Oh, yeah, yeah. Fine. I'm fine." I stand above her, not sure how close to sit. "I'm fine."

She smiles. "Well, I'm glad you're fine, Junar." An awkward pause. "You going to sit?"

"Fine. Yeah." *Sit, Junar!*

After an even longer pause, with Liv smiling the whole time, she asks, "So, you said you wanted to tell me something?"

She's amazing. Always keeping me on track. "Yes! I mean, *yes*. It's about the Champions Race."

Instantly her smile disappears. Oh, man.

"Junar, how can—?"

"You don't understand."

She's mad now. I see the flash in her eyes.

"Yeah, I *do* understand, Junar. I don't know where you—"

"I'm not going to race."

"—come off thinking that you're..." She stares at me. "You're...you're not going to *what?*"

"I'm not going to race." I shrug my shoulders and smile sheepishly. "It's not important anymore."

Liv's stare suddenly turns into sheer surprise. I've never seen her so happy.

"Oh, Junar!" She leaps at me and throws her arms around my neck. I'm laughing too hard at my good fortune to keep from falling over. Then she presses herself up, looking right into my face. Just inches away. Her hair smells like flowers, and I have this sudden, overwhelming urge to kiss her. My heart pounding too hard to think straight.

"You're important to me now, Liv. The most import—"

She drops her head suddenly and kisses me on the mouth. Feeling the warmth of her lips on mine makes my head spin. And she doesn't let up, not until Banth's voice makes her scream.

"I'm sorry to interrupt," he says, standing behind me.

Liv puts on her *I'm-the-daughter-of-the-Headmaster* act, where Banth is one of her personal servants. "Banth, just what do you think you're doing sneaking up on us like this? And—" she looks to the entrance of Eldorfold...behind her— "where exactly did you come from?"

I answer that question in my head: *probably from the same route Erik, Finn and I spotted him on earlier.* And like that time, when he was carrying something monstrous, his arms hold something large, covered with a dark sheet.

"Again, my deepest apologies, Lady ay Dalfirin, but I have something that should be of interest to Apprentice Junar." He shifts his ominous gaze toward me. I tense. For all my assumptions about the Sky Pirates, I'd just as soon blame the man standing in front of me for Dad's death.

Then with one fluid motion, he gently lays his burden on the grass and removes the canvas. Sitting just a few feet away from me is a felrell saddle. One I'd know anywhere.

Because it's Dad's.

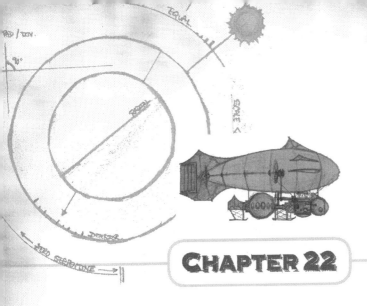

CHAPTER 22

"I'M COMING! I'M coming!" Haupstie yells from inside his cave. But with the way Banth is pounding on his door, the Brologi Chief could have saved the Inventor the trip and just knocked it down. Banth insisted that we come see Dr. Haupstien and refused to answer any of my questions until we'd done so.

"Can I help you?" Haupstie's voice crackles to life from the device hidden in the rock.

"Maurice, it's Banth. Let us in."

Maurice? Wait, wait, they're on a first name basis?

"Let us in?" crackles the device.

"Maurice!"

"Sorry, sorry, just calm yourself, my friend."

And they're friends?

Gears churn, and then the steam blasts toward our faces. The door cracks open and Banth pushes his way in with the saddle. Haupstie lets Banth through, sees the saddle, then watches me and Liv slip in.

"What's the meaning of this, Banth?" Haupstie calls to

him.

"Got something for you to look at."

Haupstie tries to protest, but Banth is already heading for the laboratory before Haupstie can close the door. Seems to know his way around. I'm really beginning to wonder about my assumptions of this Chief...or the integrity of my Inventor.

"Come, come, children." Haupstie coaxes us forward, waving with his pipe, probably more out of concern for beating the giant to the laboratory than actually making sure we are taken care of.

When we emerge into the work space, Banth is already at the center cluster of tables, setting the saddle down.

"Haupstie!" yells Banth.

"I'm coming, Banth! You're bound to give me a heart attack one of these days!"

I lead Liv forward between the panes of glass, her eyes wide. "Pretty cool, eh?"

She doesn't respond with words, just a simple nod, mouth open.

"What have we here?" Haupstie says. He dons his absurd Inventor's cap and buckles the clasp under his chin. Banth still hasn't explained anything to me, including how he came by Dad's saddle. I'm hoping that story will be shared in full with the Inventor. Here. Now.

Haupstie cycles through monocles with his fingers, then drops a different optic over each eye.

"Ligeon Manufacturing. Exquisitely maintained. Ten years old, I'd wager." Haupstie's fingers scan the leather, stopping on a red stain. "Blood."

Liv squeezes my hand.

"I'll be OK," I whisper.

Haupstie goes on. "This saddle has fallen a great distance," he says cryptically, as if he's not sure he even believes it himself. "Crushed, thus the severe deformation."

"Go on," Banth encourages him.

Haupstie swaps out his monocles for two larger ones; I can only presume they have a higher magnification level. He leans in close, this time examining the mechanical details of the rig. "Nothing out of the ordinary here," he says, hovering over the harness safety line. "I'm not exactly sure why you've brought me this specimen, old friend."

Old friend? I'm learning more than I anticipated at this reunion. But I can see Banth is growing restless. Does he have something in mind with Dad's saddle?

"Keep looking," Banth prods Haupstie.

The Inventor casts him a sideways glance, then focuses back on the examination. "If you have some useful piece of information, Banth, now would be the opportune—*wait a second...*" Haupstie pauses, then flips down an even larger optic over his right eye.

Banth leans in.

"Why...what have we here?"

"What? What is it?" Banth moves around beside the Inventor. Liv and I draw close too. Haupstie fumbles with a lever on the side of the saddle.

"That's the mechanism they use for hauling logs," I offer.

Haupstie glares at me above his mismatched monocles. "I know, my dear boy. I designed it."

"Oh." I look down at my feet and brush my hand over my hair.

The Inventor goes on, running his fingers along the work. Then places his hand on the lever. And pulls.

Nothing happens.

"See here—" he stands back— "it's jammed."

"Jammed?" I ask.

"The fall must have damaged it," Banth interjects.

"No, no, no." Haupstie flips down a second layer of green glass in front of his left eye, then hunkers down. "Here, the fulcrum in the pivot assembly. Something's..." He fights with it.

"What?!" Banth is practically on top of him.

Haupstie summons a pair of spring-loaded pliers from his helmet. He pokes and prods, then resorts to wedging the tool in the work, prying hard. Haupstie's lips draw back from his pipe stem, baring his teeth. Eventually a piece of metal pops out and flies overhead. Right toward me. I reach up and snag it.

"What's this?" I hold it up. Banth races toward me. Liv pulls my hand down to look in my palm.

"This, my dear friends," Haupstie says, taking the item from me, "is a foreign, homogenous iron-ore compound fused with an ulterior steel derivative into a previously fixed locale."

"Haupstie!" Banth fires back, stealing the nugget. "Regular people talk, please!"

"It's a tack weld."

"A tack what?" I ask, still not understanding.

"Someone intentionally introduced a new piece of metal into the system." The Inventor loosens the clasp and removes his helmet.

"So they added to your work?" I say.

"They *tampered* with my work, would be a more accurate conclusion."

"Tampered," repeats Banth. "As in, *sabotaged.*"

Haupstie thinks for a moment. "Well, if the intent was to keep the quick-release mechanism from functioning in its intended fashion by the intended operator, then yes. *Sabotage* is accurate."

I look to Banth and he looks back at me, as if his unspoken intentions with the saddle have suddenly been justified.

"Haupstie," I say, still looking at Banth, "then what you're saying is someone intentionally wanted this mechanism *not* to work properly."

"In a word—" Haupstie looks from face to face— "yes. Why? Is this saddle meaningful to any of you?"

The four of us sit in a spacious living room, each in an overstuffed red chair turned toward a low central table. The room is lit by brass lamps that use actual fire for light and, I assume, for heat. It's a much different atmospheric effect than the piercing glow of nelurime crystals. Bookcases litter the outer walls, and end tables of dark wood sit patiently beside each chair, ready to hold the cups of hot tea and plates of crackers that Haupstie's brought us. While neither is my snack of choice, my stomach is too upset not to try and settle it with something.

"This will help, Junar," Haupstie says as he hands me a spoonful of white powder. "*Sucreh* always helps everything. Except *diabellitus*. Can be quite deadly for souls suffering with that malady."

I have no idea what he's talking about, but I'll take his word for it. I stir the white stuff into my tea. Everyone looks at me as the cup rattles on my plate.

"Thank you, Haupstie." I set the cup and saucer on the end table, trying to silence my anxiety.

"Junar." Banth eyes me across the table. I lean over and take a sip of the tea as the Brologi Chief continues. "How much do you know about what your father was involved in?"

I swallow. "Involved in? You mean as a Timber Pilot?"

"Yes."

"Well, I knew he was asked to come onboard because he was one of the best pilots in Aria-Prime."

"*The best*," Haupstie interjects. He looks to Banth. "Sorry."

Banth nods, then gestures for me to continue. I feel like I'm taking a test. "I know Dad harvested timber from the Northern Range, bringing it back here for city repair and construction. Tasks included navigation through the Shoals and occasionally fighting off a Lor-Lie or two." Is that the answer he's looking for?

"How did your father handle his new position?"

I lower my eyes and stare into my tea cup for a second. *Breathe.* Then I look up to Liv. *Not this again.*

Liv prods me with her eyes. *It's OK. Tell him.*

But why on Aria-Prime should I be willing to share personal details about Dad's life with a man I hardly know and—for all intents and purposes—could have killed him in cold blood? I have my doubts.

"He took to it well."

"Junar!" Liv protests.

"What?"

"Tell him." She points to Banth.

I look the Brologi Chief straight in the eyes.

"*Tell him.*" She draws out her words. "*Now.*"

I can feel my heartbeat quicken. Just who does this guy think he is, anyway?

"You'll forgive me if I don't trust you completely, ap...*ap Banth*. See? I don't even know your family name! Just because you've mysteriously produced my Dad's saddle doesn't mean a thing, except for making you a suspect in his death since you knew just where to find it. You're not exactly the most forthcoming individual, either. For all I know, it's *you* who sabotaged his saddle—*if* that's what really happened. And what's up with your carrying body parts around, anyway? That's a little creepy, don't you think?"

"Body parts?" Banth sits up straighter.

Got him.

Haupstie looks over at Banth, then back to me. "Careful, boy," Haupstie says. "Let's keep to one thing at a time. You'd do well not to meddle in the personal affairs of others."

"Like carrying around *my Dad's saddle?*"

Haupstie says nothing.

Banth stands and walks out of the square of chairs. He appears to be thinking. Hard. He flexes his metallic hand, then pulls it to his chest, out of view. A long sigh. Turns back around. "Junar, your father discovered a secret, a very dark secret. And those over him hoped he would keep it that way...hoped he would join them in their lust for power. But because your father was a good man—a *true man*—he could not go on living with what he knew. Did you not see him restless at home?"

I blink. "Restless?"

"Concerned? Agitated? Dear Talihdym, Junar, did you not notice your own father was being *tormented?*"

"Tormented?" I'm having trouble breathing. What's going on?

"Banth, please." Haupstie raises a hand. "Give him a moment."

I lean over to take another sip of tea, but it spills on the floor. *Tormented? Agitated?* That's exactly what I'd seen. But oh, God of the Skies, had I ignored it? Had I been that stupid?

Banth presses forward, Haupstie waving him off. The Brologi Chief's eyes pierce me. "Did you not know that he was risking his *life* when he decided to confront his superiors?"

Risking his life? But...but I'm the one who forced him to confront those superiors. So it wasn't about copping out? It wasn't about *the job being too hard?* I feel sick.

Haupstie is on the edge of his chair. "Banth, please."

"And when the powers that deemed that Leif ap Jeronil could no longer be trusted with their precious, dark secret, they tried to do to him what they do to *everyone* who poses a threat to their supremacy: *they eliminate them and their families.*"

"That is quite enough!" Haupstie is on his feet.

"Oh, Talihdym." Liv's muffled cry slips out from between her fingers.

"He *must* know, Professor," says Banth, staring down Haupstie.

"But no one feeds a newborn anything but milk at first, my friend," Haupstie replies.

Banth tightens his fists. "We don't have *time* for milk."

"He's right," I say, standing. Both men look at me. "Banth, I don't know you. And to be honest, you really freak me out. But if what you're saying is even remotely true, then not only was my Dad murdered, but my Mom and I are also in danger."

Banth steps forward. "The Zy-Adair hit on your home—"

"Wasn't an attack at all, was it?" I surmise. "A raid, is more like it. Looking for Mom and me. And anything we might be hiding that would link the Guild to Dad's death."

"To their *secret*," Banth corrects me. "Remember, your father's death was but one episode in a history of tragedy. The Guild is not your enemy—but your enemy is within the Guild."

"Lucius," I conclude. "The Guild is in league with the Sky Pirates. That's the secret." Banth looks at me, eyes pleading with... *with someone.* Is he fighting back tears?

"I...I can't say more," he resolves.

"What do you mean *you can't say more?* You're the one who started this!"

"Junar..." Haupstie halts me, shaking his head. "Banth has told you more than he is allowed, at great risk to his...to himself. Let that be enough." Banth turns away as Haupstie continues. "You must follow where your heart leads you, and do what you think is right."

"So Lucius is not acting alone," I suggest. "That's what he's saying, isn't it?"

"Is my..." Liv's voice sounds as if it's going to fall apart. "...is my...?"

"No, my dear," answers Haupstie. "Headmaster Dalfirin is not complicit in these affairs, at least not as far as we know." Liv's shoulders relax as she breathes out.

"Though we're sure he suspects something," adds Banth.

"So who else do you suspect then?" I ask, glaring at Banth.

"Junar, please," says Haupstie. "Banth cannot help you further. Not now. Not ever. The conclusions are your own, as are the consequences. And this meeting never happened."

I stand there. Frustrated. For all that I do know, there is immeasurably more that I don't. The two men in front of me are clearly aware of more than they claim, but they seem incredibly reluctant to help, apparently thinking they've already done me a great service with their cryptic explanations.

"Why are you both so afraid of these people?" I finally say. "If what you're saying is true, then we could take them down. Now. We should stop their injustice and fight back! There's enough evidence right here to take to the Chancellor and have every single conspirator arrested, tried and sentenced."

The Inventor shakes his head. "What you propose is harder than you might think," he says. "Many an idealist has set off in that direction, never to return. We are not stupid, as you might suppose, nor are we without courage—or means of retaliation."

"Then what are you waiting for?"

"Perhaps we lack only opportunity," replies Haupstie.

"Then what's this?" I raise my arms in frustration. "This whole situation *is* your opportunity!"

Banth comes around the table and gets in my face, metal finger just inches away.

"Listen to me, boy. Right now, you and your mother are safe. Your father's final letter never made it to Ravenmoore—at least that's what they think. And as long as they believe your father kept his mouth shut and didn't tell you anything, then they have no reason to silence you. But the moment they suspect anything—" Banth reaches into his pocket and produces the tack weld from Dad's locking mechanism— "they'll kill you. Whatever you choose to do, that's your call. But right now, you're safe—and if I were you, I'd keep it that way. There are ears everywhere." His face saddens at his own words. "It's not just the Guild Steward you have to worry about, Junar."

"So there are more, then! You admit it!"

"I admit only what you're able to handle."

"I can handle it all," I reply indignantly.

"No, Junar. You can't," Banth replies. "What did the Ace pilots tell you about your father's death? That he died as a hero? That he died *saving their lives?*"

Anger flares in my chest. "How dare you!"

"Banth! Junar!" Haupstie pushes between us.

"Think about it, Junar. Your father's safety lever was sabotaged. You really think he was flying around, taking out Sky Pirates, with a few tons of logs strapped beneath him?"

"He was a hero!"

Haupstie puts both his hands against my chest.

"Indeed—" Banth raises his voice— "but he was *dragged* to his death, Junar. Of that I can *assure* you."

"Oh, you can, can you?" I can feel hot trails streaming down my face. "Just how would *you* know how he died, huh? Were you there? And you still haven't told me how you got his saddle either." I'm wiping away spittle with my forearm. "Coward!"

"My point is," he says, clearly trying to keep himself under control, "that the Guild Steward is not acting alone. I can't tell you, young Junar, or else I forfeit assets of my own."

"Assets of your own?" This Chief is infuriating!

Suddenly Haupstie draws close to my face. "Young man, if you value your life at all, or that of your mother and the rest of your friends, you will believe—even if on blind faith—every word coming out of this man's mouth."

"And if I don't?"

Haupstie releases me and steps back. "Then you are not

welcome back here or in any Inventor's hovel. Ever. I will make sure that a young man who treats wisdom and life with such disregard *never* comes near those dearest to me."

"Oh, so you're a conspirator, too, eh?"

"Junar!" Liv says. "Trust them, won't you?"

No one makes a move. Haupstie's defiant. Banth's behind him, somehow still as stoic as a statue. And Liv's doing her best to keep the peace and not freak out. But *I'm* freaking out! What's wrong with everyone? I push away from Haupstie, nearly fall over the chair behind me, and walk out of the circle for a second.

Breathe, Junar.

I'm trying to collect my thoughts. But the harder I focus on them, the more they seem to run wild. The Inventor is right about *milk*; if this is all true, I feel like a baby trying to eat an entire lamb in one sitting. Another deep breath. Then a thought. One final question to ask Banth. I collect myself, assure Haupstie I'm not going to choke the Chief with my bare hands (who'd drop me in a flash anyway, so I don't know why I even bother reassuring Haupstie...probably for his sake more than anything), and walk up to Banth. He's even more intimidating up close...but still afraid... of something.

"Let's say I trust you," I say. "Then prove it to me." I want to poke him in the chest, but think better of it. "Prove it to me with the truth. What *letter*, Banth?"

Everyone's holding their breath. Even me. Feels like ten minutes pass as I wait for a response from this monster of a man.

Finally Banth sighs and hands me the small bit of iron. "Your father's letter, which he made certain would be secretly delivered to your home the night before his murder."

"But how would you know anything about that, if it was a secret? The *truth*, Banth."

"Easy now, Junar," says Haupstie.

Liv is on the verge of tears, hands to her mouth.

"The courier Leif used *did* deliver the letter to your house," says Banth. "But the Guild Steward saw the courier leave the tack barn and cornered him upon his return. He's dead, I presume."

"The raid on my house...Lucius was looking for the letter.

Had he found it…"

"Dear Talihdym!" Liv says, now crying. "Had either of you been home he would've killed you both!"

Banth nods.

I feel like throwing up.

"Lucius was systematically killing anyone who had knowledge of whatever Dad knew, including me and Mom," I conclude. "That's why Lucius was so adamant I spend the night at home."

"I told you, there are devious powers at work here, Junar," says Haupstie. "Please believe that what we're telling you is the truth."

I look Banth straight in the eyes. "But you still haven't answered my question, Chief. How do you know anything about this letter?"

"Because I was the one who stole it when the courier left. Your mother wasn't home, so no hand-delivery. Just tucked in the mailbox on the porch in the middle of the night."

"You stole Dad's final letter to Mom?"

"To keep both of you alive," Haupstie interjects. "Please, Banth, this is enough."

"No," he says to Haupstie, without taking his eyes off me, "it isn't enough. But *this* is a step in the right direction." Banth reaches his mechanical hand inside his vest pocket and produces a folded vellum letter. He places it in my hand and makes me cover the wax seal with my other. Dad's wax seal.

"Junar," Liv pleads, "you can't be serious."

We're back in Eldorfold, darkness all but blotting out the starlight. Banth is gone, and Haupstie is most likely fast asleep in his hovel of gears, tubes and fire. Liv is being a good friend, but her logic is stifling my creativity. That, or the letter burning inside my flight jacket is.

"How would you even get a meeting with the Chancellor? Just because you stood next to him on a stage doesn't mean you're best friends. No one gets in to see him without a pretty good reason, and what are you going to say? 'Hey, I need to see the big man because our Guild Steward is a murderer and working with the Sky Pirates?' I don't think so, sport."

"I can fake a reason," I say.

"And will that lie hold up under the Interior Barrister who'd investigate your cause before he sees fit to involve the Chancellor at all?"

She has a point. "What if a grief-stricken son of a fallen Kili-Boranna Ace wants an audience with the Chancellor?"

"Again," Liv counters, "for what purpose? You want a pat on the back? I'm telling you, Junar, they're not going to let you in. This is the *Chancellor* we're talking about."

"But now I have this." I pat the letter under my jacket.

"And the Chancellor is going to believe an unconfirmed letter—whatever it says—from your dead father?" She stops. Looks down. "Sorry."

I shake it off. As badly as I want to rip the letter open, I feel Mom should be the first to read it. "Not if I let Mom read it, too. She can confirm breaking the seal—and his handwriting."

"Junar, you heard what Banth said. Right now, your mother's innocent. She knows nothing. Don't ruin that."

"She knows *something*, Liv. Dad had to confess his hardships to her. They were close. Really close. The night overheard them talking about his new job, he was talking about how hard the mission was." I correct myself, forgetting I'd been wrong. "About how hard it was to live with what he'd seen. But this—this letter probably points to all his conclusions, ones Mom can confirm from firsthand conversations. She can piece it together and testify against the Guild Steward!"

"OK," Liv thinks out loud, "but even if the letter is conclusive and your mother's testimony stands up, you still haven't figured out how to get a face-to-face with the Chancellor."

As always, Liv is right. For all I know, there's little I can do. Not without getting killed, anyway. I feel like someone who's just been given wings—but has them clipped before he even gets to try them. All at once, I'm incredibly empowered and yet equally helpless.

Before the move to Christiana, everything had been so much simpler. I'd give anything to go back. To Dad. And Mom, in our small house. To Lance. And working my way up through the ranks in Bellride. Dreaming of becoming an Ace pilot, and one day flying in...

...in...

"I got it," I whisper.

"Got what?" Liv turns, her eyes glimmering with hope in the starlight.

"But you're not going to like it."

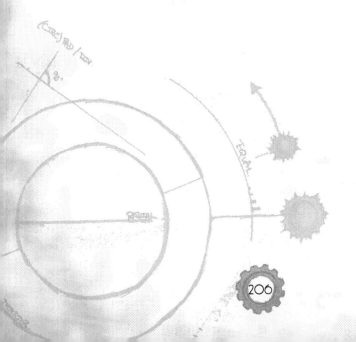

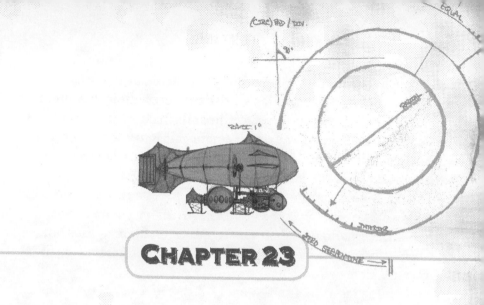

CHAPTER 23

LIV DOESN'T TAKE my second suggestion of flying in the Champions Race any better than she took it the first time. But even she can't deny its merits. Not only is the winner paraded around Christiana right beside the Chancellor, but he's granted an exclusive dinner with Aria-Prime's leader, along with up to ten friends of the winner's choice. And I can think of plenty of people willing to sit with me at *that* dinner table.

But her consent of my participation comes with its own condition: contrary to her previous statements about its faults, I'm to attempt a meeting with the Chancellor *before* flying in the race. If that fails, either by not securing an appointment or by getting me killed—a possibility I remind her of—then I can fly in the race. Which, she makes certain to point out, will most likely kill me. So, the way I look at it, I'm dead either way.

The other option is to stay quiet. To live out my days hiding the facts that surround my Dad's, and a good many other men's deaths. And that's the desire of the powers that be. To bully me into submission. To be compliant to whatever secrets are at work beneath the Guild's surface. Of course, that's not an option for me.

I decide to read Dad's letter before giving it to Mom. Not to disrespect her, but to protect her. To make sure it's safe. Dad must've had a hunch his letter might fall into the wrong hands, so I can't imagine he'd fill in with too much damning evidence. Banth assumed the same. And if the letter did get to Mom as Dad intended, he wasn't going to jeopardize her life further. Anything more would just give the traitors written proof to convict her with. But he also wouldn't want her to be unaware of the truth, so there's got to be something in the document that might benefit my investigation.

Lucius must also assume Dad shared *some* details with her, either by letter or in person; they were married, after all. But with no factual evidence, Lucius can't be sure. Yet if everything Banth and Haupstie have told me is true, I doubt it will be long before Lucius decides he doesn't need any evidence to do what he must… to silence Mom. To silence us both.

I sit comfortably in Serio's nest while he sleeps. It's late, almost time to head home and check in on Mom. But I can't risk her seeing this letter, not just yet. Plus, with Dad's funeral just a day away, I'm required to be back here at the hangar for chores, asked by Dalfirin himself to 'get back into the swing of things' if I intend to remain a member of the Kili-Boranna. Which I do—at least for now. I appreciate his unassuming nature in giving me the freedom to back out of the very system that claimed Dad's life. I don't doubt his innocence in all this. And I find great strength from Haupstie and Banth's conclusion of him. He's a good man—definitely the strictest in my life. But I'm committed now more than ever to bury myself in the Guild. To know it and all its dealings, inside and out.

I read my Dad's hasty handwriting, skipping the romantic parts. Not because I think they're sappy, but because they aren't intended for me.

What I first told you remains true, my love. The Northern Range is nothing more than a barren and stark landscape of mountains,

devoid of even the lowliest plant life, let alone great forests worthy of timbering. The mythical Lor-Lie are just that: legends to keep others away. The only threat I ever encountered were workers—men—with nelurime pistols. Zy-Adair, perhaps, but I was strongly discouraged from asking any questions until I'd been 'approved.' Something about an elite group of men, the Order, with a higher pay grade than mine.

I still don't know where the wood comes from, nor the protein cream. Another city, perhaps? It all has to come from somewhere. But of this you can be sure: I never cut down a single tree. The shipments were always there for us, ready and waiting. And then there was our method of payment. Nelurime. Satchels of it. Why these men couldn't buy it like everyone else still eludes me. But that was the trade. Nelurime, lots of it, in exchange for timber and satchels of cream.

My required silence, however, became the subject of my greatest fears only tonight. I sat with Lucius. I promised Junar I would. I know our son is disappointed in me. I would be, too, if it were me. But I couldn't possibly explain it all to him, or expect him to understand. His life always has been and always will be more valuable than my reputation. And I refuse to jeopardize his safety, burdening him with knowledge that will only damn him in the end.

I rub my knuckles over my eyes, pressing away the tears that blur my vision. Whatever sense of regret I'd felt in Haupstie's laboratory is replaced by an even deeper sense of betrayal. Toward the man I loved most. Of course, I try defending my actions. Against that reproving voice deep inside of me.

Mom barely knew, so how could you?

From the outside, anyone would have guessed what you did.

But that's the point. They hadn't guessed what I did. Everyone around me seemed to notice Dad's declining disposition. And they never tied it to weakness as I had. Only strength.

I take a deep breath, hoping for more answers in Dad's script.

Lucius is not the man I thought him to be. Though, to be truthful, he never seemed sincere. But he's hiding something, something valuable enough that he threatened my life. Threatened your lives, though he didn't come right out and say it. To his credit, however, he promised we'd be able to return to Bellride just as soon as I get home. I doubt that will do anything to mend Junar's perception of me, but at least life will gain some semblance of normalcy, and I won't have to hide in my labor. So I'm writing this letter. Just in case, I guess.

I will see you shortly, my love, as this shipment's required here in Christiana immediately. Then our family will be back in Bellride before week's end. We'll be home.

Lovingly,

Leif ap Jeronil

So Lucius is not to be trusted. And, I'm now certain, is responsible for murdering my father. As are any number of the Timber Pilots, if not all of them. Which means exposing their plot will be harder than I think. There'll be eyes everywhere.

This is less about some random Zy-Adair attack and more about a coverup. A coverup that is eroding the fabric of the Guild. A coverup that I vow I'll help unravel. 'By week's end' Dad thought we'd be back in Bellride. Instead, week's end will see his funeral.

The funeral.

The Chancellor will be there! Why didn't I think of this before?

Everything for the weekend is taken care of by the Guild. Mom just needs to show up, sit through the ceremony, and go back to the house. As for their part, I'm proud of the Kili-Boranna for going to such lengths for her. And for me, I suppose. But knowing many among their number inspired this funeral to begin with leaves me in a perpetual state of wanting to throw up. And unsure of who I can talk to. Liv's safe, obviously. And Erik. For all his arrogance, he's far too untrustworthy to keep a secret for more than a day. Finn seems safe, too. He'd be the kind of guy you want on your side if things get rough, and I know things will.

Despite his menacing disposition, Banth appears an agent of assistance, though the myriad of unanswered questions surrounding his behavior leave me feeling uneasy. The most obvious of which, mind you, is why he isn't arresting the culprits himself. Isn't he the Chief of the Brologi? Still, Haupstie trusts him, and I trust Haupstie. Mostly.

Dalfirin had also helped us race to the Timber Pilots' rescue. Of course, everyone remaining at the hangar had. Both Haupstie and Banth's denial of the Headmaster's involvement seems to place him in the clear, but I can't see him as a shoulder to rest my head on, nor a confidant for spilling my guts to. Perhaps one day, when I'm desperate. But for now, he's just too close to all of it.

Mom is better left out. At least until I figure out why the public is not getting the whole story about the Northern Range and Dad's death. Like why the Zy-Adair chose to flee from a fight for the first time in their history. *Plunder 'til death bid thee still.* Sure, I feel bad about keeping the letter from her. But better that she stay alive than become a liability to herself.

Just as with his induction, the whole city shows up to honor Dad. But only a relatively small percentage will witness the ceremony. The rest wait in lines that stretch all the way into the stadium where the procession will pass. They will pay homage to a single grey image, a life-like picture of his face made from a device only recently created, found in just two markets in all of Aria-Prime. As if anyone could afford it. A *photonical refraction chamber.* While no one says it, everyone knows it's another amazing creation by the Inventors. Most just pay to have their image captured once, like Mom and Dad, instead of buying the device. Sad that this one image is what benchmarks his funeral.

The only other person I have in the world to talk to is Lance. We're sitting on a bench outside Celebration Hall—ironically named—as it fills up with people. The public and the workers leave us alone in a floral section of courtyard that's cordoned off for *family only*.

Lance apologizes to me for the hundredth time already.

"Man, don't worry about it," I say. "Can't bring him back by saying it again."

"I know, Junar. I just...I just know how much you looked up to him."

Did he have to say that? "Yeah," I say, while gripping the bench. I look up to the sliver of sky between the balloon matrix and the city skyline. The setting suns have turned the horizon a brilliant orange with a pink fade toward the bottom. I'd rather be flying than sitting here.

"I'd give anything for five minutes in the air with the Sky Pirates that killed him, you know," Lance offers up heroically. He's silent for a while, then: "You thinking of going after them?"

"Maybe."

"'Cause you know I'd help you."

"I know you would, Lance." He's the best. "It's just that I'm not entirely sure they're to blame."

Lance looks at me. "What?"

I look around. Only a few bystanders, most working the funeral and allowing me some space. It's not the best spot for the narration of my conspiracy theory, but I'm not sure when I'll get another chance with Lance. I lower my voice and tell him all about how Banth found me and Liv at Eldorfold—leaving out the kiss, knowing he'll be distracted by it—and what Haupstie said about the saddle. Then there's Dad's cryptic letter.

It takes a minute for everything to sink in. Lance sits with his mouth open. "Man, I don't even know what to say. But if any of it's true..." He shakes his head.

"It's all true. I'm just trying to figure out what to do about it."

"I'd say!" Lance declares.

"*Shhh,*" I hush him.

"*Sorry.*" He looks around. "So what are you going to do?"

"Well, Banth's hands seem to be tied, or else he'd have

offered to do something already. Haupstie wouldn't explain it, but I think there's something up within the Brologi." I pause, finally verbalizing the conclusion I fear the most. "This coverup might be more wide-reaching than we think."

"So...that leaves you with going to..."

"The Chancellor," I say.

"The Chancellor? Holy bird crap! How do you expect to..." Lance looks away and trails off in thought. I know he'll get it. Then he glances up at me in shock. "Here? Tonight?"

I nod. "You got it."

"Oh, man! Listen, if you need a wingman, I'm good for it."

"Thanks, Lance," I say, waving him off and eyeing our surroundings for anyone out of place. "But no sense getting you caught up in this."

"I already am, man!"

I hush him again. "I mean, more than you *already are*. Lance, they killed my Dad. My *Dad*. That means they'd just as soon take out some meddling teens." I put my hand on his shoulder. "Nah, you stay clear for now. If I need you, I know where to find you."

"Unless you're dead."

"Woah, now that's harsh."

"Sorry," he recants. "But if it's true for me, it's even more true for you." And I know he's right. "I'm just saying, Junar. Watch your back. And if you won't, I'll have to."

I smile at him. "Thanks, Lance. Seriously."

"Hey, what are friends for?"

As the music begins inside Celebration Hall, Lance and I find our way to our seats. I'm in the front row beside Mom, of course—Lance, Liv, Erik and Finn are all somewhere back in the throng.

An assembly of dignitaries march in from the sides of the hall as the ceremony begins. They take their seats beside and behind us. First come the Guild Stewards of every city in Aria-Prime, with the Kili-Boranna being given the seats of highest prominence.

Lucius and Dalfirin both give me a solemn nod and sit directly behind me. I'm careful not to glare at Lucius too strongly lest my fury betray me.

Next come the House of Lords, overseers from every city. Next, the Brologi Chief and his Captains. Banth isn't even looking my way. And lastly, the Elders, retired servants of the citizens who, despite having moved out of office, still hold firm places of admiration and respect among the people. The Temple Priests sit beyond us in the front of the hall, a semicircle three deep. They had protested the funeral's location, insisting it take place at Temple Christiana to simultaneously fulfill the requirements for weekly Festival, but the sheer number of attendees had forced them to relent.

The Temple High Priest stands behind the lectern and raises his hands. It's officially beginning. And that's when my stomach twists up inside. The only person *not* here is the one I'm interested in seeing. The Chancellor.

"Please rise," says the High Priest.

The room swishes with the sounds of pant legs and jackets, benches breathing a collective sigh of relief. And right on cue, the Chancellor appears from the side entrance. Heads turn, but not a single voice utters a word. Out of respect for Dad.

My amazement intensifies when the Chancellor and his three assistants take their places on our bench, right next to me with only a forearm's length between us. He smells of musk and incense. Observing a day of grief. Talihdym has indeed smiled on me, His temple or not. This is incredible.

I look over at Opius far too enthusiastically. Of course he's used to gawking, and dips his head with the hint of a smile. Probably at my stupid grin. *Charming boy*, I can hear him think. *What a pity.*

But how do I talk to him?

This is my Dad's funeral after all, and I'm expected to give it my utmost attention. Worse still, Lucius is behind me.

Just great.

There's always *after* the ceremony, but I know the Chancellor won't stick around. Show up late, leave early. That's the way of anyone in power. Avoid the people at all costs. Not that I blame them. Masses of adoring fans can be more of a nuisance than anything else. Of course, I wouldn't mind fans. But I do mind the masses. All those watching eyes.

No, if I'm going to fulfill my promise to Liv and chance a meeting before the race, this is my shot.

The High Priest is praying. I bow my head. Thinking.

Upon his *Amen* he asks everyone to sit. The benches protest with creaks and moans; still no one talks, and I so desperately want to.

Suddenly the priests at the front begin a hymn. Not one of the happy ones I'm used to, but filled with mourning. Dissonant and minor. Their chordal chanting echoes through the hall, and I hear more than one person sniffling as they repeat the chorus. It's a somber song, almost depressing, but not without hope. I recognize it at last, a variation of the Prayer of the Kili-Boranna.

I trust in the Hand
Of the God of the Skies
To keep me safe
In the folds of his cloak
As I fall, as I fall
Catch me, Mighty Light
Into the great abyss
Your name I invoke

I look over at Opius, his eyes fixed on the priests. Then back at Mom. Crying. I can feel Lucius' eyes burning into the back of my skull, willing me to bide my silence.

Still, I must try.

I ever-so-subtly inch my way closer to the Chancellor. He notices, of course, and glances at me. He smiles again. I'm sure I'm like so many other stalkers. But he'll sing a different tune when I open my mouth.

And say what?

Suddenly I panic. He looks at me again. This time, his expression is flat. Annoyed. Does he feel the change in my mood?

Hi, Chancellor. I'm Junar. A few minor points of interest here: Lucius ap Victovin sabotaged my Dad's saddle and pinned it on a convenient ambush by the Zy-Adair. And, oh yeah, the wood that our Guild supplies to the city is not really from the Northern Range. Nothing actually grows there. Just thought you should know.

I'm doomed.

I look down at my feet. What am I thinking? This is great, Junar. Just great.

The song ends and the High Priest starts speaking again. Quoting scriptures by memory. Passages having to do with security and safety found in death. How about in life? *Any wisdom for me here, Talihdym?*

"I'd like to invite Guild Steward Lucius ap Victovin to share some words with us," the High Priest says. I glance back at Lucius. The corner of his mouth pricks into a smile as he stands. What does that mean? I watch as he makes his way up front.

And then it hits me: *This is my chance.* I don't care at all about disrespecting whatever Lucius has to say. Let people think what they want.

The moment Lucius opens his mouth to say, "Ladies and Gentlemen," I lean toward the Chancellor.

"Chancellor Opius, thank you for coming."

Surprisingly, he smiles and looks at me as any grandfather might. "You're very welcome, my boy." He pats my knee. "I'm so very sorry about your father." His is the most genuine regret I hear yet. Catches me off guard.

"Thank—thank you," I stutter. "Sir, if you don't mind, I have some grave concerns about my father's death."

His brow furrows. "Do you, now? Well, that is very responsible of you." He leans in closer, whispering. "I promise that we'll do everything we can to make sure your mother is taken care of, I promise. You, too."

What? No, no, that's not what I mean. "Sir, not those concerns. I'm sorry—"

"Son, might this wait until *after* the ceremony?" He inclines his head toward the front, then sits back.

Curse the impostor speaking up there! This is life and

death!

"Leif was the best pilot I ever had under my command," Lucius declares. "And I'm privileged to..."

"Chancellor Opius," I say again.

Lucius pauses and looks at me. Perhaps I'm a bit too loud. I feel Mom's eyes—plus about a thousand sets—staring at my head. I freeze. Then motion to Lucius to continue. I can see my command ruffles him.

"As I was saying," Lucius resumes, "I'm privileged to have known him, not only as a pilot but as a friend."

Lies.

"Chancellor Opius," I say, this time barely audible. "I believe my Dad was murdered."

The Chancellor doesn't reply at first. But I can see his face wrinkle out of the corner of my eye. He heard me.

And I know I have him.

"Murdered?" he says ever-so-quietly, turning his head. I nod. "Then you must meet with the Guild Steward directly following the funeral. He will—"

"I have reason to believe it's the Guild Steward who's to blame." Of course, everything in me wants to stand up and point. Shout down Dad's betrayer. Not whisper like this.

Lucius looks at me while he's speaking. Does he know I'm talking about him?

"Involved?" Opius looks down. "Come now, that's an outrageous—"

"Yes, outrageous, but true," I reply. The way Dad mentions Lucius in the letter, the tack weld on the saddle, the other Timber Pilots aiding in the coverup, Lucius' insistence that I sleep at home the night of the raid and Dad's murder. It's all there. But how to say it in a moment like this? I need more time.

Wait just a minute. Opius used the word *involved*. Does he believe there's a bigger issue *to be involved with*? Does he already suspect something? Perhaps it's just me being over-analytical, but I might not get this chance again. So I go for it. "Sir, do you suspect there are *more* who might be *involved*?"

He gives no immediate reply. But I'm sure he heard my

question. I'll repeat myself if I must. But he's got to answer. I'll *make* him answer. Then he looks at me, speaking in the quietest of tones. "Junar, we too believe your father was set up."

All at once Lucius' voice fades away as my heart beats wildly within my chest. I inhale a series of tight breaths, trying my best to maintain control of my emotions. But my sense of dread is overwhelmed by another feeling, far stronger. That of justification. Of needing someone to help me not feel so alone. And all at once, it's the Chancellor himself who stands with me. The Chancellor!

"Oh, praise Talihdym!" I exclaim. My voice reverberates through the hall like a clarion call to worship. Lucius stops talking. I can hear everyone behind me mumble to one another. Even the Chancellor appears quite surprised at my outburst.

Nice job, Junar. Real smooth. Think fast. Temple! This is Festival, albeit in a public hall. I raise my hands and stand up. "I've had a vision! My father, rest his soul, is seated with Talihdym in the Sky Beyond!"

At this, the entire room begins to stir. I can hear some of them now. *Poor boy, under so much stress. He must really be heartbroken. I wonder how he's coping with all this. I don't blame him.* Only the priests, perhaps concerned I might be mocking Talihdym, seem to disbelieve me. Please don't hold this against me, Talihdym.

I feel Mom touch my sleeve. "Junar, are you alright?"

"Fine, Mom," I say, looking down at her.

"A vision?"

"Uh, yeah, yeah. Saw him just now. Amazing, Mom. Really just amazing."

"That's wonderful, baby. I don't know what to say. But can you please sit down?"

"Sure thing, Mom." I sit, hoping I played it off effectively. The room is still humming with people thinking I'm either delusional or severely depressed. Or both. I'll accept *insanity* as easily as I'll accept *committed* in trying to get myself out of this one.

For the second time, I motion for Lucius to continue. The anger in his eyes is unmistakable. I'm going to pay for it, I know. But not if I make him pay for his actions first.

"As I was saying..." continues Lucius.

The Chancellor and I both look on at the Guild Steward as he revives his homily on the attributes of my Dad. I can hardly stomach it. But now the Chancellor knows, and my job is done. But sitting here, right next to him, without being able to hold a candid conversation, is eating me alive. Like the raging furnace in Haupstie's lab, but with the door clamped shut to build up the heat. I'm so close to vindication!

"Come see me," the Chancellor whispers. "After the Champions Race. Win or lose, you have my ear."

Win or lose? I glance up at him.

"I saw your name on the roster, boy. You have a brave constitution. That or you're incredibly inept in the faculties of logic."

"Thank you, sir." I think.

"You are still racing, aren't you?"

I'd fulfilled my end of the agreement with Liv, had't I? And while it wasn't the result we'd hoped for, now the Chancellor is prompting me to fly, and granting me an audience with him no matter what place I finish in. An audience that will allow me to speak freely with him. I have to fly, and the funny thing is, I don't even want to anymore. If there was any other way to meet with the Chancellor, I'd back out. Liv will understand. She'd do exactly the same.

"Why, yes," I say to the Chancellor, staring straight ahead at Lucius. "Yes, I am flying."

"You'll make your father proud."

"Thank you again, sir."

Lucius keeps staring at the two of us. Does he know he's at the center of our conversation? Does he even suspect he's about to lose everything? The Guild Steward's voice rises. "Brilliant. Brave. Honest. How can we possibly bear to live without such an esteemed man? His memory will surely follow us for a lifetime."

I hate how he speaks of Dad like he was a close friend. Like he knew him. Like he wasn't guilty of killing him.

The Chancellor leans in close. "Junar, I may have something that will help you. Help us. I'm not sure what it means. But I think you should have it. The thing is not with me, of course, but it is quickly obtained. However, no one knows of it." If the Chancellor could lean in any closer and breathe any more quietly, he did so. "I received a letter the night before your father's murder." He pauses. "*Letter* is too broad a word. A *token* is better suited to it."

"A token?" I make to turn to him, but his face is too close.

"Tonight. Come to the Great Hall, Guild Entry."

I can't even believe this is happening! By Talihdym, it's happening! A private meeting with the Chancellor. And *before* the race? This is incredible. I could kiss this man! And I don't even have to fly. Oh, Liv will be so happy.

The Chancellor touches my knee again. "Tell no one."

Just then Lucius pauses, finishing something about the tragedy that befell Dad. I look at him. And he looks at the Chancellor's hand on my knee. Or is he staring off into the distance? Lucius' face seems pale, hands gripping the pulpit. Then with a strained voice, he says the last thing I ever expect him to say.

"But, worst of all, dear friends, due to evidence gathered by the Brologi, it is clear to the Guild that Leif's death was not merely at the hands of the Zy-Adair, but a conspiracy to commit murder—from right here among our own countrymen."

With the reverence of the ceremony discarded like unsold produce from a merchant cart, the mood changes from that of a funeral to an investigative court proceeding. A collective gasp rises behind me. A beat later and people are talking openly, a few standing to shout down the injustice of such a notion. Within seconds, women are crying. Mom, most notably. She grabs my arm.

"Mom, Mom, relax." I rub the top of her hand. "Everything's going to be alright." But she's hysterical. I look to Lucius, hands outstretched, trying in vain to calm the crowd. But he's not really trying. He knows exactly what he's doing.

The Chancellor leans over, his voice having lost its endearing commiseration, instead tending toward the accusatory. "Are we so sure about the Guild Steward's involvement now, my dear boy?" Just like that, my case is dissolving. The Chancellor stands up, and I with him.

"Sir, sir, I promise you. I can prove it!"

He brushes my hands off his robe. "I would think twice before you present me with such unfounded accusations, young man. It seems you make a victim of another who fights for your cause." Then his entourage swarms around him. The priests are trying in vain to calm the funeral attendees, but the hall has reached a level of near-pandemonium. There is no silencing this mob now. But I couldn't care less what this ceremony merits for the dead. A real funeral can only be held once Dad's killers are brought to justice. Until then, this is a sham like all the rest of the Guild's operations.

"Sir, give me time to explain it all to you!" I ball my fists. "He's covering himself! It's a ploy!"

"We need to leave, your Eminence," says one of the Chancellor's men.

Then Opius looks at me with something akin to pity. His face softens. "Come see me, boy," he relents. "The offer still stands." Closer now, eyes looking to Lucius. "If this is as you say, then we'll make it right. I promise."

"Thank you, Chancellor," I say. It's not much, but it's something. I turn and watch him walk away. As soon as the Chancellor leaves the room, the High Priest is forced to dismiss the ceremony on account of disorderly conduct. Just like that, Dad's funeral is over. And I've arranged a private meeting with the most powerful man in Aria-Prime.

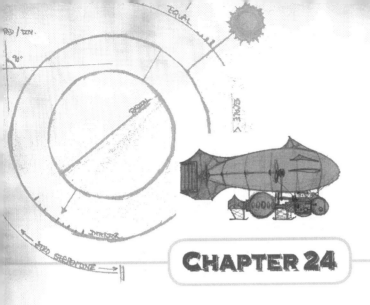

CHAPTER 24

MY FIRST DUTY, of course, revolves around getting Mom home from Celebration Hall amidst heaving emotions and a constant barrage of well-meaning, but incessantly-questioning, mourners. Once free of the funeral attendees, our progress is further bogged down by her frequent, tear-filled breakdowns, followed shortly thereafter by sudden outbursts of rage. Dad's loss had been hard enough as it is, but setting it within the context of conspiracy to commit murder has her at wit's end. And for once in my life, I don't blame her for how she's acting. For how she's feeling.

Liv is good about coming along, which I appreciate. I know she'll have plenty of questions of her own, as she obviously saw me sitting beside the Chancellor. Trying to keep the night's secret meeting from her will test every ounce of my fortitude. But she'll pardon me keeping it from her when I withdraw from the race. Which I'll do, as soon as I conclude tonight's meeting. There's no need for me to race now. Liv'd been right: there *was* another way of gaining access to the Chancellor without having to fly. Heaven bless her. I can't actually believe I'm so relieved. More than likely, the whole race will be called off anyway—or at least postponed—once I reveal Lucius' guilt. I just need to figure out how.

This cryptic *token* from the Chancellor will no doubt help, whatever it is. And as much as my heart knows I have to console Mom this evening, my head is elsewhere.

Liv escorts us up to the front door. "Need me to come in?" she asks. Mom is already stumbling inside, weeping in the background.

"Nah, I think I got it," I reply against my deeper wishes. Liv's care is unusually attractive right now, and I'm half-inclined to have her stay, more for my own concerns than Mom's. But Liv will dig tonight's meeting out of me within the hour if I do so, and I'm not about to let the Chancellor's invitation be sabotaged, not even by Liv. Talihdym knows I won't be able to keep her at bay. "Thanks though, Liv."

"Well, if you need anything, you know where to find me."

"Roger."

"I'll check back in the morning," she adds.

"Thanks, Liv."

"And if you—"

"Liv, I got it." I raise my hand. "We'll be fine."

She relents and smiles. Then, unexpectedly, she comes up the first step and kisses me on the cheek. I feel my face flush, instantly bringing up all the warmth from our kiss at Eldorfold. "See you tomorrow, flyboy," she adds, stepping back down.

I wave weakly and watch her hair wafting along in the evening breeze as she walks away over the bridge. The nelurime lamps spark to life, and casts her hair in a yellowish glow, like stardust trailing from the head of an angel. "Yeah, see ya."

A wail from inside yanks me back to reality. It's Mom, in another of her fits.

The suns have dropped below the edge of the sky rim when I finally get Mom settled in the guest room. She refuses to sleep in her bedroom, but I know that will change eventually. I prepare a cup of her favorite tea from The Moors and make sure the room's water-pressure regulator is set to keep her warm—things, I recall with a bit of nostalgia, that she'd done for me every night as a boy. I kiss her on the forehead and offer up a prayer of comfort before heading back downstairs. I can only hope Talihdym heard me like he heard my request for a meeting with the Chancellor. Perhaps our distant God is closer than we think.

I'm just about to grab my flight jacket and leave for the Great Hall when there's a knock at the door.

"Hey, how's Mom?" Lance whispers.

"She's upstairs, sleeping." I hesitate. "Or at least trying to."

"You need any company?"

Can I tell him? "Actually, I was just about to head out and get some air."

"Perfect."

There's no way of getting rid of Lance on this one. Plus, he knows everything else already. And unlike Liv, I won't need to compete with him over it. "Let me just grab my jacket."

We're out the door and strolling around the upper deck as the last strains of muted light seep from the sky. The magnanimous black shadow of the balloon matrix looms overhead, more comforting than not, an ever-present reminder of our lofty position over the world. And as Lance and I settle into conversation, night consumes the city. The nelurime lamps that had ignited during Liv's departure just an hour ago are now the only source of illumination in Christiana's deserted market square.

"So, you sat next to the Chancellor, I see," Lance says.

"Yeah, didn't expect I'd get an audience that easy."

"No kidding." Lance shoves his hands in his pockets. "Like it was handed to you. He say anything after your little outburst?"

I laugh. "Not too much. I basically said I suspected Dad's been set up."

"And then Lucius' crazy statement to end all statements," Lance adds.

"Right."

"That guy is *totally* guilty. Just trying to play the good guy now."

"And that's just what I told the Chancellor."

"He buy it?"

"I think so."

"You think so?" Lance looks at me.

"Well, it got me another meeting, didn't it?" I shrug.

"Another meeting?" Lance says, a little too loudly. He looks around in the yellow light. Then, more softly, *"Another meeting?"*

"Tonight."

"Tonight?!" Lance is beside himself. "What, like, like right now?" His eyes grow bigger. "Oh…wait a second. You *getting out for some air* and all. OK, OK. I see what you did there."

We walk to the far side of the square and move out of the center of town, heading directly for the capital buildings. "He wants to meet alone," I say, "in the Guild Entry of the Great Hall."

"Woah, alone?" Lance looks at me, his face momentarily cast in the pale yellow of a passing street lamp. "You cool with that?"

"I don't have a choice," I reply. "I mean, it's the Chancellor."

"Yeah, I guess so," Lance says a bit glumly. He's all but saying he wants to come along. I can't blame him.

"Listen, stay with me up until the gate, then hang back. It should only take me a few minutes. He said he had something small for me, and I need to share the details I have with him. I'll be in and out, and you'll be the first to know. OK?"

His face lights up like a nelurime stove. "You mean it? Man, thanks, Junar. This is awesome."

We make our way out of the square, down Kenwick Street, a left at Grandeur, right onto Middegen. There, in the soft glow of the street lights, rises the Great Hall. One of Christiana's notably larger complexes, the building is comprised of a massive central hall with smaller outbuildings attached by walkways, bridges and tunnels. The largest and innermost structure houses the two Chambers of the Council of Lords: one for the sixty men in charge of developing Aria-Prime's ever-growing infrastructure, welfare and legislation, known as The House of Lords; the other for the forty-eight Guild Stewards who govern industry and economy, known as The House of Stewards. Together they unite under the leadership of the Chancellor and are marshaled by the five Brologi Captains and their Senior Chief. While each island city has its own smaller version of this structure, it's here in Christiana that all representation gathers. And discusses. And quarrels. And discusses some more. "Put me on the back of a felrell any day," Dad would say whenever politics came up, "and leave the nit-picking to the professionals."

Lance and I walk along the high wall that runs around the complex, trying to stay out of the light as best we can.

"There it is," I say, pointing to the side Guild Entry gate about three lamps ahead.

"I'll wait over there." Lance gestures to a gap between two buildings along the far side. "If anything happens…"

"Nothing's going to happen, Lance. I'm getting a token, sharing my information with the Chancellor, and then we're getting out of here."

"Right." He nods. "Still…"

"I appreciate it, thanks." And with that, we're both off at a brisk walk to our respective destinations. At first I think my pace is making my heart beat fast, but I've only taken a dozen or so steps. *Meeting like this. In the dark. With the Chancellor. To uncover a conspiracy within the Guild.* Suddenly it all seems so cryptic, and I wonder if in fact I'm making the right choice. Why again did Lance seem so uneasy about this? It only bothers me because he's rarely wrong about hunches.

Except this time. This time I'm right, and the Chancellor is the best person to help. The *only* person to help.

I approach the third lamp. The opening to the gate lies ahead and to the left like a gaping black mouth inviting me inside to satisfy its insatiable hunger. I slow my pace and edge along the wall, taking the last few steps beyond the lamplight toward the cutout in the stone. I cast a quick look back to Lance in the alleyway. My night vision is bleached from the nelurime flare above, but I know he's there, waiting for my call if something goes wrong. And while I act like I don't need the help, knowing he's within earshot is reassuring.

I take a deep breath, then dodge around the corner to the

gate. Five steps into the darkness and I encounter the iron bars. Locked at this hour, but I suspect it will be open. For me. For my meeting with the Chancellor. I try the large thumb latch below the keyhole.

Doesn't budge. Locked.

My heart sinks. Am I too early? Or worse, *too late*. Or maybe the Chancellor forgot altogether? After all, he's a busy man, in high demand. And I'm...

...I'm a young man whose Dad's been *murdered*.

If the Chancellor doesn't show, I'll demand—

"Junar ap Leif," comes a soft voice.

Just hearing my family name sends a twinge of pain through my chest. I look between the bars, searching for a face. There, to the right of the courtyard—one of the few grassy swards in the city—a dark form emerges from the shadows. Only when he walks into the pools of light cast from the windows of the Chamber Building do I see his steady gait and bit of tufted white hair escaping from the folds of his hood.

He's come, just as he said. *Thank Talihdym.*

"Chancellor," I greet him, trying my best to keep my voice under control. Who could ever say they'd met in private with the Chancellor like this? Trouble is, I can't make it public. At least not yet. But soon, very soon, people will know Lucius and members of the Kili-Boranna were embroiled in a plot to murder Dad. *Everyone* will know.

The Chancellor approaches the gate. But doesn't unlock it for me. Instead, he reaches inside the fold of his cloak and produces something. I can't see it in the shadows. "Time is short," he says. "What is the proof you spoke of before I left?"

Proof? He wants to know everything *now*? "Uh, I hadn't anticipated...I mean, you want all the details now?" I sound so childish! He's used to hearing speeches given by great orators of high bearing. And here I am with a throat closing up from nerves.

"Well then, how many can be given in short order?"

"I...I suppose none of it, your Eminence. It's very... complex, and I..."

"Complexity is the mother of conspiracy, young man. I

would expect nothing less."

So he understands. Somehow, *just that* makes me feel at ease. I can take my time to explain the—

"Alas, I have not the hour I'd hoped for tonight. And yet, at least I have something that may do you more good than it did me." He reaches out, and I extend my hand. A small folded piece of paper alights on my palm. Then he closes my fingers over it and holds my fist tightly. "See where this takes you, young Junar. It arrived in my care on the night of your father's murder. Placed in my very bedchamber, on my writing desk. I have shared it with no one, for I do not know its meaning, and fear it was delivered by someone within my own council as a sign. A token, possibly, of your father's passing. It is too coincidental to ignore.

"I would warn you, young Junar: I believe the path before us stands as a dark one, one fraught with unmitigated danger, should there indeed be evil lurking behind your father's tragic death. Hands skilled at means such as these are not kind, and are swift, in fact, to bring wrath. Keep your wits about you, and be cautious in whom you trust." He pauses. I can see his eyes dart, looking past me. "I fear an uprising even from within my own fold."

"I know my enemies, your Eminence," I reply, trying to sound brave.

"Then it is quite certain that they also know you." The Chancellor releases my hand, then backs away from the gate. "We will meet again, Junar," he whispers. "All will be set straight with the Champions Race." He dips his head, then crosses the courtyard and disappears into the shadows.

Just like that, it's over.

I turn from the gate, staring into my shadowed hand. The warm glow of burning nelurime seeps into my palm as I walk out of the entryway. And with it, the tiny piece of paper comes to life. Red. Folded over in an artistic shape.

Of a fox.

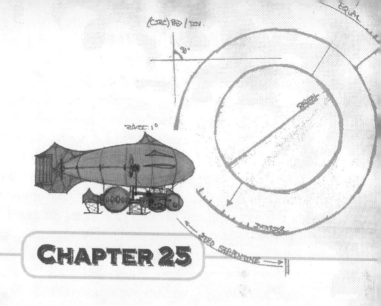

CHAPTER 25

IT'S THE FIRST time I've intentionally kept something from Lance. And I feel ashamed. "A paper fox?" he asks. "What in all the cloudy myriads does it mean?"

"I...I don't know." But of course, I *do* know. At least, I know who made it. It would be but one more in my collection.

"Woah, you OK there, 'Nar?" I feel Lance grab my elbow. Dizzy. "You don't look so hot."

"I'm fine," I say, touching my forehead to find beads of sweat along it. I need time to think this through. To put it all together. Why would the Chancellor mysteriously receive a paper fox from the Inventors on the night Dad was killed? *A warning?* Perhaps. "Maybe I'm just a little tired from the day," I tell Lance, placing the animal in my jacket pocket.

"Yeah, yeah. It's been a busy one. Let's just get back to the house."

The fox is a warning, right? As it had been for me that fateful day back in the market. Signaling a pirate attack.

We walk in silence, both trying to wrap our minds around

the strange meeting and the stranger token. For Lance's part, he's his usual amiable self. Doesn't press me, doesn't pry. He really is the perfect friend, and the only connection I have. Without him, I'd be utterly alone in all this. And yet, here it is: loneliness. Creeping into the recesses of my heart. For as much as I don't like crowds, I admit now I also don't want to be alone. Not completely, anyway. But that seems to be the threat in front of me. Just when Eldorfold has accepted me and Liv wants me. Dad is gone, Mom is hysterical, Liv is too close to the Guild, and Erik and Finn are just interested in seeing me die racing. And even though I want to run and tell Haupstie everything, suddenly an Inventor seems like the very last person I want to talk to. No doubt Banth's in league with them too.

I thought the millions of eyes hidden inside the clouds had stopped examining me. Had finally left me alone to be free of their incessant, silent torture. That they'd left me to be accepted. To belong.

But, no.

They're following me still, searching me. Even now, I can feel them. Pulling me down. Until I die. The irony of it all. That when I feel most alone, the eyes are with me. Always haunting me.

"You sure you don't want me to come in, 'Nar?"

We're on the front porch. Mom's sound asleep inside. "I think I just really need some rest, Lance."

"OK. Well, if you need anything…you know where to find me in the tack barn."

I thank him and then watch as his form melds with the darkness, slipping in and out of the street lights until he disappears. Which leaves me by myself. I hate these shivers. I pull the fur collar of my flight jacket up around my neck, take one last breath of the fresh air, then slip inside.

With just the two of us now, the house feels empty. And cold. As though I can physically feel Dad's absence. The living room doesn't feel right. The lighting, the staircase, the smell. Something's off. Half the spirit of the home has vanished. And whatever emotions I've pushed aside from the events surrounding the last few days, they're all back. All flooding back.

My knees hit the wooden floor, shoulders caving in on me like a sliding rock avalanche. Then the tears begin. Hot, fresh streams of fire run down my face. Sobbing. From deep in my gut. I see his face hovering in my mind's eye, steady and strong. Countless memories, each one slipping by slow enough for me to connect with, but too fast to savor. I want to touch his face, to hear his laugh, but both are fleeting attempts met by a sickening absence of reality. I cry all the more, curling up on the floor, knees tucked up to my chest.

Maybe I'm going crazy, not ready to come to grips with my own loss. Maybe all these suppositions in my mind are trying to assign blame to what's genuinely just...*an accident.*

But the fox in my pocket. It's real. As is the Chancellor I'd met just forty-five minutes before.

And the saddle. That's real.

And the tack weld Haupstie removed. That's real too.

Isn't it?

Isn't it all?

Suddenly ideas start forming in my head, ones I'd never dare entertain under normal circumstances. But that's just it: these are *incredible* circumstances! And I have the right to, don't I? After all, it's *my father* who's been unlawfully taken from me.

Banth never did explain how he'd come upon Dad's saddle. And that concerns me deeply. And Haupstie had rather swiftly deduced the locking mechanism had been sabotaged. He told me himself. *Sometimes things break for a reason.* It's no secret that the Inventors loathe the establishment of Aria-Prime. *Not everything's about money*, Haupstie'd said to me. *I have other ways of exacting payment from the Guild. Don't you worry.* As Dad always said, *bad blood.* Even Haupstie implied that Banth was risking his life to do as much as he'd done in bringing the saddle to light. In secret. Banth must have his own reasons to detest the very organization he works for.

Then. I see it.

Suddenly the skyline becomes clear in my head. Like flying through a storm cloud, only to emerge on the other side with the twin suns warming your back and illuminating the way before you.

I see.

While I don't truly believe Haupstie or Banth would kill Dad, I do believe men can become so desperate for a cause that they use devious means to accomplish their goals, even a *just* goal.

Like pin an accident on an establishment they detest. An establishment they want to bring down.

I'd always wondered why the Inventors weren't our leaders. Is there anything they can't do to better humanity? But not like this. Not at my expense. I've been a fool! Even with Haupstie. His false confidence, his invitation to join them, and even pretending Christiana was just as much about me as it was about Dad. Oh sure, he may not have known *then* what was going to happen, but he certainly knew *enough*.

The paper fox is indeed from the Inventors, intended as a warning, just as the Chancellor guessed. Only the warning was a taunt. To the Chancellor himself.

We're taking you down.

And then the strangest, most unsettling thought of all: if Lucius is involved, perhaps he too has his own plot against leadership. Maybe that's exactly what the Chancellor meant when he said he feared an uprising even from within his own fold. Which means members of the Guild, the Inventors and the Brologi, none of whom have full knowledge of any of the other factions' activities, are conspiring against the Chancellor.

Suddenly the most powerful, most hunted, most distant man in the world is my only friend.

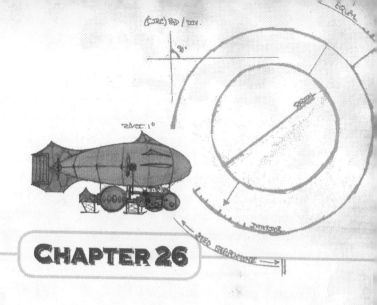

CHAPTER 26

SO FAR, THE morning has passed without incident. Almost.

"Hey, sport," comes Liv's familiar voice. "How'd last night go?"

I heft Serio's saddle off the blocks and try to avoid eye contact with Liv. "Last night?" Did Lance tell her?

"Yeah, you know, *your Mom…the whole funeral catastrophe…*"

"Right, sure," I breathe. "She slept good. Me too. I slept good. We both slept. Real good." I can feel her cock her head and stare at me from behind.

"You feeling alright, Junar?"

"Yeah. Feeling good. Why?" Everything in me wants to tell her about last night's meeting. I want nothing more than to purge myself of the secrets harbored in my head and to ramble on about the growing conspiracy. But for all I know, her own father is in alliance with Lucius, and the last thing I want to do is put her at odds with her family—or in harm's way. These are all dangerous, heartless men.

I'm rubbing an oiled cloth over the leather and she still

hasn't answered me. I look up and ask again. "What's up?"

Her arms are folded. "You're *what's up*. You just seem...I don't know. *Weird.*"

I try laughing. "You know me. Always a little *weird.*"

"Yeah...that's not it."

I stop polishing and turn to look her in the eye. *Be honest.* "Listen, Liv. This whole thing with losing Dad is hard enough as it is. Now for Lucius and the Guild to suspect foul play? I don't know. It's just a lot to handle." There. I said it as truthfully as I can. Liv looks on, then slowly relaxes her shoulders.

"I can't even begin to imagine, Junar," she relents. "I'm sorry. It just doesn't seem like—"

"Like I'm myself, I know. I guess, in a big way, I'm not."

"That's not what I was going to say."

"It wasn't?" I ask.

"It doesn't seem like you're being straight with me, sport. Like...like you're hiding something."

I can feel my face flush red. Head down. Polishing the leather again. She must be looking into my soul.

She takes a few steps forward, now resting her hands on the blocks between us. Her voice is soft in the musty stall air. "You know you can trust me, right, kid?"

Is my hand trembling? "Sure. Yep."

"With anything?"

"With anything. Roger."

"And you're going to tell me...?" I must have a fairly dumb look on my face, because my long silence provokes the kind of fiery retaliation Liv is known for dishing out to anyone who crosses her. "And here I thought we were more than friends! Just who do you think you are, Junar ap Leif?"

I know I wince at the mention of his name, because she plays off that, too.

"Hurts, does it? Hearing his name like that? Perhaps you know a thing or two about what happened, and you don't even want your closest friends to know? The people who care most about you? Who can help you? What's gotten into you, Junar?"

"*But that's just it, Liv!*" I'm practically shouting in a whisper a few inches from her face. "*I'm not sure who can help me anymore!*"

She recoils. "You're looking at one person who can. Or have you forgotten?"

"But you don't understand."

"Then explain it to me!" She glances out of the stall, then lowers her voice to match my forceful whisper. "Give me something! I know you know something, Junar. And, so help me, I'm going to dig it out of you if it kills me!"

"It just might."

She stops. One of those really awkward pauses begins. A battle of wills.

"Listen, Liv. Yes, I do have some..." What to even call them? "...*hunches*. But nothing solid."

"Then maybe I can help—"

I wave her off. "Liv, it's not that simple. Believe me, everything inside me wants to tell you. Shoot, I'm ready to explode right now!"

"*Then tell me!*"

"I care for you too much to tell you." And all at once I feel what my father must have felt when he hid what he knew in order to protect me. Our conversation in my bedroom the night he came home...in the locker room the last night we talked...and all the dozens of other times he tried to explain something to me but I cut him off.

She tightens her fists and bears down on me with those eyes. "Has anyone ever told you how stubborn you are?"

"Has anyone ever told you how intense *you* are?" I think it's funny enough to smile; apparently she doesn't.

"Not as intense as the Review Board is going to be with you."

"Review Board?"

"Oh, you didn't hear? Lucius' little comment at the funeral got us all a Full Review, coming from the Council of Lords, answering directly to the Chancellor."

"The Chancellor, eh?" I look away.

"If you think I'm hard, wait until they...hey. Junar. Junar?"

"Interesting."

She snaps her fingers twice in my face. "Kid! Kid! What's got into you?"

I look back at her. "Are they here now?"

"They who?" If she appeared confused by my behavior before, it's nothing compared to her expression now.

"The Review Board. Ordered by the Chancellor," I reply.

"Uh, yeah. Going one-on-one with every flyer from newbie to Ace. Down in Lucius' office."

"Lucius' office?" I ask.

"Yeah." She blows a lock of hair out of her face. "He insisted that he preside over every interview."

"And the Chancellor allowed that?"

"I know. Tell me about it. Wait a sec—" she's suddenly very friendly, the statements dripping off her lips like honey— "you suspect Lucius has more people involved with this than just himself, don't you. Just like what Haupstie and Banth were saying. You…you agree with them!"

"No, no I don't."

"And I bet the Chancellor doesn't even know Lucius is in those meetings?"

"I don't know."

She nearly leaps over the blocks at me. "How many do you think are involved?"

I try shushing her with my hands, but she's riled up.

"Six? Maybe a dozen? Why, that creep! He's probably got all the Timber Pilots on his payroll!"

This is not good. She can't know…that I suspect the Inventors or the Brologi just as much as I do the Guild. Did I mess up here? How in all the cloudy veils did I get stuck with a girl who can read minds?

"Who else, Junar?" she asks.

"That's for the Review Board to decide, Liv."

"And you think they'll figure it out?" Her fury is back on me. "Then tell me you don't suspect anyone else. *Tell me!*"

I gulp. "I don't know."

"Tell me!"

"*I just did!*" I say through my teeth. "I don't know, Liv!

Please, keep your voice down."

"Why?" she yells out into the tack barn. *"Because someone might be listening?"*

I push my hand over her mouth, but she bats it away. Hard.

"Oh, this is just perfect." She stomps her foot. "So you think someone within the Guild offed your Dad under Lucius' order, but you won't tell me?" She's almost hysterical now. It's like trying to extinguish a firestorm with a tea cup: the only thing I'd accomplish is successfully incinerating myself with the pointless attempt.

"Liv, you have no idea what you're talking about," I whisper. She could at least have the decency to keep her voice down like I'm doing now.

"Oh, I think I'd understand a little more if a *certain someone* would be more forthcoming with me."

"Liv, that's not fair."

I'm sure I won't survive whatever retort she has coming next, so I'm more than elated when a man appears at the stall's entrance, dressed in a High Council robe.

"Junar ap Leif?"

"Yes, that's me," I offer, probably a little too eagerly.

"The Board wishes an audience with you. This way, please," he says, stepping aside.

I move around the blocks as Liv whispers, "You're not getting out of this in one piece, Junar. This is far from over."

And somehow I feel like her words are far more telling than either of us know.

When the elevator doors open into Lucius' glass office, I see four men sitting in high-backed chairs, a fifth chair waiting for the elder escorting me. And off to one side behind his desk—which he'd no doubt begrudgingly moved to accommodate the additional furniture—sits Lucius. He eyes me without emotion, watching as I stride forward into the illusion of thin air beneath me. Is his hair permanently oiled back like that, even in bed?

"Junar ap Leif," says the elderly man in the center of the

assembly. He looks down through his spectacles to read from a parchment scroll. "I am Barrister of the Interior, addressed as *your lordship*. You have been summoned upon commission of the Council of Lords and The Chancellor of Aria-Prime to attest to your knowledge, in part or whole, as to the death of one—" he looks up from the document to amend his recitation personally— "*your father*, and aid said agencies in an investigation stemming from the claim of Guild Steward Lucius ap Victovin that the victim was murdered." The Barrister eyes me while the lord on the far right scribbles frantically in a large book. "Do you understand the situation as I have read it to you?"

"I do, your lordship."

"Very good. Then let us begin." He motions to an empty chair in front of them. "Please, please." I thank him and take my seat. Lucius is already brooding in the corner.

"And may I just say—" the Barrister removes his spectacles— "that we are deeply grieved for your loss. We understand that much of the subject matter of this proceeding may be unsettling for you. Our intent here is only to reveal the truth."

"Thank you, your lordship. I understand, as that is my earnest desire as well." He nods in approval. Lucius, however, seems disgruntled, though I don't venture a direct look.

The Barrister glances at his counterparts, asking with his eyes whether or not they would like to ask the first question. All silently incline their heads to the Barrister to begin the interview himself. He nods and stares at me. "Would you mind telling us your exact account of the events surrounding your father's untimely death as they unfolded?"

"Begging your lordship's pardon, but beginning when?"

"Presumably the morning of his accident," says the lord. "Unless, of course, you have further information for this Board to hear."

I see Lucius lean forward. This time I do look over at him, his face scowling, eyes darker than I've ever seen them. Like he knows he has a better cellwurk hand than me. I'd only ever played cards and sticks with the other apprentices—and sometimes Dad— before, and sometimes Dad, always for pieces of bird feed. But sitting here, I have the distinct impression I'm playing cellwurk with a man far more experienced than me—and for much greater stakes. However, unlike games of strategy and chance, *truth* wins here. And Lucius is outclassed, no matter how skilled he thinks he might be.

Truth always wins.

If I'm going to bring Lucius' questionable activity to light, this is the moment. The only problem is, I don't have much in my hangar, and only heaven knows if the dealer will favor me today.

I look the Barrister square in the eye. "So we move here, ya know? We're so excited. Especially Dad. But after his first mission, he's not the same."

"How so?" asks the Barrister, the secretary writing even more intently than before.

I go on to explain the onset of his melancholy moods, which turned into anxiety, which turned into depression. I hint at the sketchy conversation I stumble into between him and Mom. And even a little of our own conversations. But I focus mainly on my prompting him to talk with Lucius about his issues. Lucius doesn't even flinch when I mention his name. He just sits there, smoldering beneath the surface.

"And did he?" asks the Barrister.

"Well, yeah. At least, I think so."

"You think so?"

"He told me he was going to…the night before he died. So I was never able to…"

Dad.

Gone forever.

And that evening in the locker room…my last conversation with him. Still haunting me. Still *history*. Unmoving. Carved into stone. For all time. I'd give anything to go back and change it now.

I was a fool.

"Junar?"

I shake my head. "Sorry, your lordship. I was never able to find out how it went." I look over to Lucius, his menacing look unabated.

"And how *did* it go, Steward ap Victovin?" The Barrister

turns.

Lucius inhales, then gives a drawn-out reply as if it's too tedious and tiring to recount. "I thought just fine, Barrister. He was not as forthcoming as I would have liked, but that's surely due to the nature of his complaint."

"Which was?"

"In short—" Lucius glances at me— "that he did not feel up to the task before him."

I can feel blood rush to my face. Before, I would have gone along with Lucius' tale. That's exactly what I believed. But then I read Dad's letter. And while I don't know everything, it's clear Lucius is lying. Hiding. Now I know beyond doubt.

"Steward ap Victovin—" the Barrister turns in his seat— "why have you not spoken of Leif's reservations before?"

Slightly surprised by the shift in the investigation, Lucius sits up a little straighter.

Yeah, why haven't you, Lucius?

"I knew him, knew his kind," replies Lucius. "Eccentric. Gifted. And often overwhelmed with demands outside of their comfort-zone. In all honesty, brothers, I wrote it off."

"Wrote it off?" says one of the other lords.

"Indeed, I did."

"Don't you think that a gross oversight?" adds the Barrister.

Way to go, your lordship!

"Surely," confesses Lucius. "That is, if I hadn't heard it before."

Heard it before?

"You'd better explain yourself," prompts the Barrister.

"If I hadn't heard it from every single pilot I've ever recruited as a Timber Pilot."

What? What's he doing?

"It's a difficult job," continues Lucius. "That's the whole reason it takes the very best. Every single one of them hits a wall, handles the stress differently. In fact, I can't name a single pilot who hasn't complained of the very same issues. It's those who *push through* who become the *best*."

I can't take it anymore.

"He's lying!" I yell.

The Barrister looks at me. "Excuse me, son?"

"That's not true! Dad wasn't being overworked."

"Go on."

I look over to Lucius, but he doesn't seem threatened. That alone makes me nervous. Maybe he knows how much I'm privy to. But it's more than that. Almost as if Lucius is *smiling* behind those dark eyes. Inviting me.

"Dad wasn't overworked." I swallow hard, realizing what I'm about to say seems outlandish at best. But I have to. "He was being blackmailed."

"Blackmailed?" The Barrister rears back in disbelief. The other lords repeat the word too, while the scribe burns through a page of parchment. "Lucius, is this preposterous accusation true?"

Let's see how you slip out of this one, *Steward*.

"In all honesty, it very well could be," Lucius replies.

"What?" I cry.

"Explain," the Barrister demands, raising a hand in my direction.

"Because our team of flyers is elite, there is a certain *fraternity* among them. A *pecking order*, if you will. Even as the new man on the job, no matter how skilled or reputable he may be, there is always an initiation of sorts."

"Hazing," comments one of the other lords, nodding.

"A slang term, but I won't deny it," says Lucius. "Given Leif's Ace status, I can see how many of the others would be threatened by him, even as a newbie."

"What are you talking about?" I stare at Lucius.

"Junar ap Leif." The Barrister eyes me. "Should you continue with these outbursts, I will have you confined."

I sit back, frustrated. *Infuriated* is more like it.

"Do we understand one another?"

"Yes, your lordship."

Lucius flashes me a condescending smile. "Where was I?"

"Hazing," says one of the lords.

"Ah, yes. What I'm about to say is purely subjective, and I give you my word I have no grounds to believe such outlandish accusations are true, or have ever been made good on, but I've heard rumors that particularly successful pilots have had threats made against them if they did not step down."

"Step down?" says the Barrister.

"Give the better flying times to more senior flyers, bring in a smaller timber take to favor other pilots, you know. To Leif's credit, he wouldn't sell out to the others. I honor him for that. But based on how frequently he was going up and the short time between long routes, I'd say he was bending to their threats. It would certainly explain his fatigue, his moods…and his eventual complaining to me."

The Barrister rubs his chin. "This is all very enlightening, Steward. But it still does not explain your declaration of murder during the funeral."

"Begging your pardon, your lordship, but I think it does."

"Oh?"

Everything in me wants to scream *murderer!* and point to the Guild Steward. But I have to play this one out to the end. I have to pinpoint Lucius' frayed feather and exploit it. He'll trip up, and when he does, I'll be sure to catch him in it. Whatever *it* is.

"You see, Leif was not just *any* pilot, as young Junar will attest to. And not just because Leif was his father. How do I put this?"

Lucius leans forward on his elbow, searching for the right words.

Oh, you're good, Lucius.

"Once in a lifetime, a pilot comes along who's truly gifted. I mean, they're born with it in their blood. They talk to the birds, they read the sky, the air. Leif was one of those." He pauses and looks at me for effect. "The best I've ever seen."

For the first time in my life, the most vile thought comes to mind. Despicable thought. And I almost feel ashamed for it. *Almost.* But Lucius plunges back into his monologue before it can fully materialize.

"*Retreat* is what I heard from him. Of course, he didn't *say* that. But he didn't have to. When he told me he wanted to move back to Bellride, I knew it wasn't the pressure of the job. It was the pressure from someone within his inner circle. Someone close to him."

"And your counsel to him?" asks the Barrister, his eyes narrowing. "Consider your words carefully, Steward. Murder is perpetrated by those who kill as well as those who empower."

Lucius doesn't blink—hasn't blinked. How does he do it? "I told him I'd send him home, back to Bellride."

That's the first thing Lucius has said that lines up with Dad's letter. This snake is clearly up to something.

"Yet he flew the next morning," the Barrister concludes.

"He insisted," Lucius raises his shoulders in defeat. "What was I to do? 'One more mission,' he told me. 'Then it's over.' I pleaded with him, but he said he 'wanted to go out with dignity.' That his son would never fully respect him if he didn't try until the end to make things work." Lucius turns. "He was speaking of you, Junar."

Bastard.

The evil thought I had earlier is materializing, nearly forming on my lips.

"So you think Leif's last mission was seen as an affront to those threatening him?"

"In a word, yes," Lucius says, peaking his fingers.

"And you have a suspect?"

"I do indeed."

This ought to be good. I sit back in my chair.

"But it was the last person in the world I'd have expected." Lucius turns to me. Eyes drilling deep. And they don't avert. Or blink. And the Barrister follows them, as do the other four lords. Even the scribe stops his writing. The wicked thought stirring deep inside me finally emerges as one clear line in my head: *Lucius ap Victovin, one day, I'm going to kill you with my own two hands.*

"Junar ap Leif," says Lucius, "his own son."

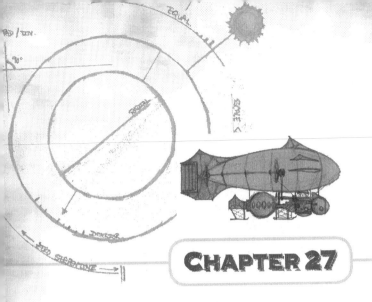

CHAPTER 27

MY HEART IS beating furiously. Sweat on my forehead. And any attempt to stop sweating—reminding myself that such involuntary evidence only succeeds in making me look guilty—just makes it worse.

"Lucius." The Barrister looks at him, his formal air deserting him. "I hope you know what you're doing."

"Oh, I do, your lordship," he assures the Barrister, eyes still riveted on me.

"Junar, do you wish to address this dangerous accusation?"

Do I wish to? Of course! But how? What? Where to even begin? I have to say something to advance my cellwurk holdings. But my heart is beating even faster. I'm sure whatever words I attempt to speak next will only get caught in my throat. The little boy in me wants to cry. To stand up and point a finger and have my parents swoop in and rescue me. But I'm no longer a boy. And I haven't been for quite some time. Dad's death left me more than without his presence. It left me a man. A man who is sitting face-to-face with his accuser. And face-to-face with the men of power who can change the direction of his life with one flick of that ink-laden quill.

"Yes," I reply, just managing to keep my voice from cracking. "I would like to know the absurd reasoning he has for such a horrible accusation. I can't even believe I have to sit here and take this!" Easy Junar, don't get all dramatic on them.

"I would tend to agree with Junar," says the Barrister. "Lucius, please explain yourself."

"Junar—" Lucius doesn't even pause— "tell us how you felt when your father first mentioned you might be moving back to Bellride."

"I was upset, but who wouldn't have been?"

"Indeed. A young man, raised in the obscurity of Bellride, suddenly finds fame and glory in the big city."

"I'd hardly call it fame and—"

"Please, you're not that bad of a flyer yourself. How long did it take for you to gain the eye of the Headmaster?"

"I—"

"You made your mark rather quickly, as I recall."

"Lucius, where's this going?" asks the Barrister.

"Please, your lordship, if I may continue?"

"Be about it, quickly."

Lucius looks back to me. "In your own accounting of the story, you even mentioned how aghast you were that your father wanted to move back to Bellride."

"Yes, but I—"

"But while your father was finding opposition, you were finding a challenge. Friendships. Prestige. And even a little *love*, if I'm not mistaken?"

"That's none of your business!"

"Gentlemen!" the Barrister admonishes.

"But it's *all* my business, Apprentice. It's *my* Guild." Lucius turns to the Barrister. "I am going somewhere, your lordship."

"I'm beginning to question that very much," replies the Barrister. "This is your last warning."

Lucius acknowledges the rebuke, then drills me with his dark eyes. "Tell me, Junar ap Leif, what business did you have with the Inventors a few weeks ago?"

"The Inventors?" The Barrister looks between us. "What's this?"

"Ask him for yourself, your lordship," says Lucius.

The Barrister seems beside himself as he stares at me. "Junar, what have you to say?"

Where *are* you going with this, Lucius? "I'm not sure what he's talking about," I say. Half-truth.

"One of the Ace pilots needed a saddle repaired," Lucius says. "Your father said you could handle it. So the work went to you. But even *it* was too *complex* of an issue to handle in-house. So you took it elsewhere, didn't you?"

I squint at Lucius. "How did you—?"

"So it's true?" concludes the Barrister. But I'm still blinking in disbelief at Lucius. "Please answer the question, Junar. You're on the record here."

"Yes, OK? I took the saddle to an Inventor for repair. Is that really a crime?"

"Repair?" asks Lucius.

"Yes, a repair!"

"Or was it sabotage?"

I jerk away. My neck and cheeks start to burn. I can hardly repeat the word. "Sabotage?"

Lucius pushes back and opens a drawer in his desk, producing a leather-bound file of documents. "Equipment reports." He unwinds the leather thong that keeps it closed. "Meticulously kept." He flips open the folio. "Tracking all our inventory and tack rotations. Signed, dated and double-checked. The saddle you repaired for…" he searches the record on top. "Ah, here it is: *Connor ap Hawthorne*, was checked into inventory and never used again. Until your father's saddle unexplainably went in for repair and was replaced with another for his final mission." Lucius passes the paper to the Barrister. "With the one you repaired."

The saddle I repaired? But that's not the one he crashed in! "That's not true! That's not the one he died in!"

"Oh?" Lucius inquires. "And how would you know that?"

Think, Junar!

Banth found Dad's saddle.

Could he have fabricated the find?

No. He couldn't. But Banth clearly has something to gain by attacking the establishment. And he has access to the tack barn if Dad's saddle had indeed been checked out for repair, which would have explained the failing locking mechanism Haupstie discovered.

Could Banth have switched the saddles on me?

A new wave of anger flares up in my chest. And fear. Because I have no grounds to justify any of this. I'm feeling closed off. Claustrophobic. And if I even breathe a word about Banth miraculously producing Dad's saddle, I'd be dead as soon as I stepped out of this room.

"Junar?" The Barrister breaks my stare.

"What?"

"Son, this is a very serious accusation Lucius is making, but I fear it is not without some credence. We must have you answer him."

"I did not sabotage my own Dad's saddle!" I blurt out.

"Your lordship," Lucius interjects, "let my last question be stricken from the record."

"I'm sorry," the Barrister says, looking to Lucius, "but we can't just—"

"Rather—" Lucius turns on me again— "Junar, how did you *really* feel when your father threatened to move back to Bellride? Were you upset?"

"Sure, who wouldn't be?"

"Mad, even?"

"Uh, I guess."

"So upset that you moved out?"

I don't answer.

"Did you, in fact, abandon your primary residence with your parents, Junar?"

"Abandon?" I ask, trying to stall on a technicality, my eyes never leaving Lucius.

"Did you or did you not run away?" the Barrister clarifies.

"I did, but it—"

"And slept in the hangar and bathed in the locker rooms and ate in the mess hall," Lucius adds. "For weeks."

"And you endorsed this, Lucius?" asks one of the lords.

"Hardly, but the last thing I wanted to do was cause further friction in the home of an Ace who was already enduring so much. Especially with his wife in such an unstable state. One wrong step and she could leave him again."

That's it.

I leap from my chair and fly across Lucius' desk, shouting, *"You treacherous hawk! Stay out of my family's business!"*

My hands are at Lucius' throat faster than I dare imagine. But my momentum topples his chair backward and spills us both onto the glass floor. The lords start flapping around us like a gaggle of crows, not sure what to do until one of them starts pulling on my arms to stop me constricting Lucius' windpipe. Then the others join in. The most sickening thing of all, however, is that Lucius is doing nothing to stop me, save maybe a minor bat at my hands. Playing the victim.

"He's lying! He's lying!" I shout as they pull me back. "You must believe me!"

Thrusting me back in my seat, now standing around to guard from another outburst, the Barrister straightens his robe and stares at me. "Young man, your actions have already spoken to your gross lack of self-control and tendency toward rage." He pants to catch his breath. "This, I'm afraid, coupled with contempt for your father's decision to move your family back to Bellride, at least gives merit to Lucius' audacious accusation of patricide. It must be entertained to its end, no matter how objectionable I may find it. Which, I'll have you know, I do. We are here for justice, not for our own likings."

"But it's simply not true!"

"Then, my dear boy, I pray you produce some shred of evidence that vindicates you."

All at once I hear Banth's warning back at Haupstie's laboratory: *As long as they believe your father kept his mouth shut and didn't tell you anything, then they have no reason to silence you. But the moment they suspect anything, they'll kill you.*

But that's before I knew Banth betrayed me. Betrayed my father.

"I have a letter."

For the first time since this interrogation started, I can see Lucius tense up. Rubbing his neck. He still doesn't know what's in the letter, or if it even existed up until this point; now, it's my only hope.

"Go on," says the Barrister, slowly walking back to his chair behind the table.

"Dad wrote it to Mom, the night before he died. Had a courier deliver it. It was Lucius who then had my house ransacked, looking for it."

"What's this?" The Barrister looks over his shoulder to Lucius, who doesn't so much as twitch. "Why ever would he do a thing like that?"

"Because," I say, feeling more confident than I had in a long time. "It implicates him, in a coverup." And I pray the little letter I withdraw from inside my jacket will trump whatever hand Lucius is hoping to play next.

Lucius strains in his seat, and I can see the torture in his face: he's desperately searching for some legal tacit to prevent this paper from traveling the five feet from my hands to the Barrister's, yet fighting to maintain his self-composure.

But it's Dad's letter. In his own hand. And it will see me through.

The lords sit in awe, each leaning forward as I present the rough papyrus to the Barrister. Not lavish, and far from ornate, the note is written by a working man. A poet of the sky. And his heart is in every line, no matter how hastily composed.

"From your father?" the Barrister looks up. I nod. "May I?" He accepts the folded note as if it were a holy relic; for this, I'm grateful. And somehow feel relieved. Here it is. My only shred of evidence. My only hope.

The Barrister opens the document with the other four men leaning in; even the secretary can't help himself, laying his utensils aside and awkwardly propping himself up to peer above the others. I watch the Barrister's lips mumble each of the lines I now know by heart.

"*The Northern Range is nothing more than a barren and stark landscape...The only threat I ever encountered were workers—men—with nelurime pistols...I never cut down a single tree...Nelurime, lots of it, in exchange for timber and satchels of cream...I sat with Lucius...I promised Junar I would.*"

When the Barrister is through, he passes the letter to the secretary who—for all his struggling—still hasn't gotten a good look at it, and takes to transcribing it word-for-word into his archive of the meeting.

And then I wait.

And wait.

The Barrister sits, puzzling. Not looking at me, and not looking at Lucius. And for all my people skills, I can't read him. That's when a sickening thought surfaces.

What if the Barrister is in on the coverup?

No. He can't be. He's the personal appointee of the Chancellor himself. Plus, he's far too genuine in his unbiased questioning, even of Lucius. Unless the Barrister only wants to conduct the interview for the sheer appearance of justice. Which means I've been doomed from the very beginning of this meeting.

The silence is killing me! But, oddly enough, it's Lucius' outburst that gives me to know I'm most likely safe. At least for the time being.

"Well?" he finally blurts out. If the Barrister's in on the coverup, Lucius would never demonstrate such a lack of confidence.

Would he?

I'm either surrounded by the best actors in all of Aria-Prime, or Dad has vindicated me from beyond the grave.

"It seems," the Barrister breathes, "that Junar has indeed produced evidence of a most unprecedented nature, written either by a crazy man or by a desperate father in witness to outrageous happenings, the likes of which we've never seen."

Lucius seems to lighten at this pronouncement. The Barrister continues. "Likewise, the Steward here purports a heinous crime of patricide with material logs, motive and a confession by Junar himself of his dealings with the Inventors."

Wait. Where's this going? The Barrister leans back in his chair, stroking his chin. I steal a glance at Lucius: he seems more confident than ever. Doesn't feel good.

"Yet I cannot, in good conscience, accuse a youth for the alleged murder of his father when the man himself writes to us, from the grave, of his son's own importance. No matter how outlandish Leif's claims may appear, unless my colleagues have further discourse, it is my recommendation that this note be tested for authenticity and a full investigation be made into the claims Leif purports of the Northern Range, as well as the dealings of one, Guild Steward Lucius ap Victovin."

The secretary raises his head as if to say something, but commits himself to his duties and continues scribbling what I understand to be the Barrister's final pronouncement in the matter.

Turning to the astounded Guild Steward, the Barrister says, "Lucius ap Victovin, on the basis of the written account of Leif ap Jeronil, I hereby confine you to your quarters until further notice. A Council-appointed Brologi Sentinel will ensure your protection, both from others and from yourself.

"Likewise, Junar ap Leif, on the basis of having the motive, means and proximity to devices which may or may not have led to the death of your father, you will be placed under house arrest until further notice. A Council-appointed Brologi Sentinel will ensure your protection, both from others and from yourself. This case will be revisited again in full, pending review of all elements entered into the record."

The Barrister is about to rap his gavel on the table and stand when the secretary finally succeeds in getting a word in. "Your lordship," he says.

The Barrister glances over at him, seemingly shocked the man even has a voice. "What is it?"

"You may be interested in this announcement," says the secretary.

"Is it very much pertinent?"

The secretary reaches within the fold of his robe and produces a small folded parchment. "I do think so."

"Do you?" asks the Barrister, now reaching for it. I'm

intrigued, as is Lucius. The lord unfolds the document, and sets some spectacles on the end of his nose. Reading. Reading some more. He looks to me. "Well, young Junar. It seems your house arrest will be interrupted for a spell. This copy of the Champions Race roster includes one Junar ap Leif, signed by the Chancellor himself. I think what our counterpart here is surmising—" the Barrister acknowledges the secretary— "is that this court does not have the permission to usurp such a document, at least not with circumstantial evidence."

"So what are you saying?" I ask him.

"I'm saying you'll be confined to your home both before and after, but not during, the Champions Race. You're free to compete."

I should be elated. I should feel vindicated. But all I feel is uneasiness. Because I'm being forced to do the thing I no longer want to do.

And Lucius is smiling to himself.

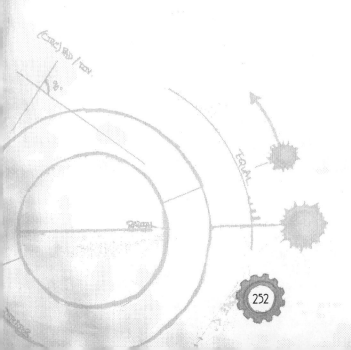

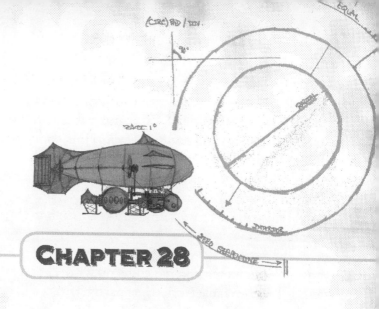

CHAPTER 28

IT'S WELL PAST midnight when the Brologi Sentinel escorts me home. Good thing. Only the God of the Skies knows how frustrated I would be with all the questions from the neighbors. And my friends. But even explaining this to Liv and Erik can wait. Right now, I have to figure out how to tell Mom what's going on.

"So you'll be here all night?" I ask the Brologi standing on the porch.

"Aye," he says, nodding.

"Then can I at least get your name?" He stiffens. "Relax, I'm not reporting you or anything. I just want to be able to tell Mom who the giant on our deck is. You know, offering *that guy* something to drink gets a little awkward."

"Denlin," he replies.

"Nice to meet you, officially," I say, extending my hand. We shake. Isn't his fault he has to watch a suspected teenage murderer. Just trying to make it easier on the guy. But more than that, I want him to know I'm grateful. Because I am. Shoot, this hulk may be my last line of defense against a prowler bent on slitting my throat. The way I figure it, there's at least three factions who want me silenced. And, house arrest or not, I know Lucius is powerful enough to come after me, no matter where I'm holed up. What I really want to say to Denlin is *you might want to ask for some backup.* But that would definitely be taken as a threat.

"So if you need anything…some water…the bathroom…ya know, just knock."

"I will," he says. "Thanks, kid." Then turns to stand by the awning post.

I walk inside, hoping not to wake Mom. Hoping to buy myself some more time. To come up with a good excuse. No sense telling her the whole truth when partial truths will do. She's already frazzled enough as it is.

"Junar? Is that you?" I hear her say.

Perfect.

"Yeah, Mom. Sorry I'm late."

She comes bounding down the stairs. "Junar! I was worried sick about you!" Her eyes are swollen, rubbed dry after a fresh bout of grief. "Where have you been?"

Start with some of the truth. "The tack barn," I say.

"Cleaning late again?"

"Not exactly." She gives me *The Look.* Yeah, hate it. No use fighting it. "There's an investigation going on."

She cups her mouth with her hands. "Your father."

I nod. "They're following through on the Steward's accusation that someone murdered him."

"So the House believes him?"

"You could say that."

"Say what?"

Give her some more of the truth.

"They have reason to believe it was him."

"What?" Mom turns pale. "Lucius?"

"Yeah, crazy, huh?"

Mom turns away, pacing toward the front window, then screams. "There's a man on our porch!"

"Easy, mom. He's Brologi. Denlin."

"Brologi? What? Why?"

Not the whole truth.

"He's just protecting us."

"Protecting us?" She glances between me and the Brologi a few times. "Junar, what's going on here?" Then *The Look* again. Even in her weakened condition, her temper is not to be crossed.

"I produced evidence that could pin Dad's murder on Lucius. So they're protecting us."

"You did? What evidence?"

"Mom, it's OK, I—"

"What evidence, Junar?"

"A letter. From Dad."

"What?!"

"The letter Dad sent to the house the night before he died. The one they couldn't find."

"The one Lucius was asking for?" she adds.

"Yeah."

"And you had it all along?" she says, moving toward me.

"Not exactly. It's...*complicated.*"

"Then un-complicate it," she says in my face.

Easy, Junar. Don't show too much of your hand.

I run my fingers through my hair.

"Lucius feared Dad had somehow implicated him in a plot, which Dad had. He'd put it in the letter. The Steward was going to make sure you never got it. Make sure it never saw the light of day. But a Brologi intercepted the letter, knowing Lucius would send his goons looking for it."

"Which he did." Mom turns away, obviously remembering the house in disarray. "I knew it was *him,*" she seethes.

"Then finally the Brologi gave it to me for safekeeping."

Mom spins back to me. "How long have you had it then, son? Why didn't you let me see it?"

I freeze, honestly not knowing what to say. My lips move. But no words come out.

"What did it say, Junar? For crying out loud!" She comes forward and clutches my shirt. "It's my *husband's last words to me!* How can you keep it from me?" Her fist comes down on my collarbone. "How, Junar? How can you do this to me?" She pummels me again.

Then something real happens. Something raw. Something that breaks my heart.

"I must know what he said." She starts sobbing. "I must know what he thought about..."

Mom collapses into me. Her head presses into my neck, right arm still weakly pounding my shoulder.

I see *it*.

Shame. She's still carrying it.

The affair.

I see it now. As if I had been blind this whole time. I see *fear*. Fear of not knowing what her husband said to her the night he left forever. About what he thought. She can only guess. Is he angry at her? Regretful? Offering forgiveness? What do his words speak from the grave?

I realize, right now, that while Dad had long ago forgiven, even forgotten—something I inappropriately saw as weakness— Mom has not. She's lived with it. Every day. Every night. Tormenting her. To the point that she now clutches me, pleading to know what few sparse lines her betrayed husband might profess over her life.

And I *feel*. I feel guilty.

Not just from withholding the letter. But from withholding something deeper. Something greater.

My *love*.

Then a sick thought curdles in my gut. Perhaps it's been *me*. Me that's perpetuated the misery of remembrance. My mistrust, my malice. Can it be my unforgiveness that's bound her to the past, so desperate for Dad's mercy before his death that she'd plead with me now for a mere scrap of paper?

All at once, my bitterness...is dying. Dwindling. The flame of anger that's burned since the night I first found out about her unfaithfulness...is starving. And here in the chasm that is my chest, I see my fingers creeping toward a flame, a fire that I've fueled for far too long. I feel the heat, threatening to blister my skin. To sear me. But I can't help but move my hand toward the light as I feel Mom's hot tears on my neck.

And that's when I decide to snuff it out. Welcoming the tendril of smoke coiling up from the wick as the funeral pyre of my hate.

"He said he loved you," I whisper in her ear, my tears now mixing with hers. "He's always loved you."

Mom shudders, a violent inhale, then a fresh wave of emotion weakens her knees, sending us both to the floor. I try to think of specific lines Dad wrote. But my memory is cloudy. "He said…"

What did he say?

Of course I don't remember. I'd skipped all the intimate parts of the letter. The ones not intended for me. But how can I disappoint her now, when she needs love the most? What would Dad say? I may not have read his admissions of love, but I know the heart behind them. His heart. And there's a good chance she'll never even see the document.

I take a deep breath. To speak for him. To speak for me.

"He said you were the most precious thing in his life," I say. And I mean it, for us both. "That he only had wonderful thoughts about you." I choke on my own tears. "That he held nothing against you, and was forced to remember the pain of the past only when you brought it up with your eyes."

Mom sobs, shuddering against me.

"He said you were his greatest choice. And…and he would have chosen you every time if he had to do it over again. And if this was to be his last mission, would you forgive him for taking us all back to Bellride once he got home?"

"Yes, yes, yes," she cries, face contorting, lips straining, then biting her fist. "Yes, my love." She groans, her body wracked with the jarring assault of loss.

There's nothing I can do but hold her. Until I whisper, "I'm sorry."

I'm sorry.

It's all I can think to say.

I'm sorry for harboring bitterness toward you. For keeping you accountable for the things you did wrong. For hurting our family. For hurting Dad. When you begged with your eyes for relief from your

memories, I added insult to injury by ignoring your silent pleas for help.
You didn't betray me, Mom. I betrayed you.

"I forgive you, Junar," she says suddenly.

Forgive me?

I'd spoken it all out loud, had I?

And all at once, I can see. Truly *see*. Like the clearing of a storm front, the oppression that's lingered around my mind is gone. I'm free! And the suns are bright and beautiful, like never before.

I'm not sure how long we've knelt here together in the front room, but as far as I can tell, Denlin the Brologi hasn't moved. And while others might feel awkward with his presence just outside the window, having him there makes me feel safe. He's not just guarding from outside attack; in some unspoken way, he's guarding the intimacy of this moment. And the moments that follow on until dawn, when the suns kiss my face and find me nestled beside my mother, who's sleeping soundly on the couch, wrapped in a blanket.

I slip away and look out the front window. The Brologi still hasn't moved a muscle. Did they train them to sleep standing up? Wouldn't surprise me.

I open the door. "Coffee?" I ask.

Denlin moves his head only a quarter turn and nods.

"Coming up." I close the door quietly.

I slip into the kitchen, grind some beans, then dump the prized black powder into the steam generator. I clamp the lid down tight and turn up the pressure until the valve needle peaks into the red. The brass contraption rattles until finally a steady black stream of fluid drips out of the lower nozzle and into the mugs I'd prepared. Holding my own under my arm, I quietly open the door and join Denlin on the porch in view of the morning suns.

"Here ya go," I say, offering the aromatic brew.

"Thank you," he replies with the faintest hint of a smile. The warm yellow glow chases the shadows away in the crisp morning air. Christiana is flying leeward to the northeast today—means summer's on its way.

I take a sip of my coffee. Nearly always scald my upper lip. "Get any sleep?" I ask him.

Denlin has his sun visor lowered so I can't see his eyes, but his head turns toward me as before.

Is that a yes?

He takes a drink from his mug.

OK. Change of subject. "Beautiful morning," I say.

"Hope Saturday's just like it," he adds. Almost a whole sentence from him. Impressive.

"Yeah. Why's that?" I ask, hoping to keep the conversation rolling.

"Are you stupid, kid?"

"Uh, excuse me?"

"The Champions Race."

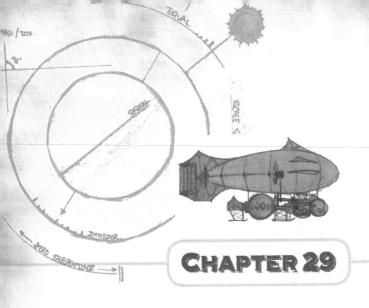

CHAPTER 29

"*I CAN'T BELIEVE* you're still going through with this," Liv says as I heave Serio's saddle up onto his back. The tack barn is in chaos as the Aces prepare their birds for the race. Serio and I don't have a stall, but I have Lance; his extra help makes a world of difference. I had to make good on his promise to be my flight leader. We're stuck all the way back at the end of the tack barn, out of the way. It's fine, though. Lance is off washing Serio's feed bin, so it gives me and Liv a moment to talk, though she's not changing my mind.

"What else can I do?" I reply. "Trust me, I really don't want to anymore. But I have orders to race now." Referring to the Board's recognition of the Chancellor's proclamation. "You know the situation better than anyone else." Though she doesn't know *every* detail—she'd never forgive me if she found out I suspect Banth and Haupstie. "Plus, I need more time with the Chancellor. And this is the perfect chance. Setting up a meeting any other way would only raise suspicions." I start buckling Serio's girth straps.

"Suspicions that might draw the Chancellor's accusers into the open," Liv says.

"Or taunt them to kill us in a meeting," I add. "It's too dangerous, Liv. You know that."

"But flying in the race is still too dangerous, kid."

Why is she so frustrating?

"Listen—" I square my shoulder with her— "we both know I have to do this. That I *can* do this. I'm going to be OK, and I'm going to get to speak with the Chancellor again."

"Are you really going to be OK, Junar?" She walks closer.

"Well, sure, I—"

"Because if you say you can guarantee it, you're lying. No one can. If you're bent on doing this, at least don't lie to me."

"Liv, I—"

But she cuts me off and grabs me by the collar. "Because I care about you, Junar. So at least let's be straight with one another. You can't guarantee your safety anymore than I can. It's the way life is. But—" She hesitates and looks down— "you *can* promise me you'll be careful. You will, won't you?" She looks up again, eyes searching mine. Deeply.

I don't want to die. Heck, who does? But she's right. I can't guarantee anything. Dad couldn't guarantee his survival. And neither can I. The truth is, I like this girl. Maybe even love her. And that demands a measure of honesty, even if she doesn't know about the Inventors and the Brologi. I can at least be forthcoming here. In this.

"I will be careful," I say. "For your sake"

"Thank you," she whispers, then pulls me down into a kiss.

When she's through, I ask, "What's that for?"

"For listening to me." She smiles, then lets me go. "Perhaps you should do it more."

"Perhaps I will," I say, smiling wide.

I hear footsteps pounding down the center aisle and look to see Lance running toward us. "Get ready!" he yells. "It's time!"

Right on time, Reginald stands in the middle of the tack barn and cups his hand to his mouth. "All birds departing for the stadium," he announces. "Last call."

"That's my cue." I wink at Liv.

"We'll see you from the crowd," she says. "May Talihdym

give you fair winds and clear skies." She turns to leave, then looks back. "And who knows: with any luck, you might just win it. Fly or die."

Lance and I walk Serio down the long hallway toward the hangar. I hear my name from behind. *Mom.*

"I'm so glad I caught you," Mom says as she runs over, out of breath.

"So am I," I say as Lance takes Serio's reins. Haven't see her run like this in—well—a very long time. She gives me a hug, and I'm glad for it. I squeeze her back. Ever since our night of crying together, there's something different between us. And I can only thank Talihdym for it, no matter how distant I think Him to be. "Thanks for coming."

"I wouldn't miss it, Junar," she says. Feels good to see her so excited. So...*happy.*

"You going up?" I ask.

"Yes!" She claps her hands. Like she's a little girl. "The Chancellor's airship!"

"The Chancellor's?" I ask, shocked.

"I know! Can you believe it?"

Stunned, I stammer, "No, I mean, well, he's kind to, and—"

"Said it was the least he could do for me. For *us.*"

Here I am, all set to race, and now Mom has the very window of opportunity I need. My brain's thinking fast. But not fast enough. I can't figure out how to join her because of the reasons I just finished discussing with Liv. Not racing is to break proclamation and invite assassination, though I know that's being melodramatic, whereas racing means risking death, but a sure way of meeting up with the Chancellor.

Perhaps I can have Mom give him a message? Maybe start outlining what I know? But that's as futile as trying to tell the Chancellor everything back at our midnight meeting. There's no time.

"I'll be in the stands for the opening ceremony," she says, "then I'm leaving with his entourage on his airship."

"Remind me to thank him," I say. "That's really kind."

"I know," she says. "I just wish that…" Her eyes glaze over, and I can see tears forming.

"I know, Mom," I say, embracing her with my free arm. "Me too. Me too."

She leans her head on me and takes a deep breath.

"I miss him," she says.

"Yeah, he'd love to be here right now," I agree, rubbing her arm.

"He'd be flying with you today, you know."

I nod. "I like to think he *is* flying with me today. With both of us."

Mom looks up at me, the tears having materialized and running down her cheeks.

"Yes. Yes, he is," she adds.

The last few pilots are mounting their birds and exiting through the hanger.

"Look at me," Mom says, standing upright and wiping her sleeve across her face. "Here," she says, handing me a small cloth with something warm inside. "Brought you something. For when you get hungry up there. It's a long flight." We already had a small satchel of water and food on our saddles, but this gift is worth all that and more. I thank her and tuck it inside my jacket. She zips me back up and gives a kiss. "Be safe," she says. "But make sure you win." Makes me smile.

"I'll try," I say.

"I love you, my son."

"I love you too, Mom." And for the first time in a long time, I mean it.

It's quite the spectacle. I swear every airship in Aria-Prime is docked along the perimeter of Christiana. As if each deck is adorned with oblong fruit, so overripe that they threaten to pull the city into the cloud-floor; she does look like she's riding rather low today.

I'm one of the last pilots to join the formation slowly circling the cloud-floor. We can hear the crowd already chanting from inside the stadium. A few of the Aces salute me as I pull up, tolerating my participation a little better than I'd expected. Probably due to my loss, I'm sure. I smile and salute back, wondering just how many of these men are in on *it*—on murdering Dad.

The lead flyer, always a non-competing Kili-Boranna, signals the cast, then breaks formation and heads toward Christiana. Coming around the balloon matrix, I can feel the pulse of Champions Stadium in the air, surging under Serio's wings. It's like one of Haupstie's electrical generators humming in his laboratory.

Haupstie.

If only he was as innocent as I once thought he was. Dad was right. *Bad blood.* I don't think he's malicious. But he's not innocent either. He's proof that even the most pure of men can succumb to the bitterness of a grudge. I know I had with Mom. For so long. Not anymore, of course. She'll be cheering in the stadium, and all is well between us. Of course, she doesn't need to know about the Board's implication of my involvement with Dad's murder. Nor should she. It's not true. No need to torment her further. It would only succeed in riling her up.

Of course, she wasn't thrilled about me racing, either. Not at first. But when I explained I was doing it to honor Dad and that the Chancellor was permitting it—even welcoming it—she couldn't *break my heart*, as she put it. Then there was the invite to ride in the Chancellor's airship. That sealed the deal.

My only reservation is the one I can least explain, though I heartily suspect: Lucius' smile.

The volume coming from the stadium is deafening as our formation flies in. I'm bringing up the rear, of course, but I'm still *in*. My dream. I just never imagined that I'd be racing under these conditions. Never. Whatever excitement I should be feeling is overshadowed by the obvious. The fact is, I can linger in the rear of the cast for the entire race. Shoot, I can just circle Christiana until it's over and then meet up with the Chancellor.

But I'd betray what little dignity I have left. And the memory of my father who told me to never give up. To always give my best. And to see things through to the end. Today, I will race. I will give it my best. With any luck, and a lot of favor from Talihdym, I might even win.

The air above the field seems to vibrate. It's a wonder that the felrell aren't spooked out of their minds. But somehow the din of noise is so constant they don't seem to mind—like the unceasing hiss of wind in their ears. Serio beats his wings against our momentum and slows, talons searching for the ground. We're the last to touch down, but no less lauded by the throng of viewers. Lance and Liv are out there, somewhere. As is Mom. So I wave.

Apart from the flags and banners and brightly colored clothes, the stadium is skirted by more airships, most belonging to the Stewards and Lords. They'll get a head start as soon as the formalities are concluded. Three years ago, Dad wasn't competing, and he got invited to watch the race from the Steward's airship from Bellride. I was so excited when he told me I could come along. I was sitting out there, in these very same seats, daydreaming about what it must be like to be competing…to be doing what I'm doing right now. It's surreal. I heard the musicians and the conductor begin Christiana's anthem. The people singing. I watched Christiana's Guild Steward offer a benediction in the name of Talihdym. I saw the Chancellor stand up, just as he's doing now. The history recited, the Commission read, and the one-hour flag waved, signaling the official start of the race.

The birds remained in the field as we left the stadium, nearly trampling one another in a frantic attempt to be the first to our respective airships. Dad bought some lamb skewers from a vendor inside the stadium before climbing into the passenger pod of the Steward's ship. Then we set out, heading toward an observation coordinate far east of Knightsbridge.

Sitting there with my eyes glued to the portal glass, I wondered what the pilots were doing back in the field, waiting there for what could only be the longest hour of their lives. Talking about the race, thinking about their individual strategies, and reveling in the fact that they are the best of the best. That they've *arrived*.

"You sure you're up for this?" asks one pilot named Rald, sitting on his bird beside me. Pretty good pilot, from what I'd seen. And not a Timber Pilot, so I'll at least give him the benefit of the doubt that he *may* not be in on Dad's murder.

"Think so," I reply, absently checking a clasp on my saddle.

"This isn't the time to *think*, kid," says another pilot behind me. I don't know his name. But I know he was in Dad's squadron.

"Go easy on him," says Rald.

"Yeah," says Daren from atop his bird. "Kid's been through a lot. Go easy." Daren forces his way in front of the other pilot and moves toward me. "Sorry about that, kid. Come on, let's have a seat."

Sitting down with Daren is the last thing I want to do. *Murderer.* But I guess it never dawned on me that the racers wouldn't just sit atop their birds for a whole hour. Not when they were preparing for an eight-hour flight. As the stadium empties of its last occupants, all the pilots slide off their birds and find places on the grass. Rald comes over to stretch out with me and Daren as attendants bring around drinks and trays of food.

Suddenly, I'm with the big boys. No Lance or Liv, not even Erik or Finn. And it wouldn't surprise me if every one of these men are complicit in Dad's death. I'm a sparrow in the raptor pen.

"You're pretty brave for going up," says Rald.

"I don't feel very brave," I admit.

"Still, it's something," he says.

"You don't have to go, ya know," says Daren. "You've already come out here. Shown your face."

I look Daren in the eyes, searching his face. I'm convinced he knows all about Dad's murder. In detail. How could he not? Yet he can sit here and lie so cleanly. He pulls out a cellwurk deck and starts dealing cards and sticks to me and Rald.

Cellwurk. *Strategy.* It's building cities and routes to expand your cloud holdings. I examine my cards.

Daren plays his first set. Builds a city, then a new nelurime route. Strong opening. "Your Dad's already a hero to all of Aria-

Prime," he says. "Given everything that's happened, no one would think any less of you if you headed back to the hangar now."

"Given everything that's happened?" I repeat, staring at my cards. "Is there something about my family that would cause them to think less of me?"

I place my first city set and build my own route. Rald plays a hand and glances over at me, then to Daren.

Daren looks over his cards, smiling. "Not that I'm aware of, Junar. Is there?" He finishes a nelurime route, preparing to build two new cities. *Intimidation*. Faking players out, getting them to back down even when you have nothing in your hand.

"I can't think of anything," I say. "Unless my Dad's death was disgraceful somehow." I cut off Daren's nelurime corridor. City building stops. *Counter*. Blocking your opponent's route, eliminating options.

Rald plays a hand, working on his own route.

"Would you gentlemen like something more to drink?" asks a female server.

"You know I would," says Daren, looking her over once. She bristles under his ogling, then refills his cup. I kindly wave her off, as does Rald.

Daren takes a sip, then exchanges cards for sticks. "He was killed by Zy-Adair, Junar. Not sure there's anything disgraceful about that. Unless you know of something disgraceful and would like to inform us." *Withdraw*. Lure the enemy into a trap. But I'm not so naive.

"What I know? I'm not so sure you'd like to know what I know." I play some sticks, edging past him, and start my own city build.

Daren doesn't even blink. "That's the trouble with being the only one who knows," he states. "Can't prove a thing. The secret is yours alone." *Subtlety*. Catching your opponent off guard.

"Am I missing something here?" Rald asks with a hesitant smile, as if emphasizing Daren's point. He lays sticks down, then gives both Daren and me a confused look. Proof he's innocent. Good to know.

"Just friendly conversation," Daren says, playing his next

card. "Isn't that right, Junar?"

I nod. "Absolutely. Especially considering there are others who'd love to add what they know to the dialogue." I play my new city. *Advance.* The only way to win.

Daren isn't looking up. He's not blinking either. I've got him. At least, I have him thinking. He grunts, then reaches inside his flight jacket. Touches something. Winces. Then he wipes his fingers in the grass. Is that blood? The injury he sustained from the Sky Pirates...*or was it from Dad?* Daren reaches for a card, then changes his mind and plays sticks that intercept my city, effectively splitting its provisions between us.

We both draw more cards. *Flank.* An attack from the blind spot is costly. "Sometimes staying silent is more...beneficial," Daren says. "Don't you think?"

"Depends on what there is to lose," I add, cutting off his siphon and building my next nelurime route. *Transition.* Altering the effects of your opponent's attack.

Rald looks between us and exchanges cards for sticks.

"I wager there's quite a bit to lose," says Daren. "*Life* is not to be played with."

"Couldn't have said it better myself," I reply.

"Hey, are we playing cellwurk here? Or having a marriage dispute?" asks Rald, obviously annoyed. "Seriously, guys."

"Don't get your feathers bunched up," insists Daren. "We're still playing. Junar here is just a little *testy*, is all. I mean, can you blame him?" Daren plays some sticks and starts his next city. To me: "Still, I suppose it doesn't matter if you fly today or not."

"Why's that?" I ask, playing my turn.

Rald plays his.

"Because no matter how much you think you know," says Daren, making his move, "someone always knows a little bit more." In one turn he reconnects the route to my second city, joins another route to my third, and finishes by using his remaining resources to build a fourth of his own. "I believe that's game, gentlemen." He stands and drains his cup, then gives me a wicked smile. One much like the Guild Steward's.

Rald throws down his cards, frustrated.

"Fly or die, boys. See you in the air," Daren says as he heads toward another group of Aces standing in the field.

"What was that about?" Rald asks me. I can't tell if he's more upset about coming in last or that he has no clue what the conversation was about.

"I'm not entirely sure," I reply. "But something tells me the whole world is about to find out." I look down and examine Daren's winning layout. "And I don't think it's going to be pretty."

Riling Daren up probably wasn't the best idea. But we're airborne now. No more talking. Which is fine by me. Just flying. And Serio and I will give Daren and his bird a run for their money.

The flying start of the race goes off without a hitch. The Commencement Official—who's taken the race flag from the Chancellor so his Eminence can board his airship and watch the competition from above—waves us off as the hour ends. All forty-seven competing pilots leap from the stadium field and clear the empty stands. We bank hard right through Christiana's top deck, buzzing the tops of buildings, and shoot out of the city into open air.

It's on.

The opening pace is fast, mostly to impress the majority of viewers whose airships are clustered around the first five-mile marker. I can see them gathered ahead, spread down either side of the lane. Ribbons stretch between green marker blimps. Even over the sound of the wind, I can hear shouts coming from open portal hatches and overflowing passenger baskets dangling from the underside of the airships.

Serio and I are in the back, keeping up with the cast easily enough. But that's not too difficult. The draft back here is so strong, Serio could almost *glide* and still keep up. A great place to conserve energy. But not to win glory. "It's all for the show," I reassure him with a pat on the neck.

Horns blare and kazoos sputter as the cast passes between the first few airships. Flags and confetti shower us from vessels above, and soon the corridor is a tunnel of hovering people-carriers, all jostling for a glimpse of our speeding mass. I bank Serio slowly to the left as we round the first turn, careening dangerously close to a D-Class that's opened the sides of its cargo hold, stuffed full of people. Despite our breakneck speed, I can still make out the wondering, wide-eyed stares of children, the men who've placed bets on their favorite flyers, and more than a few pretty faces who are hoping I'll notice them. Which I do. But not the way I would have before.

Today is about survival.

Because only Talihdym knows just how many plans Lucius has concocted to take me out. After all, once we're out of sight from the cities, who's to see what happens? It's the perfect opportunity to deal with whatever loose ends Lucius fears the most. And I know I'm top on his list. Mom is safe for now—the Chancellor will see to that.

The pace lessens as we pass out of the rows of airships, giving the birds a chance to catch their breath from the initial sprint. They'll need it going into the first set of loops.

Heading west toward The Moors, I see the next marker blimps, manned by operators who ensure the balloons stay in position. These *loop balloons* are aerial markers with special criteria. The blue ones we fly under, the red ones we go over, like a vertical zig-zag. Missing a blimp or failing to obey it is an instant disqual.

The cast starts to bunch as each pilot jockeys for position in the newly-forming line. But Serio and I sit tight in last place, waiting as the formation eventually thins out into side-by-side flying. The front of the line dips under the first blue blimp and then pulls up, climbing toward the red blimp some 500 feet above. By the time Serio and I pass under the blue blimp, the front of the line is arcing over the red one, on their way back down.

Serio starts pulling up against gravity, entering the first part of the maneuver. I look past my feet and see the lead felrell racing toward the next blue balloon. Serio's getting tense: he hates being in last place as much as I do. "Nice and steady, boy," I encourage him. "It's a long race."

We crest the first red balloon and I float in the saddle as the blood rushes to my legs. Serio pitches over and down, following the line toward the blue marker to complete the first under-over maneuver. I get pushed back into my saddle.

We finish four more under-overs and resume level flight, headed across the sky for The Moors. The line spreads out to single file with slight gaps between some of the flyers. It's as good a time as any to advance a few positions. I nudge Serio with my heels. He's eager. A little too eager. We surge around three birds before I pull in on the reins, advancing two more positions before settling sixth from the rear.

"That's enough, Serio," I say.

He chirps twice.

"Don't get testy with me. One step at a time."

More airships hover around The Moors like fat pigeons trying to stay aloft. Piled full of spectators, each craft lumbers slowly in the wind, pilots attempting to keep their ships stationary for a good view of our arrival. Already, air horns are blatting, and even a few fireworks get set off—usually fanfare reserved for the finish line. Apparently, a few fans are a little too excited.

We follow the course rules and circle The Moors three times, each to the cheers of the city's inhabitants. They're lining the perimeter of the outer decks, crammed up to the rails.

From here we head to Fairvale, pointed due south. We fly straight and level for about twenty minutes before the next obstacle comes into view: a series of ever-widening vertical loops. Set up much like the under-overs, these loops have more markers with blue ones indicating the bottom half of a loop and red indicating the top.

I wave to the pilot in the first balloon as we duck under his marker and begin our descent under the loop's belly. The birds in front of us jostle for position as they prepare for the long climb up the outside. The line lifts in front of me and suddenly everyone's climbing toward the suns, wings beating black against the stark contrast of the brilliant sky bowl. I squint from behind my goggles.

Higher and higher Serio climbs, slowly arching over onto his back until I'm dangling from the tops of my feet. Blood rushes to my head. I raise my chin and see the leaders already leveling out at the bottom of the loop, heading to the start of the next one. Serio stops beating his wings, gliding the rest of the way over the red balloons until we're racing toward the cloud-floor, my gut pressed against my spine.

Something catches my eye below. Abnormal. A bird bumps out of formation. Pushed out? The felrell tries to correct. But the speed is too great. I blink once; the bird slams into the side of the last red marker. The balloon jerks down and away from the impact. The felrell and his rider cartwheel off course. At least five flyers swerve to avoid the out-of-control bird and wayward blimp.

The injured felrell is still spinning wildly, pilot strapped in. With any luck, his bird will right, but he doesn't have much time. The cloud-floor's coming up quick. And while I'd love to help, there's simply nothing to be done. A rescue attempt in such a situation is out of the question.

That's when I notice the blimp pilot. Not sure if his harness broke or if he opted not to wear one. Either way, he's free-falling, fast.

"Let's get him," I say to Serio. "Forget the race." Doesn't matter if I finish, right? That audience with the Chancellor is mine, no matter what. So this is an easy call.

Serio screeches, then fails to pull up with the rest of the cast at the bottom of the loop. He's focused on the flailing man, now his *prey*. About 1,000 feet above the cloud-floor. After three powerful digs of air, Serio folds his wings and we dive. The hunt is on. The acceleration pushes me back in my saddle, and the air roars in my ears.

The pilot is coming up fast, having halved the distance to the floor. I hear him screaming. Must be terrifying. I don't have to tell Serio what to do next. It's instinct. The man disappears under Serio's head just as Serio flares his wings and tightens his lower body, talons spread wide. I feel the sudden jerk of more weight and pull in the reins. We're still clipping along pretty good, and Serio's slow in pulling up. The cloud-floor is closing...200 feet...100 feet...50 feet. I can smell the nelurime.

Serio blasts a path through the clouds, leaving a long vapor trail behind us. The sky turns a foggy yellow. Dimming. I hold my breath, reticent to inhale the stuff. Serio pumps his wings as I continue to ask him to climb.

Climb! Climb!

The yellow won't let go. I'm gritting my teeth, grunting. Then, finally, blue sky returns. We're coming out of it.

"He-yoh!" I praise Serio.

Our passenger below is still shrieking. Probably has no idea what's going on, poor guy. I lean over the side of my saddle and try to get a glimpse. "Hey! Hey, down there! You OK?" The man stops yelling and looks around, realizing for the first time that he's no longer falling. "I said, *you OK?*"

He looks up in my face with a mix of terror, confusion and sheer relief. All he can do is nod. I suppose he might be more terrified to know that Serio could have very easily gouged him by accident. Honestly, I'm just happy his yelling is from fear and not from being impaled. Felrell are tamable, but they certainly aren't safe.

As we climb back to altitude, I realize we're alone; the other pilot and his bird never pulled up. The speed of the loss makes my gut tighten. I look up and see the long brown line of felrell heading toward Fairvale, about to begin their first circumference of the city.

"Looks like we missed that obstacle," I say to Serio. "We're disqual." I lean over my saddle and yell down to our passenger. "What d'ya say, man? Want a lift back to Fairvale?"

The pilot nods.

"Coming right up," I say, and point Serio toward the city.

By the time we get there, the cast has moved on, heading East toward Dunmorrow, then to Bellride, and from there, Knightsbridge. The crowd gathered on the upper decks backs away as Serio flares, hovering in a gap between buildings. He releases the man, who spills onto the the wooden deck, pats himself down, and looks up with an elated expression on his face. Serio alights on the ledge—another reason for disqual, but what's the use now?.

The spectators cheer so loudly I only know what the pilot's saying by reading his lips. I try and reply to his thanks, but realize a gesture is probably the best. I give a quick salute and lean Serio off the edge. We tip over the side, aiming straight down. Then

Serio opens his wings and soars back up toward the top deck.

Then reality hits me: whatever illusions I had of winning the Champions Race as a First Year apprentice are now gone forever.

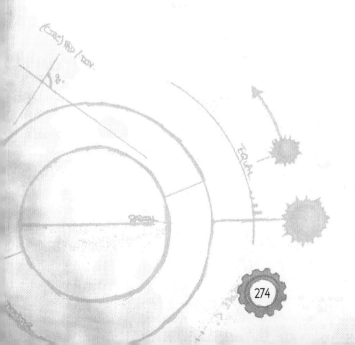

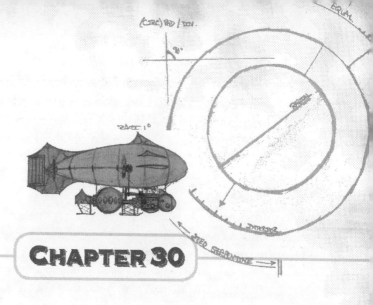

CHAPTER 30

I'D FAILED TO complete the first loop coming into Fairvale. Which means Serio and I are disqualified. Sure, we'd just saved a guy's life. And I'm not minimizing that. But the fact is, the Champions Race is over for us. For me.

"What do you want to do, pal?" I ask Serio.

He screeches.

"You sure?"

Another screech. As if he knows exactly what I'm asking. And I know exactly what he wants to do.

"Suits me just fine," I reply. Just because we can't win it doesn't mean we can't fly it. And I know that if Dad were here right now, it's exactly what he'd want me to do.

"Fly on, my friend," I command. "Fly on!"

It's taken us the better part of half an hour to complete the sections we missed and get back on track, though still well behind the cast. Doing this right meant going back and completing the missed loops, circling Fairvale, and maneuvering through all the other obstacles by ourselves. We circled Dunmorrow, then Bellride, and now we're coming up on Knightsbridge for three passes around the city. Which leaves only one section before returning to Christiana.

The Shoals.

I can hear Liv scolding me. Telling me not to do this, that I already have the meeting with the Chancellor secured. Shoot, I even hear my own voice telling me not to do this. That the flyer who died back in Fairvale could've been me, especially if Lucius was plotting something there. Which I'm certain he was. And still is. And if I were him, I'd do it in the Shoals. I can't get his smile out of my head.

There's quite a large gathering in and around Knightsbridge. It seems all the airships from the previous few cities have moved over here to see the racers off on the long northern leg. And one vessel stands out in particular: the Chancellor's, designated with the burgundy flags of his office.

As I approach the city, preparing for my three passes around, I notice a flagman in a marker blimp waving the signal for caution. But the weather's fine, and I don't see any indications of another accident. The rest of the cast is far ahead. Then the flagman points toward the Chancellor's balloon. I see the entry door to starboard cranking open. Inside are a number of attendants cautiously assisting the Chancellor to the opening. He's motioning to me.

Serio slows, soars around the airship once, and then eases into a lumbering hover. Fellrell aren't the best at flying stationary by nature, but they *are* trained to ease the nelurime nets into the nel-vats.

"Hello, my dear boy!" the Chancellor calls out.

Suddenly Mom appears next to him. "Hi, Junar!" she yells.

"Hi, Mom! Good to see you, Chancellor."

"Listen," he says, "the judges saw what you did back there, boy. It's been recommended to me that I pardon you."

"Pardon me?" I ask. "Are you serious?"

"Quite so. You saved a man's life. I think that deserves some grace. So, how about it?"

"Hear that, Serio?" I'm shocked. Truly. I look to Mom, and then the Chancellor. "Thank you, your Eminence!"

"I'll see you later, then," he says with a wide smile. "Race on, my dear boy!"

We're heading due north at speeds I know Serio is straining to keep. But if the Aces are flying fast, we must fly faster. I won't lose my bird over this, as the Chancellor and I already have a secure appointment. But now that winning the Champions Race is a very real possibility, even if a remote one, I can only imagine what the added authority might bring me, should I need to leverage the people against the warring factions of Aria-Prime. Not only do I want to win, but I might very well *need* to win.

Far against the horizon, I see a speckled mass blurring where the clouds and sky meet. It's the rest of the cast, maybe an hour ahead of us. No doubt Serio's been watching them long before I noticed. Just one more reason he's keeping this pace.

The long straightaway gives me a lot of time to think about what might happen next. About what might come of my next meeting with the Chancellor. Where we'll meet, who'll be in on it. Probably in the House of Lords. The Chancellor will be surprised, no doubt, by what I know of Banth and of the Inventors. But surely Lucius' involvement won't come as any surprise. The creep.

I'll want Liv there. And Mom and Lance. Don't know what I'd do without them. And to be honest, I can't believe how much they've put up with me. Mom especially. I want to go back and undo the things I said to her over the years. The ways I treated her. Of course, I know I can't. But it feels so good to be clear with her again, like it used to be when I was little. As far as I'm concerned, I have the rest of my life to write a new story with her. And winning this race for her and Dad is a pretty good start. Though right now, winning feels like it's very far away.

I can feel *cloud gaze* setting in: the long impassive stares a pilot gets during extended hours aloft. You run out of things to think about, and the monotony of the endless cloud-floor dulls your perception. I've heard about more than one good pilot driving his bird into the floor, unable to stay up due to pure exhaustion. And the worst part is, the pilot never even knew what he was doing. Or so they say.

I slap myself in the face. Hard. Then again. Almost dozed off. "How you doing, Serio?" I say, slapping the side of his neck.

He bobs his head.

I shove the reins under my thigh and pull my goggles down to rub my eyes. Blinking. They water. Plenty of cream still on the exposed skin of my face too. With this many hours aloft under the twin suns, a pilot can't be too sure of his skin protection. I replace the eyewear. As my tears dry, I look to the horizon again, and this time it's not hard to see the cast, nor the massive rock formation growing out of the cloud-floor, nor the storm that's permanently set around it.

This is my first glimpse of the Shoals, the monstrous gauntlet guarding the passage into the Northern Range. At first, the rocks appear out of the horizon like knife blades protruding from a sheep hide. But with every beat of Serio's wings, the scene grows more massive; the spires take on bodies wracked with cliffs and chasms and gaping holes. Lightning flashes illuminate long arms of rock that jut up at odd angles, eventually disappearing into the storm, swallowed by the raging tumult of grey and black clouds. The natural architecture stands as a veritable fortress, a foreboding guardian three times the height of our floating cities. Whose victor is rewarded with the valuable storehouses of timber beyond. No going over this one. Only through.

The whole scene sends a shiver down my spine. Seems otherworldly, like it doesn't belong on Aria-Prime. For some reason, all I can think about is Banth. He seems otherworldly. Like maybe he'd retire here in the Shoals, and all these spires would keep his myriad of dark secrets company.

Serio blurts something out and I do my best to interpret, eyes scanning up ahead. That's when I notice the cast is gone. Vanished.

"Where'd they go, boy?" I ask.

Serio cries out again. My eyes more keen now. Then I see it: a green marker balloon tucked just inside the cleft of the tall spire to the west. I would have missed it entirely had not a flash of lightning kissed the sliver of fabric poking out. The full balloon comes into view as Serio adjusts our course. But to my astonishment, the marker is far smaller than I imagined it would be against the looming rock finger, like a speck of ink on a piece of papyrus. It's also the only balloon I've seen that's tethered to the rock, its line stretched taut against the churning air.

A shiver goes down my spine as a gust of wind reminds me the air's about to get dirty. "Dad must have flown through here," I say, more for my own ears than Serio's. The thought of it makes me sad. That in one of my world's loneliest places, my father had flown this route amongst men he believed were his confidants—only to discover they would be his greatest betrayers. I wish I'd been able to fly with him. To keep him company. To defend him against their fateful subterfuge.

With the balloon marking our first hard right bank into a collection of rock fingers, each at least as high as any of our anchor mountains, Serio breaks the gait he's been holding for the last several hours and accelerates into a wide turn. The pilot seems to startle awake as he fumbles for the right flag. Green. *Continue forward.* Then red. *Danger ahead.*

Serio bleats, then beats the air with his wings, gaining speed. We pass under the marker balloon and stare down a corridor composed of dozens of tendrils of red granite arching skyward. Doesn't seem so bad. Definitely the coolest place I've ever flown in. The light dims as we pass under the first arch. The turbulent air carries the scent of moist stone.

A torrent of wind slams against the side of my head, helmet smacking against my ear. Something else strikes the right side of my body. Motes swirl in my eyes. Serio does a barrel roll, and suddenly the corridor is spiraling faster than I can track. If not for my safety line, I'd be free-falling. Serio's on his own, trying to right himself, as I've lost the reins.

Finally coming level against the horizon, or at least against gravity, I recover the lines and touch the side of my head. Serio has all but slowed, jostling against the wind. My gloved hand brushes against something lodged against my head. A feather. From Serio. The gust must have been so strong it flipped Serio's wing up into my body. Could have snapped my neck. I thank Talihdym for whatever mercy He's just extended, and and take a deep breath.

"Easy does it," I say to Serio. "Let's try this again. And watch the crosswind." I prod him with my heels.

He screeches, then dips his head and presses back down the corridor.

I soon discover that every gap between fingers brings with it a new stream of wind, channeled through the layers—much like a water flow careens around rocks on an anchor mountain and then plummets off the side toward the cloud-floor. Serio's halved his speed to account for the violent shifts, and before long he's developed a steady rhythm of slowing in the gaps and accelerating in the shadows.

It's certainly not the kind of time either of us would like to be making, but I'd also like to avoid being plastered against some barren wall in this God-forsaken place. How the Timber Pilots actually make it through here while hauling shipments is a miracle, and makes me appreciate them all the more. Well, one in particular.

Whatever distance Serio managed to close during the trip north is lost now. The large majority of pilots know this route like the backs of their hands.

Serio screeches again.

"Let's just do our best, friend. There's still a long way to go."

Our path takes us through a rolling labyrinth of natural tunnels, caves dotted with massive columns, and chutes that bring us dangerously close to the cloud-floor. We pass in and out of the stormy light, all the while buffeted by gusts strong enough to impede Serio's motion entirely, forcing us back to search for a different route.

There are no marker balloons in here. Any attempt to place one would be an exercise in futility. Which means there's no governance. And that makes it the perfect place for Lucius to—

The air shakes above my head, but not from the wind. Something far more violent. I instinctively raise my arms over my head, reins still in hand. A quick glance up reveals a shower of stone plummeting from a dust cloud about 500 feet above. And the whole ceiling starts to move.

A second explosion occurs somewhere ahead, followed by a third. Serio veers hard to port, missing a falling boulder the size of my house. Small pebbles pelt my helmet and leather jacket, and I can smell an acrid odor in the air. That's when more thunderous cracks start echoing through the sunlit chamber we're in. And I notice the walls. Shifting.

Collapsing.

Serio darts forward to avoid a cluster of falling rock, his head swiveling, spying for an escape. The tunnel ahead is closing too quickly for us to pass through. Suddenly my mind is back in the clouds outside Christiana, my first chance to impress my new Headmaster. And Liv. Everything's closing in, getting smaller and smaller, faster than Serio can fly. Faster than I can think.

Something grazes my helmet and then strikes my left shoulder. Hard. I yell, but can't hear my own voice over the cacophony around me. My chest heaves. It feels as if my entire left arm has just broken off. Breathless, I glance down. The arm is still there, but a large tear in my sleeve is ringed with red, and my whole left side is throbbing.

There's a new surge in Serio's movement. As I've unconsciously let go of the reins, Serio is making the next decision for both of us. He's mounting up toward the first blast. I'm sure he's been hit in the head. This is crazy! We're dodging massive chunks of rock, Serio even using his talons to propel himself off them, climbing the debris in the air. Then I see something flutter through a gap in the ever-widening expanse of stormy sky.

Wings.

I blink against the shooting pain in my chest as Serio climbs out from within the destruction. More wings. Birds. And pilots.

As my gut suspects, this is no accident. And whoever set off these explosions is sticking around to make sure the job is done. Which, to my surprise, and probably theirs—if they could see us—

it isn't.

Serio surges past a mammoth section of spire as it pitches from its perch and plunges into the cloud-floor. The only thing to accompany us into the open sky is a towering plume of smoke and dust, now enveloping our escape and shielding us from the three felrell I see circling up ahead. Hidden in the cover, I realize we've just been given a precious few moments to regroup. To think.

But the pain is too distracting. That, and I'm getting lightheaded. I look down to see my left hand drenched in blood. "They're going to kill us, Serio." Saying it out loud makes it feel even more real. They're Timber Pilots, no doubt, and completely under Lucius' control. Explosives aren't their only weapons either, I bet. Gotta have crossbows. Which is more than we have. And we're still pinned within a massive bowl in the Shoals whose ridge lines are shrouded in thundering clouds. At least we're still alive. For the moment. We could have been crushed somewhere below.

Below.

Where the corridor continues on through the rest of the course, there's a new gap, this one much smaller than the original. But a gap nonetheless.

"Only one way out of this one," I say to my steadfast bird, pointing to the hole. "Listen, I know you're tired. But I need everything from you. Everything to get us out of here and catch back up with the cast. We can't outshoot them, but we can outfly them. And there's safety among those in the cast who are still loyal to the Chancellor."

I take a deep breath and steal myself from the excruciating pain. Our dust cover is dissipating and the three pilots are tightening their circle, closing in for the kill.

"You up for this? One last push?" To his credit, Serio lets out a shrieking cry that makes the hair on the back of my neck stand up. "My sentiments exactly."

I flick the reins with my good hand and strike Serio with my heels, giving him a loud *he-yoh!* The result is the exhilarating rush of pure acceleration as he darts from cover and dives straight for the small space amongst the rubble.

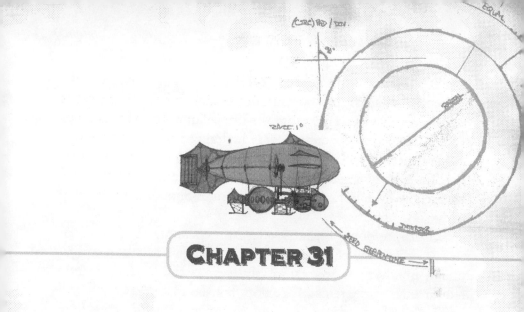

CHAPTER 31

THE WIND IS darting in the crevices of my helmet, pushing my goggles against my eye sockets. I release the reins entirely, holding onto the saddle with my right hand. Left arm is done. I glance over my shoulder to see the three pilots in hot pursuit, obviously having noticed our sudden departure from the fog of their ruthless ambush.

Serio screeches again and I look forward just as a crossbow bolt flies past my head. The fletchings of a second are so close I swear they've brushed my cheek. I lean forward to make myself less of a target, but the strain on my frame grates my shoulder until the pain makes me vomit against Serio's neck. The wind carries away whatever spittle remains, and I look up to see we're less than 300 feet from the entrance to the corridor. I hold my breath as Serio folds his wings and we surge into darkness.

Fortunately, Serio's eyes adjust faster than mine, as I'm flying blind. I blink a few times and see we've entered a narrow chute that curves around to starboard. And there's light up ahead.

I keep low and look behind us. To my surprise, the first of

the three pilots doesn't make it through the small gap. At least, not successfully. His bird is a little too high, and the pilot smacks his head against the upper ledge. The force flips him off backward, but he's caught by his safety line. He's dragged the rest of the way through the gap and into the chute, his corpse dangling from his bird. The next two pilots enter with far less issue, skirting their ill-fated fellow flyer, but I lose sight of them as Serio makes the slow turn to our right.

"You're doing great." I offer him encouragement, but the words catch in my chest as the pressure it takes to talk seems to inflame my shoulder even more. My eyes search for another tactic to outmaneuver the remaining pilots, but the space between spires causes a flicker effect with the light, making it difficult to see. I try my best to catch a glimpse of what's outside this corridor. Perhaps open air, or an alternate passage. But the next section of solid rock walls is upon us before I can see much of anything, and this time we're banking to port.

I force another backwards glance and see the two pilots closing the distance. I assume their birds are refreshed, having made the crossing north at a reasonable pace with the of the cast. One of the pilots emphasizes just how close he really is by sending another bolt over the top of Serio's right wing.

I look forward, studying the way ahead, only to find the tunnel terminates in a rock wall. Dead end? But it can't be! A lightning bolt flashes somewhere above. Light. Coming down a chute. Probably a steep ascent.

"Get ready for a climb," I say to Serio, pushing myself back in the saddle. I know he feels me adjusting.

We race out of the chute, my eyes assessing the rise in front of us. But neither Serio or I make the right judgement, and I realize it too late. The passage skyward is nearly *vertical.*

Serio flares, instantly bleeding off speed. I manage to save myself from tumbling backward by clinging to his neck. But we're still not going to make the steep pitch—at least, not gracefully. The far wall comes up quick, and Serio extends his talons, absorbing the impact with his legs. I'm jarred, and my shoulder explodes in another round of pain. My right hand grabs a handful of feathers as Serio beats his wings, fighting his way up the wall.

I hear myself grunting, trying to suppress the torturous throbbing in my arm. Even Serio is making some sort of beastly noise in his efforts.

With a sudden leap skyward, Serio thrusts himself off the rock and we're flying again. He's extending as much wing as he can, shoving air beneath us and climbing hard.

"Go! Go!" I yell, trying my best to encourage him. The chute leads straight up, grey sky ahead. "Just a little further!"

I hold tightly to the saddle horn and look below. My heart sinks. The two pilots have made the transition with ease. But of course they would; they've flown this passage before. I feel like a fool for thinking either of them might be caught off guard as we were. Even if we make it to the top, my bird and I will both be driven through with crossbow bolts.

Serio is pumping his wings with everything he's got, still not even halfway up this chute. I wish I could help lighten the load.

Lighten the load.

Junar, you're crazy.

But the thought won't let me go. And I'll miss the opportunity if I hesitate longer than I'm doing. Or reason myself out of it. Because it's truly crazy.

In one swift motion, I unclip my safety line and push my hips away from my saddle, still holding on with my good arm. I look between my legs, straight down, guessing the distance and angle to the first pilot, who's directly below me. My heart is racing. I really can't believe this is about to happen. "Fly or die," I tell Serio. Then I let gravity strip me away.

The sudden change of direction not only jars my stomach, but also my shoulder. Yet the pain keeps me sharp. I'm wide awake, falling in slow motion. Aware of every bit of stone knocked from the chute walls by Serio's wings. Aware of the smell that a recent rain shower has left on the rock walls. Aware of the feathers rippling on the bird rising to meet me…who's surprised as I am by my sudden drop, ducking his head so I have a clear shot at his pilot.

My legs slam into the rider, driving him out of his saddle. I hear his crossbow clatter away. Bad arm feels as though it's been ripped clean off my body, the good arm hooked around the saddle horn at the elbow. But momentum is too high, and my right arm breaks free with a jolt. More pain. My body tumbles from the bird's back and collides with the pilot in midair, who's still tethered by his safety line. I hear him yelp as my body gets wedged lengthwise between the line and his chest, our torsos facing one another. He cradles me for a moment before the fisticuffs begin, his gloved hands pummeling any target he can manage. But in such cramped quarters, the blows are far from debilitating. Right now I can't believe I'm still alive.

One of his punches connects with my bad shoulder. Flecks of light shoot across my vision. Then everything dims.

No, no, no! Not now!

I grunt, push aside the pain, and will myself back to consciousness.

Come on, Junar!

Knife. On my belt. Sheathed.

I don't know how this is going to work with one good hand, but I'm fumbling for the tool. More blows land. At least a few elbows to my ribcage.

I order my left hand to grab the handle. Just the effort to make a fist brings tears to my eyes. I pull the blade free. That's when the pilot starts spewing curses at me. Thinks I'm going to stab him? The punches cease and he starts pulling on my bad arm.

I hear myself scream. A deep scream. So deep it triggers a response I can't control. My left hand—the knife still held tightly in it—swings past my face and hits the line. And that's all it takes. My right hand is fixed to the safety cord as the pilot falls away.

But not before he grabs onto my boot.

His weight's too great. My right hand slips. Down the line, dangerously close to the severed end. I attempt to throw my left arm up for added strength, but it's immobile. That last action with the knife did it in. Can hardly feel it.

The pilot's climbing my legs. Right hand's on fire. I try kicking, but the man has my ankles pinned together, and his weight's too much for me. His fingers wrap around my belt. I try wiggling, but my hand's reached the end of the rope.

Something dark moves down and to my left. Then screeches. Serio!

His massive form passes just below me as his beak opens to envelope the pilot's legs. The pilot yells, his weight suddenly free of my body. But my hand is done, and my fingers slip off the line.

A short fall. And I'm on Serio's neck. I can't believe it! I manage to thank my bird—barely—as another crossbow bolt passes wildly over my head. I move down into my saddle as Serio completes the loop he's on and comes around, now flying down the chute at the remaining pilot. With talons extended, Serio spreads his wings, flaring in the path of the enemy.

Everything is still for a moment. Serio and I are floating down the passage, suspended in a flash of lightning. Drops have begun to fall, suspended for a split second beside me. I wonder if the other pilot has diverted his path in the shadow of Serio's display. But I know impact is imminent.

Crack!

The hard blow ripples through Serio and rattles my head. My frame crumples as my chin strikes the vertebrae in his neck. More flecks of light. The taste of iron in my mouth.

And we're falling. Tumbling through the air. Both birds clasped in a death roll, their talons intertwined, beaks open. My right arm is lodged around my saddle horn. The rock wall is spinning, as are the dark clouds above.

I catch a glimpse of the basin floor, a curving elbow that slides into the darkness of the corridor we've come from. I'm dizzy. Seconds away from impact. And I'll be on one side of this pile or the other.

Talihdym, please be with Mom.

At the last moment, I'm thrown from my saddle, airborne. The birds spin beneath me.

I shut my eyes.

Ku-thud!

The impact slaps my teeth together. Ears ringing. It feels as if every organ in my body has been displaced. I'm aloft for another second, bounce off a bird's body, and then skitter across the smooth basin floor into the dim light of the tunnel. Rain's splatting the rock floor just a few feet away. A sharp pain in my head. Heat. I'm suddenly tired. Like all I want to do is close my eyes and take a long nap. Sleep would feel so good right now.

"Come over here so I can kill you," says a gravelly voice.

I blink a dozen times, trying to shake off the adamant pull to darkness. Raising my head produces more swirling motes in my vision. I hear slow footsteps. Dragging.

"I swear, if it's the last thing I do..." the man's voice says again. And I recognize it.

I'm able to prop myself up on my good elbow. The other pilot is limping toward me; I've seen him before. I blink. A thick trail of blood follows him, coming from a severely mangled leg. There's also a pretty good gash in his head. We seem a picturesque pair. Though the one thing he has that really seems to matter is a crossbow. Pointed straight at me, his hands shaking.

I see Serio in the background, a mass of wings and feathers. Little movement. An ache swells deep in my chest. Then the pilot steps in my way.

I stare along his weapon and look him in the eyes. "Daren," I say, spitting blood. "Why am I not surprised..."

In the same moment, we both realize there's no bolt in his crossbow. Probably knocked free in the impact. Daren swears, but I can see by the look in his eyes as he steps toward me that he's just as content to beat me to death.

I glance behind me and start backing away, hip dragging on the rock. I'd like to stand, but my head still isn't right. I look back at Daren just as he falls forward. Yelling something unintelligible. Somehow I'm hoping his crossbow has spun free. But it hasn't. In fact, he takes a moment to roll over and withdraw another bolt from his thigh pouch.

Now I'm starting to panic, which I find humorous: of all moments to be panicking, my brain chooses this one?

I feel a surge of heightened awareness, the need for sleep diminishing. I'm able to sit up, but not stand. Daren has his bowstring nearly cocked. I start looking around for something. Anything. A rock. A handful of dirt.

A crossbow.

The one from the pilot I cut loose. Just to my right! I crawl across the floor, eyes fixed on the weapon.

"Leaving so soon?" Daren cries from the ground. He can see his partner's corpse as easily as I can. "Found a friend? You can't hide, you little runt. I'm going to skewer you just like your father tried to skewer me." He coughs. Then I hear the click of his bowstring. "Hold still!"

Great Talihdym, he's *aiming!*

I'm almost to the body. Maybe I'll use it to hide behind, after all. The weapon is a few feet beyond it anyway.

Thwap!

The bowstring snaps taught, followed by a quick glance off the stone, and then a sharp pain that explodes from my calf. I'm screaming something aloud. I know I am. I can't hear myself, but I can see Daren smiling. He's still laying on his side, reaching for another bolt already.

"Skewered like a sheep," he mumbles to himself.

When I can breathe, I look toward the spare crossbow again.

Crawl, Junar! Crawl!

I pull myself forward again, but the bolt protruding from my leg binds me to the rock floor. I dry heave from the agony it produces.

Talihdym, help me! Please!

Where is He? Isn't He supposed to help those in need? Well, I'm in need!

"Might as well roast you for dinner tonight, too," Daren says. But I don't care. I'm going to end this, one way or another. I'm using my good arm and my good leg, alternating them to push myself forward. Closer.

Daren's bowstring clicks into place again.

Talihdym!

But He's not there to help me. He hasn't been this whole time. Or else none of this would've happened. Mom's affair, Dad's death, my demise. If He really cared, He'd help me now.

No, I'm going to have to do this myself. And I will. One hand and foot at a time.

All.

By.

Myself.

"Where do you think you're going?" comes the pilot's strained voice.

My right hand grabs the handle. The weapon is cocked, but the bolt is still a few feet away. No sense calling on Him now. I clamp the handle between my teeth, then stretch out for the bolt.

"Come out, come out, wherever you are," Daren says. I can hear him struggling to his feet. I'll have no cover once he's standing. "Where are you, little sheep? You know, killing you is going to be even more fun than killing your Daddy. Because I get to see your body after you're dead."

My fingers straining, blindly grasping. Stupid bolt.

I have it.

Crossbow under my chin, fingers loading. Snapped in place. Right hand on the handle.

"I see you," says Daren.

"I see you too," I say, rolling onto my back and pulling the wooden trigger.

Daren looks at me in surprise, then down at the fletchings protruding from the center of his chest.

"Never understood why everyone else had burn marks, but you had a chest puncture," I say. "Finishing what Daddy started. No more flying for you, just dying."

His mouth hangs open, hands limp. The weapon clatters to the floor. In one motion, his head sags forward, knees buckle, and his mass collides with the ground.

Then silence.

I watch his body for a second. To make sure he's really dead. And then I realize I killed him. *I've killed a person.* My eyes catch the man beside me. *Two people. I've killed two people.* I want to vomit, but there's no use. Nothing's there. I'm dizzy again, but I don't think it's from pain or shock or blood loss. It's from reality. Of what I've done.

A squawk. In the light.

The pile of birds.

"Serio!" I yell, surprised by the amount of effort it takes. "Serio," I say again, hoping the bird that's moving is him. "I'm coming. I'm coming." I notice that I've already let go of the crossbow. I'm using the same awkward motion as before to inch my way back into the rain.

I see rustling, but I still can't tell which bird it is. Wings, feathers, talons. Closer, I see a large pool of blood soaking the ground, feathers stuck in the congealing mire.

"Serio!" I cry, suddenly hoarse. "Serio, it's OK. I'm right here."

More struggling. Serio's attempting to get up. My heart is nearly bursting! He pushes up from the pile, stretching his wings, and gives a loud screech. He's whole!

"Serio!" I yell.

His head cocks sideways. And he fails to recognize me.

Teeth clenched, I can only think of one thing to say. "Curse you, Talihdym."

CHAPTER 32

I'M GOING TO kill this bird if I drive it any harder. Not knowing its name makes it easier, though. That, and I just don't care. All that matters is getting back to Christiana. So I can kill Lucius.

My left arm is caked in my own blood, the rest of me in Serio's, all of it now dried in the wind. And as I ride this nameless bird southbound through the clouds, I can't help but replay my actions over and over again in my mind. Had I not been so stupid in leaping from Serio's back, none of this would have happened. I'm a fool. A careless, reckless fool.

Dad would be so mad at me. And I can't help but feel that I let him down. That I've misused the wonderful gift he purchased for me. That I've broken my word to him. My eyes had been so big, he said, when I first saw Serio. Sitting there in the hangar with his head cockeyed, staring at me.

"He's all yours," Dad said. "Take good care of him and he'll take good care of you."

"I will, Dad!" I replied. "Oh, I will!"

I'm not sure who I hugged more that day, Dad or Serio. But

Dad had made my dream come true. I'd never forget it.

And now? Now I left my best friend, a mass of broken bones and feathers, soaking in his own blood on a rock floor in the most barren place on Aria-Prime.

"I'm sorry, Dad," I whisper to the wind, my tears collecting in the bottoms of my goggles. "I'm so sorry." We were going to win it. The Champions Race. Me and Serio. And Dad.

As the specks transform from smudges on the horizon into a cast of felrell, I feel my heart quicken. I drive the poor felrell so hard I can hear him wheezing like one of Haupstie's steam engines. Any time the bird tries to slow, I answer with a sharp jab to his sides. The truth is, we both might die before we reach Christiana. I can tell my blood loss has made me incredibly tired. My calf is throbbing, my shoulder is all but divorced from my body, and my heart...well, my heart is beyond repair. But I knew that already. No use crying out to Talihdym. He's not listening. But I suppose, deep down, I already knew that too.

I reach inside my jacket and withdraw the small packet of food that Mom gave me. I'm not hungry. But I need all the strength I can get. For what's to come. Though, I'm not entirely sure what my plan is once I return. I'd love to march up and stab the traitor in his throat. The boldness of the thought surprises me. But I'm not thinking the clearest. At this point, I doubt I could walk more than a few feet. No, I'd need to see a doctor. That much, I'm sure they'll make me do. Then I'll be seen by the Chancellor. And then I'll need to think on my feet, because Lucius won't be far behind. To finish the job he started. The one his men failed to do. No, the one *he* failed to do.

Up ahead, I see some of the pilots looking back. Hear some shouting. Then more of them look back. Suddenly the cast parts as I approach, making room for me. I must be a sorry sight.

"Hey'o there, Junar," calls out one pilot. "What—what's happened to you?"

I try and measure the tone of his voice: genuine surprise,

or mockery? Of course, this pilot could know of the plot, and he's genuinely surprised I made it out of the ambush. But he doesn't seem to be looking for any of the other three pilots, and his voice sounds earnest.

"The Shoals tore me up pretty good," I say. "But we made it through." I pat the ailing bird on his neck; the pilot doesn't even notice it's not Serio. But why would he? I'm surprised he even knows my name. Had Dad not been so well-revered in the Guild, I doubt he would.

"You need to see a doctor," says another pilot to port.

"What gave you that impression?" I say with a sneer. Does he think I haven't accounted for the obvious?

The man seems put off, however, and I almost feel bad.

A few more flyers check in on me, and that's when I realize that the pilots staying furthest away are the quiet ones. At first I thought maybe they didn't see me, but then I catch a glimpse of a man I recognize. A Timber Pilot. He's about four bird-lengths ahead of me. Glances back. Sure, he's got goggles and a helmet on. But that doesn't mean I can't read his face. It's flat, unmoved. Not disdain, not shock, not annoyance. Just flat.

I look to starboard, three birds across, and see another pilot eye me down. This one gives a subtle nod, as if recognizing my presence as…as I don't know what. As having bested three of his partners? As him telling me he's going to kill me himself? It's surprising how many men Lucius has been able to employ in his attempt to cover up murder…to cover up a Guild conspiracy. Are they really so loyal? Or are they just as power-hungry as he is?

Christiana is growing on the horizon, and I can't be happier to see her. I'm cold. In fact, much colder than I noticed before. Yet, I can feel my helmet soaked in sweat. Still can't feel my left hand, and my calf is aching so badly I'd do anything to remove it from my body. That, and I'm hungry. *Ravenous* is a better word.

"Almost home, boys," shouts one pilot from up ahead. "Best of luck."

Those words somehow take everyone from the methodical pace they'd probably been keeping since the Shoals to a sudden surge back into race gait. Like a bundle of wool that's spun out into a long piece of yarn, the formation of birds and pilots stretch out toward Christiana, accelerating toward the final cluster of marker balloons. And beyond them, it seems every airship on the planet has gathered for our arrival.

As expected, I find my place at the back of the pack. This bird isn't responding to my heel pricks any more. I have no remorse, either. Right now, I can only think of what I'm going to do to Lucius. And as far as I'm concerned, we can't get to Christiana fast enough.

We pass the first marker balloon since leaving the Shoals. The flagman waves us into a series of wide turns in the course. Nothing too strenuous. Hundreds of airships line the course, waving flags, blasting air horns, and screaming as we fly by. Normally, I suppose, I'd be stirred. I've dreamed of this moment my whole life. Never did I picture it going this way. I see more than a few faces turn from glee to horror as they watch me bring up the rear. I'm probably not the joyous sight they were hoping to see. Children point, women look away. To them, I must represent the darker side of what can happen on the Champions Race. If only they knew. So much evil lurking beneath the surface.

For my bird's sake, I'm glad there aren't any vertical loops. He'd never make them. Shoot, I'm not sure I'd make them. I realize now this last part of the course is merely for show. And maybe to give beat-up flyers, like me, an easy go of things. In all the years I came to watch this race, I never realized what these boys go through. Of course, my plight is an exception. Isn't it?

The cheering grows louder as we near the city, the afternoon suns warming the air. More marker balloons constrict our path toward the top deck and into Champions Stadium. Suddenly there's a disruption in the front of the pack. Birds are slowing down; the cast is separating. Within a few seconds, a hole opens ahead of me as the long piece of yarn bunches back up into a tuft of wool. The next thing I know, I'm surrounded by flyers.

"Go ahead, Junar," says one of the lead pilots. I must look as confused as I feel, because he repeats himself.

"I—I don't understand."

"We want you to take the lead," he says. But not everyone

shares his sentiment. Must be two dozen pilots looking away from me as I glance around. But the rest seem as earnest as this first pilot. "You deserve it."

"No, no." I wave him off.

"We insist," he adds, and then flares his bird, trailing behind me.

One moment I'm struggling to keep up, the next I'm out in front. The pandemonium in the air around me is, as Haupstie might say, *electric*. And it only grows as we file into Champions Stadium. I feel guilty, like I'm winning out of pity. It's not an authentic win. Not a *true* win. But I'm in such pain that I can't think of a way to fix it. Arguing is pointless, as I don't have the energy or the voice. And there's nowhere to fly to. My bird will be lucky enough to land on the grass in one piece.

The deafening roar around the field keeps me focused for the few remaining seconds it takes to fly through the finish line: a thin, silk tape suspended thirty feet above the field. The tape snaps against my bird's beak...something Serio should have enjoyed. The crowd is euphoric. Ironic that my brush with death would cause them so much ecstasy.

I give the command to flare. The bird knows he's done and lands in the open field. His talons no sooner touch the ground than his legs give out. His chest strikes the ground and I pitch forward, my gut impaled on the saddle's horn. It's not the first time, but it sends another wave of agony through my weakened body. I struggle for the release on my safety line, only I can't prop myself up. People are yelling, closer. I hear footsteps.

Feet.

Hands.

Someone's tugging on my jacket.

"Easy! Easy!" someone yells.

"Cut it, gently. *Gently!*" says another voice.

"Watch his head!"

I've lost control. My body is not my own, now carried in the hands of countless others. I can feel their hot breaths on my face, my body jostled between half a dozen men, carried off my bird and across the grass. All of it is set to the music of a constant roar, echoing throughout the cavernous hall, of which I'm its epicenter.

The cries of the people are suddenly much closer. I open my eyes. I see nothing but the torsos of the men carrying me. They start yelling, commanding people to make room. To step away.

Then I hear my name. Not spoken by anyone I know. But by those I don't. Hundreds of them. No, *thousands*. And said in rhythm, until it becomes a chant.

It's surreal. My name. Lauded by those I don't know, but they know me. Or at least they think they do. Oh, if they only knew the conspiracy playing out before them. And this, my chance! If only I could stand on my own two feet, if only I had the energy to say something, to silence them. To shout from the housetops everything I know. I feel more tears welling up, not from physical pain, but the pain of knowing I'm powerless to leverage the audience that is, right now, in the palm of my hand.

"Hold, hold!" says someone at my feet. Then a gap appears to my right.

"Junar!" I'd know that voice anywhere.

"Mom," I say, but my own ears can't hear it.

"Junar! Great Talihdym, you're alive! Thank you, God of the Skies!"

He didn't save me, I did. And he certainly didn't save Serio. He didn't save Dad. But I don't have the energy to argue with her. Nor is this the time. I see her face hovering over me, tears lining her face.

Another face appears to my left. "It seems the heavens have looked favorably upon you, my dear boy," says the Chancellor, straining to be heard above the throng. He cups my face with his hand. "I could not be happier. Well done."

"Thank you," I say, relieved to be looking up into his kind eyes. "I need to tell you—"

"Now, now," he chides, "there will be time. Trust me." Then, spoken close to my helmet-covered ear: "I know as well as you the Shoals could not have done what I see before me." He withdraws his head and smiles, sad, yet knowing.

"Thank you," I say again, so grateful to have an advocate like him in my corner. This will be solved as soon as I'm able to stand before my accuser. Justice will be measured out in full. I'll make sure of it myself.

I feel the strong hand of fatigue closing its fingers tightly around my body. I can't resist any more. The grip is simply too strong, and my heart is too tired. Until I have the strength to rise, there will be comfort in the dark.

So I let go.

And fall.

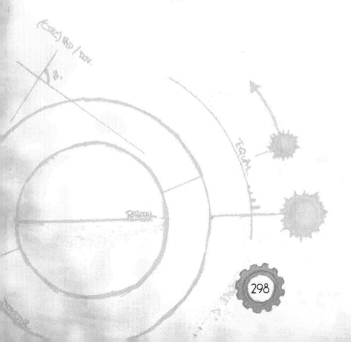

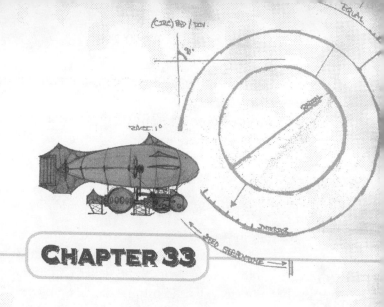

CHAPTER 33

THEY'VE TOLD ME it's been three days. I feel like I've lived this scene before. Brass pipes in the ceiling, a calming, whirring sound. The same room, the same nurses. Except, this time, I'm strapped to a bed. Couldn't move even if I wanted to. And now, after a dozen checks by the staff and a number of different medications, the same doctor is standing over me.

"We really must stop meeting like this," says Dr. Remkovich, staring at me through his spectacles. "But it seems you insist on getting into trouble. So the fault certainly isn't mine." He's just as spry and wiry as I remember from two months ago, adorned with tufts of hair on the sides of his head.

"Yeah, I'll try and curb the habit from now on," I muster, still surprised at the raspy sound of my voice. "They tell me it's bad for my health."

"Ha! I'll say!" he declares with a wave of his hands. "And it seems to me you've met more than the hard side of the Shoals, if you ask me." I just stare at him, not sure how much of my story to divulge. Dr. Remkovich shoos the nurses from my room and closes the door, then turns back to me. "So, someone was using you for target practice, I see."

"It was a branch. From…"

"Yes, from where exactly?"

"From…"

"My boy, I know a crossbow bolt injury when I see one."

I close my eyes, taking a deep breath. "Fair enough," I relent.

"Let me guess—" he pushes his spectacles back up his nose— "someone didn't want you getting that patch on your jacket, did they?" He points to my flight jacket hanging on a chair back; affixed to the sleeve is the unmistakable emblem of a Champions Race winner. Someone's already sewed it on. Probably Mom.

Trying to match his tone, I say, smiling, "*Strongly disapproved of it* might be more accurate."

"Ah, very well. Two sides of the same coin, I suppose."

"Hey, Doc, any chance I can get unstrapped here?" I look down at my body with my eyes.

"Ah, yes, yes. Very good," he says, fingering the thick leather straps along my body. "Just precautionary. Can't have you thrashing yourself to death now, can we?"

"Not my favorite way to die," I say as he finishes the task. Dr. Remkovich helps me sit up. It's a slow effort, filled with new waves of pain. But I'm happy to be awake, alert, and knowing my body is on the mend.

"I still can't feel my left hand," I say.

"Or probably your whole left arm, if I'm right."

I look down at the sleeve-length cast, trying to feel any sensations along the arm. That's when I realize something even more disturbing. "Doctor, I—I can't…"

"Move it. As I suspected."

"Suspected?"

"I'm afraid the break in your shoulder has produced some nasty side effects," he says.

"Like what?"

"Like paralysis." He pauses. "I'm sorry, my boy. I don't think you'll ever move that arm again."

"Wait, wait," I say, "I don't think I understood you." He stares at me in silence. "Once the cast comes off..." I try speculating, waiting for him to finish my sentence. "Then I'll, you know..."

Dr. Remkovich shakes his head slowly. "Whatever you decided to hit your shoulder with did some serious damage. I'm surprised the impact didn't kill you, truthfully. Your neural strands have been severed."

"Neural strands?"

"Ah." The doctor shakes his head. "Forgive me. How your brain communicates with your limbs. The paths have been cut." He chops the air with the flats of his hands. "Terminated. Sliced. Like goat cheese!"

"But they'll heal," I insist.

"Not that I've ever seen," Dr. Remkovich adds, bringing his goat-cheese-cutting hands back to his sides. "But I have seen *modifications* done in such circumstances."

I take the information in as best I can, looking down at my limb. *Modifications.* All at once, I don't see my arm anymore, but a mechanical version of it. Just like Banth's. The idea of having a metal body part sends a shiver down my spine. "I try and steer clear of Inventors," I say.

The statement has a far different result than I imagined it might. Most people act as if you'd used Talihdym's name in vain or something. But not Dr. Remkovich. He looks disappointed. Sad, almost.

"Methinks that in your future," the doctor says, pushing his spectacles up, which had slipped down, "you might keep as many friends as you can, even if you don't understand all their motives."

"Wait, what?"

"Well, you're free to go," he says, turning around and heading for the door.

"Wait, wait! Why did you say that? Hold on!" I lean forward in a poor attempt to get up. I want to stop him. But instead I'm met with a wave of blinding agony. So much agony, I pass out.

I've missed another day, they tell me. But the good news is I'm going home. No one has been allowed to see me, so I'm eager to see Mom. And Liv. Not that I've been awake enough to talk with them anyway. The nurses tell me there've been guards at my door since I arrived. Apparently, there's an investigation looking into people that might want to kill me. Shoot, if they'd just interview me, I could fill them in.

They said Dr. Remkovich checked on me again, but I was out. Now they're rolling me down the hallway in a fantastic wheeled chair. I think it's made even more fantastic by the satchel of medication they've started me on. Small pills. Something about infection. And pain relief. All I know is that I feel much better. But I'm having a hard time focusing on things. My head feels funny.

At the end of the hall I see a mob of sheep.

Wait, no.

People.

They're definitely not sheep. They're people. Clapping their hands in excitement. Hardly able to contain themselves. Suddenly one of them blurts my name out, and the mass of them are moving toward me.

I blink twice. Mom. It's Mom! "Boy, am I glad to see you," I say.

"Oh, my baby," she says, kissing my cheek and giving me an awkward hug, arms half wrapped around my wheeled chair. "How are you?"

"I'm...I'm here," is all I can say.

"Glad you're OK, sport," says another female voice. This one younger. Glowing. I blink some more and see an angel. No, it's not an angel; the glowing's in my head.

"Hi, Liv," I say. Next thing I know, she kneels beside me and kisses my other cheek. Shoot, I could get used to this.

"Everyone wanted to come and see you," she adds.

"Everyone?" I ask.

Liv steps aside.

There's Erik and Finn, Danos, even Lance.

Headmaster Dalfirin reaches a hand toward me. I shake it

groggily.

"Good to see you're alive," he says.

"So am I," I say to a smattering of laughter down the hall. It all feels rather surreal. But I couldn't be happier to see them all. My friends.

"If we could," says a strong, imposing voice from behind me, "I'd like to get our young hero home."

I try and turn around to see the face, but my cast won't let me.

"It's alright," says the voice, now moving into my field of vision. "Been watching out for you over the last few days."

Banth.

He's...he's been *here?* As one of the guards?

So they stationed Brologi outside my door. Of course.

"Thank you," I say. Suddenly it seems we're quite the pair, Banth and I. I shudder again to think what my arm might become. His mechanical hand sits on the handle beside my head. "And thanks to your men," I add. "I heard something about an investigation."

"An investigation that's got the whole city talking," adds Liv, as if she knows something no one else does. And knowing her, that's probably not far from the truth.

"As I said, we need to get him home," says Banth.

I settle back into my chair as they roll me down the hallway. My right hand brushes against something cold, wedged between my right thigh and the cushion of the seat. I pull it out: a small brass plate, maybe two inches square.

Level 10, Inner Deck, Home 24, Sub B. REMKOVICH.

Fortunately, my exposure to the general public has been limited, due to a gag order placed on our home by the Guild. Some take it as evidence that the Guild is trying to hide something. Which I know they are. But I take it as a relief from having to be a creative liar, which is harder than people think. Not only do you have to keep a nonexistent story straight over multiple tellings, but you have to restrain yourself from telling a truth that you desperately want to blurt out. Medications compound both of these immensely. You also have to keep your stories straight for the various people you're accountable to.

For now, only Mom, Liv and Lance know that I was attacked. And Dr. Remkovich, I guess. To everyone else, questions about an 'investigation into a threat against my life' are met with vague answers about the dangers of flying the Champions Race. I can only hope that some of the Kili-Boranna still loyal to the Chancellor have leaked the story. Not that they had too much to leak in terms of first-hand knowledge. But they saw three of their number hang back in the Shoals, never to return again. And they obviously met a pulp-beaten specimen of human excrement who'd somehow misplaced his bird. It was enough to start things moving, but probably not enough to draw any conclusions. That, I know, is my job.

Thankfully, the troop of Brologi stationed around our home is successful at keeping the public away. And even though I don't fully trust their allegiance to the Chancellor, I also don't think they mean me and Mom any harm, or else Banth would have killed me himself a long time ago.

The next few days are pretty quiet. Aside from the daily ebb and flow of cheering fans wanting to catch a glimpse of the course-torn winner of their beloved race, the house is pretty quiet. Lance spends two more days with us before he's summoned back to Bellride, and Liv has all but set up shop in our first-floor guest room. I won't lie: having her around is about as good as it gets. Like, *I wish she'd never leave* kind of good. Mom loves her company too, I can tell. Plus, Liv keeps me appraised of everything happening outside, especially at Kar-Christiana.

Apparently the Chancellor himself has ordered all timber and nelurime harvesting suspended in Christiana until the investigation is complete. The pilots attend to their birds twice a day and then go home, instructed that they must be at the disposal of the Council of Lords at a moment's notice. I'm sure they're all ticked. Having your wings clipped is never fun. I should know.

And then there's Serio. My faithful friend. Physical pain

and disability aside, nothing hurts as badly as losing him. I can hardly take it. He should be in the hangar, resting. Rewarded with fresh grain, cool water and as many sheep as he can devour. Instead, his body is decaying on some rock ledge hundreds of miles north of here. And it's all my fault. No time for proper goodbyes, no time for prayers for his crossing into the Great Sky. I just *left*.

I'm walking now, and it feels good. My calf has moved from 'sharp pain' to a 'dull ache,' good enough for me to move around the house without crying. And from what I'm told, my arm cast will be coming off in four weeks. That's longer than I want, but shoot, I'm not sure what difference having it off will make. My arm's busted for good, unless I want to become Banth II. The thought of that makes my chest hurt. Something between panic and fear. I pat the brass card in my pocket, the one I found in the wheelchair of Dr. Remkovich. Not exactly sure why I've been carrying it around. Maybe my head is busted too.

"Well, look at you," Mom says, the same thing she's said every morning since I arrived home. I suppose it's her way of encouraging me in my healing process.

"Good morning, Mom," I say, giving her a peck on the cheek.

"Made you some coffee. Come on over." She gestures toward the kitchen table. "Need me to pull out—"

"I'm fine, thanks," I say, waving her off and pulling out my own chair. I want to do as much as normal people do. No sense going senile at seventeen.

Mom goes over and pours me a mug of black liquid, preparing it the way I like it with honey and goat's milk.

"Is Liv up yet?" I ask.

"Up and gone," Mom says.

"Already? Seems a bit early, even for her."

"She said something's going on today." Mom hands me the coffee. Always smells better than it tastes, but I can't stop drinking it. "Something with the investigation."

"She wasn't more specific?" I ask, taking a sip.

Mom shakes her head. "No, sorry, Love."

There's activity on the front porch. Talking, lots of talking. Then yelling.

"What in Talihdym's name is going on now?" Mom declares. She moves out of the kitchen and toward the front windows, drawing back the curtain. I hear an audible gasp followed by the sight of her hand moving to her mouth.

"What? What is it, Mom?" I can't get my body from behind the kitchen table fast enough. But I don't have to. Suddenly the front door flings open and Liv appears, hair falling out of her braid, face red from exertion.

"They've arrested him!" she blurts out.

"What? Who?!" asks Mom, a look of deep concern crossing her face.

"Him, him! *Lucius!*" Liv says, walking toward me. "The Brologi have taken Lucius ap Victovin into custody by order of the Chancellor and the findings of the Council of Lords! You did it, Junar!"

I'm stunned. Gusts of twenty different emotions assault me until I recognize there are tears falling into my coffee cup. Liv is hugging me on one side, Mom on the other. I hear them crying too. And laughing. And…and…I don't know what else. It's all too much. Surreal. Like I'm about to wake up from a perfect dream I don't want to end.

"Please, please," I say to Liv, forcing her away for a second, "tell me again."

She smiles widely, smearing tears across her cheeks. Her next words come out slowly and steadily. "Lucius ap Victovin, Guild Steward of the Kili-Boranna at Kar-Christiana, has been arrested on the grounds of premeditated murder of Leif ap Jeronil."

I drop my head, half laughing, half crying. "I just can't believe it."

"But there's more," she adds. "The Brologi have also arrested three Timber Pilots whom they have reason to believe are directly responsible in carrying out your Dad's murder, with even more on a list that they're working through." The crowd outside our home has apparently received the news too, as cheers and applause go up. "The boy who proved his father's murder," Liv adds. "That's what they're saying about you. Ever since the story broke about the information that you brought to the Chancellor. The Review Board, the investigation following the race, they're saying it's all because of you, Junar."

And they're right, I know. Not anyone else. Not the Inventors or the Brologi, not the Guild. Not even Talihdym.

Me.

And Serio. We did the impossible.

"You can't bring him back," Mom says, her face buried in my neck, "but you've vindicated his name. Thank you," she says, sobbing with every repetition, "thank you, thank you, thank you."

Then I realize it's over. The battle. Of carrying this alone. It's not just Dad's vindication, it's *my* vindication too. I'm not crazy, and things are being seen for what they truly are. "I just can't believe it," I say again, "and I didn't even meet with the Chancellor."

"Oh! I almost forgot," Liv says. "He wants to meet with you!"

"Who?" I ask.

"The Chancellor, silly. *Who.* He's requested an audience with you. Something about *a promotion*," she says with a sing-song voice, dancing around the table.

"You're kidding. When?"

"*Someone's getting pro-mo-ted!*"

"Ha, Liv! Stop!" I'm laughing now. "When?!"

"At your convenience. When you're well. They say you pick the time."

I let out a deep sigh and set my coffee mug on the table. The emotions are overwhelming. I feel like life can finally move on. Like all is right with the world. I look at Liv and think about marrying her. I look at Mom and wonder what her future holds. And then I realize that for the first time in a long time, there can be some peace in my little section of Aria-Prime. The only person I'm not square with is Talihdym. But given his track record, I doubt he's noticed.

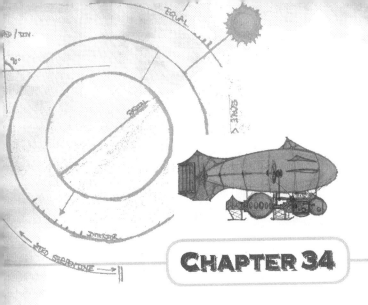

CHAPTER 34

"WHAT A FINE night for dining," says the Chancellor, "and even more so for celebrating." His hand is on my shoulder like a songbird alighting on a feeder, escorting me across the vast expanse of his private dining room floor. "Thank you for coming."

"Shoot, thanks for having me, sir."

"*Opius*, please," he says. "You're getting back to your old self, I see."

"Leg's manageable," I reply, "but they say my arm will never be the same."

"I'm so sorry to hear that," the Chancellor says, looking at my cast as it hangs limp in the sling around my neck. "Most valiant efforts leave deep wounds. But your people are grateful, I'm grateful, and dare I say, your father is grateful." His mention of Dad puts a lump in my throat. Opius walks us toward a grand table set ostentatiously for two. "I would imagine we have much to discuss," he adds, rubbing his hands together with a grin, "and a fine spread over which to discuss it."

He's happier than an eight-year-old in a felrell hangar. I

can't help but smile at him, which improves my sudden melancholy.

"Come, come!" Opius says.

He motions me to an ornately carved chair. Two attendants seat us and draw our napkins into our laps. I've never been waited on like this before. Feels a little awkward, but I won't lie. "This kind of luxury could grow on a guy like me," I say.

"As well it should, Junar! How fitting." He holds his palms toward heaven and looks at me. "Shall we?"

I hesitate.

Prayer.

And using formal hand gestures. Talk about awkward.

I nod some sort of assessment that satisfies him, but I largely ignore his invocation to Talihdym—or as I've come to know him, the deaf, indifferent myth that is Talihdym. Opius' eyes are closed, his face set in earnest to his task. I'm squinting like a child, looking at the food, the candles, the table and high-backed chairs, the marble floor, the paintings and arched doorways, the ceiling painted in a display of the starlit heavens.

His prayer concludes and four male attendants appear, two to serve us each various trays of food, two to pour water flavored with lemon wedges and sliced cucumber. I've never had fruit and vegetables in my water before. But it tastes really refreshing. The food attendant offers me tray after tray, presenting some of the most mouthwatering food I've ever seen. Succulent smoked lamb, roasted potatoes with rosemary, asparagus fried in some sort of cream, steaming bread loaves with sweet cheese, and platters of fresh fruit. I've never used so many different serving utensils in all my life: tongs, oversized spoons, wide forks—one would think I'd been given a tool box just for eating.

I make a messy cut in the lamb with the edge of my fork. One of the attendants offers to help me cut it, but I refuse. If this tastes half as good as it looks, I may never leave this place.

"Well, you don't have to," says Opius.

I'm taken aback. I look up at him, a slice of roast lamb two inches from my mouth. "Excuse me?"

"You said, 'I may never leave this place,' and I'm saying, you don't have to," explains Opius.

I said that out loud? "I—I don't understand." My mouth is suddenly twitching at the bite that I'm lowering back to my plate. Is he serious?

"Shame on me," says Opius. "Eat! Eat! All in due time."

I'm slightly confused, but I fear I may drool on myself, so I eagerly stuff the slice of lamb into my mouth. It's lightly charred on the outside, but sweet and tender in the center, with an aroma of smoke that's otherworldly.

"Glorious, isn't it?" Opius asks, stuffing his own mouth. "My late father's recipe, which he inherited from his father."

"Just the smell is incredible," I add, hacking away with my fork in order to separate another piece.

"Wood chips soaked in water, but from a tree you wouldn't be familiar with," he adds.

"Why's that?"

"It's long ago extinct," he says. "But these chips are from my private supply. *Cedar*, they called it."

I nod, eating my next bite and savoring the flavor.

We continue enjoying the food, my hunger driving me forward. I'm so glad Opius doesn't want to talk right now. I'm in no mood to answer questions when this feast is in front of me. But he seems to be really enjoying himself too, so the feeling might be mutual.

"Ah, and these!" Opius claps his hands as the attendants bring out new trays of colorful food.

"More?" I ask in wonder.

"Yes! These are of particular interest, my favorite, I must say." The display is like nothing I've ever seen. Some sort of white meat, scattered with reds and pinks, spilling out of thin orange bodies as if the creature was broken open to make this meal. The smell is altogether new, inviting my nose with a pallid sweetness that's completely foreign. "Go ahead!" Opius says with enthusiasm. "You're going to love it."

I pick up one of the crispy *talons*—though it doesn't look like any talon I've ever seen—and dip the exposed meat in the clear yellow fluid in a bowl on my plate, as Opius instructs. Any reservations I have, however, are scattered as soon as the tender flesh hits my tongue. The taste is like eating the finest lamb I've ever had, but less pungent, and more refined. More delicate. It's... it's...

"Incredible!"

"Ha!" Opius claps again. "See? There you have it! I knew you'd love it!"

"What—what—" I'm still chewing, making a mess of myself— "what is it?" I wipe some of the yellow fluid away from my lips with my napkin.

"A little-known creature," he replies. "But plentiful, I assure you."

"No private supply?" I smile.

He nods. "This one isn't going extinct anytime soon."

We both consume as much of the white flesh as our stomachs allow us until finally Opius and I are laughing, demanding that the attendants take all the platters away. I think I'm delirious. It's been so good. But I couldn't possibly eat anything more.

"Dessert?" Opius asks.

I shake my head.

"Oh, come now! You must."

"Sir—Opius, I'm sorry." I extend my hand to wave him off. "I really can't. I might, you know..." I gesture from my open mouth to the floor.

Opius lets out a deep laugh. "I completely understand," he says. "You're a man after my own heart. *Major on the main course,* I always say. Good man." He waves off his attendants, then stands. I follow his motioning and join him as he walks to a large set of archways that open to a wide balcony, running the length of his deck-edge estate. The view is beautiful, a panorama of the horizon that no one gets except a pilot on the back of a bird. He indicates a chair that looks like it's been woven from vines. Contrary to my suspicion that it might collapse under my weight, the piece of furniture supports me fully, giving only slightly to my body. Comfortable. In front of us is a low table bearing candles, as well as a parchment pad, an elegant quill and an inkhorn. Opius takes up his own chair and sits back.

"Now this is the life," he says. "A feast worthy of celebration,

followed by a painting in the sky by the Great Talihdym Himself."
And he's right about the painting part: the growing sunsets *are*
incredible. Vibrant. Dramatic. Though I hardly think Talihdym
has much to do with it.

The air is warm with a slight breeze out of the west as
Opius and I stretch out in our chairs. There's hardly any air traffic
around Christiana tonight. All the felrell are tucked in. And the
only airship I see is a lone A-Class moving in from the horizon.

An attendant appears to offer us another glass of flavored
water. Opius lets out a long sigh, then asks, "I'd like to hear about
your experience in the Champions Race. And the Shoals."

I look over to him. "All of it?"

"Yes, son."

The truth is, I'm not sure I want to recount *all of it*. Serio's
death is still too fresh in my mind. And deeply connected with his
is Dad's.

"Even the hard parts," Opius adds, reading my hesitation.

"OK," I say, mustering my resolve. So I share everything,
starting with the cellwurk game on the field before we left the
stadium. Opius seems to take note when I mention Daren's name.
Then Opius and I both recall our sides of the story as I get to the
collision outside The Moors, and I express my gratitude for his
pardon of my actions.

"The pilot that died," says Opius, "did you know him?"

I feel ashamed. "I'm sorry, Opius, I must confess that I still
don't know who it was."

"His name was Rald," he replies. "Eighth year. Was a good
man from what I understand."

My stomach tightens into a knot.

"But, go on," insists Opius.

I so want to think through the implication of Rald's death
in light of our card game with Daren, but it will have to wait. I
share about the encounter in the Shoals. Every detail. Everything I
remember. My final encounter with Daren. And my final moments
with Serio. All the way up to the finish line and passing out.

"I'm sorry about your bird," Opius finally says. "They tell
me your father bought him for you." I nod. "That only makes it all

the more difficult," he adds.

And he couldn't be more right. It's really like Dad died all over again. The wound is still so fresh, I feel like crying.

"So would you like to know about Lucius, then?" Opius asks me after a moment.

"I would, sir. Very much. I mean, *Opius*."

"He's been executed."

"What?!" I nearly fall out of my seat. "Executed?"

"He was found guilty of high treason, conspiracy, attempted assassination, and," he pauses to look at me, "your father's murder."

The news is abrasive, to say the least. But the strange part is, I don't feel the release I thought I would, the peace from knowing my father's killer was brought to justice…or in this case, *gone forever.*

"You look unhappy," Opius points out.

"No, no," I say, shaking off a shiver in my body. "It's just that, well—"

"You weren't expecting such a swift decision from the Council?"

"I guess you could say that. I mean, the people don't know, do they?"

"No, son. The Council of Lords insisted that you be the first. Once all the evidence was in and the Review Board submitted their findings, everything pointed to Lucius." Opius looks out to the flame-red horizon. "Really, we had no choice. Justice demanded he pay the ultimate price."

"It's just so sudden," I reply.

"Yes, it is sudden. But justice must be swift."

"Heck, I suppose so," I say. "When will it be public?"

"Tomorrow," he says. "I'll be delivering the news myself, with representation from the House of Lords and the House of Stewards. You can be there too, if you wish. You'd be my honored guest."

Honored guest? This is so much to take in.

"So, will you come?" he asks.

"I'm not sure what I should say."

"Say yes, Junar. For all you have been through, for all your family has been through, stand with me as we put to rest one of Aria-Prime's darker chapters."

I take in a deep breath. "OK, I'll do it."

"Splendid!"

"But I don't have to say anything, right?"

"Not if you don't want to." He smiles knowingly.

"I don't."

"Very well," he says, leaning back into his chair and taking in the sunsets.

I follow suit, but I can't relax.

Lucius.

Dead.

I can't even imagine it, let alone embrace it. But it's the way our government deals with traitors, I guess. And heck, with such a precarious world as ours, there's little room for murderers. My eyes drift through the panorama before me, noting the slight drop in temperature as the suns start sneaking out of view. That lone A-Class is still heading toward the city, slowly becoming a dark silhouette.

"What of the others?" I ask.

"The others?" Opius replies, looking sideways.

"Those who helped kill my father. The Timber Pilots. Have you executed them too?"

"That remains to be seen," says Opius. "I would like to think we won't have to, but that's not up to me."

"It's up to the Council, then?"

"Precisely. They hold the investigations, they determine the punishment."

"I see."

"It won't be as swift as it was with Lucius," he adds. "Plus, we suspect that there are far more people involved than we know."

"Who do you suspect?"

"The Timber Pilots, to be sure. But there are others, even as you and I had discussed." Our night meeting at the gate. I remember well. "Surely even you saw hints of involvement."

"Certainly," I say. "Shoot, I feel like a lot of people could've had a hand in it, but nothing conclusive. Not like what you had on

Lucius."

"You didn't see their actions as conclusive because…?"

"Because when I told them I suspected Dad was murdered, they had their own story of how it went down. Nothing added up."

"Nothing added up?"

"Shoot, take Liv for example."

"Liv?"

"Sorry, Olivia ay Dalfirin."

"The Headmaster's spunky daughter, yes. I like her. And, from the look of it, it seems you do too, young Junar."

I can feel my face flush, but I'm past denying it. Not with everything that's happened, and with how much she's been there for me.

"Yes, I do," I say. "Liv always suspected Lucius."

"Did she now."

"Yeah, but she always disapproved of my tactics, especially the bit about me entering the Champions Race. She was really upset."

"I can imagine."

"And she seemed to side with Banth and Haupstie's suspicions, which made no sense."

Opius sits upright. "Banth and whom?"

"Haupstie." I realize my error too late. "He's…a friend. Old family friend."

"I see," says Opius, suddenly more interested and leaning on the arm of his chair. "Go on."

"Well, they recovered Dad's saddle. Said it'd been sabotaged. But I saw through it."

"Did you now."

"Sure. I mean, how do you produce a saddle that's fallen into the cloud-floor like that? Impossible. A disgruntled Brologi Chief and a bitter old Inventor, what more would you expect? Trying to get back at the government that's marginalized them both."

"Inventor?" says Opius. Shoot. Didn't mean to let that slip. "As in Dr. Maurice Haupstien?"

"You…you know him?"

"Know him?" Opius says rather loudly. Then suddenly more composed: "I know *of him*. Brilliant man, from what I understand."

"Shoot, the guy's a genius. But probably too smart for his own good."

"I would agree. That's what most believe drove him crazy. And sent him, along with the other Inventors, underground, despising our system. Tragic. If only they didn't loathe the Light as they do."

"Well, it certainly seemed like they were trying to pin this whole thing on more than just Lucius," I surmise. "But I never understood why. Or on whom."

"The Inventors have always hated accountability and transparency, you know," says Opius. "Be careful, my dear boy, for they are a crafty lot. Anarchists, every last one of them, I'm reticent to say."

"Yeah, I'm seeing that." My thoughts drift back to Haupstie and Banth. Even Liv, to a certain extent. *Misguided* is all. But not bad people. "With this all behind us now, and with Lucius gone, I'm looking forward to things getting back to normal."

"Well said," Opius acknowledges. "Tell me, were there others who saw Lucius' actions? Surely people close to you suspected him? Brought it up in passing. You know."

"Besides Mom and Liv? Not really. Ran it by a few of the other First Years when we gathered."

"And they are?"

"You want their names?"

"It wouldn't hurt," he says, handing me the parchment and quill from the table. "Their testimonies will only aid in our ongoing investigation. Maybe weed out other Timber Pilots. Anything they've seen, no matter how small, will be of great assistance."

I scribble down Lance, Erik, Finn and Danos, then place the writing set back on the low table. "Anything to help."

Opius takes the pad, looks at it with satisfaction, and returns it to its place. "Well," he says with a lighter tone, "I think that about covers it."

"Yes, I guess it does," I reply, but I'm distracted. The A-Class that's been tracking in from the horizon is getting unusually close.

Definitely straying from the typical approach pattern; the airship port is on the other side of the city. And it's moving fast.

"Are you alright, young Junar?" Opius asks. "You seem uneasy."

I lean forward, glance at him, then back to the airship. "It's just that that airship," I say, pointing. "Seems a little off course."

"This one here?" He indicates.

"Yeah, yeah." I nod. "I think something might be wrong with his steering linkage or throttle assembly. He should have moved into the circumference of the matrix by now."

"I'm sure he's fine, Junar," insists Opius. "Sit back. Relax."

I don't expect the Chancellor to understand. He's a politician. I'm a pilot. "Sir, something is definitely wrong."

I hear the propellers now as the airship comes under the arch of the balloon matrix and heads straight for us. The setting suns still keep the vessel in shadow, but I'm straining to see inside the cockpit. Maybe the pilot has passed out or something.

"Come, come," says Opius, "I'm quite sure they have it under control. I'd like to discuss a promotion with you."

"Chancellor, sir, this could be serious. We may need to get you out of here."

"Nonsense." He waves me off. "They've got everything under control."

Suddenly I hear the engines strain as they're thrown into reverse. She's slowing, but just. Close enough now that we should be taking cover. Close enough for me to see...

A crimson flag.

"Chancellor! The city's under attack!" I'm on my feet and pulling him out of his chair.

But he's not moving.

"Quick, sir!"

Opius is smiling.

"Come, come, everything will be fine," he says.

I look back at the airship. Am I missing something? But with the vessel being so close, the insignia of the Zy-Adair is unmistakable, emblazoned on the side of the blimp's canvas. My heart is racing.

The ship spins to port, momentum sliding it right up to our portico. The gears disengage and stall the propellers. The ship sits nestled against the Chancellor's building.

"What's going on?"

"I think it's best if you sit," says Opius.

"Sit?" I look at him, then back to the airship. "Heck, I mean no disrespect, but what's wrong with you, sir?"

The side passenger pod opens and a leather-jacketed pirate appears, shoving the concealed gangway across the open space between the airship and the balcony. I jump back as it slams onto the railing. The Chancellor is standing, but serenely, with his hands clasped in front of him.

"Is this some kind of joke?" I ask, staring between him and the five Sky Pirates now walking down the plank.

"*Junar!*"

My name. From somewhere up above.

"*JUNAR!*"

Someone's screaming my name. Someone I know well. Better than anyone in the whole world.

Mom.

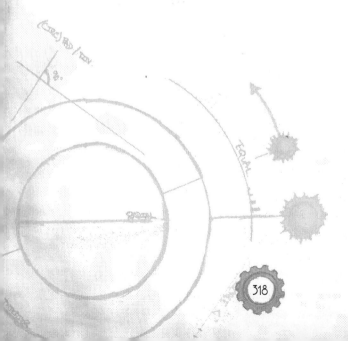

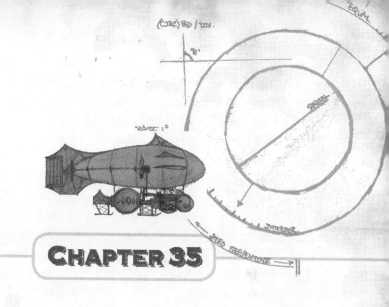

CHAPTER 35

I LOOK UP to the passenger pod door and see Mom's face. Her hands are bound, and there's a red cut on her head. One of the pirates is prodding her down the plank with a cutlass. She's stumbling 3,000 feet above the cloud-floor on a thin, metal walkway.

"What's going on?" I ask angrily. I spin the Chancellor around, my head trying to piece everything together. Five pirates jump down and gather around me, Mom still on the plank. She's crying.

"Hands off him, Junar ap Leif," says a voice, the owner of which is coming down the gangway behind Mom. "Unless you want dear old Mummy to go exploring for your father."

I know that voice. I look up and see a face appear behind Mom's. "*Lucius.*"

"Miss me?" he asks, yanking Mom to a halt.

"You let her go right now!" I demand, moving away from Opius. But the pirates are on me, nelurime pistols in one hand, cutlasses in the other.

"Tsk, tsk, Junar," Lucius says with a wave of his finger.

"Getting jolted by 10,000 volts of high-frequency electricity isn't exactly something you can walk away from."

"Junar, run!" Mom blurts out.

But Lucius takes the wind out of her with a shameless punch to the side.

"Do that again and I'll—"

"You'll what, Junar? Come up here and deal with me yourself?" he chides me as he pulls a gag up over Mom's mouth.

"You let her go, Lucius! She's got nothing to do with this."

"Oh, but she has *everything* to do with this," Lucius corrects, drawing the words out. He yanks her against his chest and lays the cutlass against her throat.

"You took my father. You're not going to take my mother."

"Ah, but you see, I can. And I will. Unless you answer the Chancellor's questions the way you're supposed to."

I turn toward the Chancellor. I'm met with nelurime pistols pointed at my face. Opius has backed away. "I can't believe you're in on this! I *trusted* you!"

"And that's something you can still do, if you like, my dear boy," says Opius.

"Not likely. You told…you told me…" The one man in all of Aria-Prime that I trusted. This whole time. I feel like a fool. "You told me he was dead," I say, pointing to Lucius.

"And he is," agrees Opius. "At least to the people of the floating cities. But he's very much alive to the Zy-Adair. Their *leader*, in fact."

"Their leader?!"

"Along with the other men who conspired with us against your father," says Opius. "Have to maintain the appearance of order, you know. The public demand justice, and there was too much evidence against Lucius. Thanks to you. Can't let this sort of thing slip, or you lose control. Plus, that's simply too many men to jail—or kill. So messy, anyways. No, no, Lucius and his Timber Pilots will serve me better as antagonists."

"Antagonists? I don't understand."

"And I don't expect you to, Junar. At least, not right now. You're young, and know little of what it means to govern. To rule.

But you will, in time, I believe. In every society, there must be order. And that order is established through strict parameters. Calculated parameters. Life, death, tyranny, justice. They are all measured systems, and someone has to do the arithmetic."

"And you're not the man," I spit back.

"Then who is, Junar? You? The public? Maybe your beloved Talihdym?"

Talihdym?

"Ah, you put so much faith in your unseen God," says Opius. "Please, he's about as interested in you as—"

"He's not interested in me," I mumble. And it makes me sick to my stomach to think that Opius and I agree about Talihdym.

"Excuse me?"

"Enough of the speech, Opius," I say. "You've never been very good at giving them anyway." I hear Lucius chuckle from the gangway.

Opius flattens out his robes with his hands, collecting himself. "So, you have a choice to make, Junar. And the outcomes are entirely your own to calculate."

"But I thought you just said—"

"These ones are yours. Consider it your first step in learning to rule. You see," Opius says, stepping closer to me, "I like you. There's room for you in the Order. And I think...*we* think you have something that your father didn't."

"Oh, and what's that?"

"The drive to do what it takes," replies Opius.

"My father did *everything* it took."

"No, not everything," says Opius. "He *could have been something* with us, had he truly possessed *everything*. But he was *weak*."

"He wasn't weak!" I shout. "He wasn't!" Tears on my cheeks. Had Opius told me this a few weeks prior, I would have agreed. And maybe that's what they wanted all along. So what had changed? What had changed that they missed?

Opius steps away, looks up to Lucius, then back to me. This isn't going the way he wants it to. I'm not sure what he wants, but I won't let it go his way.

"Junar, your father got in the way. And so did you, to a certain extent. But the Order took it in stride. A *fortuitous intrusion*, you might say. But an intrusion all the same. And one we must deal with."

"So you're going to kill me," I say. "Because I know about your coverup, and whatever *this* whole setup is." I gesture at all the pirates and Lucius.

"Kill you? Please. Do you think I'm a monster?"

"Truthfully?"

"I don't kill those who scorn me. I make them *suffer*. I'd no sooner kill a bird. But I would break its wings." He looks up, like he's dreaming. Takes a deep breath. "You, Junar? I imagine I'll send you to a forgotten prison. For a very long time." Then he looks at my face. "But I will kill your mother."

I lunge at him. Two of the guards cross their cutlasses and bar me from moving further. I smell the odor of nelurime charging up their weapons.

"Easy, my dear boy," says Opius.

"I thought you said you don't kill those who cross you!"

"I don't, but your mother has never crossed me, so killing her does what I first said. *It breaks your wings*."

I look to see Mom struggling against Lucius, but her knees are weak. He's holding her up from behind, his blade still resting against her skin.

"What do you want?" I ask Opius, teeth clenched together.

"I want you to work for me."

"Work for you?"

"Yes, now that Lucius is gone, I need a hero. Someone to run the Kili-Boranna with excellence. Someone the people will love and follow. And someone who will follow me."

"You just don't get it, do you?" I say, measuring my words out. "I'm not going to follow you. *Ever*."

"And that's where *you* don't get it, Junar. Yes, I have your mother. And I think you'd do just about anything to save her. But I also have something you don't."

"What's that?"

"Power, Junar. Power to shape how people think. To shape

how they behave. They enforce Life Control on their own because they fear over-expansion. They cover themselves in paste every day, even though they don't have a clue what it's made of, all because we tell them to. They adhere to whatever rules we put in place because they don't want to repeat the past. And they forget their history in a desperate effort to evade what they've done, what they've left behind. Because the guilt is crushing. They'll do anything to make things better for themselves and their children rather than face the blackness of their own souls. Things that are inconvenient are easy to ignore, and if it doesn't benefit them directly, what's the use? That, my dear boy, *is* power, power that you know nothing of. But I'll teach you.

"Think it about, Junar. This is the only chance I'll give you. Ultimate power over Aria-Prime within the Order. Join me, and your mother and friends live long, healthy lives. Or, the second scenario, which doesn't end too happily."

My head feels as if it's going to explode, like the pressure inside the nelurime steam engines whirring above me. But I don't need to think this through. Not this decision. I made it the day I knew Dad was murdered.

Fight.

Fight until there's nothing left to fight for.

In an action so fast I even surprise myself, I spin to my left, catch the first pirate off guard, and strip his pistol from him. I flip the weapon in my hand and duck. I feel my calf explode in pain, but it's inconsequential now. My mind is wide awake and clear. I know the small cluster of pirates wouldn't fire this close to each other, as we're all aware of the damage a nelurime weapon can have. But from inside their circle, I've got nowhere to shoot but out. And shoot I do.

The first jolt surprises me. I've never discharged this technology before. I feel the hair on my neck stand up as the fingers of electricity explode from the tip of the weapon and connect with two pirates, striking them square in the chest with brilliant white sparks. They fly backward, their leather armor on fire, blades and pistols clattering to the ground.

From my squatting position, I pivot around and pull the

trigger again, and again, and again. The pistol answers each time, loosing tendrils of bright blue light that leap into the chests of the pirates.

Opius ducks quickly, moving to hide behind his vine-crafted chair. But I'm not interested in him. Only Mom's safety.

I look up the gangway. She's nearly back inside the passenger pod, with Lucius yelling orders to the pilot. The propellers are spinning again, the plank scraping along the railing.

It's all I can do to leap up on the railing, my leg fighting against me. I run along it for five paces, then jump. Both feet connect on the moving gangway, but I have to drop the pistol to keep from falling over the side.

I glance up the walkway to the door. Lucius has reappeared, straining to shut the hatch. Below me is open air. But before it's sealed, Lucius points a pistol out of the remaining space. He takes aim, and I hear Mom's voice yell something in the background. The weapon discharges. I duck, the electricity veering wide. I'm not hit.

But I'm off balance.

I'm falling left. And my arm won't move, no matter how much I tell it to stop me. Without it, I've already judged my momentum: I'm going over the side. As I pass the point of no return, I reach for the lip of the gangway with my good hand. And connect. My body swings out into the air like a pendulum swaying under the plank. Right hand holding fast.

The airship is 300 feet from the Chancellor's portico now, and he's standing, staring at me, praying to a deaf god that I fall. And he'll get his wish, I know that. There's no way I'm climbing back up. I hear Mom screaming behind her gag. Then a heavy blow, followed by silence.

My right hand is straining. Losing grip. I hear footsteps above me as the wind blows harder in my ears. I look up. It's Lucius.

"Maybe the Chancellor won't kill you," says Lucius. "But I will."

I think to plead for my life. But I won't give him the pleasure. I'll die, defiant. The sole of his boot explodes onto my knuckles. The pain is excruciating and my grip releases, no contest.

My stomach jars upward. Free fall. I know the sensation well. But I'm not afraid.

Not this time.

Which strikes me as peculiar, especially as I look up into the last face I'll ever see. Lucius', staring down at me with wild glee in his dark eyes. The airship spins, as does Christiana, further and further up into the dim sky. No one to rescue me, no Serio to swoop in and save the day. No Talihdym to cradle me with clouds. No father to encourage me, no mother to tell me everything's going to be alright. Just open air, the same air I've loved to soar through. Alone. Just as I've always wanted to be. It's fitting that I should die this way, now embraced by the wet clouds I spent so many years learning to harvest.

The clouds.

The clouds, and a million sets of eyes, burrowing deep into my soul. Calling me. Waiting for me. The sickening feeling of death. Enveloped in darkness, I close my eyes, and wait to experience what no one has ever returned to tell of.

Impact.

ACKNOWLEDGMENTS

This manuscript was made infinitely better by the scouring eyes of my tireless Proofies. Their love for Aria-Prime combined with their unsurpassed attention to detail made this book shine. I can't thank them enough for their selfless dedication. I only hope their names will be immortalized in this section which is forever dedicated to their greatness. They are: Matthew Sampson, Josie Crihfield, William Jepma, Noah Arsenault, Sophie Sureau, Delanie Douglas, Emma McPhee, Evan C. Keegan, Sarah Pennington, Raptor Elytra, Ryan Paige Howard, Trista Vaporblade, David Sampson, Sierra Huntley, Wilby Kingston, Juliette Sureau, Andy Miller, Caleb "Sgt. Caz" Baker, Joanne Suhr, Nathan Reimer, Aaron and Sarah Novak, Naomi Wilson and Leah Atkins.

David Buckles, my dear friend, whose real-life heroics in combat as a medevac pilot have saved countless soldiers while flying HH-60M Blackhawks for the 10 Aviation Regiment, 10 Mountain Division. You inspire me, and Sky Riders everywhere. Fly or die.

My amazing friend, Brett Peryer, whose sharp wit and insightful dialog on the state of the union have kept me sane, and challenged me to be a better patriot of both my country and the Kingdom. Thank you for being my sounding board, and for protecting our nation's borders.

Dave Tewksbury, the spirit of Haupstie, and the smoke in the Inventor's pipe.

Wayne Thomas Batson, my writing companion. So grateful for the Lewis/Tolkien friendship that's been bestowed upon us. It never ceases to amaze me how privileged we are. A toast to the journey thus far, and the untold hours logged online. May many more boards overhear talk of far-off worlds and heroes in the ranks.

The Brick Store Pub in Decatur, Georgia, where this tale was first told amongst friends, Wayne Thomas Batson, Gregg Wooding, and Jennifer Lee.

To my remarkable sister and brother-in-law, Natalie and Joe Smith, who continue our family's legacy of flight, and keep our friendly skies safe.

And to my faithful co-pilot, Jenny, who has pushed me to soar higher than I dared and farther than I dreamed.

Fly or die,

ch:

Look for Book 2 of
The Sky Riders...

RAISING THENDARA

AN INVENTORS WORLD NOVEL

CHRISTOPHER HOPPER, author and co-author of numerous novels, including *Rise of the Dibor*, *The Lion Vrie*, and *Athera's Dawn*, has gathered awards and nominations including The Silver Moonbeam, The Lamplighter, The Clive Staples, and The Pluto. He is also a multi-album recording artist, pastor, visual designer, and restaurateur. His prolific writings in both book and blog form have captured the imaginations of loyal readers around the world. He lives with his wife, Jennifer, and their four children in the 1000 Islands of northern New York, and has been known to ride felrell on occasion.

To find out more about Christopher,
go to christopherhopper.com

And for the latest Sky Riders news and merchandise,
check out iskyriders.com

MORE GREAT TITLES FROM SPEARHEAD BOOKS...

The Miller Brothers

Mech Mice: Genesis Strike

Hunter Brown and the Secret of the Shadow

Hunter Brown and the Consuming Fire

Hunter Brown and the Eye of Ends

Wayne Thomas Batson

Ghost: A John Spector Novel

The Door Within

Rise of the Wyrm Lord

The Final Storm

The Dark Sea Annals: Sword in the Stars

The Dark Sea Annals: The Errant King

VISIT SpearheadBooks.com

27622583R00194

Made in the USA
Lexington, KY
16 November 2013